MONSTERS OF THE DEEP

David Wingrove is the Hugo Award-winning co-author (with Brian Aldiss) of *Trillion Year Spree: The History of Science Fiction*, and co-author of the first three *Myst* books – novelizations of one of the world's bestselling computer games. He is also author of *The Roads to Moscow* trilogy. He lives in north London.

MONSTERS OF THE DEEP

BOOK 9

DAVID WINGROVE

FRAGILE
BOOKS

First published in trade paperback and eBook in Great Britain in 2017 by Fragile Books.

Copyright © David Wingrove, 2017

A CIP catalogue record for this book is available from the British Library.

Trade paperback ISBN: 978-1-912094-57-8
eBook ISBN: 978-1-912094-56-1

Printed in Great Britain by 4edge Limited.

Fragile Books
5a Arundel Square
London
N7 8AT

www.fragilemedialtd.com

CONTENTS

For Brian and Margaret Aldiss

Whose love of things Chinese and of
the vast worlds of the imagination
set me upon this path.
With much love.

'For every one of us it is the same.
Worlds end or open as we go.'

MONSTERS OF THE DEEP

Book Nine

'Wasps and ants have a mean fate:
how could their power be enduring?'
—*Tien Wen* ('Heavenly Questions') by Ch'u Yuan, from
the *Ch'u Tz'u* (*Songs Of The South*), 2nd Century BC

'Can't teach a true peach being a prisoner
Skin all round and stone within'
—Jukka Tolonen, 'Last Quarters', 1972

INTRODUCTION

Chung Kuo. The words mean 'Middle Kingdom' and, since 221 BC, when the First Emperor, Ch'in Shih Huang Ti, unified the seven Warring States, it is what the 'black-haired people', the Han, or Chinese, have called their great country. The Middle Kingdom – for them it was the whole world; a world bounded by great mountain chains to the north and west, by the sea to east and south. Beyond was only desert and barbarism. So it was for two thousand years and through sixteen great dynasties. Chung Kuo *was* the Middle Kingdom, the very centre of the human world, and its Emperor the 'Son of Heaven', the 'One Man'. But in the eighteenth century that world was invaded by the young and aggressive Western powers with their superior weaponry and their unshakeable belief in Progress. It was, to the surprise of the Han, an unequal contest and China's myth of supreme strength and self-sufficiency was shattered. By the early twentieth century China – *Chung Kuo* – was the sick old man of the East: 'a carefully preserved mummy in a hermetically sealed coffin' as Karl Marx called it. But from the disastrous ravages of that century grew a giant of a nation, capable of competing with the West and with its own Eastern rivals, Japan and Korea, from a position of incomparable strength. The twenty-first century, 'the Pacific Century' as it was known even before it began, saw China become once more a world unto itself, but this time its only boundary was space.

The War Of The Two Directions

It had begun with the assassination of the T'ang's Minister, Lwo K'ang, some thirteen years earlier, the poor man blown into the next world along with his Junior Ministers while basking in the imperial solarium. The Seven – the great Lords and rulers of Chung Kuo – had hit back at once, arresting one of the leading figures of the Dispersionist faction responsible for the Minister's death. But it was not to end there. Within days of the public execution, their opponents had struck another deadly blow, killing Li Han Ch'in, son of the T'ang, Li Shai Tung, and heir to City Europe, on the day of his wedding to the beautiful Fei Yen.

It might have ended there, with the decision of the Seven to take no action in reprisal for Prince Han's death – to adopt a policy of peaceful non-action, *wuwei* – but for one man such a course could not be borne. Taking matters into his own hands, Li Shai Tung's General, Knut Tolonen, had marched into the House of Representatives in Weimar and killed the leader of the Dispersionists, Under Secretary Lehmann. It was an act almost guaranteed to tumble Chung Kuo into a bloody civil war unless the anger of the Dispersionists could be assuaged and concessions made.

Concessions were made, an uneasy peace maintained, but the divisions between rulers and ruled remained, their conflicting desires – the Seven for Stasis, the Dispersionists for Change – unresolved. Amongst those concessions the Seven had permitted the Dispersionists to build a starship, *The New Hope*. As the ship approached readiness, the Dispersionists pushed things even further at Weimar, impeaching the *tai* – the Representatives of the Seven in the House – and effectively declaring their independence. In response the Seven destroyed *The New Hope*. War was declared.

The five year 'War-that-wasn't-a-War' left the Dispersionists broken, their leaders killed, their Companies confiscated. The great push for Change had been crushed and peace returned to Chung Kuo. Or so it briefly seemed, for the War had woken older, far stronger currents of dissent. In the depths of the City new movements began to arise, seeking not merely to change the system, but to revolutionise it altogether. One of these factions, the *Ping Tiao*, or 'Levellers', wanted to pull down the great City of three hundred levels and destroy the Empire of the Han.

For a while the status quo had been maintained, but three of the most senior T'ang had died in the War, leaving the Council of the Seven weaker and more inexperienced than they had been in all the long years of their rule. When Wang Sau-leyan, the youngest son of Wang Hsien, ruler of City Africa, became T'ang after his father's death, things looked ominous, the young man seeking to create disharmony amongst the Seven. But Li Yuan, inheriting from his father, formed effective alliances with his fellow T'ang, Tsu Ma, Wu Shih and Wei Feng, to block Wang in Council, out-voting him 4 to 3.

Now, looking beyond the immediate political situation, Li Yuan wants permanent solutions to the problems of over-population and civil unrest. To achieve the former, he is willing to make deals with his enemies in the Above – to relax the Edict of Technological Control that has kept Change at bay for so long, and to reopen the House at Weimar, in return for population controls. As for civil unrest, he has devised a somewhat darker scheme: to 'wire up' the whole population of Chung Kuo, so that they can be traced and tracked and rigidly controlled.

For the first time in years, then, there is real hope that peace and stability might be achieved and chaos staved off. But time is running out. Chung Kuo is a society badly out of balance, and close – very close – to total breakdown.

In Wu Shih's great City of North America, the first signs of social unrest have already manifested themselves in movements like the 'Sons of Benjamin Franklin', and in a growing desire amongst the *Hung Mao* – the Europeans – for a new nationalism. But the problems are not merely between the rulers and the ruled. Amongst the ruled there are also divisions. Divisions that run deeper than race ...

PROLOGUE **In The Space Between Heaven and Earth**

SPRING 2209

'Heaven and earth are ruthless, and treat the myriad
creatures as straw dogs; the sage is ruthless, and
treats the people as straw dogs.

Is not the space between heaven and earth like a
bellows?

It is empty without being exhausted;
The more it works the more comes out.
Much speech leads inevitably to silence.
Better to hold fast to the void.'
—Lao Tzu, *Tao Te Ching*, 6th Century BC

IN THE SPACE BETWEEN HEAVEN AND EARTH

Wu Shih, T'ang of North America, stood at the top of the ruined, pitted steps, looking down at the men. Behind him, headless, the huge statue sat, embedded in its chair of granite, hands on its knees. Overhead, spotlights set into the floor of the Above picked out the figures at the foot of the broad white stairway. Five men. Five old, greybearded men, well-dressed and senatorial. Company Heads. *Americans.* Wu Shih studied them, his contempt barely concealed. His left foot rested on the statue's fallen head, his right hand on his hip.

One of the men, taller than the rest, stepped out in front of the others and called up to him.

'Where are they? You said you'd bring them, Wu Shih. So where are they?'

Dead, he would have liked to have said. *Your sons are dead, old men.* But it wasn't so. Wang Sau-leyan had saved their lives. There had been an agreement in Council and the traitors were to go free, unpunished, the price of their treachery unexacted. It was foolishness, but it had been decided.

'They are here, *Shih* Lever. Close by. Unharmed.'

Wu Shih paused and looked about the ruins of the old city. From where he stood, high above it all, the floor of the Above was less than fifty *ch'i* overhead, a dark and solid presence, stretching away to every horizon. Facing him, beyond the darkly-shadowed outline of a toppled obelisk, could be glimpsed the wreckage of the Capitol building, a huge, silvered pillar thrusting up through its ruined dome – one of many that rose to meet the smooth, featureless darkness of the City's underbelly.

He had brought them here deliberately, knowing the effect it would have on the old men. Overhead, its presence vast and crushing, lay the City that he ruled – a City that rose two li – almost a mile by their ancient measure – into the air, stretching from the Atlantic to the Pacific, from the coast of Labrador to the Gulf of Mexico in the south. While here below ...

Wu Shih smiled. Here, in the darkness beneath the City's piles, lay the ruins of old America – of Washington, once-capital of the Sixty-Nine States of the American Empire. And these men – these foolish, greedy old men – would have the Empire back; would break a century and more of peace to have it back. Wu Shih snorted and looked down at the massive granite head beneath the foot.

'You have signed the documents?'

A moment's silence greeted his words, then Lever answered him, the irritation in his voice barely restrained. 'It's done.'

Wu Shih felt a ripple of anger pass through him. It was the second time Old Man Lever had refused to address him properly.

'All of you?' he demanded. 'All those on my list?'

He looked up from Lincoln's head and sought Lever's eyes. Lever was staring at the fallen stone, his face suffused with anger, his expression so eloquent that Wu Shih laughed and pressed down on the heavy stone, forcing the nose firmly into the dust that lay everywhere here.

'You haven't answered me.'

Wu Shih's voice had changed, grown harder, its flattened tones filled with threat. Lever looked up at him, surprised by the command in his voice – unaccustoned, clearly, to another's rule. Again this spoke volumes. These men were far gone in their dissent – had grown fat and arrogant in the illusion of their power. Li Yuan had been right to see them as a threat – right to act against them as he had. There was no respect in them, no understanding of their true relationship to things. The old man thought himself the equal of the Seven – perhaps, even, their superior. It was a dangerous, insolent delusion.

Lever turned his head away sharply, spitting the words out angrily. 'We've signed. Everyone on your list.' He beckoned to another of his party, who came forward and handed him the document.

Wu Shih watched, his eyes half-lidded, seeing how Lever turned back to face him, hesitating, as if he expected Wu Shih to come down the steps and take the paper from him.

'Bring it,' he said, and put out his left hand casually, almost languidly. Wang Sau-leyan may have forced the Council to make this deal with their enemies – this 'concession', as he called it – but he, Wu Shih, would show these men exactly where they stood. He saw how Lever turned, uncertainty in his face, looking towards the others as if for guidance, then turn back and begin to climb. Each step was a small humiliation. Each a belittling of the man. Then, when he was only three steps from the top, Wu Shih raised his hand, commanding him, by that gesture, to stay where he was.

Lever frowned, but did as he was bid.

'Kneel,' Wu Shih said, his voice soft, almost gentle now.

Lever turned his head slightly, as if he had not heard properly. 'What?'

'Kneel.'

Wu Shih's voice had been no louder, no harder, but this time it was command not reminder.

Again Lever hesitated, half turning, the muscles in his face twitching, conscious of his fellows down below, watching him. Slowly, huffing as he did, the old man knelt, his face raised, eyes glaring at Wu Shih. This was a protocol he had clearly thought he could avoid. But Wu Shih was unrelenting. He was determined to have the form of Lever's respect if not the actuality, knowing that in such forms lay power. Real power. The bowing of one man before another: it was a gesture as old as it was profound. And even if true respect were not forthcoming here, he could still insist on one of its components – obedience. Simple obedience.

Leaning forward, Wu Shih plucked the paper from Lever's outstretched hand and opened it. Its original – verified by retinal print and scan – was already on file. Yet there was more power in this – this written paper, signed by the hand of each and given here at this place where the dream of America had died – than in the purely legal form of their agreement. It was little understood by them, but ritual was more than empty show. It was power itself. Was what gave form to the relationships of men.

Wu Shih folded the paper, grunting his satisfaction. Half turning, he made a signal. At once, a brilliant light fell on a nearby building. For a moment there was nothing, then a door opened in the plain white face of the building and from the darkness within stepped a group of young men. The Sons. Gaunter, less proud for their fifteen month incarceration. But dangerous. More dangerous than Wang Sau-leyan would ever contemplate.

Wu Shih raised his hand, dismissing the old man.

Lever backed away, moving slowly down the steps, then, at the bottom, turned and went amongst his fellows, making his way across the littered wasteland towards the building where the young men stood. Wu Shih watched a moment, then turned away. In his hand he held their guarantee of good behaviour – their pledge to govern themselves better than they had. But he had seen the hate, the irreverence in Lever's face. Was such a guarantee worth having in the face of such open defiance?

He smiled. Yes, for it would give him the excuse to act, without the intercession of that meddler Wang.

As he made his way from there he knew for a certainty that this was not the end of this, only a temporary respite. There would come a time when he would have to face these men again.

'Americans ...' he said beneath his breath, then laughed softly, looking back at the headless statue, silhouetted against the lights from above. The Supernal, they called themselves. Dwellers in the Heavens. Supremely great and excellent. Exalted.

He laughed. So they might believe, but if they so much as spat he'd make it hell for them.

Leaf shadow fell on the pale, slatted rocks on the far side of the pool. Li Yuan, T'ang of Europe, stood on the low, humped bridge, listening to the sounds coming from the rooms across the water. Low trees obscured his view of the courtyards and the house, but the sounds came clear to him; laughter, light-headed with relief; the chatter of excited female voices, and beneath both, unremitting, the bawling of a newborn child.

He stood there, in perfect stillness, looking down at his dark reflection in the lotus-strewn water. It was a child. A son – of course a son – there would not be laughter if it were otherwise. He stood, unmoving, not knowing what to think, what to feel at that moment, the world – the tiny world of tree and stone and water – suspended all about him.

A son ... He shook his head, frowning. There should be more than this, he thought. I should be glad. I too should laugh, for today the chain is forged anew, the Family strengthened. But there was nothing – only an empty space where feeling ought to have been.

Across from him one of the nurses stepped out onto the balcony of the birth room and saw him. He looked up in time to see her turn hurriedly and go back inside; heard her warning to them and the sudden silence that followed, broken almost at once by the high-pitched cries of the newborn. He stood there a moment longer, then moved on slowly, his heart strangely heavy, for once totally unprepared for what lay ahead.

Mien Shan lay there, a tiny figure in his grandmother's huge bed – the same bed where his father, Li Shai Tung, had come into the world. She was propped up on pillows, her dark hair tied back from her sweat-beaded brow. Seeing him she smiled broadly and lifted the tiny bundle in her arms, offering it to him.

'Your son, *Chieh Hsia*.'

He took the child from her, cradling it carefully, conscious of the others in the room watching him. With one hand he drew back the blanket and looked down at the child. Dark hair lay finely on its long, pale scalp, glistening wetly in the overhead light. Its eyes were screwed shut and its thin lips formed ugly, awkward shapes as it yelled incessantly, one thin arm and tiny hand reaching blindly, repetitively into the air. It struggled against him as he held it, as if sensing his unease. Even so, he laughed, feeling how small, how light it was. So fragile and yet so determined. His son. Once more he laughed, and sensed the mood in the room change, growing more relaxed.

He looked down at Mien Shan and smiled. 'Good. You have done well, my love.' He glanced across, seeing how his other wives, Lai Shi and Fu Ti Chang, blushed with Mien Shan at the endearment, and felt an unexpected warmth. They were good, kind women. Nan Ho had chosen well for him.

He sat beside Mien Shan on the bed and turned to face her, holding the child in one arm. Behind her, on the wall above the bed, was a copy of the *Luoshu* diagram – the 'magic' numbers used as a charm for easing childbirth. Normally the sight of such superstitious nonsense would have angered him. But this was no moment for anger.

'Was it hard?' he asked, lifting her chin gently with one finger, making her look at him. She hesitated, then gave the slightest nod, remembered pain in her eyes.

He took a deep breath, trying to imagine it, then nodded, his lips and eyes slowly forming a smile. 'I honour you, sweet wife. And thank you, both for my son and for myself.'

For a moment he looked at her, an unusual tenderness in his features, then, giving the slightest bow, he leaned forward and kissed the wetness of her brow.

He turned, facing the others in the room. Besides wives, nurses and doctors, several of his Ministers were present – witnesses to the birth. Li Yuan stood up, still cradling the child, and took a step towards them.

'You will announce that the Families have a new heir. That Kuei Jen, first son to Li Yuan, was born this morning of his wife, Mien Shan, in good health and in a state of physical perfection.'

He nodded vigorously, holding the child firmer, seeing how they all smiled at that. 'A strong child. Like his grandfather.'

There was a murmur of agreement and a nodding of heads. But then Li Yuan lowered his head in the sign of dismissal and, with bows of respect, the others left, leaving Li Yuan alone with Mien Shan and the child. The babe in his arms had settled and was no longer crying. Now it looked up at him, open-eyed. Huge, dark eyes that peered out from the mystery of birth. And, lowering his face gently, he kissed brow and nose and chin with a tenderness that took him by surprise.

'Kuei Jen,' he said, smiling down softly at the child. 'Welcome, my son. May the world be kind to you.' And, looking up, he saw that Mien Shan was watching him, tears trickling down her cheeks.

The room was dark, ill-ventilated. The old man in the bed coughed, a dry, hacking cough, then sniffed loudly. 'Draw the curtains, Chan Yin. I want to see you all.'

His eldest son went to the far side of the room and drew the heavy, silken curtains back a fraction. Brilliant light spilled into the room, cutting a broad swathe through the shadow.

'More,' said the old man, leaning forward from his pillows. 'And open the doors. It's like a sweat box in here.'

Chan Yin hesitated and looked across at the doctors, but they simply shrugged. Pulling the curtains back fully, he pushed open the bronze and glass doors that led out onto the balcony then stood there, feeling the freshness of the breeze on his face and arms, looking out across the gardens towards the distant mountains. After a moment he turned back, facing his father.

In the sudden brightness Wei Feng was squinting at him, a faint smile on his creased and ancient-looking face. 'Better,' he said, easing himself back onto the pillows. 'It's like a tomb. Each night they tuck me up and bury me. And yet, when the morning comes, I am still here.'

Chan Yin looked at his father with concern and love. He hated seeing him like this, so old and powerless. His memories rebelled against this image of Wei Feng and would have had his father strong and vigorous again. But those were childhood memories and he himself was older, much older now. Forty this next birthday. He sighed, then crossed the room to stand with his brothers at the bedside.

Hsi Wang stood there in his Colonel's uniform, ill at ease in this situation, his usual good humour subdued. Since his father's stroke he had been only half himself, his normally untroubled face overcast. Tseng-li, the youngest, stood right beside his father, his hand resting lightly on the old man's shoulder, his beautiful face looking down into his father's. From time to time Wei Feng would turn slightly and look up at him, smiling.

The stroke had almost killed Wei Feng. Only expert surgery had saved him. But pneumonia had set in shortly afterwards. Now, a month from the first heart attack, he was much better, but the experience had aged him greatly. The left side of his skull was shaved bald and his right arm lay useless on the covers. There had been a blood clot and certain areas of his brain had died, amongst them those which controlled certain of his movements. Not even expert prosthetics could bring back the use of his right arm.

'My sons,' he said, smiling, looking from one to another, the simple words heavy with emotion. For a moment the coughing took him again, and Tseng-li bent his huge, tall body, kneeling, holding the old man's hand more tightly until the spasm passed. Then Wei Feng spoke again, looking mainly at his heir, Chan Yin.

'The doctors tell me I shall live.' He smiled sadly, then nodded. 'Even that seems strange now ... the thought of living.' He took a long, shuddering breath, then spoke again. 'But being such a friend to death these last few weeks, I have had the chance to study him – to look him in the face and come to know him. Like an enemy one comes to respect for his great skill and cunning.'

Hsi Wang laughed shortly and Wei Feng looked up at him, smiling, indulging his laughter. 'It is good to hear you laugh, Hsi. I have missed your laughter.' He licked his lips slightly, then carried on. 'I have stood beside him, you see, and looked back. Into the light. Looked back and seen the shape of things, here, in this shadow world of ours.'

Chan Yin narrowed his eyes, listening, watching his father's face, and saw how the old T'ang's eyes seemed to look out past Hsi, as if he really could see something that was denied to their vision.

'For the first time I saw clearly. How things are. How they will be.'

Wei Feng turned his head and looked at his eldest son once more. 'Which is why you are here. You especially, Chan Yin. But you also, Hsi and Tseng. As witnesses. Custodians, if you like.'

They waited while Wei Feng took his breath. From the open doors came the sound of the wind in the trees and the buzzing of insects. A faint breeze moved the curtains gently, cooling the air in the room.

'There is something I want from you, Chan Yin. Something no father ought to ask of his eldest son. But I have seen what is to come. And, because I love you, I want you to swear to me that you will do what I ask of you.'

Chan Yin shivered, seeing the strange intensity in his father's eyes, and nodded. 'Whatever you ask, father.'

Wei Feng was quiet a while, watching him; then he sighed and looked down at his useless arm. 'I want you to swear to me that you will support Li Yuan. Support him in whatever he asks, and for whatever reason he gives. *Whatever* he asks of you, do it.'

He paused, a sudden ferocity in his face, as if he was seeing things again from the side of death. Looking back at the world of shadows and light.

'Do it, Chan Yin! You must! For upon Li Yuan's shoulders rests the fate of us all. Deny him and the Seven will fall, as surely as I will some day die and you inherit.'

For a moment Chan Yin was silent, thoughtful, then he looked up and met his father's eyes, smiling, understanding the full import of what was being asked of him.

'I swear to do as my father wishes. To support Li Yuan, whatever he asks.' He bowed low, then turned, facing his brothers. 'This I swear as a sacred trust, which you, my brothers, bear witness to.'

Wei Feng lay back again, relaxing, looking up at the three faces of his sons. 'You are good men. Good sons. A father could not ask for better sons.'

Leaning forward, Tseng-li kissed his father's brow. 'It isn't chosen, father,' he said softly, smiling at him once more. 'It simply is.'

Li Yuan sat at his desk, beneath the portrait of his grandfather. Across from him the face of Wu Shih, ten times its normal size, stared down at him from a huge wall screen.

'You talk of troubles to come, Yuan, but things have been quiet for some time now. The Lowers have not been so placid these past ten years.'

'Maybe so, but things are happening down there, Wu Shih. I can feel it. We are sitting on a powder keg.'

'And more powder every day, neh?' Wu Shih moved back a fraction, his features formed into a frown. 'Then maybe it is time, Yuan. Time to implement what we have already decided.'

Li Yuan sat there a moment, then nodded slowly. The decision had been made the day before, in Council, the terms for the 'new deal' agreed between the Seven. It remained only to put it before the representatives of the Above.

In principle the package was fairly straightforward. Five changes to the Edict of Technological Control, in specialised areas. Stricter monitoring controls. Changes to the Personal Liberty Act. More money to be spent on low level health care and maintenance support. Minor concessions concerning space travel. The reopening of the House of Representatives at Weimar. And in return, the House would set up the legal machinery for population controls.

Wu Shih sighed deeply and tugged at his plaited beard. 'My instincts cry out against giving those bastards anything. But as you have rightly argued, we have a problem and it will not go away. So...' He shrugged and raised his hands, as if in surrender.

'We go ahead then? We ratify the document?'

Wu Shih nodded. 'I see no point in waiting, Yuan. Even our cousin Wang is in agreement. Indeed, his amendments to the Edict changes were most thoughtful. It is clear the problem worries him as much as you or I.'

'Perhaps ...' Li Yuan looked away a moment, deep in thought, then turned back, facing the giant image of Wu Shih, meeting those plate-like almond eyes. 'We should have done this sixty years ago. Now ... Well, maybe it is already much too late. Maybe we are only building walls of sand against the tide.'

'Yet we must try, neh? We are Seven, after all.'

The tone of irony in Wu Shih's voice did not escape the young T'ang. Li Yuan laughed, then fell serious again. 'These are uncertain times, dear cousin. But whatever happens, remember that I count you as my friend. As brother to my father.'

Wu Shih stared back at him, his expression giving nothing away, then he nodded. 'You have my support, Li Yuan, in whatever you do. And yes, I will be an uncle to you in all things.' He smiled, relaxing. 'Well, so much for business. Now how is that child of yours? How is Kuei Jen?'

Li Yuan's face lit from within. 'He is ...' He hesitated, seeking the correct word, then laughed, finding nothing better than what had first come to mind. 'He is beautiful, Wu Shih. Simply the most beautiful thing I have ever seen.'

Michael Lever stood there on the balcony overlooking the ballroom of his father's mansion, remembering the last time he had been there, fifteen months before, at the great Thanksgiving Ball his father had thrown for the Supernal. Outwardly, things seemed to have changed very little; the pillars and balconies of the great hall were festooned as before with red, white and blue banners, while at the far end of the hall, beside a full-size replica of the ancient Liberty Bell, a twelve-piece band, dressed in the dark blue military uniform of the Revolution, played the battle tunes of the old American Empire – forbidden tunes that spoke eloquently of another age when the Americans ruled their own land and the Han were safe within their borders. Looking about him, it was easy to believe that this evening and the last were somehow connected, and that the fifteen months that had elapsed between were merely a dream, a dark delusion. But there was no connection, and those days – four hundred and sixty-three days, to be precise about it – had been no dream.

He pushed back from the edge, a feeling of hollowness, of a tiredness that went beyond mere physical exhaustion, making him feel giddy for a moment. There had been a breach. Whereas, before, he had looked at this with casual, accepting eyes, now he saw it clearly.

It was the same, and yet it was wholly, utterly different.

Like himself. Oh, he knew how he looked. He had stood there for a long time, earlier that afternoon, staring at himself in the full length mirror. He was gaunter than he'd been back then, and there was a haunted, slightly melancholy look about him that had not been there before, yet otherwise he seemed the man he'd been. But he was not that man.

From the beginning they had kept him – as they'd kept all the Sons – in isolation. At first he had not been frightened, but had nursed his anger in silence, expecting his release at any moment. Yet as the days wore on and no word came he had found his mood changing.

For several days he had bellowed at his guards and refused the food they brought. Then, changing his tack, he had adopted a more civil air, demanding firmly but politely to see whoever was in charge. Unexpectedly, his request had been granted.

He could still remember how it had felt, knelt before the man in that tiny, awful cell. Even thinking of it made him feel cold, apprehensive. Before that moment he had never felt fear, never had to bow his head before another man. But now he knew. And that knowledge had changed him. Had made him a different man. Now, when he looked at things, he saw not a world that was his to make and shape, but a world in thrall to power and desire, a world corrupted by the dark currents of domination and submission.

In the light of which his father's anger, earlier, at Wu Shih's treatment of him had seemed childish, almost laughable. What, after all, had he expected? Gratitude? Respect? No. For the relations of men were flawed – deeply flawed – as if they could not exist without the brutal mechanisms of power.

And now this. This celebration of his homecoming ...

He shuddered, then turned, making his way down, knowing he had no choice; that this evening had to be faced and overcome, if only for his father's sake. Even so, he did not feel like celebrating.

I have been on my own too long, he thought, feeling a faint uneasiness as the murmur of the crowd below grew louder. I'll have to learn all this again.

At the turn of the stairs, he paused, trying out a brief, apologetic smile, conscious of how awkward it felt, of the way the skin stretched tightly across his face. Then, reluctantly, like a prisoner being taken to the place of punishment, he moved on, down, into the body of the hall.

Charles Lever stared at his son, a broad grin splitting his face, then drew him close, holding him in a bear hug for the dozenth time that evening.

All about them, pressed close on every side, the pack of friends and relations laughed delightedly and raised their glasses to toast the two men, their joy unbounded.

'Have you told him yet, Charles?' one of them called out.

'Not yet,' Lever called back, holding his son's head between his hands and staring once more, as if he could not have enough of the sight.

'What's this?' Michael asked quietly.

'Later,' the old man answered. 'There's plenty of time.'

Much had changed, but he knew that tone in his father's voice. It was the tone he used when he wanted to avoid something awkward. Michael pressed him, softly but insistent. 'Tell me. I'd like to know.'

Lever laughed. 'Okay. I wanted to keep it a while, but I guess now's as good a time as any.' His smile broadened again. 'I've asked Ted Johnstone about Louisa. He's given his consent to bring things forward. I thought we could announce it tonight – make it a double celebration.'

Michael felt himself go cold. Louisa Johnstone ... He looked down, licking his lips, then looked back at his father. 'No,' he said softly, almost inaudibly.

'What did you say?' his father asked, leaning closer.

'I said no. I don't want that.'

'No?' Old Man Lever laughed, as if at a good joke. 'Hell, Michael, you can't say no. You've been betrothed to the girl fifteen years now. All I'm saying is that we bring the wedding forward.'

Michael looked about him at the expectant, joyous faces, then looked back at his father. Charles Lever had grown more solid by the year. His head rested like something carved upon a bull-like neck, the close trim of his ash white hair accentuating the robust power of his features.

That is how I will look, forty years from now, he thought. *But do I have to be like him as well?*

'Not now,' he said, wanting to let the matter drop; to save it for some quieter, less public moment, but his father was insistent. He slapped Michael's shoulder, as if encouraging a fighter.

'No, come on, Michael! It's a great time to announce it! It'll give everyone something to look forward to. And it'll help us put this thing behind us.'

Michael stared at his father, then shook his head. 'Please, father. I'm not ready for it. Let's talk about it tomorrow, neh?'

Even that, that attempt at the old, father-son tone, had been hard; had stretched his resources to their limit. But it was as if Charles Lever hadn't heard. He shook his massive head and gripped his son's arm firmly.

'Don't be silly, Michael. I know how you feel, but this'll help you snap out of it. A woman, that's what you need! And sons! Plenty of sons!'

'*Help* me?' The sharpness in Michael's voice made Lever jerk his head back, surprised.

Michael glared at his father, something breaking in him. 'Don't you understand? Don't you fucking understand? I don't *need* help. I need to be left alone. Sons... What use are fucking sons when I feel like *this*?'

The great room had gone deathly silent. A hundred faces stared at him, shocked and uncomprehending.

'There's no need ...' Old Man Lever began, but Michael made a dismissive gesture.

'You push me, father. You always did. But I mean it. I'm not marrying the girl. Not now, not ever, understand me?'

'*Michael!*'

But suddenly he was beyond words. He turned away, pushing through the crowd roughly, ignoring the shouting at his back; seeing only the floor of the tiny cell, the guard above him, that ugly mouth leaning close, shouting abuse, teaching him about how things really were.

PART EIGHTEEN Monsters of the Deep

SPRING 2209

'Humanity must perforce prey on itself,
Like monsters of the deep.'
—William Shakespeare, *King Lear*, Act IV, Sc. ii

'Go into emptiness, strike voids, bypass what he
defends, hit him where he does not expect you.'
—Tsao Tsao, (AD 155–220) Commentary on Sun
Tzu's *The Art Of War*

CHAPTER 77

EARTH

In the clear, golden light of dawn the seven 'gods of the soil and grain' stood at their places on the huge earthen mound. Dressed in dragon robes of imperial yellow, each held an ancient ceremonial hand plough, the primitive wooden shaft curiously curved, the long blade made of black rough-cast iron. Here, at the Temple of Heaven, at the very centre of the universe, the New Year rites were about to be enacted, the furrows ploughed, the sacrifices made to Hou T'u, 'He Who Rules The Earth', and Hou Chi, 'He Who Rules The Millet', as they had been since the time of T'ang, the founder of the Shang dynasty, three thousand seven hundred years before.

For a moment longer they stood there, while ten thousand blue-cloaked servants waited silently about the foot of the mound, the seven gold-clothed figures forming a single burnished eye at the centre of the dark circle of earth, and then it began, the pure tone of the bell sounding in the silence, followed by the low, monotonous chanting of the officials.

As one they bent, moving outwards, pushing the ploughs before them, seven black furrows forming in the earth like the spokes of a giant wheel.

Turning, Li Yuan looked across the circle of the mound, seeing his fellow T'ang spread out along the rim, their dark, silhouetted figures like pillars holding up Heaven itself, their yellow-gold silks fluttering like banners in the early morning breeze. For a moment the illusion was perfect. For the briefest moment he was back a thousand years, at the very centre of the ancient Middle Kingdom, the offerings made, the harvest guaranteed. But then, raising his eyes, he looked beyond his cousins, beyond the pleasant arbours and orchards of the Temple grounds.

The veil fell from his eyes. There, like a vast glacier dominating the skyline, lay the City, its pearl-white walls surrounding them on every side, towering over the lush greenery of the ancient gardens. For a moment he felt almost giddy. Then, checking himself, he stood straighter, listening to the chant, to the ancient words that spoke of the harmony between the ruler and the earth and of the balance of forces that must be maintained if the Kingdom was not to fall. For a moment he let himself be comforted by the ancient formula – by the thought that they might yet keep that age-old bargain and maintain the threefold link between Earth and Man and Heaven. But it was hard to concentrate. His eyes kept returning to the whiteness. To the giddying whiteness that encircled the tiny, earthen mound.

It was like death. Death on every side. And when, for the briefest moment, he let his attention stray, he grew conscious of the lie that lay behind their apparent unity. For in that moment of vertigo he had seen the Great Wheel break and spin aimlessly, like a cartwheel tumbling down a cliff face.

He shuddered and closed his eyes momentarily, wishing it were over, then looked down, noting the earth that clung to his boots and stained the hem of his silks. As on another day, eleven years before, when they had lain his brother, Han Ch'in, in his tomb.

Later, in the sedan returning to the *Chi Nien Tien*, the Hall of Prayer for Good Harvests, he thought of all that had happened since that day. Of the War-that-wasn't-a-War, of his father's death and of the failure of his marriage to his dead brother's wife, Fei Yen. All had left their scars. And yet he had come through; had endured all that pain and suffering, to reach these calm heights from which he might look back. This hilltop of contentment.

Yes. And that was the strangest thing of all. For there was no doubting how he had felt these past few weeks. His child, his wives – these, more than anything, had become his comfort, his delight. Outside the small circle of his family the storm clouds were gathering. There would be War again. Or worse. And yet he was happy. When he sat there, bouncing Kuei Jen on his knee, or carrying him against his shoulder, feeling his soft warmth and hearing the soft pattern of his breathing close by his ear, he would feel his cares fall from him. For a while there would be nothing but himself and the child, as if all else were a dream. And even afterwards, when he had to go out from that magic circle and face the problems of his world, he would carry that warmth – that light – within him, like a charm against the world's darkness.

The sedan swayed gently, tilting slowly backwards as the carriers climbed the broad, white marble ramp that led up to the great three-tiered tower.

Happy. Yes, he was happy now. And yet it was not enough.

Climbing down, he looked about him, attending closely to all he saw, as if this were the last time he would witness all of this. It was that thought – that strange and frightening glimpse of finality – which made him look away as Wu Shih came across.

'What is it Yuan?' Wu Shih said softly, speaking to his ear.

He turned back, smiling, taking the older man's arm. 'It's nothing, cousin. Just a fleeting thought.'

Wu Shih nodded, understanding. 'Then come. Let us make our sacrifices.'

The Seven stood in line before the great altar, their offerings held out before them. A bell sounded, high and pure in the silence, and then the chanting began again. Candles flickered in the shadows. New Confucian officials came forward, their saffron robes whispering against the stone floor, and took the offerings from the T'ang, turning back to lay them before the statue that crouched, thrice lifesize, on the altar.

Shang Ti, the Supreme Ancestor, looked down on his seven sons with blind, impassive eyes. He was Yang, Male, the personification of Heaven itself and the great arbiter of the weather. Appeased by sacrifices, he would provide good harvests; would look after the black-haired people. Neglected he would spurn them. Would bring plague and desolation. And death.

Or so it was said. So the officials chanted.

Li Yuan, standing there, was conscious suddenly of the great line of kings and emperors who had preceded him. Of that ghostly throng who stood with him, in his person, before the altar. Had they felt as he felt now? Or was he alone in doubting the efficacy of laying paper offerings before a blank-eyed statue?

It was not the first time he had questioned his beliefs. Often, in the past, he had looked squarely, critically at the rites and customs he, as T'ang, was obliged to perform. Yet this morning the ritual seemed more hollow than ever, his actions sheer pretence. And though he had questioned things before, he had never experienced so profound a mistrust of his own words and actions.

What, after all, did they mean? What did any of it mean?

Oh, he could see the beauty in it. Could even feel some part of him stir, responding to the powerful sense of tradition, to the great weight of years that the rituals evoked. But beyond that – beyond that simple, almost aesthetic thrill – there was nothing. Nothing at all.

He watched it all happening, distanced from himself, and tried to fathom why. These three things – the darkening clouds of circumstance, the great, enduring chain of tradition and the bright yet tiny circle of his own, individual happiness – how did they come together? Where did they meet and make sense?

As they bowed and backed away, he looked to either side of him, but on the faces of Wu Shih and Tsu Ma, of Hou Tung-Po and Chi Hsing, on the broad moon face of Wang Sau-leyan and the Regent Wei Chan Yin, there was nothing but a solemn certainty. Whatever they thought of this, it was hidden from him behind the walls of their faces.

They descended the steps in silence, slowly, almost casually now that the ritual was over, making for the great tent and the breakfast that had been laid out by their host Wei Chan Yin's servants. It was there, beneath the golden awning, that Wang Sau-leyan came across to Li Yuan, addressing him for the first time since his son had been born.

He faced Li Yuan, smiling, seemingly at ease, a tumbler of *ch'a* cradled in the palm of one hand. 'Well, cousin, and how is the child?'

It seemed an innocuous question – the kind of politeness one might have expected from a fellow T'ang – yet it was as if a shadow had fallen over Li Yuan. He felt a sudden tightening in his chest and – briefly, absurdly – experienced a powerful, overwhelming fear for his son. Then it passed. He was himself again. He forced a smile, lowering his head the merest degree, acknowledging his cousin's query.

'Kuei Jen is fine. He is a strong and healthy child. Heaven has blessed me, Wang Sau-leyan.'

Wang smiled, no sign of calculation in his face. 'I am pleased for you, cousin. A man should have sons, neh?'

Li Yuan stared back at the young T'ang of Africa, surprised by the almost wistful tone in Wang's voice, thinking to see something in his eyes, but there was nothing. Wang nodded and turned away, his business done. And Li Yuan, left to watch his back, stood there a moment, wondering, that small, hard nugget of fear returning, like a stone within his flesh.

Main was packed. Thirty, maybe forty thousand people were crammed into the broad two-li long concourse, banners and streamers of bright red ersilk waved energetically above their heads. At the northern end of Main, before the bell tower, a raised podium had been constructed. There the crowd pressed thickest, held back by a double line of green-uniformed Security guards.

As ninth bell sounded from the tower the lights dimmed, a hush falling on the great gathering. A moment later, cloaked in a veil of brilliant white laser light, the huge statue of the goddess descended slowly onto its pedestal.

As the figure settled there was a strong murmur of approval. Kuan Yin, Goddess of Mercy and Fecundity, sat, Buddha-like on a giant lotus, a new-born baby cradled lovingly in her arms. Her face in the brilliant white light was benign, radiant with compassion.

There was a moment's silence, then, with a great popping of crackers on every side and the creaking of rattles, the crowd began to celebrate. The sick and lame, held back by the crush, now renewed their efforts to get to the front, to receive the goddess's blessing.

On the podium nearby, separated from the crowd by a wide corridor of armed guards, the dignitaries looked on, turning in their high-backed chairs to talk amongst themselves. The guest of honour – the man whose money had paid for the giant statue – was a squat, balding Hung Mao named May Feng. His company, EduCol, had benefited from GenSyn's relaxation of food patents and – developing one of those patents – had increased food production significantly over the last twelve months, perhaps by as much as four per cent throughout City Europe, winning the praise of both T'ang and people. After years of ever-stricter rationing and growing discontent, it had reversed the trend and brought new stability to these levels. But what most of those gathered in Main to celebrate EduCol's generosity didn't know was just how poor, nutritionally, the new product was, nor the amount of profit the Company had made on their new soy-substitute; for while the new process cost only one-sixth of the old, the product price was roughly the same.

To May Feng's right sat a big, slightly corpulent Han named K'ang A-yin, a local gang leader, operating this and the surrounding stacks under the protection of the *Kuei Chuan* Triad. Behind K'ang stood two of his henchmen, their eyes shifting uneasily in their faces as they surveyed the massive crowd. K'ang himself was studying the merchant, noting the fashionable cut of his silk *pau*, the absence of rings on his fingers. K'ang looked away, tucking one hand under the other in his lap. He, at least, knew how much profit EduCol were making. Five hundred per cent, if reports were true. And he could use a cut of that, to buy himself more muscle and finance a few schemes. But May Feng knew nothing of that yet. As far as he was concerned, K'ang was simply a businessman. The man to deal with at these levels.

K'ang smiled and looked past May Feng at his friend, the local *Wei*, or Commandant of Security, who was standing off to one side of the podium. 'Well, Captain Franke. It's almost time ...'

Franke bowed his head, then turned, calling down to his lieutenant. A moment later the great curtain, which was draped across the width of Main behind the bell tower, twitched then began to draw back. From the tunnel beyond a procession of carts, heaped with the latest range of EduCol products, began to make its way out into Main towards the crowd.

At the far end of Main, on a balcony almost two *li* from where the dignitaries were sitting, a tall, bearded *Hung Mao* lowered the field glasses from his eyes and turned, making a curt hand signal. At once the group of men and women gathered about him turned, making their way down the steps and out into the crowd below.

Mach watched them a moment, seeing how they went amongst the crowd, handing out the leaflets, their voices murmuring old slogans, the catch-phrases of ancient discontents. And after they'd moved on, he saw how those who had glanced at the leaflets now held them out to their neighbours, angered by what they'd read, their own voices raised.

He smiled, then turned away again, moving out into the corridor. Two guards were standing there, staring up at one of the public service screens.

'You'd best get downstairs,' he said, showing them his ID. 'It looks like trouble.'

They looked at his badge, then nodded, moving past him quickly, the noise from the crowd growing by the moment.

Mach stood there a moment longer, looking up at the screen. Li Yuan was talking to his citizens, telling them about the committee that had been set up to investigate the possibility of changes to the Edict and the reopening of the House. Mach moved closer, spitting up into the face of the young T'ang, then, drawing his gun, he turned, following the guards down.

On the podium May Feng was standing now, concerned. The noise from the far end of Main was growing all the while, rising above the sound of the firecrackers. People at the front were turning their heads, anxious, conscious that something was happening back there.

'What is it, Shih K'ang?' the merchant asked, fingering his girdle-pouch nervously.

K'ang frowned, trying to conceal his own concern. 'I'm not sure. I ...'

His words were drowned out as deck communications cut in, the voice harsh and accusing.

'Death to all profiteers and thieving First Level bandits! Death to all those who would steal the rice from your children's mouths! Death to those who profit from the misery and need of others! Death ...'

The litany went on, fanatical, endless, stirring up already excited passions into a frenzy; turning fear into a sudden blinding panic that spread amongst the masses like a brushfire. K'ang watched as the thin line of green gave and the crowd spilled out towards the podium and the giant statue. Without thought, he turned and, his henchmen close behind, leapt from the back of the platform, making for the safety of the tunnel. It was not a moment too soon, for the front edge of the crowd, impelled by the pressure of bodies from behind, broke like a wave against the podium, bringing its supporting stanchions crashing down.

For a moment May Feng kept his balance, then he went down, his mouth formed in a perfect 'O' of surprise before he was lost to sight, trampled beneath the stampeding crowd. There was a steady roar within the great space now, like the sound of a great wind blowing from the north. As if caught in the grip of that wind, the great statue shuddered, then, with a slow, soundless motion, it fell, crushing more than two dozen people beneath it.

All was chaos now. There was gunfire from the far end of Main and the sound of small explosions, of falling ice. And over everything was the voice, chanting its litany of death, death, death.

There were three of them, not counting the stallholder. Becker was standing at the back of the partitioned room, browsing the shelves of second-hand tapebooks that crowded the walls. Haller lounged in a chair nearby, staring up at the overhead FacScreen, one hand lazily holding a squeezetube of prawn-flavoured protein paste.

Lehmann was talking to the owner, Pai Mei, his back to the doorway. 'Don't worry,' he was saying. 'Just get down behind the counter when things start. And remember – no one will harm you. I guarantee it.'

Pai Mei, a thin-faced, hard-looking man hesitated. K'ang A-yin was a bastard, but who knew what this one was like? Yet if the albino failed, K'ang might think that he, Pai Mei, had put him up to it. He shuddered, then gave a reluctant nod. It was a no-win situation.

Just then the ragged curtain was tugged back and two men came in. One was tall, going to fat, the other smaller, lither, but more dangerous-looking altogether. His bare arms were heavily-muscled and his head was shaved, the skull painted in an intricate pattern of red and green that indicated he was a *chan shih*, a fighter. They were K'ang's men.

The fat man stopped and looked about him. Glancing sourly at Pai Mei, he touched the *chan shih*'s arm. 'Move them. I want to speak to Shih Pai in private.'

The small man tapped Haller on the shoulder, indicating that he should go and quick. Smiling, apologetic, Haller got up and went. Becker, turning, saw how things stood and, shoving the tape back hastily, scuttled out after Haller. Only Lehmann remained, his back to the newcomers.

'You,' said the fat man, coming up behind him. 'Out of here! I've business with Shih Pai.'

Lehmann turned, facing them. The *chan shih* seemed easier now that there was only Lehmann in the room. He relaxed, looking about the room, for that brief moment inattentive. The fat man, meanwhile, was staring at Lehmann curiously, as if he ought to know him. But even he, for that instant, was off his guard.

Lehmann struck. With one quick movement he kicked the *chan shih* beneath the chin, then turned to face the fat man. Panicking, K'ang's lieutenant tugged at the gun in his pocket, trying to free it. He had just levelled it when Lehmann punched it from his hand, breaking the man's wrist with the downward blow. His second punch floored the man. Lehmann stood over him, looking down, his fist raised, waiting to see if he would try to get up.

Haller and Becker stood in the doorway, smiling. They had seen already how Lehmann operated. Becker looked across at Pai Mei and laughed. The stallholder had gone white. He was staring at Lehmann in astonishment.

'I thought that all three of you ...'

Pai Mei left the sentence unfinished.

Becker stepped into the room and knelt down beside the *chan shih*, feeling for a pulse at the neck. The small man was dead. 'Shame,' Becker said darkly. 'I would have liked to have seen his expression when I slit his throat.' Haller, coming up beside him, laughed at that, but Lehmann was unmoved. He stood there over his wheezing victim, tensed, perfectly still, making sure.

'That's it, you see,' Becker said, looking up at the stallholder, then drew a large, razor-sharp knife from beneath his tunic. 'They never expect trouble from a single man. That's how they think. And in the moment that they least expect trouble, that's when they're at their weakest.' He smiled again and looked across at Lehmann, as if to say, 'Isn't that so, *Shih* Lehmann?' But Lehmann ignored him. Becker looked down again, shrugging, then got to work, cutting into the flesh at the neck, blood oozing out over the bare, unswept floor.

Pai Mei looked away, feeling sick.

He looked across. Lehmann was crouching now, talking to the fat man. K'ang's man was making hoarse, gasping noises, as if he'd damaged his windpipe, but he was listening very carefully as the albino spelt out what he was to tell his boss. At one point he laughed dismissively and turned his head away, but Lehmann grasped his chin in one long, pale hand and turned his head back savagely, forcing him to look up into his face. The fat man shut up at once, fear returning to his eyes.

Becker had finished now. He wrapped the head in a towel and dropped it into a bag. Haller, in the doorway, was looking past him, his attention on the FacScreen and the media speculation about what tomorrow's meeting of the Seven might bring for the people of Chung Kuo.

'Big things are happening up there,' he said at last, looking down at Becker, ignoring the pool of blood that had formed about his feet. 'Big changes are coming.'

'As above, so below,' said Lehmann, pulling the fat man to his feet. Then, taking the bag from Becker, he thrust it into the man's one good hand.

Watching him, the two men laughed, enjoying the fat man's discomfort. But Lehmann didn't smile. Lehmann *never* smiled.

The *tong* boss, K'ang A-yin, sat back in his chair, drawing the back of his hand across his mouth, then looked around him at the eight men gathered in the room. The Zwickau riot had shocked and angered him, but this latest news was too much. K'ang was trembling with rage. Only with the greatest effort did he keep himself from shouting.

'Okay. What the fuck is going on? Who the fuck's this *Hung Mao*?'

There was an awkward silence from his men, then one of them – Soucek, his lieutenant – spoke up.

'We don't know. I sent a runner to Pai Mei's. He only confirmed what Feng Wo said. The pale *Hung Mao* killed the *chan shih*. The others hacked his head off. Why, we don't know.'

'And no one knows the bastard?'

Soucek shrugged. 'You want I should do some asking?'

K'ang looked away a moment, considering, then shook his head. 'No. I've a better idea. Chao, Kant ... I want you to find out where he's staying and hit him. When the fucker's asleep. I want him dead, him and his two side-kicks. And I want their heads, back here, on my desk, by the morning.'

Soucek made to say something, to insist, perhaps, that he be given the job of killing the *Hung Mao*, but K'ang raised a hand. 'No, Jiri. Not this time. I want you to go and see Whiskers Lu and find out all you can about what happened earlier. If the *Yu* are active again, it threatens us all. And if it's something else, I want to know, understand?'

Soucek nodded.

K'ang stood, looking about him, more at ease now that he was taking the initiative. 'Good. Then let's get going. Let's sort these fuckers out, neh? Then we can get on with making money.'

They came two hours later. Lehmann was expecting them. Haller's bunk was empty, Haller fifty *ch'i* down the corridor in the public washroom. Becker's was occupied, but by a dummy, while Becker crouched behind the false partition, gun in hand. Lehmann lay beneath the thin blanket on the upper bunk, masked and waiting. He too was armed.

There were no locks at these lowest levels, so it was easy for K'ang's man to pull the slide-to back a fraction and roll in the gas grenade. It exploded with a dull plop, followed instantly by the hiss of escaping gas. Lehmann counted, knowing they would make certain before coming through. Sure enough, on a count of thirty, the slide-to was heaved aside and two men came into the room, machine-pistols raised. A third waited outside.

He didn't give them a chance. Poking the muzzle of the rocket-launcher from the blanket, he squeezed the hair-trigger and watched the far wall explode. There was no sign of the two men. Wall, floor and men had gone. A great, gaping hole had opened up, revealing the level below. Fractured cables sparked. There was screaming from below and the sweet stink of super-heated plastics hung in the air, stronger than the gas.

From further down the corridor two shots rang out. Haller had done his job. He appeared a moment later, gun in hand, looking across the gap into the room. 'Messy,' he said, grinning through his mask. 'Maybe K'ang will talk now.'

'We'll see,' Lehmann said, sitting up and wrapping the big gun in the blanket. 'Either way, he'll know now that we aren't so easy. He'll be more careful in future.'

'That's good,' said Haller, slipping the gun back in his shoulder-holster, 'It was a bit too easy for my liking.'

Lehmann said nothing. He simply looked at Haller and shook his head. They had a lot to learn.

From where it soared, high above the wood, the hawk could see the figures down below, amongst the trees. The leading group had stopped now in a clearing, resting their mounts, their necks strained back, hands shielding their eyes as they looked up at it. Further back, partly hidden by foliage, a second group waited. These last were smaller but more numerous and in its dark, instinctive way, it knew these to be men; knew they were on foot.

It circled patiently, its keen eyes searching for that sudden, distinctive movement that would betray its prey. For a time there was nothing, then, as the wind changed, there was a flutter of sound and a brief blur, as a guinea-fowl broke cover far below.

With a cry the hawk fell, turning, straining after its prey. For a moment it seemed as if the other bird might yet regain its perch, then, with a sickening thud, the hawk struck.

A roar of triumph erupted from the men below.

In the clearing the three men leaned forward, watching the hawk spread its wings wide, slowing its fall, the fowl held tightly in its talons, then settle on the ground amongst the trees to their right.

Tsu Ma leaned down, patting the dark neck of his mount fondly, then turned his head, looking across at his fellow T'ang. 'Well, cousins, what do you think?'

Wu Shih placed one hand carefully on the pommel of his saddle and turned slightly, inclining his head. They were talking of their cousin, Wang Sau-leyan, T'ang of Africa. 'I don't trust him,' he said. 'He has been too quiet these past six months. Too damned polite.'

'He's up to something,' Li Yuan added, sitting straighter in his saddle. 'Something deep. Something we can't see yet.'

Wu Shih nodded. 'I agree. I am not certain about much in these troubled times, but of this I *can* be sure … Wang Sau-leyan has not changed his nature. He is still the same devious little shit-eating insect he always was.'

Tsu Ma looked past them momentarily, watching his falconer run across to where the hawk had brought down its prey, his lure out, ready to draw the hawk off, then looked back at Wu Shih.

'I think you are right,' he said. 'But exactly what it is … Well, it's very strange. My servants in his household have heard nothing. Or almost nothing …'

'*Almost* nothing?' Wu Shih stared at him intently.

'Just that there is a woman in his life. Or so it seems. A *Hung Mao*. He has her smuggled in. Late, when he thinks no one will see. I'm told he even visits her.'

Li Yuan looked away. 'How strange. I would not have thought it. A *Hung Mao* … And you think it is serious?'

Tsu Ma shrugged. 'Maybe it is nothing. Or maybe this is why our cousin has behaved himself so well recently. Perhaps he has been distracted.'

'In love, you mean?' Wu Shih roared with laughter. 'The only one that ingrate will ever love is his own reflection. Love!' He shook his head, then reached down, slapping his horse's flank. 'No … that moon-faced bastard is up to something. I guarantee it!'

'*Chieh Hsia* …'

A servant stood at the edge of the clearing, his head bowed.

'What is it, Cheng Yi?'

At Tsu Ma's summons, the man came across, his body bent double, and took his T'ang's foot, kissing it, before falling to his knees beside the horse.

'News has come, *Chieh Hsia*. There have been riots in City Europe. Many have died ...'

'Riots ...' Li Yuan urged his horse forward sharply. 'What in the gods' names has been happening?'

The servant bowed his head lower, answering as if his own T'ang had spoken. 'It began at Zwickau *hsien*, *Chieh Hsia*, at the dedication ceremony for the new statue, and spread quickly to surrounding stacks.'

'And many have died?'

'That is so, *Chieh Hsia*. A great number. Tens of thousands, some say. Amongst them the merchant, May Feng.'

Li Yuan looked across at Tsu Ma, alarmed. May Feng had been a leading figure in the new peace. Had sat on committees to discuss the proposed Edict changes and the reopening of the House. What's more, he represented a whole class – of powerful First Level merchants – who had been won back to the Seven and their cause. And now he was dead.

Li Yuan leaned towards the man, anxious now. 'What happened? How did he die?'

The servant swallowed. 'It is not clear how he died, *Chieh Hsia*. All we know is that his body was returned to his widow shortly afterwards. He had been cut open, it seems, then stuffed with dirt like a sack and sewn up again.'

Li Yuan sat back. 'Do we know who was responsible?'

'It is too early yet to know for certain, *Chieh Hsia*. Early rumours attributed it to the *Yu*, but General Rheinhardt believes that the *Hung Mun* had a hand in this.'

Again, Li Yuan felt a ripple of shock pass through him. The *Hung Mun* – the Triads, or Secret Societies – had kept out of things before now. But that was clearly changing. If they *were* involved ...

'I must get back,' he said, turning his horse, looking from Tsu Ma to Wu Shih. 'If the *Hung Mun* are involved, I must act.'

'No, Yuan,' Tsu Ma said, putting out a hand to him. 'I would counsel against acting too rashly. Take some measure to calm things down, by all means, but consider before you take action against the brotherhoods. Your father's scheme, for instance ...'

'Buy them off, you mean?' Li Yuan sat back, shaking his head. 'No, Tsu Ma. I will not bow to them in my own City!'

'Nor am I asking you to, cousin. Pursue your father's scheme – offer them funds, assistance, power of a kind – while all the time undermining their position.'

Li Yuan narrowed his eyes. 'What do you mean?'

'The new force. Karr's *shen t'se* ...'

Li Yuan looked down, then he smiled. 'You know of that?'

Tsu Ma nodded. 'My cousin's business is my business. How can I know how I might help him unless I know his needs, his plans?'

Li Yuan turned, looking to the older man. 'And you, Wu Shih?'

Wu Shih shrugged. 'You have a special force, I take it. Good. Then use it. Do as our good cousin, Tsu Ma, says. Play a double game. Buy time. For it's time we need right now, not another War. Not yet.'

Tsu Ma nodded. 'Wu Shih is right, Yuan. Fight a war against the brother-hoods now and it would weaken us greatly. And who would benefit?'

'Wang Sau-leyan.'

'Exactly. So do not be goaded into a futile war.' Tsu Ma smiled bleakly. 'Oh, the time will come – and not so long from now – when we must take on the *Hung Mun*. But let us pick that time, neh? Let us be prepared for it.'

'Besides,' Wu Shih added, coming alongside him, 'we have problems enough already, neh? The *Yu*, the Younger Sons ... Why add to them?'

Li Yuan was silent a moment, calming himself, then reached out, tak-ing Wu Shih's arm. 'Thank you, cousin. And you, Tsu Ma. But we must get back, neh? There is much to be done. Besides, watching the hawk has whet-ted my appetite for other sport.'

Tsu Ma stared at him a moment, then laughed. 'For once, Yuan, your meaning escapes me, but let it pass. You are right. There is much to be done. Nonetheless, we must meet more often, neh? Just the three of us.'

'It shall be so,' Wu Shih said, giving a brief, decisive nod. 'We shall be like the three brothers of the peach garden, neh?'

Li Yuan, watching the two older men, felt the darkness subside a little. So it would be. So it *had* to be from now on. *The Three*, he thought, trying the term out in his head for the first time, and finding it not strange but strangely comforting. *Yes, we shall be The Three.*

There was a sudden flutter of sound. Behind Li Yuan, on the far side of the clearing, the hawk lifted, stretching its wings, then settled on its kill once more, ignoring the lure.

CHAPTER 78

IN THE WORLD OF LEVELS

Jelka was stretched out on the sunbed, looking out across the brightly-lit expanse of tiles to where her two school friends splashed noisily in the pool. Beside her on the chair lay the compact computer notepad she had been using, its display screen lit.

For a moment she watched their antics thoughtlessly, enjoying the warmth on her skin, the faint scent of jasmine and pine from the nearby rock garden. Then, with a tiny shiver, she returned to the matter she had been considering.

Yesterday had been the last day of school; the end of her childhood, of twelve years preparing for her adult life. Ahead of her, tonight, lay the ordeal of the College Graduation Ball, and beyond that the rest of her life – fifty, sixty years of it, maybe, needing to be filled.

But how?

She turned over, lying on her back a moment, conscious of how it felt to be herself, seventeen, in a young woman's body, the future open to her.

She stretched her legs, flexing her toes, exercising the muscles of her feet and calves and thighs, as if warming up for an exercise session, then relaxed again. *The Marshal's daughter* ... that was how she was known. As if she had no separate identity of her own.

Jelka shook her head, exasperated, then turned onto her stomach again. The Marshal's daughter ... If she had been his son, her future would have been mapped out long before today. Cadet school, a commission, and then the service. Fifty years of service: of dodging assassins' bullets and attending official functions; of investigating murders and pandering to the whims of some old Minister; of unearthing corruption scandals at First Level and tidying up after riots beneath the Net. Such was her father's life, and there were far worse ways of spending one's time, but it wasn't that. It was having a say in her future. As a son to the Marshal she would have had no say in things.

Not that being a daughter had made all that great a difference. Had it not been for Hans Ebert's duplicity – for the betrayal of his T'ang and the murder of his father – she would have been married now, her future set, determined. And no way out.

She shuddered, recollecting her aversion for the young Major. That was something her friends had never understood. Something which, when she mentioned it, brought looks of incredulity. Hans Ebert ... why, he had been every schoolgirl's dream, surely? A prince amongst men. She laughed sourly, remembering how often she had heard him called that. Moreover, as heir to the richest Company in Chung Kuo, she could have expected a life of idleness, of unremitting luxury.

Yes, but Hans Ebert was also cruel, and arrogant and devious.

She looked down, recalling her father's hurt when Hans had finally been exposed; a hurt mingled with grief at the death of his brother and his wife, and of his oldest friend, Klaus Ebert. She too had felt a similar grief, but also relief that Hans was gone from her life; a relief that was like a huge stone lifted from her chest. She sighed and shook her head. Maybe that was why it was so important now to get it right; to make sure that her life from here on was her own.

It seemed simple enough, but there was one small complication. She was a woman. For her friends that seemed to pose no problems. Only five of the sixty girls in her year were not yet betrothed, and of those, three were actively pursuing a husband. Eight were already married and two – her close friend Yi Pang-chou amongst them – had already presented their husbands with a child. Against which, only six of her year were going on to Oxford, and in each case it was not so much to fulfil their own needs as to make them the perfect companions for their high-flying husbands.

But so it was in this god-awful world of levels. To be a woman – an intelligent, capable young woman – it was unthinkable! One had to be a drudge, a whore, an ornament ...

'Jelka?'

She hesitated, then turned, lifting her head lazily, as if she had been doz-
ing. 'Hi ... What is it?'

Anna was crouched beside her, towelling her dripping hair. Beyond her
stood the stocky figure of Yi Pang-chou. She was grinning, a faint colour in
her cheeks.

'You should have joined us, Mu-Lan. What have you been doing?'

She smiled at the use of her nick-name, then sat up, stretching, conscious of how her friends were watching her.

'I was thinking. And making lists.'

'Making lists?' Anna laughed. 'Lists of what? Men you'd like to marry?
Why, you could have any man you chose, Jelka Tolonen, and you know it.'

Jelka shrugged. 'Maybe. But it wasn't that kind of list. I was jotting down
my options.'

'Jotting down my options,' Yi Pang-chou mimicked, then giggled.

Jelka smiled, good-humouredly. 'I know how it sounds, but here,' she
handed the comset across to Anna. 'Go on. Have a look. Tell me what you
think.'

Anna studied the screen a moment, then turned, passing it up to Yi Pang-
chou. 'I can't see the point,' she said, looking at Jelka with a slightly puzzled
frown. 'It's so much effort. Why not simply enjoy yourself? Take a rich husband. It doesn't mean you have to be in his pocket. These days a woman has
much more freedom.'

Jelka looked away. Freedom! As if Anna had any understanding of the
word's true meaning. What she meant was the freedom to go to countless
entertainments; to drink and play to excess and to take young officers for
lovers. Beyond that she had no idea. For her this world of levels was enough.
But then, she knew no different. She had not seen how beautiful it was outside.

Yi Pang-chou had been studying her list. Now she looked back at Jelka,
puzzled.

'This entry for Security. I thought they didn't accept women in the service.'

'They don't. Or not yet. But I thought I'd apply. I'm as qualified as any cadet, after all. And I can fight. So why not? I thought I'd apply for the auxiliary

forces, specialising in space operations.'

Anna raked one hand through her long dark hair, then laughed. 'You're strange, Jelka. You know that? If you really want to meet young officers, you should attend a few more parties. You don't have to sign up for the service!'

'And you've a one-track mind, Anna Koslevic!' Jelka laughed, then grew serious again. 'I know it's hard to understand, but I want to do something with my life. I don't just want ... well, I don't want to waste it, that's all.'

'Like us, you mean,' Yi Pang-chou said, coming across and sitting beside her on the edge of the sunbed.

'No ... I didn't mean it like that. I ...' Again she laughed, but this time her laughter was tinged with a certain desperation. 'Look, I can talk to you two. I can say things without you being hurt by them. So when I say that I want something more than what I'm being offered, it's not to put you down. It's ...' She shrugged. 'I don't know. Maybe I want something that I simply can't have, but why not try for it?' She looked from one to the other. 'Do you understand?'

'Sure,' Anna said, nodding. 'It's simple. You want to be a man. You want to go out there and do things. You want to break skulls and ride horses. Like your 'ex', Hans.'

Jelka shook her head. 'No. I want only to be myself. But why should that be so difficult? Why should I be denied that?'

'Because it's how things are,' Yi Pang-chou said, stroking the back of her hand. 'There's us and there's them. Women and Men. Yin and Yang. And it's a Yang world.' She smiled sadly. 'Don't fight it, Mu Lan. It'll only make you unhappy.'

She looked down. Maybe so. But she would never be at peace unless she tried. Besides, there was always Kim. He, if anyone, would understand.

Anna leaned close, placing her hand on Jelka's knee. 'Anyway. Let's forget about all that for now. It's almost six and our escorts are coming at eight, so we'd best get ready.'

'Escorts?' Jelka looked up, eyeing her friend sharply. 'You didn't say anything about escorts!'

'Didn't I?' Anna laughed innocently. 'I guess it must have slipped my mind. Anyway, let's go through. I'll lend you one of my chi pao ... the blue and grey silk with the black edging. And then I'll make you up. Maybe it'll take your mind off all this nonsense ...'

Jelka sat there, looking from one to the other, then laughed. 'All right. Just this once. But I hope you haven't said anything. Anything, well ...'

'Anything *true*?' Anna put on an earnest face, mirroring Jelka's own, then burst out laughing. She leaned across, kissing Jelka's brow. 'Come. Let's get ready. Before those big, hulking Yangs arrive!'

The main building of the Bremen Academy for Young Women – a huge *yamen* in the old northern style – dominated the open space at the top of the stack. On the great terrace overlooking the lake it was hot, the music loud. On the dance floor the press of young, well-dressed bodies filled the dimly-lit darkness, the rich, cloyingly-sweet scents of the dancers tainting the air, their drunken laughter echoing out across the water.

It was late now, almost midnight, and the Ball had reached a fever pitch of intensity. For the young women, the days of hard work were behind them, the long vacation ahead, while for the young men, cadets and commissioned officers alike, there was a sense of temporary surcease from the rigours of duty. Tonight was a night for celebration, for high spirits and wild excess. Some lay in the corridors leading off the terrace, slumped in drunken stupor, while others cavorted wildly at the edges of the crowd, howling maniacally, their formal jackets unbuttoned or cast aside. Most, however, had found partners and could be found pressed close in that central darkness, washed over by a heavy pulse of sound, willing victims of those old, insistent currents.

Jelka stood there at the centre of that great crush, cradling an empty glass, alone at last and conscious, for the first time that evening, just how awful it was. The heat was stifling, the noise oppressive, while to every side the crowd pressed in on her relentlessly; a great tide of bodies, male and female, jerking and swaying to the ancient rhythms of the pipes and drums.

For a moment longer she stood there, hemmed in, wondering if she should wait for her escort to return from the bar, then she turned and began to make her way across. She was aware of the unnatural excitement in the faces that she passed; of the feverish brightness of their eyes, the sudden, excessive animation of their features. There was something strange and frightening about it all, a sense of primal urgency, almost of hysteria.

Outside it was cooler, quieter. Jelka stood there at the top of the steps, gulping in the cold, refreshing air and staring about her, as if waking from some dark and threatening dream. Overhead, a very real-looking moon shone down on her from the artificial sky, casting a painted light upon the distant mountains, while to her left a faint breeze rippled the dark lake's surface, scattering petals on the white stone arch of the bridge that led across to the island and the great watchtower.

Away, she thought. *I have to get away.*

She set her glass down on the steps, then made her way down, out onto the path that led to the bridge, half running now, as if pursued. Halfway down, however, she stopped and turned, staring back at it all, her mouth wide open, as if stupefied. Then, with a faint shudder, she went on.

At the foot of the watchtower she stopped again, staring up at its brightly-lit face. It was two minutes to midnight. Twelve years she had been here at the Academy; twelve years, not including the time she had spent in exile with her father and that time she had been ill, after the attack. And in all that time she had never – not once – felt at home here. She had stood there earlier, listening to the other girls say how much they'd miss the dear old place; had heard them profess to a genuine love for its strange old ways and nonsensical rules, but for herself she felt nothing; only a strange relief that it was over. And a sense of emptiness – of something unfulfilled in her.

She turned briefly, looking back, wondering if she had been missed yet, then moved on quickly, climbing the broad yet shallow steps up to the open doorway. Inside, in the shadows just inside the door, a couple were leaning against the wall, kissing, her hand at his neck, his arm about her lower back. She hesitated, watching them a moment, then tiptoed by, making her way up to the first level and the little room at the front of the tower, above the clock.

She closed the door behind her, then went across and sat on the box beside the window, her elbows on the mock-stone of the window ledge, looking back across the lake at the crowded terrace. From a distance it seemed a kind of madness, a mass delirium. As if, for once, they had glimpsed the hollowness of it all. Glimpsed it and turned away, drowning themselves in this frenzy of thoughtless activity.

She rested her chin on her hands and sighed. Coming here tonight had been a mistake. She should have trusted to instinct and stayed at home. But now it was too late.

Too late for what?

That small, inner voice – that never-resting, ever-questioning part of her – was what kept her at a distance from it all; was what made her different from the others. At school she had always been something of an outsider, right from the first. Not that she had been unpopular; it was simply that she had never formed any of those close relationships that the other girls seemed to need. Some had tried, like Anna and Yi Pang-chou, but they could only get so close before she clammed-up on them. 'It's because of the attacks,' Anna had said to her once. 'It's only natural that you should mistrust the world after what happened to you.' And maybe that was true. Maybe those experiences had shaped her. But the explanation was somehow insufficient, for she had always felt like this. From the cradle on. There had always been a space unfilled in her. A lack. But tonight it was different. Tonight the sheer intensity of what she felt was new to her.

Looking back at the dance floor, she saw not celebration and the joyous blossoming of new life, but a mechanistic orgy of self-denial; of deadness incarnate. It was pretence; pretence on a vast scale. It began with the great City in which they lived and spread like a virus to infect every pore, every cell of their individual beings. And now there was nothing. Nothing but meaningless activity and a desperate filling of the hours. A wilful forgetting.

She turned her head, her eyes sweeping the familiar landscape of the College grounds, taking it all in. The star-filled sky, the moon, the distant mountains; it was false, every last tiny bit of it. The arched stone bridge the lake, the ancient building. Manufactured, all of it; a substitute for life, conjured from nothingness.

Too late.

She shuddered. It was true. Never had she felt so alienated from it all. Never so alone.

I am trapped, she thought. *Trapped in the world of levels.*

On the steps beside the dance floor there was movement. A young cadet officer had stepped out onto the top step and now stood there, looking about him, a glass in each hand.

Jelka shivered and drew her head back, into the shadows.

He looked down and spotted the empty glass, then turned back, craning to see where she had gone. Then he came on, negotiating the steps smartly, elegantly, his manner – the very way he walked – assured and arrogant. Unquestioning. On he came, along the path and up onto the gentle arch of the bridge. For a moment he stood there, looking about him casually, as if taking in the view, then he walked on, glancing up at the watchtower, as if he could see her, there in the shadows beyond the window frame.

She moved back, then stood, looking about her. There was no way out. The floor above was locked. But maybe he would go away. The couple …

She heard noises from below; an angry grunt and then a murmured, 'Excuse me, I …', followed by the sound of booted feet ringing on the stairs.

She turned, facing the doorway, watching as it slowly opened.

'Ah, there you are,' he said softly, smiling at her. 'I thought …'

He held out her glass to her, as if she should take it, but she simply stood there, staring at him. He frowned, not understanding, then, stooping carefully, watching her all the while, he set the glasses down.

The jacket of his dress uniform seemed to glow in the light from the window. The rich scent he wore filled the tiny room.

He hesitated, then came closer. 'You should have said,' he said gently. 'I thought you liked the music.'

She could feel his breath on her cheek now; could smell the sweetness of the wine. As if in a dream she saw his right hand lift and press gently against her left shoulder, as if they were about to dance.

'Don't …'

'Just one kiss,' he whispered, his mouth close to her ear. 'Just one tiny, little kiss …'

She moved back, shrugging off his hand. '*Please* …'

She saw the movement in his face. The sudden anger, softening instantly.

'One kiss,' he persisted. 'You know you'd like to.'

She laughed sourly. 'You know that, do you?'

He laughed, the uncertainty in his eyes fading quickly. 'Of course. That's why we're here, isn't it? Young girls like to be kissed. It's only natural. And you're a very beautiful young woman, Jelka Tolonen. Very beautiful indeed.'

He made to touch her once again, to lift her chin and kiss her, but she pushed him back sharply, the palm of her hand thudding against his chest.

'No. Understand me, Lieutenant? Other 'girls' might well like it, but I don't wish to be kissed. I simply want to be left alone.'

He looked down at where her hand had struck his chest, then back at her, angry now. 'You shouldn't have done that.'

Again she laughed. Who was he to tell her what she should or shouldn't do? She glared at him angrily, then made to push past him and go down, but he grabbed her arm roughly and pulled her about.

'You'll kiss me, understand?'

She stared at him, for that brief instant seeing things clearly. Here it was again. As in that moment when she had faced Hans Ebert in the machine, the day they had been officially betrothed. Yes, and as in that moment when the wall to the practice room had been ripped aside and the three assassins had burst in. To possess her or to kill her, there seemed no other choice for them, these half-men. Like the pure Yang they were, they had either to dominate or destroy.

Maybe so. But she would not acquiesce in it. Would not permit it.

She lifted her chin challengingly. 'Are you drunk, Lieutenant Bachman, or just suicidal?'

His right hand was clasping her wrist. Slowly he increased the pressure on it, drawing her closer, his eyes watching her all the while, his smile brutal, unforgiving now. Slowly she moved closer, drawn in towards him, until only a hand's breadth separated them.

His left hand reached up and held her shoulder, his fingers digging into her flesh, holding her there.

'Kiss me and I'll break your neck,' she warned, her voice cold now, dangerous.

He laughed, unimpressed. 'Oh, I've heard the rumours, Jelka Tolonen. I've heard how you fought off the assassins that time. You're a real tigress, neh? A regular Mu Lan. But you will kiss me. And you'll not break my neck.'

There was a moment's softness in his face, a moment's relaxation, and then he tugged her towards him savagely, his face pushing out at hers, his mouth straining to find hers.

And then he was gasping, doubled up, groaning where her knee had come up hard into his stomach. Jelka stood back, breathing unevenly, looking down at him, then she turned and went down the stairs hurriedly, leaping the last four and barging unceremoniously past the couple in the doorway.

'Hey ...'

Outside, she almost ran into her friends.

'Jelka ...' Anna said, holding her arms and looking up into her face.

'What is it?'

She drew herself up straight, then shook her head. 'It's nothing ... Really.'

'Are you sure?' Yi Pang-chou said, concerned. 'You look dreadful. Your face ...'

'I'm okay,' Jelka answered, rather too harshly. Then, relenting a little. 'Look, it's all right. I've sorted things out. Let's go back now, okay?'

Beyond the two young women, their escorts looked on, not certain whether amusement or concern were the right expression. 'Where's that randy bastard Lothar?' one of them called. 'Don't tell me you've worn the young ram out!'

'Enough!' Anna said sharply, turning to them. 'Can't you see something's happened?'

'Too fucking true it has!'

The voice came from behind them. From the watch-tower. Bachman stood there in the doorway, one hand to his stomach, his face distorted with anger.

'You should ask the bitch what she's up to, leading me on and then kneeing me in the fucking stomach!'

Jelka turned, a cold, hard anger transforming her. If he said another word ...

'She needs a fucking beating, that's what she needs, the spoilt little brat! She needs someone to knock some manners into her ...'

'Lothar!' one of the young officers hissed. 'Remember who she is, for fuck's sake! Her father ...'

'Fuck her father!' Bachman snarled, then straightened up and pushed himself away from the doorway. 'I don't give a shit if she runs and tells her father! That's the way of these bitches, neh? The least sign of trouble and they run and hide behind their father's skirts!'

If his words were designed to provoke, they seemed to have little or no effect. Jelka stood there, strangely relaxed, as if a weight had suddenly lifted from her.

'Lothar!'

'Don't worry,' she said calmly, distanced from the words. 'I fight my own battles.'

'Jelka, come on, this is just silly ...' Yi Pang-chou tugged at her sleeve, but Jelka shrugged her off.

She was half crouched now, facing him, watching him approach. He was clearly not so sure now. His hurt anger had been enough until now, but suddenly it was not so good an idea. Besides, a small crowd was forming on the steps beside the dance floor. It wouldn't do to make a scene ...

'Ah, fuck it ... she's just a girl.'

Jelka's smile was like ice. 'What's the matter, Lothar Bachman? Are you scared you might be beaten?'

Anger flared in his eyes anew. Slowly, his fingers trembling, he unbuttoned his jacket and threw it aside.

'Okay,' he said. 'You've had your chance.'

'Why, you pompous little powder-monkey!'

The reference eluded him, but the tone, cold and mocking, had its effect. With a bellow he charged at her, throwing himself forward in a kick which, if it had connected, would have shattered her lower ribcage. But she was too fast for him. As he fell, she turned, her whole body describing an arc, and kicked, the satin of her dress ripping, the hard edge of her foot smashing down into his shoulder. He cried out, but she was far from done. Savagely she kicked and punched, a kick, a punch, another kick ...

'Jelka!'

She moved back, crouched, her bent arms raised before her as if to fend off another attack, her eyes flicking from side to side.

'Gods ...' one of the young officers said, his face pale. 'She's killed him! She's fucking well killed him!'

But Bachman wasn't dead. Not yet. Not unless four broken limbs and two shattered collarbones could kill a man.

'Kuan Yin!' Anna said, kneeling over the young man and looking back at her. 'What have you done, Jelka? What in the gods' names have you done?'

Nothing, she thought, straightening up slowly. At least, *nothing you'd understand.*

K'ang A-yin, gang boss of the Tu Sun *tong*, looked about him, then nodded, satisfied that all was well. His head-quarters was four decks up from the Net, on level 50. A respectable height for a man who, not so long ago, had had nothing but the strength of his hands and the wit he had been born with. He had bought and converted one side of a corridor, turning it into a suite of rooms, some of them interconnected offices, the rest – by far the greater part – his personal quarters. Between was one long room created out of three living spaces, which was where he held his meetings and greeted his guests.

It was an oddly luxurious room for this low level. The floor was carpeted and wall-hangings covered the bareness of the ice. A long sofa, made of ersatz leather, took up the whole of the left hand wall. Nearby was a low table, and, against the far wall, stood a bar. To anyone born into the Lowers, as K'ang had been, it was impressive, yet underlying its apparent luxury was a basic shabbiness. The carpet was faded and worn, the leather scuffed and shiny in places; the bottles lining the glass frontage of the bar were genuine enough, but their sour contents had been distilled in vats not far from where they now rested.

K'ang A-yin, standing in the doorway, felt a profound satisfaction in what he saw. The walls were free of graffiti, the floor swept clean. It smelt good and in many ways it resembled those images of the Above that filtered down through the medium of the MedFac soaps. As ever when he expected someone new, he was looking forward to that first look of surprise in their face. Rubbing his hands together, he laughed throatily and turned to his lieutenant.

'Well, Soucek? What do you think the bastard wants?'

K'ang's lieutenant, Soucek, was an exercise in contrast to his boss. A tall, almost spiderish man, he had a face designed for mourning; long and bony, with slate grey eyes that were like the eyes of a dead fish, and lips that seemed drawn by the finest of needles to a tight slit. He was a man of few words.

'A deal. Maybe a partnership.'

'A partnership ...' K'ang laughed, but his eyes were cold, calculating. He had lost four men to Lehmann already, and there was the growing feeling amongst the rest that this new man was some kind of power. He cut his laughter off abruptly and turned away, sniffing in deeply.

He had toyed with the idea of bringing Lehmann here and killing him. That would be simplest, easiest. But something stopped him. He had failed once, and besides, maybe he could use him. Make him a lieutenant, like Soucek. The idea attracted K'ang. With such a man in harness who knew what he might achieve? He might even drive Lo Han back in the north and gain access to the lucrative drug trade that came down from Munich stack.

And who knew what might come of that?

K'ang looked up again, meeting Soucek's eyes, a faint smile on his well-fleshed face. 'Okay. Set things up. Let's meet the bastard.'

K'ang was sitting on the leather sofa; cradling a tumbler of wine in his left hand, when Soucek came in.

'He's here.' Soucek laughed; a strange sound coming from that humourless face. 'And he's alone. There's no sign of his two henchmen.'

K'ang took that in, then nodded. 'Good. Bring him in. And make sure there are three or four of our best men in here with us. I don't want to take any chances. Is he armed?'

'Maybe,' said Soucek. 'He said he'd kill the first man that tried to frisk him.'

K'ang laughed uncomfortably. Waving Soucek away, he got up heavily and walked across to the bar. Refilling his glass, he went through what he knew of Lehmann once more, looking for a handle. The strangest thing was that Lehmann had no history. One moment he hadn't been there; the next, there he was. His two associates, Haller and Becker, were faces from the Munich underworld. They had worked for Lo Han before they'd crossed him. Somehow Lehmann had bossed it over them, then, without warning, had muscled in on his, K'ang's, territory. And that was it. The sum total. Except that Lehmann was trained. And, if the reports were accurate, he had heavy munitions. The sort Security used.

So was he a plant? A Security infiltrator? The possibility had made K'ang check through his contacts, costing him dearly for a simple 'No'. But even before he'd had it confirmed, he had ruled it out. Why should Security bother with the likes of him? They had bigger fish to fry. And anyway, he paid his dues – not light ones either – to keep their eyes turned aside.

Whatever he was, Lehmann didn't fit. And K'ang, who wanted some kind of peace in those stacks and levels the *Kuei Chuan* Triad allowed him to control, needed him to fit. A deal would be best, but if not a deal, then he'd try again. And again, until Lehmann was a corpse.

That thought was in his mind as he turned to face the door.

Soucek was standing there, one thin-boned hand on the jamb, his body turned away from K'ang, looking out into the corridor. From another door, behind K'ang and to his right, came three of his best men. Killers. Good men to have behind you in a situation like this.

K'ang sipped at his wine, then nodded to himself, knowing how he would play it. As he watched, Soucek backed into the room slowly and stood to the side. The shape of his gun showed clearly through the thin material of his trousers, his hand hovering close by. K'ang smiled at him, as if to say, 'Leave this to me,' then moved forward a pace.

At that moment Lehmann came into the room.

There was a sudden, perceptible heightening of tension in the room. Two things were evident at once. Lehmann was tall, taller even than the gangly Soucek. And he was an albino. Skin and hair were a deathly white – a pallor emphasised by the whiteness of his simple, armless tunic and his close-fitting trousers. Even his gun, which he held loosely in his left hand, the barrel pointed at the floor, was painted white. White ... the colour of death.

K'ang heard the sharp indraw of breath of the men behind him. The muscle in his right cheek twitched, but he controlled it and slowly raised a hand in welcome, meeting the albino's eyes. He smiled, exuding confidence, but at the pit of his stomach he was experiencing something he hadn't felt in years. Fear. A plain, naked fear.

At first Lehmann let K'ang A-yin do all the talking, knowing that his simple presence there, silent amongst them, the big gun resting in his hand, was eloquent enough. He had seen at once how it was – saw where the real power lay – and, behind the solemn mask of his face, had smiled.

'I can use you,' K'ang was saying for the third time. 'With me you could go far. I'd reward you well. Look after you.'

K'ang was a big man, broad at the shoulders and well-muscled, but some of that muscle had gone to fat and there were definite signs of a paunch developing. K'ang had grown lazy, self-indulgent. Like most of these low level tong bosses he had grown accustomed to the small luxuries that surrounded him. Moving up, he had cut himself off from the immediacy of the Lowers; had forgotten what had given him his power. Soucek, his deputy, was the real power here. Neither knew it, but the time would have come when Soucek challenged him for control. Now there was no need, for he, Lehmann, had pre-empted that struggle.

He let his eyes stray a moment, letting no sign of his distaste for the drabness, the sheer ugliness of the room, register on his face. This was the worst of it, he sometimes felt; not the claustrophobic inwardness of everything here, nor the over-crowded poverty of life in the Lowers, but the ugliness, the unmitigated absence of anything that pleased the eye. More than that he missed the mountains, the cold, sharp freshness of the air. Missed the purity of the ice.

'All right,' he said, the words so sudden, so out of context, that K'ang's face wrinkled up, not understanding.

'I said all right,' he repeated, tucking the gun into the strengthened web holster inside the top of his trousers. 'I join you as lieutenant. Equal to Soucek here.' He indicated the tall, gangly man without looking at him. 'My two men ... they work with me still, right?'

He could see that K'ang didn't like that. It meant divided loyalties. For a moment K'ang hesitated, then he nodded and held out his hand to make the bargain. It was a large, strong hand, but warm and over-fleshed. There were rings on three of the fingers. By contrast Lehmann's hand was like steel, inflexible and cold.

'One further thing,' Lehmann said, extending the handshake unnaturally, seemingly oblivious of K'ang's unease. 'Your man, K'ang Yeh-su.'

K'ang looked down at his hand, then back up at Lehmann. 'What of him?'

'Get rid of him.'

'Why?'

'Because he warned me. Sold me information about you.'

There was a movement in K'ang's face that betrayed not merely surprise but shock. K'ang Yeh-su was his nephew. His sister's son. For a moment he said nothing. Then, 'Why do you tell me this?'

'Because he's weak. Corrupt. He would sell anyone for the same price.' Lehmann hesitated, then added. 'And because I'm your man now, aren't I?'

For a moment longer he held K'ang's hand, then, as if he had tired of the game, released it. But K'ang hardly noticed. Freed, he turned away and signalled to one of his men. 'Bring Yeh-su. Say nothing to him. Just bring him.'

'Jelka? Is that you?'

Jelka turned, making her way back down the unlit corridor to her father's study.

'Yes, papa?'

The Marshal sat at his big oak desk, a stack of papers to one side, a file open before him, his hands, one flesh, one golden metal, resting on the page. He looked tired, but then he always looked tired these days. His smile at least was as strong as ever.

'How did it go?'

She hesitated. He would find out. He was sure to find out. But not yet. Not before she'd had time to think things through. 'I don't know ...' She shrugged and gave a little sigh. 'It's not my thing, really. I ...'

He laughed softly. 'You don't have to tell me, my love. I know that feeling only too well. I used to think it was me, but I know better now. We're not party people, we Tolonens. Our ancestors were made of sterner stuff, neh? All that northern ice – some of it must have got into our blood!'

His laughter was warm, wonderful, and for a moment she simply stood there, basking in it. But in the morning he would be different – when he discovered what she'd done. So maybe it was best ...

She moved closer, until she stood there, facing him across the desk, looking down at him. 'I ... did something tonight, papa. I ... hurt someone.'

'You hurt someone?' He frowned, trying to understand, then gave a short laugh. 'What? You mean, you broke their heart?'

She shook her head. 'No. One of the young officers, it was. My escort for the evening. Lieutenant Bachman. He tried ...'

Tolonen sat forward, his face changed; suddenly stern, implacable. 'What? What did he try?'

She looked away briefly, wondering how it had got to this point; why she had let it get out of control. 'He tried to kiss me, papa. Against my wishes. He was persistent.'

He sat back, indignation and anger writ large on his face. 'Bachman, you say? Colonel Bachman's son?'

'Yes, papa. But please ... listen. I hurt him, you see. Hurt him badly.'

'Badly? How badly?'

She swallowed. 'I think I nearly killed him. If Anna hadn't shouted at me ...'

He narrowed his eyes, then shook his head. 'You mean, you nearly killed a man, and all because he wanted to kiss you?'

'It wasn't like that, papa. He ... he was awful. It was as if I didn't exist. As if he had the right ...' She shuddered and looked down, realising she had clenched both her fists. 'Even so, in the end I provoked him. I *made* him fight me. I could have walked away, but I didn't. I don't know why ... I ...' She stopped, looking back at her father. 'Do you understand, papa? Something snapped in me. Something ...'

He stared back at her a moment, then nodded. His voice was soft now, almost a whisper. 'I understand, my love. It's how we are, neh? Brittle. That time I killed Lehmann in the House. It was like that then. As if I had no choice. As if I'd lost control.'

For a moment they were silent, staring at each other. Then, with a tiny shudder, Tolonen looked away, fixing his gaze on the file in front of him. 'He'll live, I take it?'

'Yes.'

He looked up again, a strange kind of pride in his face. 'So what did you do to him? Kick him in the balls? Break his nose?'

'I wish it were that simple. I ...' She shook her head, suddenly exasperated with herself. 'It wasn't even as if I was angry at that point. It was like ... like it was just something I had to do. I ... well, you'll think this strange, but it was like it was Hans in front of me. Hans Ebert. And I had to stop him coming after me. That's why I broke both his legs, to stop him. And his arms.'

He stared at her, astonished, then sniffed in deeply. 'Aiya ... And were there any witnesses to this?'

'About a thousand ...'

For a moment he sat there, deep in thought, then, remembering something suddenly, he got up and went across to the other side of the room, where a long worktop filled the alcove.

'Something was delivered about an hour back,' he said, searching amongst the papers there. 'It wasn't marked urgent and I was busy, so I left it. It's here somewhere.'

She watched him, wondering what was going on in his mind at that moment. Did he really understand why she had done it? Or was he only saying that? He would stand by her, certainly, because that was his way, but for once that was not enough. She needed him to understand. Because if *he* didn't understand ...

'Here,' he said, turning back to her and slitting open the package with his thumbnail. 'If it's as you said. If it was a fair fight ...'

He fell silent, reading through the brief report. She watched him come to the end of it, then read it once again. He nodded, as if satisfied, then looked back at her.

'We'll sit down, tomorrow, first thing, and make a report. In your own words, exactly as it happened. Then I'll go and see Bachman, sort something out about his son's medical expenses. The rest ... well, I think it's straightforward enough. It'll teach the lad manners, neh? And maybe wake a few of them up, into the bargain.' He looked away, giving a tight bark of laughter. 'They're growing soft, these young men. Soft ...'

'Papa ... ?'

He looked back at her, seeing how she stood there, close – suddenly very close – to tears, and came across, holding her to him tightly.

'It's all right, my love. It's all over now.' He looked down into her face, then gently kissed her brow.

'You understand, then? You understand why I did it?'

He nodded, his grim smile fading into concern. 'It's how we are, my love. Brittle. Easily angered. But strong, too, neh? Stronger than iron.'

CHAPTER 79

FATHERS AND SONS

Li Yuan stood inside the doorway, looking across to where the T'ang of East Asia lay in a huge, canopied bed. The room was bright and unexpectedly airy. A warm breeze blew in through the open doors that led out onto the balcony, the scent of apple blossom strong in the air. Yet underlying it was the faintest hint of corruption. Of sickness and age.

'Wei Feng ...' Yuan said softly, his heart torn from him at the sight of his father's oldest friend.

The old man turned his head on the pillow, his voice faint, almost inaudible. 'Shai Tung? Is that you?'

Li Yuan swallowed and moved closer. 'It is I, cousin Feng. Shai Tung's son, Yuan.'

'Ahh ...' Blind eyes searched the darkness from whence the voice had come, looking past the young T'ang of Europe. The voice was stronger now, more confident. 'Forgive me, Yuan. I was dreaming ... Your father and I were walking in the meadow. We stopped beneath a tree ...'

Yuan waited, but there was nothing more. 'How are you, cousin?' he said gently, fearing the old man had drifted back into sleep.

'Ah yes ...' Wei Feng's laughter was weak; the merest shadow of the great roar of delight Yuan remembered from his childhood. Yuan felt his stomach muscles tighten with pain at the thought. Was it all so quickly gone?

'Where are your sons?' Yuan asked, surprised to find himself alone with the old man. 'Should I summon them, Wei Feng?'

The old man's head came round, his blind eyes staring up into Yuan's face. The hair had not grown back on the half of his skull that had been shaven and the flesh there was a pale ivory, mottled, almost transparent. One could see the bone clearly.

'No, Yuan,' the old man said determinedly. Old age and sickness had robbed Wei Feng of much, but his mind seemed as sharp as ever. 'It is you I wished to see. I ...'

The old man swallowed drily, unable to continue. Li Yuan looked about him, then saw the jug and the cup on the table behind him and went across. He poured a little of the water into the cup, then brought it back, supporting Wei Feng's head while he sipped, then, setting the cup aside, wiped his lips for him with the cloth.

'Thank you, Yuan. You are your father's son.'

Once again, it was painful to see the thin, watery smile the old man gave and recall the strength of former days. It made him feel that this ought not to be – that this great fall from health and potency was a kind of sin against life itself. He looked away momentarily, robbed of words. Why had he not felt this for his own father?

There was a moment's silence and then the old man reached out, his frail hand searching for Li Yuan's. Yuan took it, clasping it in both of his, holding it firmly yet tenderly, his fingers stroking its back.

Wei Feng's face looked up into his, the clouded eyes turned inwards. It was a drawn and ancient face, creased deeply by time and care, the skin blotched and discoloured like faded parchment.

'I am dying, Yuan. My surgeons tell me otherwise, but I know it is only days now before my time here is done and I go to join my ancestors. That does not distress me. Life has been good. I have been fortunate, both in my friends and in my wives and sons. I look back and see much happiness. But I am not sad to be leaving the world Above, for I have seen what is to come. Dark clouds are forming, Yuan. A great storm is coming. A storm so dark, so fierce it will be like nothing ever witnessed by the eyes of man.'

A faint shudder passed through him. For a moment his face was pained, then it cleared, a look of wonder filling those ancient features.

'I have been dreaming, Yuan. Strange, powerful dreams. Again and again I have seen it ...'

'Seen what, cousin Feng?'

Wei Feng laughed as if amused, but the amusement quickly faded from his lips. His voice was a hoarse whisper.

'An egg it was, Yuan. A great egg nested in the earth. They give painted eggs to celebrate a marriage, neh? Or to invalids, to wish them a speedy recovery. But this egg was different. It was like the great egg itself – the hun tun – from which the ten thousand things came forth. Moreover, it was purest white, like a great stone, polished and shining in the light that came from nowhere. It lay there, nestled in the dark earth, and the people came from all around to see it. It was huge, Yuan. The biggest man seemed as a child beside it. I stood there, amongst the crowd, watching, waiting for the egg to hatch. Across from me, behind the blood red curtains of her sedan, a bride sat waiting in a high-backed chair. I glanced at her, studying her in silhouette, then looked back at the egg. Between my looking away and looking back it had changed. Now it was stippled with tiny cracks that ran from base to tip. Slowly they darkened. A bell sounded – a single, perfect note, pure and high. As if at a signal, the shell shattered into a thousand tiny pieces. And now a man stood there, clothed in darkness, his back to me. He was huge, taller than any man I had ever seen.'

Wei Feng paused, getting his breath, his thin, darkly-blotched tongue tracing the length of his lips.

'Shall I get you more water, cousin?' Li Yuan asked, but Wei Feng shook his head.

'Let me finish.' The old man swallowed drily, then went on. 'I looked across again. The curtains of the sedan were drawn back now and I could see the bride. She was smiling. The kind of smile that lasts ten thousand years. Her wedding dress hung in tatters from her bones. Nails of black iron secured her to the chair. I looked back. The man was turning. Slowly, he turned. And as he turned, all those who fell beneath his gaze dropped to the ground, writhing in agony, as if smitten by some sudden, virulent plague.'

Slowly the old man's grip on Yuan's hand had tightened. Now it relaxed, a look of puzzlement coming into that ancient face.

'And the man, Wei Feng ... you saw his face?'

Wei Feng frowned deeply, then gave the tiniest of nods. 'It was him, Yuan. It was DeVore. But changed somehow. Enlarged. Made somehow greater than he was in life.' The old man shuddered, then turned his head away. 'I have had this dream a dozen, twenty times and each time I wake before he turns to face me fully. But I have no doubt. It *was* him. That profile. I could not forget it. Yes, I can see him even now, smiling, his hands outstretched, facing his bride.'

Li Yuan shivered. *Dreams*. Was this where the first signs appeared – in dreams? And was all that followed merely a working out of what was first glimpsed in dream?

'What time is it, Yuan?'

Li Yuan turned, looking out. 'It is late, Wei Feng. The afternoon is almost done.'

'Ahh ...' Wei Feng nodded. Then, unexpectedly, he drew Yuan's hand to his lips and kissed the great iron ring – the ring of power Li Yuan had inherited from his father and his father's father, the great seal of the *ywe lung*, the wheel of seven dragons, imprinted in its face.

Li Yuan frowned, disturbed by the old man's gesture. This was not something done lightly, nor on whim; he could see that by the way Wei Feng stared up at him, his sightless eyes imploring him to understand. But he understood nothing; only that this dear, kind man – this confidant and ally, this strong and friendly presence from his childhood – would soon be gone from the world. Gone, as if he'd never been.

And afterwards, outside in the cold and silent corridors, he stopped and looked down, noticing for the first time that there was earth on the hem of his gown. Earth ... He lifted his hand, staring at the great iron ring, then walked on, his movements stiff with regret, knowing he would never see Wei Feng alive again.

It was late afternoon before Li Yuan got back to Tongjiang. Stopping only to shower and change, he went directly to his study and sat there at his desk, his Chancellor, Nan Ho before him, Chang Shih-sen, his secretary at his side. Outside, in the Eastern Garden, his three wives sat beside the lotus pool, laughing and talking, their maids in attendance. For a moment he looked out, watching them, the shadow of his earlier meeting with Wei Feng forgotten, his eyes drawn to the new maid – the wet nurse – seeing how she attended to the hunger of his eight-week-old son, Kuei Jen. She was a pretty young thing, well-formed and with a delicate, pouting mouth. He felt his sex stir at the thought of what that mouth might do and looked down, a faint thrill of anticipated pleasure rippling through him.

He turned back, facing his Chancellor again, a faint smile on his lips.

'You wish me to arrange something, *Chieh Hsia?*'

Li Yuan laughed. 'Am I so transparent, Master Nan?'

'You are a man, *Chieh Hsia*, with a man's appetites. Besides, your First Wife, Mien Shan suggested it to me only the other day. She too, it seems, has noticed your interest.'

Li Yuan studied Nan Ho a moment, then nodded. 'Arrange it, Master Nan. We have but one life, neh?'

'It is done, *Chieh Hsia*. Now ... if we might begin.'

It was the kind of gentle admonishment Li Yuan had come to expect from his Chancellor. Another might have viewed it as impertinence, but he knew better. Master Nan had been with him since his sixth year, first as his body servant, then as his Master of the Inner Chambers. Recognising his qualities, Li Yuan had side-stepped the usual channels when he had come to the dragon throne eighteen months back and promoted the industrious Nan Ho – a man without family connections – to his most senior administrative post. It had been a bold and unexpected move and had caused ripples at the time, but he had had no reason to regret his decision. Nan Ho had proved himself the perfect statesman, attending to Li Yuan's business as if it were his own. Indeed, there was no more loyal servant in Chung Kuo. Unless it was Tolonen.

Li Yuan sat back, staring at the great stack of state papers that were piled up to the right of his desk. This was his daily burden – the great weight he had taken on at his father's death. Reports from his *Hsien L'ing*, commissioned studies on the effects of proposed legislation, warrants to be signed or queried, petitions from senior Above citizens, preparatory drafts for Council, Security summaries and more. Endless, it all seemed. Enough to keep a room full of clerks busy for a week.

He half turned, looking up at Chang Shih-sen. At this customary signal, Chang handed him the first paper. For the next hour or so the great pile slowly diminished, but they were far from done when Li Yuan sat back and, with a laugh, gestured for Chang to take the rest away. He turned, facing his Chancellor.

'Look at us, Master Nan, sitting here while the sun is shining outside! Let us deal with these tomorrow, neh?'

Nan Ho made to comment, then changed his mind. He could see that Li

Yuan was determined not to work that day. Smiling, he bowed low. 'As you wish, *Chieh Hsia*. But I must remind you that you have dinner at your cousin, Tsu Ma's estate this evening. We must be there at nine. Wu Shih has confirmed that he will be attending.'

'Good ... Good!' The young T'ang clapped his hands.

'Then come. Let us join my wives. It is a fine afternoon, neh?'

They went outside, Nan Ho sending a servant running to bring wine and tumblers. The women were beside the pool, laughing, sharing some secret joke. As the men came out, they turned, almost as one, their laughter fading, then stood, bowing their heads, the maids kneeling in their T'ang's presence.

'Where is my son?' Li Yuan asked, looking about him, surprised not to see the wet nurse there amongst the group by the pool.

'He is here, *Chieh Hsia*,' a voice said from just behind him.

He turned, smiling, remembering suddenly what he had agreed with Nan Ho earlier. The girl handed the child to him, then knelt, the faintest colour in her cheeks. She knew. He could tell she knew.

'Kuei Jen ...' he said softly, transferring his attention to the child in his arms. 'And how is my darling little boy?'

The child stared up at him, cooing softly, his dark eyes round with curiosity, his face the tiny image of his mother's. Li Yuan looked across, laughing, and saw how Mien Shan was watching him, her eyes moist with happiness, and for the briefest moment he thought of Wei Feng and what he had said to him on his sick bed. Life *was* good, if one let it be.

He turned, facing the sun. Then, as if compelled, he lifted the child, holding him up at arm's length, as if offering him up. And when he turned back, the child cradled against him once more, he saw how they looked at him, in awe, as at that moment when he had stepped down from the Temple of Heaven, wearing the dragon robes for the first time.

'My son,' he said, looking about him, fiercely proud, seeing how his words affected them, even the seemingly imperturbable Nan Ho. 'My *son*.'

On the east coast of North America it was dawn, and amidst the low, flower-strewn screens of the Tea House of the Ninth Dragon it was busy. Maroon-cloaked waiters moved between the crowded tables, their faces impassive, the heavily-laden trays they bore swept effortlessly above their patrons' heads. At the tables, wizen-faced grey-beards sat there in their stiff-collared jackets, smoking and playing *Chou* or *Siang Chi*, ignoring the muted screens set high up on the pillars on every side. From two big speakers set either side of the long *ch'a* counter, the romantic strains of 'Love At The Fair' drifted across the tea house, competing with the babble of the old men. It was a timeless scene – a scene as old as history itself. For three thousand years old men had gathered thus, to smoke and talk and drink their bowls of *ch'a*.

Kim sat at a small table at the back of the tea house, up a level, on a narrow verandah overlooking the main floor, a white and maroon-glazed *chung* of freshly-brewed *Min Hung* – 'Fukien Red' – in front of him, a small bowl of soyprawn crackers by his elbow.

He had first come here three months back, to kill an hour before a meeting, and had found himself still sitting there three hours later, his appointment forgotten, the tiny notepad he carried filled with jottings, his head bursting with new ideas. Now he came here most mornings at this hour, to sit and sip *ch'a*, and think.

Sometimes he would go down amongst the tables and sit there for an hour or two, listening to the homely wisdom of the old men, but mostly he would sit here, looking out across the busy floor, and let his mind freewheel. Today, however, was special, for earlier this morning – after a tiring all-night session – he had put the finishing touches to the first of the five new patents he had been working on: patents he had first conceived here at the Ninth Dragon.

He smiled, wondering what the old men would have made of it had he shared some of his ideas with them: whether they would have thought him sage or madman. Whichever, there was no doubting that they would have found them strange. His idea for a new kind of protein machine that could operate in space, for instance: that had been conceived here, at this table, while watching the old men blow their smoke rings in the air.

In one sense the problem had been a simple one. For the past two hundred years, most scientific engineering had been done at the microscopic level, using two basic 'tools', NPMs and NPAs. The standard NPMs – natural protein machines – that Companies like GenSyn used to engineer their products, whilst extremely versatile, were highly susceptible to heat variations, operating within a very limited temperature range. NPAs – non-protein assemblers – made of harder, more predictable molecules, were stronger and more stable than the NPMs and were therefore used wherever possible in the manufacture of most technological hardware. However, when it came to the more sensitive areas of genetic engineering, most Companies still used NPMs.

In terms of cost it didn't matter which one used, under normal conditions, but these days an increasing amount of manufacturing was done in the great orbital factories, under sterile, zero-gravity conditions.

At present the potentially much cheaper conditions of manufacture that appertained in the orbital factories were applicable only to non-living processes: for the production of basic 'hardware'. For all other processes – for food production, say, or bio-technology, where NPMs had to be used – the savings were partly offset by the need to maintain an atmosphere on board the factory ships and to keep that atmosphere at an unfluctuating and – relative to the surrounding cold of space – high temperature. Cut out that need and the savings would be the same as for those factories that used NPAs; that is, somewhere between fifteen and twenty per cent of the total manufacturing cost.

It was a huge saving, and the development company that could patent a protein-based nanomachine that could operate in extreme cold and under vacuum conditions was certain to enjoy vast profits.

Kim drew the *chung* towards him and raised it to his mouth. Lifting the rounded lid he tilted it gently and took a sip of the sweet black *ch'a*.

It was a problem he had set himself a long time back – long before Li Yuan had given him the means to set up his own company – and for a while he had thought it insoluble. How could one make a living thing that operated in the absence of those very things that sustained it – heat and air? The two processes seemed and surely were inimical. Even so, he had persisted, and, sitting there, watching the smoke rings curl from those ancient mouths and climb the air, had glimpsed how it might be done. Now, three months on from that insight, he had finally worked it out – down to the smallest detail. He had only to write the process up and patent it.

He set the *chung* down, smiling, the tiredness in his bones balanced against the sense of achievement he was feeling. Not only was his solution aesthetically pleasing, but it also kept well within the rigid guidelines of the Edict. The principles he'd utilised were old and well documented; it was merely the way he'd put them together that was new.

Smoke rings. He laughed, and took a deep swig of the *ch'a*. It was all so very simple, really ...

'Shih Ward?'

Kim turned. The Head Waiter, Chiang Su-li stood there, his head bowed, a few paces from the table.

'Yes, Master Chiang?'

Chiang bobbed his head, then handed across a message tab. 'Forgive me, Shih Ward, but a messenger brought this a moment back. He said I was to place it directly into your hands.'

'Thank you, Master Chiang.' Kim fished in the pocket of his jacket for a five *yuan* coin, then held it out, offering it to Chiang.

Chiang made no move to take the coin. 'I thank you, Shih Ward, but it is enough that you honour us with your presence at our humble tea house. If you will allow me, I will bring a fresh *chung* of the *Min Hung*.'

Kim stared at Chiang a moment, surprised, wondering what he had heard, then smiled. 'That would be most pleasant, Master Chiang. It is a most excellent brew.'

Chiang bowed, pleased by the compliment, then turned away, leaving Kim alone.

For a moment Kim sat there, staring at the blank face of the message card, tempted to throw it away unread. Old Man Lever had made over a dozen 'offers' this last year, each one more outrageous than the last. It was five weeks since the latest and Kim had been expecting something any day. So what was the old tyrant offering now? A partnership? A half share in his empire? Whatever it was, it wasn't enough. Nothing – not even the whole of ImmVac's vast holdings – could persuade him to work for Lever.

Kim looked out across the smoke-wreathed floor and sighed. When would Lever finally understand that he didn't want to work for him? Why couldn't he just accept that and leave him alone? What drove the old man that he kept on upping the terms, convinced that it was only a question of finding the right price?

Death, Kim thought. *The fear of death, that's what drives you. And you think I can find an answer to that. You've convinced yourself that I can succeed where a hundred generations of taoists and alchemists have failed, and unlock that last great secret. And maybe you're right. Maybe I could. Or at least some counterfeit of immortality – a hundred years of youth, perhaps.*

Yes, but the truth is that I wouldn't, even if I could. Not even if it meant that I too could live forever.

He shuddered, the strength of his aversion for the old man surprising him; then, curiosity overcoming his anger, he pressed his thumb against the release pad.

For a moment a combination of tiredness and false expectation made him sit there blankly, a look of incomprehension on his face. Then, with a laugh, he understood. Michael ... The message was from Michael Lever, not his father.

Even so, it was fifteen months since he had last seen Michael Lever, that night of the Thanksgiving Ball, and though they had been friends, much had happened between times. He could not be certain that the man he had known was the same as the one who wanted to see him now. Indeed, if the rumours were true, he had changed a great deal. But for good or ill?

Besides which, Michael wanted to meet him tonight, at ten o'clock. Normally that wouldn't have been a problem, but after a night without sleep ...

Kim smiled. There were pills he could take to keep him awake. Besides, it would do him good to have an evening off to see an old friend. And maybe Michael could give him some advice. He'd been out of circulation, sure, but things hadn't changed that much while he'd been away. What he knew about the market was still valid.

Kim set the card down, watching the message slowly fade, then looked across. At the ch'a counter, Master Chiang was setting out his tray with careful, precise little movements that were characteristic of the man. Kim watched him a while, then looked down, smiling. Yes, it would be good to see Michael again. Very good indeed.

The door was open, the tiny reception room empty save for a dust-strewn desk and an unpainted stool. Emily Ascher stood there in the doorway, holding tight to the stack of files and boxes that was balanced beneath her chin, wondering if she had come to the right place. For a moment she thought of checking the note Michael had sent her, but there was little point; she knew what was written there. *Suite 225*, it read; *East Corridor, Level 224, North Edison stack.* Turning, she nodded to her guide, dismissing him, then went inside, putting the files down on the desk.

She straightened up and looked about her, noting the shabbiness of the place. The walls were strewn with old posters, the floor bare, unswept in months. It had the look of a repossession.

'So this is it, eh?' she said softly and smiled to herself. She had expected something grander; something more in keeping with the Michael Lever she had worked with before his arrest. But this ...

She went across and closed the door, then turned, hearing voices from beyond the inner door. Male voices, laughing.

She slid the door open and went through, into a big, open-plan office. Michael was sitting on the edge of a long laboratory-style desk on the far side of the room. Nearby, sprawled in a chair, sat a second man; a short-haired athletic-looking man of about Michael's age. Seeing Emily, the two men fell silent, looking across at her.

'Mary ...' Michael said, pushing up from the desk and coming across, clearly delighted that she was there. 'You found us all right, then?'

She smiled, barely conscious of the use of her adopted name. 'It was no trouble. I've been down this way before ... on business.'

'I see ...' He stood there a moment, simply smiling at her, then turned suddenly, as if he had forgotten, and put his arm out, indicating the other man. 'I'm sorry ... look, I've forgotten how to do all this. This here is Bryn ... Bryn Kustow. He's an old friend. He was at College with me. And ... well, other things. And this, Bryn, is Mary Jennings.'

Emily met the young man's eyes and gave a brief nod, understanding. By 'other things' Michael meant that Kustow had been arrested. He too had been one of Wu Shih's 'guests' these past fifteen months. She could see it in his eyes. Could see how much the experience had changed these young men.

'It's not much as yet,' Michael went on, looking about him at the big, unfurnished room, 'but we're going to make it something.' He looked back at her. 'That's if you're going to join us.'

She narrowed her eyes. 'Pardon?'

He took a step closer. 'Look, I know how it is. It's a big decision. And you might think that you don't want to risk making an enemy of my father, but ...'

'Hold on,' she said, laughing. 'You're not making sense. What decision? And why should I be making an enemy of your father?'

There was a moment's puzzlement in his face, and then he laughed. 'Shit … I didn't say, did I?'

'No. You just told me to come here. Friday, first thing. And to bring what I'd need to start work at once. I thought …'

'You thought this was just another of my father's Companies, neh? You thought you'd still be on the payroll.' He looked away, embarrassed now. 'Look, I'm sorry. I'll spell it out. Then, if you don't like what you hear, you can just turn round and leave, and no one will be the wiser, okay?'

She stared back at him a moment, then looked across at Kustow, seeing how closely he was watching her; as if recruiting her for some secret brotherhood.

'You're setting up on your own, aren't you?' she said, looking back at Michael. 'A partnership. You and *Shih* Kustow here. Is that right?'

He nodded.

'And you want me to join, right? As what? Personal assistant to you both?'

Kustow sat forward. 'At first, yes. But hopefully it won't stay that way. We plan to run things differently. We'll match your present salary, of course. But you'll also be on bonuses. A share of profits. If things go well, you can buy in. Become a partner.'

'I see. And all I have to do is break contract with ImmVac and make an enemy of the most powerful businessman in City North America?'

Michael reached out and gently touched her arm. 'Look, it's okay. You can say no. And we won't blame you if you do. But just consider things a moment. It's a whole new venture. Something that won't come along twice in your career. To be in at the start of something like this …'

'And my contract with ImmVac? There's a hefty breach clause, you realise?'

'We've budgeted for that,' Kustow said, matter-of-factly. He stood up and came across, standing next to Michael. 'All you've got to do is decide whether you want in or not.'

'And just what *is* this venture?'

Kustow smiled for the first time. 'Near-space technologies. The kind of things our fathers wouldn't normally touch.'

She laughed. 'Too right. That field is sewn up tight.'

'Right now it is,' Michael agreed, 'but change is coming. There are rumours that the Seven want to make a deal with the Above. A deal that'll mean a radical rewriting of the Edict of Technology. Things are going to open up, and when they do, we plan to be there, at the cutting edge.'

'I see. And all I have to do is say yes.'

The two men looked at each other, then back at her, nodding.

She was quiet a moment, considering. It was a big decision. If she took this step there was no turning back. Old Man Lever would make damn sure of that. No, she had seen how he'd reacted that night Michael had said no to him; had been witness to the private scenes afterwards. You didn't cross swords with Charles Lever. Not unless you wanted to make an enemy of him for life. Common sense, therefore, told her to say no. To turn round and get out of there at once. But for once common sense held no sway. After all, she hadn't come to America to carve herself out a safe career. She'd come here to do something positive; to change things. It was time, then, that she stopped running; that she dug in and did something she believed in.

She looked back at them. They were watching her; sombrely, expectantly. How well she knew that look. How often she'd seen it, back in the old days, in City Europe. 'Okay,' she said, smiling broadly. 'Count me in.'

'Great!' Michael said, beaming, slapping Kustow on the back. 'Bloody great! All we need now is a research scientist and a patents man.'

'That and a lot of money,' Kustow said, grinning, his eyes meeting Emily's briefly to thank her. 'A huge pile of money!'

Old Man Lever strode out onto the podium of the great lecture hall and looked about him imperiously. His gaze swept across the empty tiers, then returned to the two great screens that dominated the wall to the right of where he stood.

'I like it,' he said finally, his voice booming in that great echoing space. 'I like it a lot. It's exactly what I envisaged.'

Behind him, the four man design team looked amongst themselves with expressions of relief and triumph. It had been hard going satisfying the Old Man, but now it was done, the building finished to his precise specifications. And not before time. In three weeks the hall would be filled to bursting for the inauguration ceremony. Before then there was much to do: laboratory equipment had to be installed, personnel hired and trained, not to mention the countless items of decor – Lever's 'final touches' – that had to be seen to between now and then. Even so, to have reached this stage at all seemed a miracle of sorts. Six months back, when things had been at their worst, not one of them had believed the project would ever see completion, not because what was asked of them was impossible, but because of Lever's constant meddling in their work – his abrupt changes of mind and irritating refusal to trust their judgement at any stage. The pay had been good, true, but he had ridden them hard.

Not that their experience was unique. In every area Old Man Lever had not only insisted that they hire the best in the field but that he be allowed to sit in on their consultation sessions. More than once he had overridden specialist advice, determined to stamp his own view on things, only to return, each time after a long, frustrating delay, to the very thing he'd first rejected, and with never a word that he'd been in the wrong.

But so it was with Lever. It was as if the man were obsessed. As if this one project, this single huge building and what it held, consumed him, blinding him to all else. And now, standing there at the centre of his creation, he glowed with a satisfaction that seemed much more than the sense of achievement one usually got from a job well done.

'Where's Curval?' he said, half turning towards them. 'Has anyone seen the man?'

'I'll bring him, Mister Lever,' the Architect said, recognising that tone of impatience in the Old Man's voice.

Fourteen and a half billion it had cost. Twice the original estimate. But not once had Lever balked about the cost. 'Money's irrelevant,' he had said at one point, to the astonishment of the Project Accountant. And so it had proved. Never once had he skimped or cut costs. No, the problem had been one of time. Of getting the thing done in time for the ceremony.

Curval arrived, making his way between them, the great geneticist hesitating, glancing at them uncertainly before he walked out onto the broad platform. 'Good luck,' one said softly, almost inaudibly. 'Poor bastard,' another mouthed silently as they turned to leave, bringing a knowing smile to his colleagues' faces. So it was. Their dealings with Lever were, thank the gods, almost over; Curval's, poor sod, were only just beginning.

'Ah, Andrew ...' Lever said, turning, smiling at the man and extending his hand. 'I wanted to talk to you. To make sure everything's going to plan.'

Curval bowed his head and took Lever's hand, allowing his own to be pumped and squeezed indelicately.

'It all goes well, Mister Lever. Very well indeed.'

'You've signed the two men you mentioned last time we talked?'

The last time they had talked had been the day before, less than eighteen hours earlier, in fact, but Curval let it pass.

'I got onto it at once, Mister Lever. The contracts were signed and verified this morning. They'll be here tomorrow, first thing, ready to get down to work.'

'Good.' Old Man Lever beamed his satisfaction. 'That's what I like to hear. So you've got your team now? Everyone you need?'

Curval hesitated. He knew what the Old Man wanted to hear. He wanted to hear a resounding yes; that they had the best team possible – a team good enough to tackle the big questions and overcome them – but both he and Lever knew that that wasn't so.

'It's as good as we'll get, Mister Lever. If we can't crack it with this team, no one will.'

Lever stared at him a full ten seconds, then gave a terse nod. 'It's the boy, neh? You still think we need the boy?'

Curval took a long breath, then nodded. 'I've looked over some of the things you showed me and there's no doubting it. You can't counterfeit that kind of ability. You either have it or you don't.'

'And he has it?'

Curval laughed. 'In excess! Why, he's head and shoulders above anyone in his field. He's quick of mind, and versatile, too. If anyone could make a quick breakthrough, it'd be Ward.' Again he hesitated. 'Look, don't mistake me, Mister Lever, the team we've got is good. Exceptional, I'd say. If anyone can find an answer, they can. But it'll take time. All I'm saying is that having Ward would give us an edge. It would help speed things up considerably.'

'I see.' Lever looked about him thoughtfully, then turned back to Curval, smiling. 'Okay. I'll come and visit you tomorrow. It'll be good to meet the team at last. I can give them a little pep talk, neh?'

Curval nodded, his face showing no sign of what he thought of the idea, then, with a low bow, he backed slowly away.

For a while Lever stood there, as if in trance, a deep frown lining his grizzled features. Then, abruptly, he turned about, marching off the platform and out through the open door, his silks flapping out behind him as he made his way through the maze of rooms and corridors to the entrance hall.

Beneath the great twist of stairs – that huge, unravelled double helix that filled the north end of the massive domed cavern that was the entrance hall – Lever stopped, looking about him, as if coming to himself again.

Waving away the two servants who had hurried across, he went over and stood before the blank partition wall that rested in the centre of the floor between the stairway and the huge entrance doors. This, this great screen, was the first thing that visitors to the Institute would see on entering the building, and as yet he was still to find something to fill it. But fill it he would. And with something quite exceptional.

Lever lifted his chin, then turned away, feeling a sudden rush of pride at the thought of what he'd accomplished here. Here it was, the first stage of his Dream completed. He had brought it this far, by force of will and brute determination, and he would take it even further, right to the shores of death itself. He smiled, all trace of the uncertainty he had felt back in the lecture hall gone from him. He had a right, surely, to feel proud of what he'd done? No Emperor or President had ever done so much.

He looked about him, then nodded, suddenly determined. For some reason, young Ward didn't want to work for him. A dozen times now he had turned down his offers. But that didn't mean that he had to give up. No. If anything it made him more determined. He was used to having his own way, and he would have his way in this eventually. Because this was too important not to give it his best shot. And if that best shot meant getting Ward, he would get Ward. Whatever it took.

Yes. Because here, at this place he had specially created for the purpose, they were ready to begin. In the days to come they would take on Death himself. Would track him down and face him, eye to eye. Yes. And stare him down.

Kim pushed away the empty starter plate and looked about him, noting how busy the restaurant had suddenly become, then turned back, meeting Michael Lever's eyes across the table.

'It's strange, isn't it?' Michael said, a faint smile on his lips. 'I'd never have thought that I'd feel awkward in a place like this, but these days ... well, I see it with new eyes, I guess. The wastefulness of it all. The excess. Being Wu *Shih*'s guest made me realise how much I'd taken for granted, how much I *hadn't* seen.'

Kim frowned, concerned. 'You should have said. Look, I'll cancel the main course, if you want. We can go elsewhere.'

Michael shook his head. 'No. It's okay. Besides, I'll have to get used to this again if I'm going into business on my own account. I learned that with my father. This is where the deals are made, in the restaurants and private clubs, with a full mouth and a swollen belly, over a plate of expensive delicacies and a tumbler of brandy.'

Kim laughed softly, enjoying the new Michael Lever. There was a depth of irony to him that hadn't been there before his imprisonment; a sharp, self-deprecating humour that suited him perfectly. Before, he had been his father's shadow, but now he was himself; leaner but also stronger than before.

'Do you really hate it all that much?'

Michael looked down. 'I don't know. It's like I said, it's hard to see it now the way they do. Being locked up all day ... it gave me the chance to do a lot of thinking. To look at our world afresh.' He met Kim's eyes again. 'My father can't understand that. To him it's as if I've been away at College or something. He can't see what I've been through. He thinks ...' He huffed out, hurt and exasperated. 'Well, he thinks I'm just being awkward, wilful, but it's not like that.'

Kim leaned towards him, covering his hand with his own. 'I understand,' he said, thinking back to his own experiences of confinement. 'It changes you, doesn't it? Throws you back upon yourself.'

Michael nodded and looked up at him, smiling, grateful for his understanding.

'I'm sorry. This whole business with your father. It must be hard for you.'

Michael shrugged. 'It hurts, sure, but I've known worse. Besides,' he said, brightening, 'you've not told me what *you're* up to. Have you made your first million yet?'

Kim laughed. 'No, but it sure as hell feels as if I've spent it setting things up!' He sat back, relinquishing Michael's hand. 'You know how it is, creatively we're strong, but financially ... Well, to be honest with you, Michael, I could do with some outside investment, but it's a question of finding someone I can trust. Someone who won't attach too many strings.'

'Ahh ...' Michael looked away, thoughtful a moment. 'You know, Kim, I thought I knew everything there was to know about business, I thought no one could teach me anything new, but I'm having to learn it all again, from scratch. Without my father's money, without the power that ImmVac represents, I'm just another face, fighting for my share of a hostile market.'

'Hostile?'

'My father. He doesn't like the idea of me going it alone. He thinks I should be back home, running errands for him.'

'You mean he's actively trying to stop you?'

'Actively, no. Or at least, not as far as I know. But you know how it is. The word's out that my father's angry with me, and it's a brave man who'll risk offending Charles Lever for the sake of trading with his son. I've been cut dead a dozen, twenty times these past two days alone by so-called 'friends'. But there are ways round that. Bryn and I have been working on making contacts in the East Asian marketplace. It'll cost us, sure, but at least we can do business. Here in North America things are dead as far as we're concerned.'

'I see.' Kim leaned back, letting the waiter who had appeared clear the plates. 'So how are you funding all this?'

Michael smiled. 'I've personal accounts. Money my mother left me. About fifteen million in all. It's not enough, but it'll get us started.'

Kim narrowed his eyes. 'That sounds ambitious.'

'It is. But tell me, Kim, how much do you need? A million? Two?'

'One and a half,' Kim said, as the waiter returned, setting down a plate of steaming hash before him. 'One point two if we trim back to basics.'

'And that covers what? R & D? Production? Distribution?'

'R & D is covered. I do all that up here.' Kim tapped his skull and smiled. 'No. My costing is for the initial production run, manufacture to fitting, allowing for a three month payment schedule. We start fairly small, keep borrowing to a minimum and finance expansion from profits.'

Michael leaned towards him, interested. 'You've got something ready to go, then?'

'Pretty well. I've been working on a few things this last year. Some didn't pan out, but two of them ... Well, let's say that I'm hopeful.'

'These are new inventions, I take it?'

Kim nodded.

'And you've patented them, I hope?'

'Not yet.'

Michael whistled through his teeth. 'But that's madness, Kim! What if someone raided your offices? You'd lose it all.'

Kim shook his head. 'They could strip the place bare, but they'd get nothing. As I said, it's all up here, in my head. When I'm ready I'll set it all down and take it along to the Patents Office and register it. But not before I've sorted out the practical details.'

Michael smiled, impressed. 'It sounds good. Look, Kim, why don't *we* do business? You need funding, we need a bit of specialist advice. Why can't we trade? I mean, I'll have to talk to Bryn and get his agreement, but I don't see why we can't help each other out, neh?'

Kim stared at him, confused. 'Wait a minute. Have I got this right? Are you offering to back me? To put up the funds?'

'Why not?'

'But I thought you needed that money for your own venture?'

'We need ten million to get us started, sure, but that leaves more than enough for what you want. And no strings. Or at least, just the one – that you look over our proposal and give us your technical advice on what we propose.'

Kim was smiling broadly now, his dinner quite forgotten. 'That's great. Really great. But just what is your proposal?'

'Near-space technologies,' Michael answered him, looking past him momentarily, as if seeing something clearly in the air. 'It's the coming thing, Kim. The coming thing ...'

Wei Feng lay on the great oakwood bed, his eyes closed, his long, thin face at rest. His hands lay one upon the other above the sheets, the slender fingers stiff, paler than the white silk of the coverings, a kind of darkness beneath their pallor. At the foot of the bed stood his three sons, heads bowed, the white of their clothes in sharp contrast to the rich colours of the room.

The long illness had wasted the old man. He was a thing of bone beneath the frail white gown he wore. His right arm and shoulder had atrophied, as if death had taken that part of him earlier than the rest. His lidded eyes rested low in the pits of their sockets and his thin-lipped mouth was a mere pale gash in the emaciated wasteland of his face. The hair on the left side of his face had not grown back, and the scars of the operations showed blue against the ivory of his skull. When Li Yuan entered the room his eyes were drawn to the stark ugliness of Wei Feng's head in death. He shuddered involuntarily, then turned to greet the eldest son, Chan Yin, with a silent bow.

Li Yuan stood at the bedside a long time, looking down at his old friend, recalling through misted eyes how this kind and lovely man had once twirled him round in the air, his eyes alight with the joy of what he was doing, and how he, Li Yuan, had squealed with delight at it. He glanced down at the narrow bones of the hands, the wasted muscles of the arms and grimaced. Had it been so long ago? No ... He shook his head slowly. Fifteen years. It was barely an indrawn breath in the long history of their race.

He turned away, leaving the tears on his cheeks, stepping back as if in a dream, then reached out to embrace each of the dead man's sons; holding Chan Yin longer than the others, feeling the faint trembling of the man against him.

Chan Yin stood back, a sad smile on his face. 'Thank you, Yuan.'

'He was a good man,' Yuan answered, matching his smile. 'I shall miss both his advice and his friendship. He was a second father to me.'

The forty-year-old nodded slightly, for a moment seeming younger than the nineteen-year-old Li Yuan. Before this moment, power had reversed the traditional status of age between them, but now they were both T'ang, both equals. Even so, Chan Yin deferred. Li Yuan noted this and frowned, not understanding. There was no sign in his cousin that he had inherited. Only a puzzling humility and deference towards himself.

'What is it, Chan Yin?'

Chan Yin met his eyes. Beyond him his younger brothers looked on. 'My father entrusted me to give you this, Yuan.'

From the white folds of his mourning cloak the new T'ang took a letter. It was white silk, sealed with blood red wax, the traditional instrument of the Seven. Li Yuan took it and stared at it, then, reluctantly, he prised the seal open with his fingernail.

Chan Yin reached out a hand to stop him. 'Not here, Yuan. Later. When you are alone. And then we shall meet. Just you and I.' He paused, and raised his voice as if to let it carry to his brothers. 'But remember, Li Yuan. I am my father's son. His death changes nothing.'

Li Yuan hesitated, then bowed his assent, his fingers pressing the hardened wax back into place. Then, with a brief, questioning glance, he turned and left the death chamber.

CHAPTER 80

WAVES AGAINST THE SAND

I t was low tide. In the deep shadow at the foot of the City's wall, a flat-bottomed patrol boat made its way between the tiny, grass-covered islands that dotted this side of the river, the tight beam of its searchlight sweeping slowly from side to side across the glistening shallows. Just here, at the great Loire's mouth, the river was broad, almost three li wide. Upstream lay the Bay of Biscay and the grey-green waters of the North Atlantic. Downstream, in the bright, mid-morning sunlight, one of the big Mid-Ocean vessels was making its way down the deep water channel towards the port of Nantes. On the far bank, beyond the perimeter fence and its regularly-spaced gun turrets, could be seen the needle towers and blast pits of the spaceport, the pure white of the City's walls forming a glacial backdrop far to the south. As the patrol boat slowed and turned, making its way round the low hump of a mudbank, the water seemed to shimmer. Almost imperceptibly the vibration took form in the air, a low bass growl that grew and grew in strength. A moment later the sky on the far side of the river was riven by a long, bright streak of red.

On the roof of the City, two li above the river's surface, a group of officers watched the rocket climb the sky to the south-west. To their backs, close by, five craft were parked about an open service hatch: a big, black-painted cruiser, three squat Security gunships, and a slender four-man craft with the *Ywe Lung* and the personal insignia of the T'ang of Europe on its stubby wings. Uniformed guards of the T'ang's élite squad stood by the ramps of each craft, heavy semi-automatics clutched to their chests, looking about them conscientiously.

For a moment the small group of officers were still, their necks craned back, following the arc of the rocket, then, as the echoing boom of the engines faded from the sky, they turned back, resuming their talk.

Marshal Tolonen stood at the centre of the group, his aide close by, clutching a small documents case. Facing Tolonen stood Li Yuan's new General, the fifty-two-year-old Helmut Rheinhardt. He and most of his senior staff had come out to Nantes to see the old man off.

'I admire your thoroughness, Knut,' Rheinhardt said, picking up on what they had been saying, 'but forgive me if I say that I feel you're taking on much more than you need. For myself I'd have let other, younger eyes do the spade work and saved myself for the fine sifting. From what you've said, there's plenty enough of that, neh?'

Tolonen laughed. 'Maybe so. But it's a principle I've stuck to all my life. Not to trust what I'm told, but to look for myself. I've an instinct for these things, Helmut. For that small betraying detail that another wouldn't spot. From here things look fine with GenSyn's North American operation, but I've hunch that they'll look a great deal different from close up.'

'You think something's amiss, then, Knut?'

Tolonen leaned closer. 'I'm damn sure of it! I've been working through the official records these past three months and things simply don't add up. Oh, superficially things look all right. The numbers balance and so forth, but ...' He sniffed, then shook his head. 'Look, Klaus Ebert was a conscientious, honest man. He kept a tight rein on GenSyn while he was in control. But things were different at the end ...'

'Hans, you mean?'

Tolonen looked away, a shadow falling over his granite features. 'It looks like it, I'm afraid. Most of the North American operation and its subsidiary companies were handed over to Hans for the eighteen months before Klaus Ebert's death. And it's in that period that almost all of the anomalies occur.'

'Anomalies?' It was Li Yuan's Chancellor, Nan Ho, who made the query. He was returning to the group after briefly visiting his craft to take an urgent message. Rheinhardt and his officers bowed and moved back slightly, letting Nan Ho re-enter their circle.

Tolonen hesitated, then nodded. 'Accounting irregularities. Forged shipment details. Missing documents. That kind of thing.'

It was a bland, almost evasive answer, but from the way Tolonen met Nan Ho's eyes as he said it, the Chancellor knew that it was more serious than that. Something else was missing. Something that, perhaps, couldn't be mentioned, not even in company like this.

'Besides,' Tolonen went on, changing the subject, 'it will be good to see old friends again. My work has kept me in my study this past year. And that's not healthy, neh? A man needs to get out in the world. To do things and see things.'

Rheinhardt laughed. 'It sounds like you've been missing the service, Knut! Maybe I should find you something to do once all this GenSyn business is finished with. Or maybe you would like your old job back?'

There was laughter at that; a hearty, wholesome laughter that rolled out across the roof of the City. Hearing it, Jelka Tolonen looked up from where she was sitting on the steps of the nearest gunship and frowned. How familiar such manly laughter was, and yet, suddenly, how strange, how alien it sounded. She stood, looking out past her father's men, towards the distant horizon.

It was a beautiful day. The sun was high and to her back, the air fresh with no trace of wind. Cloud lay to the west, high up, over the shining ocean, a faint, wispy cirrus feathering the deep blue of the sky. It was beautiful, simply beautiful, yet for once she felt no connection to that beauty, no resonance within herself; as if some part of her had died, or fallen fast asleep.

A week had passed since the incident at the Graduation Ball, but she had still to come to terms with what had happened. When she thought of it, it seemed strange, unreal, as if it had happened to someone else, or in some other life. Yet what concerned her more was the constant, nagging sense of unease she had felt these past few weeks; that sense that things were wrong, seriously wrong, with the balance of her life.

As far as Lieutenant Bachman was concerned, her father had smoothed things over, just as he'd said he would. Even so, she had slept badly this last week, haunted by dreams in which she was a machine, a dreadful spinning thing with blades for arms, scything down whoever strayed across her blind, erratic path.

And where was her softer self in these dreams? Where was the girl she knew existed beneath that hard metallic shell? Nowhere. There was no sign of her; of the girl she felt she ought to have been. Or was it true what her father had said that night? Was it simply that they were made of sterner stuff? Of iron?

Of all this she had said nothing. At home she had acted as though nothing were happening deep within her. As if it were all done with and forgotten. Yet she knew it was far from over, for she was undergoing a change – a change as profound and as radical as any being suffered by the greater world beyond her. And maybe there was even some connection. Maybe the change in her mirrored that outer change – was some strange kind of recognition of the reality of events?

She looked down at herself, at the simple dark blue one-piece she was wearing. It was what she always wore when she accompanied her father, its neat, military cut fitting in with her surroundings. Yet today it felt different. *Wrong*.

'Jelka?'

She turned, surprised, facing her father.

'I didn't hear you ...'

'No ...' He smiled and reached out, holding her upper arm gently with his bright, golden hand. 'You were miles away, weren't you? What were you thinking of?'

She looked down. 'That I'll miss you,' she said, hiding behind the partial truth.

'And I you,' he said, drawing her close and embracing her. 'But it won't be long. Ten days at most. Oh, and guess who I'll be seeing?'

She shrugged, unable to guess.

'*Shih* Ward ... you know, young Kim, the Clayborn lad ... the scientist.'

'You're *seeing* him?'

He held up a small white envelope. 'I'm having lunch with him, it seems. Li Yuan wants me to deliver this personally. The gods know what it is, but it'll be nice to see the young fellow again.'

'I ...' She licked at her lips, wanting to say something, to give him some message to pass on, then shook her head. 'I'll miss you,' she said finally, hugging him tightly.

He grinned. 'Now, now. You'll be all right, my boy,' Then, realising what he'd said, he laughed. 'Now, why did I say that?'

'I don't know,' she said quietly, burying her head in his chest. 'I really don't know.'

The canvas filled the end wall of the studio, dominating the room. It was not merely that it dwarfed the other paintings – for the new piece was easily ten, maybe twenty times the size of the artist's earlier work – it was the colour, the richness, the sheer scale of the composition that caught the eye and drew it in.

To the left of the canvas, what seemed at first glance to be a huge, silver-white mountain, resolved itself into a tangle of bodies, some human, some mechanical, the metallic figures unexpectedly soft and melting, those of flesh hard, almost brutal in their angularity. Looking more closely, it could be seen that this great mound of bodies was formed of two great chains, linked hand to hand, like a gigantic coil of anchor rope, the whole thing spiralling upwards into the blue-black darkness of deep space at the top right of the canvas: a huge double-helix of men and machines, twisting about itself, striving towards a single, brilliant point of light.

In the foreground, beneath the toppling mass of bodies, was the great ocean, the Atlantic, incongruously calm, its surface shimmering in the sunlight. Yet beneath its placid skin could be discerned the forms of ancient ruins – of Han temples and pagodas, of stone dragons and palaces and the skeletal framework of a rotting imperial junk.

It was shanshui – 'mountains and water' – but shanshui transformed. This was the new art. An art of symbiosis and technological aspiration that was the cultural embodiment of the old Dispersionist ideals: Futur-kunst, or Science-Art, as it was called. And Heydemeier, the artist, was its leading exponent.

Old Man Lever stood before the painting, some twenty ch'i back, his face creased into an intense frown. He had brought Heydemeier over from Europe six months back and installed him here, giving him whatever he needed to pursue his art. And this – this immense vision in oils – was the first fruit of that investment.

He turned to Heydemeier and nodded. 'It's good. Very good indeed. What is it called?'

Heydemeier drew at the thin black cigarette and gave a tight smile of satisfaction. 'I'm glad you like it, Shih Lever. I've called it 'The New World'.'

Lever laughed briefly. 'That's good. I like that. But why so big?'

Heydemeier moved past the old man, going right up to the canvas. For a while he studied the fine detail of the picture, brushing the surface of it lightly with the fingertips of one hand, then he turned back, facing Lever.

'To be honest with you, Shih Lever, I wasn't sure it would work, coming here to America. I thought it might be a step backwards, but there's something very different about this place. It's more alive here than in Europe. You get the feeling that this is where the future is.'

Lever was studying the young man hawkishly. 'And that's where this comes from?'

'Partly.' Heydemeier drew on the cigarette again. 'Now that it exists I realise that this was what I was always striving for, even in the smaller works. What was lacking was a sense of space – of outwardness. Being here, away from the confinement of Europe, freed that. Allowed it, if you like.'

'I can see that.'

Heydemeier half-turned, indicating the great swirl of bodies. 'So. There it is, Shih Lever. Yours. As we agreed.'

Lever smiled. 'It's an important work, Shih Heydemeier. I don't need experts or advisers to tell me that. I can see it with my own eyes. It's a masterpiece. Maybe the start of something wholly new, wouldn't you say?'

Heydemeier looked down, trying to conceal his pleasure at the old man's words, but Lever could see that he had touched his weak point – his vanity. He smiled inwardly and pressed on.

'I mentioned my advisers. Well, to be frank with you, Shih Heydemeier, it was on their word that you came here. They said you were the best. Without equal, and with your best work ahead of you. So it has proved. And that's good. I can use that. I like working with the best. In everything.'

Lever went across, standing there face to face with the artist. 'You're a clever man, Ernst Heydemeier. You understand how things are – how they work. So you'll not take offence when I say that my interest in you was strictly commercial. A Company like mine – like ImmVac – needs its show pieces, its cultural totems, if you like. And the more prestigious those totems, the better. They give a company great face. But this ...' He reached out and gently touched the surface of the painting, a look of genuine awe in his face. 'This goes beyond that. This transcends what I asked of you.'

Heydemeier turned, looking back at his work. 'Maybe. But it makes you wonder sometimes ... Whether you'll ever create anything half as good again. Whether you can ever make something more ... original.'

He turned back, meeting Lever's eyes. 'But that's the challenge, neh? To surprise oneself.'

Lever watched him a moment, then nodded. 'It's yours, Ernst. The painting, I mean. Keep it.'

'Keep it?' Heydemeier gave a laugh of surprise. 'I don't understand ...'

Lever looked past him, enjoying the moment. 'On one condition. That you paint something for me.'

Heydemeier looked down, then gave the tiniest shake of his head. His voice was apologetic. 'I thought you understood, Shih Lever. I thought we'd discussed this already. I don't undertake commissions. This ...' He looked up, meeting Lever's eyes unflinchingly. 'This was different. Was my rent, if you like. Repayment of your hospitality. But what you're talking of ... that's different again. I have to be free to paint what I want. It just doesn't work, otherwise.'

'I understand. But look at that. Look at it again, Ernst Heydemeier. That's a moment in your life – in your career – that you won't repeat. Oh, you may paint things which are better technically, but will you ever recapture that one moment of vision? Besides, I could re-sell this tomorrow and make, what, five, maybe ten million yuan. As to what it'll be worth ten years from now ...' He paused, letting that sink in. 'And what am I asking for in exchange? Three, maybe four days of your time.'

Heydemeier turned away, his discomfort and uncertainty evident in every muscle of his long, gaunt body.

'I don't know, Shih Lever. I ...'

'Okay. I won't force the issue. Keep it anyway. Let it be my gift to you. But let me tell you what it was I wanted. Just hear me out, okay?'

Heydemeier turned, facing the old man again. Whatever he had expected from this meeting, it had not been this. He stood there, bemused, his earlier composure shattered.

'All right,' he said resignedly. 'I'll listen, but that's all ...'

'Of course.' Lever smiled, relaxing now he had brought him this far. 'It's a simple little thing really ...'

Twenty minutes later, as Lever was climbing into his sedan, a messenger came. He tore the envelope open impatiently, knowing even before he glanced at it who it was from. This was the second time in the last twenty-four hours that his son, Michael, had written to him about the freezing of his accounts.

'Damn the boy!' he said, angry at being chased-up in this manner. 'Who the hell does he think he is! He can damn well wait ...'

He held the letter out stiffly, waiting for his secretary to take it, then, changing his mind, he drew it back.

'No. Give me brush and ink. I'll give him his answer now.'

'There,' he said, a moment later. 'Maybe that will teach him manners!'

He stepped up into the sedan again, letting the servant draw the curtains about him, but the satisfaction he had felt only moments before had gone, replaced by a blinding fury at his son. Well, Michael would learn just how decisive he could be when pushed to it. It was about time he understood how things really were.

He shuddered and sat back, reminding himself of the day's successes – of the unexpected thrill of the auction that morning, the pleasant and productive lunch with Representative Hartmann, and his 'negotiations' with Heydemeier, but this last – this final matter with his son – had taken the bloom off his day.

'Damn the boy!' he said again, turning the heavy ring on his left-hand index finger, unconscious that he was doing so. 'Damn him to hell!'

Jelka crumpled up the note and threw it down, angry with herself. Angry that she couldn't find the words to express what she had been feeling that night.

Or maybe it wasn't that at all. Maybe it was simply that she had wanted to hurt the young lieutenant; that, in a funny way, she'd *needed* to. But if that was true, what kind of creature did that make her?

She sat back, taking a long breath, trying to calm herself, but there was so much darkness in her; so much unexpressed violence. Why, she couldn't even write a simple letter of apology without wanting to hit out at something!

She stood, looking about her at the chaos of her room. Sketches of uniforms and weaponry, of machines and fighting soldiers cluttered the facing wall, while to her left a number of old campaign maps covered the face of her wardrobe. A combat robe hung over the back of the chair beside her unmade bed, while nearby, in a box in the corner, a selection of flails and staffs and practice swords reminded her of how long she had spent perfecting her skills with each. Above the box, high up on the wall, was a brightly-coloured poster of Mu-Lan, dressed in full military armour. Mu-Lan, the warrior princess, famed throughout history for her bravery and skill.

Mu-Lan ... the name her girlfriends called her.

She swallowed, her anger turned to bitterness. He had made her this. Year by year he had trimmed and shaped her. Year by year he had moulded her, until she was this thing of steel and sinew.

Or was that fair? Was her father really to blame? Wasn't it true what he had said that night? Wasn't it simply that she was of his blood, Tolonen, with the nature of their kind? Hadn't she glimpsed something of that on the island that time? Hadn't she seen her own reflection in the rocks and icy waters of that northern place? So maybe it was true. Maybe he wasn't to blame. Even so, *if she had had a mother ...*

She caught her breath.

If she had had a mother ... What then? Would it all have been different? Would she have turned out normal?

She laughed; a strange, bleak sound. What, after all, was normal? Was 'normal' what the others were? For if *that* was so, then she didn't wish to be normal. But to be as she was, that was dreadful, horrible ...

Unbearable ...

She went through to the kitchen and took a refuse sack from the strip beside the freezer, then returned to her room. She stood there, looking about her numbly, wondering where to start.

Mu-Lan, perhaps ...

She went across and ripped the poster from the wall, stuffing it down into the sack. Then, in a frenzy, she worked her way around the walls, tearing down the pictures and sketches, the posters and the maps, thrusting them all down into the sack, grunting with the effort. Finally she emptied the weapons box into the sack and tied the neck.

She stood back, looking about her at the bare walls. It was as if she had been dreaming all these years; sleepwalking her way through the days. Oh, there had been moments when she had woken – like the time she had defied him over the marriage to Hans Ebert – but for the most part she had colluded in her fate. But now all that must change. From here on she must be mistress of her own destiny.

Lifting the sack she went back through, into the kitchen. Waving the serving girl away, she stood there, over the portable incinerator, half in trance, thinking of her mother.

In some other world, perhaps, it was different. There, beneath an open sky, she was herself, complete. For an instant she pictured it; imagined the log house on the hill beside the forest, the stream below; turned and saw, as if in memory, her father standing in the doorway, her mother – the image of herself – beside him, his arm about her shoulder. Felt herself turn, her skirts swirling out about her naked legs, her bare feet running on the sunlit grass ...

She closed her eyes, the pain of longing almost over-whelming her. *In some other world ...*

The click of the incinerator brought her back. She looked about her, as if coming to from the depths of sleep, then shuddered, the tension in her unabated. What wouldn't she give to be able to live like that. To *be* like that, open and whole.

Maybe so. But that was only dreams. This here was the world she inhab-ited. This massive, brutal world of levels. This Yang world, heavy with the breath of men. And what were her dreams against the weight of that reality?

And yet she would become herself. She *would.* For to be like them – to be 'normal' in the way that they were normal – would be a living death for her. A slow and painful suffocation. And she would rather die than suffer that.

She had been running from it. All her life she had been running from it. But now, suddenly, she was awake. That moment at the Graduation Ball ... she understood it now. That – that awful moment when she had turned and goaded him – had been the moment when she had stopped running. The moment of awakening, when she had turned, quite literally, to confront the very thing she hated.

'I'm sorry.' she said softly. 'It wasn't *you* ...'

She shivered, understanding finally what had happened to her. It wasn't Bachman she had meant to hurt. It was what he represented. He ... well, he had been like ... She looked about her, her eyes coming to rest on the figure of the kitchen god, squatting on the shelf above the cooking utensils, and nodded to herself.

Yes. It was as if she had been confronted by the clay figurine of an evil demon; a figure that she had had to smash to be free of its enchantment.

And was she free?

Jelka looked down at her long, slender hands, seeing them clearly, as if she had never seen them before. No, not free. Not yet. But she would be. For she was awake now. At long last, she was awake.

'Mary? Have you got the file of old MemSys contacts?'

Emily looked up from behind the desk screen and met Michael Lever's eyes, conscious of the slight edge in his voice. This business with his father was getting to him, especially since the Old Man had frozen the accounts.

'It's here,' she said, reaching into her top left-hand drawer and taking out the bulky folder. 'Not that it'll do you any good. None of them will talk to us, let alone contemplate trading with us. They're all scared as Hell of taking on your father, Michael. You'd be better off trashing this and starting anew.'

'Maybe.' He hesitated, then came across and took the folder from her. 'Even so, I'm going to try each one of them again. Someone's got to give.'

'Why?' There was a strange hardness in her eyes. 'Your father holds all the cards. Every last one of them. And you've got nothing.'

'Maybe,' he said again, not challenging what she'd said. 'But I've got to keep trying. I can't go back. Not now.'

'No.' She said it softly, sympathetically, knowing how much pressure he'd been under these past few weeks, and how well he'd coped with it. The old Michael Lever wouldn't have coped, not one tenth as well. 'As for the other matter ... I'll let you know if we hear anything, okay?'

He smiled uncertainly. 'Okay. I'll get to it.'

When he was gone, she sat back, combing her fingers through her short blonde hair. The other matter – the freezing of the accounts – was what lay behind his current tenseness. If the Old Man refused ... She took a deep breath, trying to see ahead. What would she do if Michael gave up and went back to his father? She'd be out of a job, for a start. Worse than that, Old Man Lever would make sure she'd never work again. Not in North America, anyway. And maybe other places, too. Wherever his long arm reached.

But strangely enough her own fate didn't concern her half so much as the prospect of Michael giving up after coming this far. She'd survive. She always did. But Michael ... If he gave up now it would destroy him – cripple him emotionally. If he gave up now he would be tied – tied forever to his father's will, whether his father lived or no.

She shuddered and looked about her at the room in which she sat. In three short weeks they had built this thing from scratch. And though it was as nothing compared to MemSys and the great ImmVac corporation, it was at least something. New growth, not an expansion of the old.

Yes, and left alone it would have grown and grown. Michael and Bryn were a good team. Innovative, capable, resourceful. As good as any she had worked for these past three years. The Company would have been big. As it was, it was likely it would be dead, and probably within the hour.

'Nu shi Jennings?'

She looked up again. It was Chan, the guard. He'd slid back the outer door and was looking in at her.

'What is it, Chan Long?'

'There's a messenger here,' he said quietly, ominously. 'From ImmVac. I think it's an answer.'

She nodded. Chan knew as well as anyone what was going on. That was his business. And like her, he knew what it was likely to mean. She smiled tightly, feeling sorry for the man.

'Okay. Search him and show him through. But show the man respect. It's not his fault.'

Chan gave a small bow and slid the door closed again. A minute or so later the door slid fully back and Chan came through, ushering in a tall, dark haired Hung Mao in the bright red uniform of ImmVac's messenger service. From the way he glanced at Chan as he passed, it was clear he had not welcomed being body-searched, but Emily was taking no chances.

She stood, coming round the desk. 'You have a message, I understand? From Shih Lever.'

He hesitated, then gave the slightest nod of his head. Inwardly Emily smiled ironically. If she had been a man, his bow would have been low, to the waist, perhaps, but as she was merely a woman ...

'I have a note,' the man answered, looking away from her, as if he had dismissed her. 'It is to be given directly into the hands of young Master Lever.'

She took a long, deep breath. Young Master Lever. How clearly those words revealed Old Man Lever's attitude towards his son. How subtly and damagingly they placed Michael.

She moved closer, until her face was almost pressed against the man's. 'I will tell *Shih* Lever that you are here. If you would be seated,' she pointed past him, indicating the chair on the far side of the reception room. 'He is a very busy man, but he will see you when he can.'

As she turned away, she could see it in her mind. The thing to do was to keep the messenger waiting – an hour, two hours, maybe even to the close of business. That way the message would get back to Old Man Lever that his son was not to be treated like a troublesome infant, but respected as a man. That was what she would have done, anyway. But she was not Michael. Michael wanted an answer. Wanted an end to the tension and misery of not knowing.

She hesitated, then slid back the door. Inside she closed it behind her, then went across. Kustow was sitting to the left behind his desk, Michael to the right. They watched her cross the floor, their eyes filled with a tense expectation.

'It's here.'

She saw how the colour drained from Michael's face. He closed the Mem-Sys folder then turned in his chair, looking across at Kustow.

'Well, Bryn, what do you think?'

Kustow sat back, eyeing his partner sombrely. 'I think he's given you the finger, Michael. That's what I think.'

'But he can't,' Michael said quietly. 'Surely he can't? I mean, it's my money. *Legally* my money. If I took the matter to court ...'

Kustow shrugged fatalistically. 'You'd win, certainly, but not for several years. You, better than anyone, should know how expert your father's lawyers are at drawing things out. And in the meantime you've got nothing. Not even this ...'

'Maybe, but what gives him the right? What gives him the fucking right?'

For a moment all of the anger and frustration he was feeling was there in Michael Lever's face. Then, with a shudder, he took hold of himself again and looked across at Emily.

'Okay. Show him in. Let's hear the worst.'

She went back and brought the messenger through, watching as Michael took the envelope from him and slit it open. He read it through then, his hand trembling, passed it to Kustow at his side.

'Okay,' he said, meeting the messenger's eyes, his whole manner suddenly harder, more dignified. 'Tell my father that I note what he says and that I thank him for his generosity.'

'Is that it?' the man asked, staring back at him.

'You may go,' Michael said, letting nothing of what he was feeling enter his voice. 'You've done what was asked of you.'

When the messenger had gone, Michael turned, facing Kustow, his shoulders hunched suddenly, his eyes miserable, the pretence of dignified defiance cast off. 'That's it, then. The end of things ...'

Kustow studied the note a moment, then looked back at him. 'Is that what you want?'

'No. But what are our options? There was seventeen million in those four accounts. Without it ...'

'Without it we start again. Trim things down. Reassess our priorities. Work out what we can do. We've still got my money.'

'Two million. Where will that get us?'

'It'll get us started, that's what. As for the rest, we'll come up with something. We can borrow from the East Asian markets, maybe. Or from his major business rivals.'

'But you said you didn't want to borrow. You said that that would make us vulnerable.'

Kustow smiled. 'True. But I said that before your father turned nasty on us.' He handed Michael back the note then put his arm about his shoulders. 'Look at it this way, Michael. Your money would have given us a cushion – might have made the ride a little less bumpy – but it was never the main component of our strategy. Talent, ability, innovative ideas, that's what this Company was going to be based on, and it still can be. But I can't do it alone, Michael. I need you. And you need me.'

'But what about our plans ... ?'

'As I said. We scale things down. Put a rein on our ambitions for a time.' He shrugged. 'Look, this'll set us back, I don't deny it, but it doesn't have to put an end to things, not unless you want it to. So what about it, Michael? Are you going to crawl back to him, your tail between your legs, after all we've done and said, or are you going to spit in his eye and carry on?'

Michael glanced at Emily, then turned back, studying Kustow closely, his eyes recalling all they had been through those past few years. Gripping Kustow's arms firmly, he nodded.

'Okay,' he said quietly. 'We'll do it your way. If it fails we're no worse off, neh?'

'Not the tiniest bit ...'

Again he nodded, a smile slowly returning to his lips. 'Okay. Then let's do it. Let's spit in his eye.'

It was a dark-lit, shabby place that stank of cheap perfumes and sour liquor. The carpet underfoot was threadbare, the walls covered with inexpensive erotoprints. The girls, lined up against one of the walls, were in character; they too were cheap and worn, their faces over-painted, their bodies mere parodies of desire.

'Well?' said K'ang, turning to face Lehmann, a grin splitting his big face. 'What do you want? It's my treat. I always bring my boys here, once a month. Gives them a break. A bit of fun.'

Lehmann looked about him, letting no sign of the disgust he felt show in his face. 'No,' he said simply.

'Come on ...' K'ang made to take him by the arm, then remembered how he felt about that and backed off. 'You're sure? I mean, if it's not your thing...'

The look on Lehmann's face warned him not to say what he was thinking. K'ang shrugged and turned back to the others.

'I'll have the fat one,' said Ling Wo, K'ang's chief adviser.

'Which one?' said the Madame, coming across to him and winking. She herself was grossly fat and, like her girls, wore little or nothing about her genitals, as if such crude display could make her more desirable. Ling Wo let her fondle him and leaned close to whisper in her ear.

'Have them both!' she said and laughed raucously, slapping his shoulder. 'Shih K'ang here will pay, won't you, dear?'

K'ang laughed loudly and said, 'Of course. Have both, Ling Wo!' But his eyes said something different, and Ling Wo chose between the girls.

Lehmann, watching, saw the Madame look from one man to the other, then turn to her girls and make a face.

One by one the others made their choices, K'ang's three advisers first, then Peck, the new man from the south who had joined them only a week back.

Peck was an old acquaintance of Soucek's and had worked for K'ang

A-yin years before. Now he was back, after some trouble with Security. He had come in as lieutenant, to strengthen the *tong*. Or so the story went. To Lehmann it read otherwise. Peck had been brought in to counter him. To bring the odds back in K'ang's favour. Not that it mattered.

Then it was Soucek's turn.

'I'll pass this time, *Shih* K'ang.'

K'ang laughed. 'What do you mean, pass? Since when did you ever pass? You gone off girls or something?'

Soucek lifted his big, long head and met K'ang's eyes. 'I'll pass.'

K'ang went quiet. He looked from Soucek to Lehmann, then looked down at the floor. When he looked up again he was smiling, but his eyes, as ever, were cold. 'You don't like the way I treat you, Jiri, is that it?'

Soucek shook his head. 'You treat me fine, K'ang A-yin, but I just don't want it this time. Next time, okay. But now ...' His face was hard, expressionless.

K'ang looked across at the remaining girls, including the one he always had – the best of them, though it said little for her – and then smiled. 'Okay. You sit here with Lehmann and chat, neh?' And at that he laughed. He turned to Lehmann. 'Mind you, Stefan, you'd be better off fucking your brains out than trying to get a decent conversation out of Jiri there.'

Then, laughing, the Madame on one arm, the girl on the other, he followed the others inside.

Lehmann waited a moment, then turned, looking across at Soucek. 'Why didn't you go in?'

Soucek met Lehmann's eyes. 'I was watching you. Seeing how you saw it.'

'And?'

'You don't like all this, do you?'

'What does it matter what I like? You're K'ang's man.'

'That's not forever.'

'Nothing's forever. But that isn't what you meant, is it?'

Soucek was about to answer when the Madame came bursting in again. 'You boys want anything? Drinks?'

Lehmann looked at her blankly, then. 'Yes. Wine will do.'

Soucek half-lidded his eyes, curious. He had never seen Lehmann touch alcohol before. The Madame left the room, then returned with two drinks, setting them down on a small table at the far end of the room.

'There. You'll be comfy over here.'

Lehmann looked at her again, such hostility behind the blankness of his face that the Madame's smile faded momentarily, then came back stronger, as if to cover up the unease she felt in his presence. 'If there's anything else you need, just call.'

They waited until she went, then sat, Lehmann with his back to the wall, Soucek facing him. The two drinks rested on the low table between them.

'Tell me about Peck,' Lehmann said.

'Peck?' Soucek laughed coldly. 'Peck is *ying tzu.*'

Lehmann lowered his head slightly. He had heard of *ying tzu* – shadows – and their services. They were trained specialists, contracted out to gangland bosses. Like the *chan shih* they were a staple of the underworld here, though far more rare.

'That costs.'

Soucek nodded and reached out to take his glass, but Lehmann put out a hand, stopping him. 'Why are you telling me?'

'A warning.'

Lehmann studied him carefully, his gaze penetrating. 'Just that?'

Soucek smiled again, his thin-lipped mouth an ugly, lifeless thing. 'No.' He hesitated and then looked down. 'Because you're strong.'

'And K'ang isn't?'

Soucek looked up. 'He's strong. In some ways. But you ...' He shook his head.

Lehmann was silent a long time after that. Then he picked up his glass and sniffed at it. 'I'm K'ang's man now.'

Soucek watched him; saw him put the glass down untouched. 'Now?'

Lehmann's eyes seemed to soften marginally, as if he was pleased that Soucek had understood him, but still he didn't smile. Soucek looked down at his glass and nodded to himself. In this as in all else from now on he would copy Lehmann. If Lehmann shunned women, he too would shun women. If Lehmann touched no drink, he too would do the same. For there was a secret in all this, he saw. A kind of strength. *Macht*, the others called it, in the old slang of these parts. *Power*.

'What do you want?'

Lehmann's question surprised him. *To be like you*, he thought, but what he said was different. 'I don't want to be here forever. I ...'

He stopped and turned in his chair. Six men had come into the room. Two of them had been talking when they came in, but on seeing Lehmann and Soucek there they had fallen silent. As Soucek watched, the Madame came out and, with a glance across at Lehmann and himself, leaned close to one of the newcomers and whispered something to him. Then, with a broad, false smile, she came across again.

'Well, we are busy tonight!' she said with an excessive gaiety that struck Soucek as rather odd. Then, looking at their glasses, her smile widened again. 'You want fill-ups?'

Soucek turned and looked down at the glasses. They were empty. He looked up at Lehmann, surprised, but the albino's face was blank.

'Why not?' said Lehmann tonelessly, lifting the glasses and handing them to her.

Soucek watched Lehmann a moment longer, then turned in time to see the Madame usher the men out through a door she hadn't used before. She was the last to go through and as she did, she turned, taking an almost furtive glance back at them.

As soon as she was gone, Lehmann was on his feet and crossing the room towards the exit.

'What's happening?' began Soucek, jumping up.

Lehmann turned suddenly, like an acrobat, his balance perfect. 'Just sit there,' he said softly. 'Pretend nothing's happening. If she asks, tell her I've gone for a piss. And whatever you do, don't touch the drink. It's drugged.'

At the door Lehmann paused, slipping to one side as it irised open. No one. He went through quickly, using the far wall of the corridor to stop and turn himself, his gun out and searching, then relaxed. The corridor was empty.

Crouching, he set the gun down, then took off his wristband and turned it inside out. Quickly he tapped out the contact code. At once the tiny screen came alight, blood red. There was a moment's vague activity, then the screen's colour changed and a miniature of Haller's face stared back at him.

'What the hell time ... ?' Haller began, then saw it wasn't Becker. His manner changed at once. 'What is it?'

Lehmann spelt out the situation, gave the location and told him what was needed. 'You've got eight minutes maximum. Bring Becker. Go in at the front. And remember, no noise.'

He cut contact, put the wristband back on and picked up the gun. Then, pausing only to look back along the corridor, he began to run. There would be a back entrance. Sealed maybe. Guarded probably. But he would face that when he got there.

It was a narrow side alley with three ceiling lamps. He stood in part shadow, looking down. There was one man, his back to him, expecting nothing yet. Unhesitant, Lehmann moved quickly between the distinct pools of light and came behind the man silently, wrapping the fine, hard wire about his neck with a graceful looping of his hands. The man's cry of surprise and pain was cut off sharply, almost before it formed. Lehmann let the lifeless body fall, the wire embedded deep in the flesh.

He tested the door's frame for weaknesses, pushing at it, then leaning hard against it. Moving back from it, he took a breath, then kicked twice, in two separate places. The door fell inwards, the crude latches snapped off.

Quickly he moved through the dust cloud, conscious of the noise he'd had to make. Almost at once he was facing one of the Madame's girls who had come out of her room to see what was happening. He grabbed her, one hand about her mouth, then pushed her back into the room, looking about him. She was alone. With a quick, strong movement, he snapped her neck and lay her down. Then, shutting the door behind him, he went back for the dead man.

He had been lucky so far. No one else had heard, and no one had seen the corpse lying there in the shadows by the door. Quickly, grunting with the effort, he dragged it inside, then set the door back in place behind him.

Would they be missing him yet? Getting suspicious? It was almost five minutes now since he'd gone for that piss. Was Soucek all right?

He put the dead man in with the corpse of the whore, then came out again. For a moment he stood there, listening. Things seemed okay. He took a breath, then went on, half running down the long, dark passageway, following it round. There was a door to the left. He paused, lifting the flap. Peck was inside, naked, on his back, a busty blonde riding him vigorously. Lehmann dropped the flap silently and went on.

At the door to the reception area he stopped again, listening. He could hear Soucek's voice, and the Madame's. All seemed fine. He went through.

He saw the relief on the Madame's face, and knew at once what she'd been thinking. 'I've changed my mind,' he said, before she could say anything. 'There's a girl down the end there, I ...'

He saw her smile widen and again could read her thoughts. *You like to watch.* He looked away, as if he had been caught out, and stood back as she pushed past. Soucek had stood up. Lehmann nodded and signalled for him to come.

As she opened the door Lehmann came behind her and put his hand over her mouth so that she couldn't cry out. He felt her tense, could feel the sudden fear in every muscle of her body. She was staring at the two corpses wide-eyed.

'You can join them or you can help me,' Lehmann said quietly. She nodded and he released his grip. She was breathing heavily, trying to control herself.

'Just do what you were going to do. Give us three minutes, then send them in.'

She turned, surprised. Her mouth worked silently, its hideous rouge making ugly shapes, then she nodded. She made to step past him, but he reached out and held her. 'Remember,' he said, drawing her up with one hand until her face was just beneath his. 'Say a thing and you're dead. Those others, they're dead anyway. My men are coming here now. But you ... you can live. If you do what you're told.'

She swallowed, then found her voice. 'Okay. I'll do what you say.'

He pushed her away, disgusted by the foulness of her breath, the painted corruption of her face. He would kill her when it was done.

When she was gone, Soucek turned to him. 'What do you want me to do?' he said quietly. He had drawn his gun.

Lehmann reached out and took the gun. 'No noise. Use your knife. Or this.' He handed Soucek a garrotte with short, matt black handles. 'Or best of all, use your hands.'

Soucek stared at him. 'Are you serious?'

'Yes. Now, no noise. Understand?'

'Why?'

Lehmann glared at him. 'Just do it. Right?'

Soucek nodded, chastened by Lehmann's look.

They went out and down the passageway. At the turn, Lehmann stopped and pointed over to the right. 'There,' he whispered. 'In that doorway.

They'll not see you when they come round.' He turned and pointed back a little way. 'I'll be there, ahead of them. When they're past, you come up behind them. You should be able to take two of them at least.'

Soucek's eyes widened, then, remembering what his informer, Masson, had said about Lehmann's ferocity, nodded and got into place in the doorway. He had only moments to wait.

One of them came through on his own and stood there, listening. Distinct sounds of sexual pleasure were coming from several of the rooms now. Soucek, from his hiding place, saw the man hesitate, then turn back to the door, beckoning the others through.

They moved quickly, as though this had all been planned and rehearsed. But as they turned the corner Lehmann came at them. One went down at once, a knife in his throat. A second followed a moment later as Lehmann kicked high and shattered his nose. From behind them Soucek moved quickly, thrusting with his knife then swinging his blade high, catching the one who was turning back on him in the chest.

There was the faintest groan from one of the men, but otherwise it was a strangely silent struggle, a violent, desperate conflict, fought in the deep shadow of the passageway, as if in the blackest of nightmares. In less than a minute it was over.

Soucek stood there, panting, his arms shaking, and looked across at Lehmann, amazed.

'Mutes,' Lehmann said, as if it explained everything.

Soucek laughed softly. 'But they were talking. I heard them ...'

'That one ...' said Lehmann, pointing to the one who lay there, the big throwing knife deeply embedded in his throat. 'And that one over there.' The man he indicated was face down, a garrotte wound tightly about his neck. 'The rest had been operated on.'

Soucek bent down and looked. It was true. Four of the dead men had had their larynxes surgically removed. 'Why?' he asked, looking up.

'It's an old trick. I saw it at once.'

From the nearest room the sounds of pleasure grew louder briefly, then died away. Then, from the end door, stepped two more figures. Soucek tensed, reaching for his knife, but it was only Haller and Becker.

'Just in time, I see,' said Haller, grinning.

'Keep your voice down,' said Lehmann in a fierce whisper. 'You've brought the bags?'

Haller half turned. 'Becker has them.'

'Good. Then let's get these bodies through to the end room and tidy up.'

They worked quickly, taking the corpses down and piling them onto the bed beside the whore and the house guard. Then, while Haller cleaned up in the corridor, Becker got to work.

Soucek looked away from the grisly work and stared at Lehmann. 'I don't understand. What's going on?'

Lehmann watched Becker a moment, then turned to face Soucek. 'Who did this, do you think? Who would set K'ang up this way?'

Soucek thought a moment. 'Lo Han?'

'Exactly. It had to be Lo Han. K'ang A-yin threatens no one else. And Lo Han would have heard that both I and Peck had joined up with him. He'd be worried by that. He'd think there was a reason.'

'Maybe. But why this? Why the silence? The secrecy?'

Lehmann looked down at Becker again. 'You could say that I didn't want to inconvenience *Shih* K'ang, or interrupt his pleasure, but the truth is I want to meet Lo Han. To find out a bit more about him.'

Soucek made to speak, then stopped. Lehmann turned, looking at what he'd seen. It was the Madame. She stood in the doorway, her mouth open in horror, watching Becker.

'How did he pay you?' Lehmann asked, looking at her coldly.

For a moment she seemed not to have heard him, then her eyes jerked away from what Becker was doing and looked back at Lehmann. 'What?'

'What did Lo Han give you to set this up?'

'I ... I ...' she stammered, then, turning aside, she began to heave.

Lehmann looked away, disgusted. 'Never mind. You can tell *Shih* Soucek here.' He looked back at Soucek. 'We'll be gone in a while. Tell K'ang that I got tired of waiting. Tell him I've gone looking for other sport.'

'And if he asks what?'

'Tell him it's drugs. Tell him I've gone to get some drugs.'

The restaurant had been cleared, guards posted at every entrance. Beneath the broad, slatted steps, élite marksmen lay behind low, makeshift barriers, their high-powered rifles covering the approach corridors, while in the busy kitchens Wu Shih's own personal taster sampled each dish as it was presented to him, sending them through only when he was completely satisfied.

At the centre of the dark, tiled surface Marshal Tolonen sat facing Kim across a table crowded with silver trays of delicacies. Briefly the old man turned away, talking quietly to his ensign, then he turned back, facing Kim again.

'I'm sorry about all this, Kim, but Wu Shih is determined that nothing happens to me while I'm in his City. It might seem a little much, but such measures are necessary these days. We live in difficult times.'

'Difficult but interesting, neh?'

Tolonen laughed. 'So some might say. For myself I'd prefer things a little duller and a little safer.'

'And is that why you're here, Marshal Tolonen? To make things a little safer?'

'Call me Knut, boy,' he said, leaning forward and beginning to fill his plate with various bits and pieces. 'But yes, you might say I'm here to make things safer. Between you and me, I'm not quite sure what it is I'm looking for, but I know the smell of rottenness when I catch a whiff of it, and there's something rotten buried in these levels, you can be sure.'

'Is there any way I can help?' Kim asked, reaching for a plate.

Tolonen looked back at him. 'It's nice of you to ask, but until I know what exactly's been going on here, it's hard to say what I'll need. I'll bear it in mind, though, boy. And very kind of you, too. Oh, and by the way ...' the old man felt in his jacket pocket with the fingers of his golden hand, then passed a sealed note across the table to him, 'Li Yuan asked me to hand this to you personally.'

Kim took the note and, setting down his plate, turned it between his fingers, studying the great seal a moment. He glanced across, noting how the Marshal was busy filling his plate, then looked down again, slitting the envelope open with a fingernail.

Inside was a single sheet, handwritten in Mandarin; the message brief and familiar.

Dear Kim,

You have been much in my thoughts of late. Working on the proposed amendments to the Edict, I have often stopped and thought how helpful it might have been to have had you at my shoulder, advising me. But before you mistake me, this is no appeal for help, but a heartfelt thank you for all you have done in the past. I merely wished you to know that should you ever need help, in any way, you have only to ask. I hope all goes well for you.

With respect,

Li Yuan.

He looked up. Tolonen was watching him, smiling faintly. 'So ... how's it all going?'

'Things are fine, though there's not much to report, really. I've been holding fire on the business front, while I've been working on some new patents.'

'Patents, eh?' Tolonen narrowed his eyes, as if he thought the whole thing slightly dubious.

Kim laughed. 'Nothing illegal, I assure you. In fact, to be honest, I was surprised to learn what could actually be done within the existing guidelines. I've spent a long time recently, checking out what was already on file ...'

Tolonen interrupted him. 'I'm sorry, boy, I don't understand ...'

'At the Central Patents Office,' Kim explained quickly. 'It was hard work sifting through all that stuff, but worth it in the end. Originally, all I wanted was to check whether existing patents had been registered in any of the areas I was working in.'

'And were there?'

'One or two, but nothing even vaguely like what I proposed. However, in looking through the register, I noticed that there were whole areas – areas permitted under the Edict – which had essentially gone undeveloped these last one hundred and twenty years.'

Tolonen eyed him curiously. 'Whole areas? You mean, like whole fields of research?'

Kim shook his head. 'In the context of what's there – and we're talking about several billion patents on file – you'd probably consider these 'gaps' quite small, but in terms of the research possibilities, they're vast. I could have spent months there, simply locating more such 'gaps'.'

'I see.' Tolonen took a mouthful of tender pork and chewed for a moment, considering. 'Have you ever thought of speeding the process up?'

'How do you mean?'

Tolonen turned his head slightly, indicating the access slot just beneath his right ear. 'One of these. I'd have thought it would make your job a whole lot easier.'

'A wire?' Kim looked away, suddenly uncomfortable. 'I don't know.'

The old man leaned towards Kim. 'Looking at things from the outside, it strikes me that more than half your work involves what you might crudely call 'processing' information. Now, if you were to find a way of speeding that up, you'd get a lot more done, surely?'

'Maybe.'

Tolonen laughed gruffly. 'The only thing that surprises me is that you hadn't thought of it yourself. You're usually way ahead of me. Way ahead!'

Kim looked down, busying himself for a moment filling his plate. When he looked up again, Tolonen was still watching him.

'So what is it, lad? Are you afraid? Is that it?'

'I ...' Kim hesitated, not wanting to say what it was. How often had he thought this one through. How often he had yearned for a faster way of doing things, and come to the same conclusion. Yet against the logic of the thing was a deep ingrained fear of being wired – of somehow being controlled.

'The operation's simple,' Tolonen said. 'And I'm certain, if you wanted it done, Li Yuan's own surgeon would perform the task. Surgeon Hung is the best there is. And so he should be. He learned his skills from his father, who did this. Fifty years I've had this. Fifty years! And it's been a godsend, especially these past six months, what with all this GenSyn business.'

'I don't know,' Kim said, meeting his eyes again. 'It would make things easier. There's no doubting that. I just wonder ...'

'What? That it might impair some other part of you?' Tolonen laughed, and reached across, holding Kim's shoulder briefly with his human hand. 'I've never had your kind of talent, so maybe I'm not the one to comment on such things, but I've found my own wire nothing but a help all these years. All I know is that I couldn't have coped without it. Seriously.'

Kim gave a tiny nod. 'Maybe.' But he still seemed unconvinced.

'Well,' Tolonen said, leaning back again, the pearl white chopsticks gleaming in his golden hand, 'you think about it, boy. And if you want it done, I'll arrange everything for you. It's the least I can do.'

Later, alone in his office, Kim sat there at his desk, toying with the graphics display on his comset and thinking about what Tolonen had said. Maybe he should get wired. Maybe he was just being silly about the whole thing. After all, it wouldn't hurt to be able to process things a little faster. No, nor was there any evidence that the procedure impaired creative thought. Quite the opposite, if reports were true. In fact, there wasn't a single reason not to be 'wired', nothing but his own irrational fear. Even so, he held back, unable, finally, to commit himself.

So what was it? What was he afraid of?

Control, he thought, unwilling even to utter the word, however softly. *I'm afraid of losing control again.*

And maybe that was paranoia, but he wasn't quite convinced. After all, hadn't he been the one called in by Li Yuan to look at the feasibility of wiring up the whole population? Hadn't he seen for himself how easy it would be to take that first simple step?

And if he took that first step by himself?

It isn't the same, he told himself for the hundredth time; *the two things are completely different.* And so it was. The kind of 'wiring' Tolonen had in mind was nothing like the process Li Yuan was looking into, yet his mind refused the distinction, preferring to connect them. Wires in the head. They were a means of control. And if he took the first step, who was to say that someone else might not take the next, making him their beast?

Nonsense, a part of him replied: *you're talking fearful nonsense now, Kim Ward.*

But was he? Or was his instinct sound?

He huffed, exasperated with himself, then turned, startled, hearing the faintest rustle of silk behind him.

A young Han stood there, head bowed, a small tray held out before him. 'Forgive me, Master. I have brought *ch'a*.'

Kim relaxed. It was only his book-keeper, Nong Yan.

'I'm sorry, Yan. I thought I was the only one here.'

Nong placed the tray down beside him, then turned, smiling. 'And so you were, Master. I came in half an hour ago and saw that you were working, so I thought it best not to disturb you.'

'Ah ...' Kim nodded, yet he was surprised. Had he been that deep in his thoughts, then, that he hadn't heard the door? He set the comset down and reached across, lifting the chung and pouring two bowls of the steaming ch'a. Looking up, he offered one to the young book-keeper.

'So how are our finances, Yan? Are we in desperate straits yet?'

Nong took the bowl with a terse nod, then squatted on the edge of the desk, beside the comset. 'You know how things are, Master Kim. All bills are paid, all commitments met. Even so, the underlying problem remains as before. We are under-capitalised. If we are to expand ...'

'... we must get new funding,' Kim finished for him, studying the details of the diagram he had sketched out on the comset's screen. 'I hear what you say, Yan, but until I hear from young Shih Lever, we must struggle on as we are.' He took a sip from his bowl, then looked up at the young man again. 'You're happy, I take it, Yan?'

'Happy, Master?' Nong Yan laughed, his softly rounded face lighting up briefly. 'I have a fine wife and a good Master. Why should I not be happy?'

Kim smiled. 'Good. Then have patience with me, Yan, and we shall all be rich men.' He tapped the surface of the comset's screen with a fingernail, indicating the faintly webbed smoke-ring shape there. 'Once the patent has been registered things will begin in earnest. Until then, we hang fire. You know how it is in this business, Yan. The least said in public the better.'

'So it is, Master.'

'Good.' Kim reached across, clearing the screen, then looked back at Nong Yan. In the few moments he had been distracted by the young book-keeper, he had come to a decision. Taking Tolonen's card from his wallet, he studied it, memorising the contact number, then tucked it back into the top pocket of his jacket.

Setting the ch'a bowl down, he leaned forward, tapping out the number on the comset's pad, then turned, looking up at Nong Yan. 'Thank you, Yan. If you would leave me now ...'

As the ensign's face appeared on the screen, Kim turned back, and, with a confidence he did not wholly feel, asked to be put through to the Marshal.

The doubts remained. Even so, he would have it done. Besides, it would be good to visit Tolonen; to sit and talk to him at length. Yes, and to see his daughter, Jelka, once again.

There was a moment's delay and then Tolonen's face appeared. 'Kim! It was good to see you earlier!'

Kim gave the slightest bow. 'I felt I ought to thank you for the meal, Marshal. It was quite excellent.'

The old man laughed heartily. 'It was, wasn't it!'

'As for the other matter ...'

'You've thought it through, I take it?'

Kim nodded.

'And?' Tolonen asked eagerly.

'And I'd like to accept your kind invitation.'

Tolonen leaned back, delighted. 'So you're going to have it done, eh? Good! Excellent! I'll arrange everything. Just let Hauser here know when you want to come over and we'll organise it all. You won't regret it, Kim, believe me!'

'No,' he said, smiling, reassured by the old man's genuine delight. Yet when the screen went dead, he felt the tightness return and wondered briefly if he had acted for the good.

Too late, he thought. And even if that wasn't entirely true, he knew that he had taken a vital step towards it.

Ten days. He would have it done ten days from now. And as he framed the thought, an image came to mind: the image of a young woman, tall and straight and elegant, with hair the colour of the sun and eyes the deep blue of a summer's sky.

Kim frowned, wondering if she would remember him. Whether, in the long months that had passed since they'd met, she had ever once thought of him. He leaned forward, tapping out his personal code, summoning up the diagram again, but his mind was no longer on the patent.

Does she remember me? he thought, a sudden longing to see her face overwhelming him. *Does she?*

And if she did? What then?

He looked down at his hands where they rested in his lap – tiny, childlike hands, scarred and stunted by his experience in the Clay – and wondered what she had made of him that time, remembering how her eyes had met his own. Had he been wrong, or had something passed between them in that instant?

For a moment he sat there, undecided, then, angry at himself, at the doubts that constantly assailed him, he stood and, clearing the screen once more, hurried out, calling farewell to Nong Yan as he went.

The white silk envelope lay open, empty on the desktop. The chair behind the great desk was unoccupied, the portrait of Li Kou-lung, great-grandfather to Li Yuan, looked down imperiously on a room where nothing stirred. An ornate dragon lamp cast a pool of yellowed light about the desk, throwing heavy shadows on the tiled, mosaic floor. On the desk beside the lamp, a faint wisp of steam still drifting up from its untouched surface, rested a shallow bowl of soup, the long, straight, silver handle of the spoon jutting out horizontally, the dark line of its shadow dissecting the jaundiced whiteness of the silk.

Li Yuan stood in darkness beside the carp pool, Wei Feng's letter held loosely in his left hand as he stared out into the shadows. He had dismissed the servants and ordered that no one should disturb him, no matter how urgent the need. Now he stood there, unmoving, deep in thought, trying to see, in that utter, impenetrable darkness, his way through to clarity: to formulate a decision – a degree of certainty – from the sudden chaos of his thoughts.

Once before he had stood where he stood now, both figuratively and literally, facing this same matter. Back then anger and frustration – and a feeling of betrayal – had formed the thought in him, 'Why Seven?', and then, as now, he had passed through the anger to a feeling of peace and to the realisation that he had survived the worst his enemies could throw at him. Yet there was a difference, for now he understood that such peace, such respite, was temporary. Whatever he did, however he acted, his enemies would multiply. Cut off one head and two more would grow in its place, as in the legend. But now, with Wei Feng's letter, something new had entered the calculations of power. Now that thought – 'Why Seven?' – was given more than a tentative expression.

Li Yuan sighed. The old man had seen how things stood; had seen the divisions that lay ahead if things remained as they were, and had said to him directly, unequivocally, 'Take power, Li Yuan. Grasp it now, before all Seven go down into the darkness.' Those, his words, had been mirrored in his son, Chan Yin's face. He understood now; knew what that look of deference and humility had meant. And Chan's words, 'I am my father's son', they too took on a new significance.

At first he had not believed what he had read. Slowly, one finger tracing the words, he had mouthed them to himself, then had sat back, oblivious of the servant who had brought his evening soup, trying to take in the profound significance of Wei Feng's final message to him. How would he, in Chan Yin's position, have behaved? Would he, like Chan, have submitted to his father's wishes?

He frowned, realising he did not know himself as well as that. To give away his birthright. To bow before another when there was no need. He shook his head. No, even filial duty broke before such demands. Chan Yin would have been within his rights to ignore his father's dying wishes; to have dismissed them as the addled ravings of a sick and disappointed man. But he had not.

Beyond this question of duty and birthright lay a second, more complex one; the matter of acting upon Wei Feng's wishes, and the likely political repercussions. Ignoring the morality of it a moment, he could not, even in practical terms, accept what Wei Feng had offered him. He could not be the new T'ang of Eastern Asia in Chan Yin's place. While the letter stated this as Wei Feng's wish, and though Chan Yin and his brothers might agree to and accept the terms of this document – two factors which might make his inheritance incontestable in law – there was not the slightest possibility that the other five T'ang would allow it. Even Tsu Ma would act to prevent it if he knew. No, if he even so much as mentioned the possibility it would have the effect of isolating him in Council and achieve in an instant what Wang Sau-leyan had long striven to do.

Chan Yin would inherit. The chain would remain unbroken. But in the dark something else had come to the young T'ang of Europe. Some deeper scheme that might build upon what Wei Feng had freed him to contemplate. A scheme whereby the Seven might become both simpler and more effective. Might become – he dared to whisper it aloud – 'Just three of us. Tsu Ma. Wu Shih. And I …'

And, once uttered, the idea took root in the depths of him, became a growing seed that he might now begin to nurture with the water of thought and the sunlight of action.

Returning to his study he stood there in the doorway, looking across at the portrait of his great-grandfather, a man he had never known, wondering how he would have viewed such things and whether he, in similar circumstances, would have thought or acted differently. He could ask, of course, consult the old man's hologram, yet he sensed it would do little good. Li

Kou-lung's responses had been programmed in a different age; an age of solid certainties when even to think of such matters would have been considered a sign of frailty. Sighing deeply, he crossed the room and pulled at the bell rope, summoning Chang Shih-sen, his secretary.

He stood there, waiting, staring down at the shallow bowl, then reached out and, with one finger, gently breached the cold, congealed surface, thinking to himself, *Three. Just Three*, before raising the finger to his mouth.

Li Yuan turned from the desk as Chang Shih-sen entered, drawing himself up straight.

'Call Wei Chan Yin for me,' he said, all sign of tiredness gone from him, replaced by a strange excitement. 'Ask him if he will come here. At once. He will be expecting my message.'

Chang Shih-sen bowed and turned to go, but Li Yuan reached out and held his arm a moment. 'And Shih-sen ... ask him to bring Tseng-li, the youngest. I have a use for him. Then rest. I will not need you for a while.'

CHAPTER 81

THE CHAIN OF BEING

In the formal gardens surrounding the great House at Weimar, song birds were singing in the cypress trees, greeting the dawn. The great House itself was empty, as it had been these past eight years, since Wang Hsien, father of the present T'ang of Africa, read the Seven's Edict of Disbandment, but in the pavilion to the east of the vast, ziggurat-like mass of the assembly building, a conference was taking place. There, in the shadow of the nearby City, fourteen men – the seven Chancellors of the Seven and seven greybeards, ex-Representatives of the House – sat about a huge circular table, discussing the future of Chung Kuo. On the ceiling directly overhead was a huge chart of Chung Kuo, the boundaries of the new Hsien, the administrative districts, marked in red against the background white, like capillaries on the surface of a clouded eye. For eleven hours now they had talked, with only two short breaks for refreshments, but now it was almost done.

Nan Ho, seated at the table, looked up from the silk-bound folder in front of him and smiled, meeting the eyes of the pig-tailed old Han facing him.

'You are a stubborn man, Ping Hsiang, but not unreasonable. What you ask for is far from what my Masters would have wished. But, as I have said many times this night, we are not here to impose. No. We must come to some new compact between Seven and Above. For the sake of all.'

There was a murmur of agreement about the table and from Ping Hsiang a taut smile and a single nod of the head.

'Good. Then let us agree on this final point. Let us delay the implementation of the package of measures agreed earlier until ten months after the House has passed the proposal. That way no one can say we have not been fair and open.'

'And the draft of these proposals?' Ping Hsiang asked, looking to either side of him as he spoke.

'A document is being prepared, even as we speak, and will be ready for the signature of all before we leave. You will all be given copies to take with you, naturally.'

Nan Ho saw the grins of pleasure at that news and smiled inwardly. He had brought them a long way this night, from open hostility and mistrust of the Seven and their motives, to a new respect, and maybe even a grudging admiration for the men who ruled them. On the way he had gained all that his masters had entrusted him, as spokesman of their negotiating committee, to gain, and had given no more – less, in fact – than they had empowered him to give. All in all, then, it had been a successful round of negotiations, and the irony was that, now that it was done, the men sat facing him positively glowed with satisfaction, as if they had put one over on him.

But then, that was the art of negotiation, surely? From the simplest marketplace haggling to the subtle art of statecraft, the principle behind it was the same: one had to forget the value of the thing one wanted, and begin negotiations from a point beyond. To over- or under-value, that was the basis of it; the one and only secret. But to do that one had also to know, with pinpoint accuracy, just what the thing desired was truly worth. So it had been today. He had spent long months establishing clearly in his mind just what it was the two sides wanted from this meeting.

And now it was done.

Nan Ho stood, looking about him, then clapped his hands together sharply, summoning the pavilion's servants. At once, two dozen shaven-headed young men entered, heads bowed respectfully, bearing trays of food and wine. He watched them move about the table, offering refreshments, then turned away, going across to the long window that curved away to either side.

Out there a new day was beginning, sunlight glittering off the upper windows of the House, stretching down the smooth, pearled flanks of the great building towards the deep shadow at its foot. Yesterday, before the meeting, Nan Ho had had the great doors unlocked and had gone into the House, pacing its empty corridors and lobbies until he came out into the echoing vastness of the central debating chamber. There, surrounded by tier upon tier of empty seats, he had imagined it, a year from now, filled with the elected Representatives of the Above – ten thousand voices clamouring to be heard above the din – and for a moment had found himself beset by doubts. Yet he knew that there was no stepping back from this course, no real alternative to this compact between Seven and Above. It was as Li Yuan argued, it was this or nothing. And so he had shrugged off his doubts and gone to the negotiating table with a clear, hard mind, softening his stance only when it was clear to those sat opposite him that he was bargaining from a position of strength, not weakness. Only then had he relaxed, bowing like the reed before the wind, making unexpected concessions. The Seven's demand for a maximum of two children per married couple was softened to three. A provocative 'retrospective action' clause, never intended to be part of the final package, was fought for and then abandoned. A proposal to extend the voting franchise from the top fifty to the top one hundred levels – a measure as abhorrent to the Seven as it was to the seven greybeards facing Nan Ho – was pressed and then dropped. And so it went on, false bargains being made, while real concessions were gained.

There were footsteps just behind him. Nan Ho half turned, then formed his features into a tight, polite smile. It was Hung Mien-lo, the Chancellor of City Africa, Wang Sau-leyan's man.

'Well, Chancellor Nan,' Hung said softly, his voice not carrying beyond their circle, 'we have what we came for, neh?'

Nan Ho looked beyond Hung Mien-lo at the greybeards gathered on the far side of the table. 'So it seems,' he said, mistrustful of the man. 'But it is not the power we give them that worries me – for that is little enough – as what they might yet take for themselves. There is no stepping back from this course. To close the House a second time ... It is inconceivable, neh?'

Hung Mien-lo smiled. 'Maybe. And yet stranger things have happened.'

Nan Ho shook his head, disturbed by the thought. 'No. To close the House again is unthinkable. Our task henceforth is a simple one. We must find ways of harnessing that power.'

'Like 'Pockets' you mean?'

Nan Ho narrowed his eyes, trying to gauge what the other meant by his comment. 'Pockets' – tai – were Représsentatives who had been bought by the Seven, and who had, in the past, exerted considerable influence over the House. But in the period leading up to the War-that-wasn't-a-War the Seven had tried to swamp the House with 'Pockets' and the institution had fallen into disrepute. The impeachment and arrest of the *tai* in the Spring of 2201 had, in effect, been a declaration of independence by the House from the Seven, and had led directly to the War.

Nan Ho shrugged. 'In this, as in all else, the past shows us the way to the future.'

'The past ...' Hung Mien-lo laughed softly and leaned closer. 'And when the future finally comes? What then, Master Nan? How do we block the future? How harness it? For it *is* coming. You and I know that, even if our masters don't.'

Nan Ho stared back at Hung Mien-lo a moment, his face impassive, then, seeing that the scribes were finished, the document prepared, moved past his fellow Chancellor, leaving the questions unanswered.

The two bodyguards looked about them nervously as the sedan was set down, unused to being so far down the levels, but Michael Lever, stepping down from the carriage, seemed not to notice their unease. He looked about him, noting the stark neatness of his surroundings, then crossed the narrow hallway.

There was no entrance hall, no suite of offices isolating the inner workings of the Company from the outside world, merely a big double door, decorated, like many Company premises, with the Company logo. Lever smiled, amused by the simplicity of it all. He reached out to touch the delicate, shimmering web, then drew his fingers back sharply, surprised to find the strands warm, the background deathly cold.

He took a step back, studying the design. At the centre of the web was a tiny, smiling spider, while above it was the Company name, *Ch'i chu* – Spider – written in English and Mandarin.

This was the first time he had visited Kim at his facility and, despite all Kim had said, he was surprised to find it all so low-key. Why, there wasn't even a camera over the doorway ...

The doors shuddered, then, unexpectedly, melted away, leaving only the logo, hovering in the empty darkness. One of the guards made to come past him, but Michael raised a hand. Then, a faint smile of amusement on his lips, he stepped through.

There was the faintest crackle of static, the feeling of having passed through the flimsiest of barriers, and then he was inside. A tall, slightly balding Han stood before him, his head lowered, his hands folded before him respectfully.

'Welcome, Shih Lever. We were expecting you.'

Michael laughed. 'I see you were.' He turned, watching the door shimmer back into existence.

'Two holograms,' the Han explained, straightening up. 'One for the door, one for the logo. And behind them a security force field. It was Kim's idea.'

Michael nodded. 'It's clever. But I prefer more solid things.'

'Perhaps so. But solidity is a relative thing, Shih Lever. If the field had been turned on, you would have found it hard enough to walk through, hologram or no. But forgive me, let me introduce myself. My name is T'ai Cho.'

Michael lowered his head. 'T'ai Cho ... I am delighted to meet you. Kim has spoken of you often. He is fortunate to have such a good friend and guardian.'

The Han bowed, but his face remained expressionless.

'The good fortune has been mine alone, Shih Lever. The honour of serving so fine and talented a young man falls to few in this life. I would have counted my life as having had little meaning had I not met Shih Ward.'

Michael nodded, impressed by the Han's words. Yet if what Kim had told him were true, he owed T'ai Cho not merely his chance in life, but life itself. When Kim had come out of the Clay, it was T'ai Cho who – as his tutor in the Reclamation Project – had not merely recognised and fostered Kim's talent, but had interceded at a crucial moment to prevent his death.

'But let us not stand here talking, Shih Lever. Let me take you through. Kim is working just now – finishing something he began last night – but he will not be long. Maybe you would like to watch. If you would follow me ...'

'Thank you, T'ai Cho. It will be a real pleasure.'

He followed T'ai Cho through. There were two small offices off to the left of the corridor, but the main work space was a big L-shaped room at the end. There he found Kim, sitting with his back to the door, crouched forward, facing an experimental environment – the vacuum-sealed transparent box five ch'i to a side. The top half of Kim's head was hidden within a bulky headwrap, a dozen or more wires trailing off into a console to one side, while his arms were inside the box, enclosed in skin-tight armatures as he operated the nano-fine waldoes. Two lab-coated technicians sat on the edge of the desk nearby, so engrossed in what Kim was doing that they didn't even look up as Lever came into the room.

Michael went across and stood behind them. As far as he could see nothing was happening. Or – and the thought struck him as strangely amusing – as if Kim were only pretending to do something. The delicate appendages seemed to cut and mould the air, drawing out fine lines of nothingness, the tips of the waldoes sparking and flickering, but it was all to no apparent purpose. He felt a vague twinge of disappointment. There seemed no point to what Kim was doing; no discernible result. Michael squinted, trying to make out something he had missed, but it was no good. There really did seem to be nothing there.

He turned, looking about him. There were benches, cabinets, various items of machinery, most of them inexpensive, older models, all of it so unexpectedly shabby that he found himself making unwarranted comparisons: setting all of this against the state-of-the-art efficiency of his father's labs. It all seemed wrong somehow; too small, too cobbled-together. How could anything worthwhile be produced in conditions like this?

For the briefest moment he wondered whether he might not be mistaken in his plans to work with Ward, but then he remembered his father's interest and what he had heard from his European contacts. And then there was what he himself knew about the boy's abilities.

The boy ... He turned, studying Ward in profile, then looked away, conscious of how his thoughts had betrayed him. Appearances. With Ward it wasn't possible to judge things on appearances, for he was not what he seemed. Nineteen now, Ward seemed little more than a child, a boy of twelve, thirteen at most, his diminutive stature the result of his childhood in the Clay. That experience, down there in the darkness beneath the City's foundations, had shaped him, inwardly and out, making him – at a glance – different from those he went amongst. Michael smiled. Compared to the tall, well-fed citizens of First Level, Kim seemed but the unfleshed suggestion of humanity – a throw-back to an earlier evolutionary stage. Physically, Kim had so little substance. But appearances were deceptive, for there was a fire in his eyes, a strength even in his smallest movement that belied that

first impression. And one further thing. Ward was reputedly the finest the-
oretical scientist in the whole of Chung Kuo.

He looked back. Kim was watching him, his dark eyes curious. 'Michael
...' he said softly, greeting him. 'One moment and I'm done.'

He watched. Where there had been nothing, a fine point of pure white
light blossomed, a fine web of threads spreading out like buds from the radiant hub then turning back on themselves until they formed a tiny, spher-
ical net, the whole thing taking on detail and complexity until it seemed to
glow with an intense energy. It began to turn, slowly at first, then faster, the
glow fading and returning until it formed a regular pulse.

Michael shook his head, astonished. It was beautiful. He glanced at Kim
and saw how he was leaning forward now, his lips parted, his breathing
shallow. Michael shivered then looked back, his eyes drawn to the spinning
helix of light.

It span, faster and faster, and as it span brief, brilliant pulses of light
flashed from its glowing heart, each pulse striking one of the tiny stud-like
targets that dotted the inside walls of the chamber. Slowly the light intensi-
fied until he had to half-lid his eyes, then turn aside, his eyes squeezed shut,
one hand shielding his face. But even then he could still see it through the
flesh of his eyelids, spinning at the centre of the void, like a tiny, burning
star, flashing magnificently.

For a moment longer it maintained its perfect equilibrium at the centre
of the vacuum, then, with a noisy crackle of static, the light abruptly died.

Michael turned, blinking, staring into the darkness of the chamber, then
looked across. For a moment Kim sat there, perfectly still, then, with a tiny
shudder, he sat back, pulling his arms from the waldoes.

'Kuan Yin!' Michael said softly, shaking his head.

Kim turned his head and looked at him, a faint, almost apologetic smile
on his lips, then, tugging off the head-wrap, he came across, taking Lever's
hands. 'Michael ... It's good to see you. How are things?'

Michael smiled. 'I'm fine. But what *was* that?'

Kim half glanced back at the empty chamber, then shrugged. 'It's something long-term, that's all. A problem I've set myself. I thought I had a solution, but, well, let's just say that it's not stable.'

Michael laughed. 'Yes ... but what was it? It looked beautiful.'

Kim moved past him, then turned back, a rough sketch in one hand.

'Basically, it's a switching device. It's meant to transmit energy at a molec- ular level. The trouble is, it has to be able to maintain its form and turn at phenomenal speeds – at the speed of molecular reactions themselves, to be accurate. At present, however, it's very fragile. The least molecular interfer- ence from outside and it breaks up. As you saw. Add to that the fact that it's far too big for practical use, and you can see just how far I am from solving things.'

Michael glanced at the paper Kim had given him, but the equations meant nothing to him. They might just as well have been written in Shang dynasty Mandarin. 'Maybe, but it's certainly impressive.'

Kim laughed. 'You think so? Well, maybe, but sometimes it feels like I'm grasping at nothingness itself. And I ask myself, what if I'm wrong? What if all the talent I have isn't enough? What if the universe is *different* from how I conceive it? What if it won't conform to the pattern in my head?'

'Then you change the pattern, surely?'

Kim studied Michael a moment, then looked away. 'But what if I *am* the pattern?' For a moment Kim stood there, perfectly still, staring into the empty chamber, then, as if remembering suddenly where he was, he looked back, smiling. 'All that aside, how did it go? Is it still on?'

It was Michael's turn to look away. 'I'm sorry, Kim. The Old Man wouldn't budge. And without those funds ...'

Kim reached out and touched his arm. 'I understand. And it's all right. We can make do as we are for a while longer. But you ... you needed that money, didn't you?'

Michael met his eyes and nodded.

'So? What will you do?'

Michael smiled stoically. 'I've a scheme or two. The Old Man won't put curb and bit on me that easily.'

Kim nodded, but he could see how disappointed – and, beneath that, how angry – Michael was at his father for freezing his accounts.

'It was such a small amount,' Michael said quietly. 'Less than he spends on some of the old memorabilia he buys. But that's how it is. We have to live with it, neh?' He reached inside his jacket and took out a letter. 'Here. I thought this might help.'

Kim took the envelope without looking at it. 'What is it?'

'A letter of introduction, to the Hang Su. Credit Agency.'

'Credit?' Kim laughed, recalling the difficulties he had faced in going to the Credit Agencies when he had first set up Ch'i Chu. The message had been the same everywhere he'd turned. Find a major sponsor or forget it. That was how things worked here. Big fish and little fish. But he had been determined to keep his independence. He had struggled on, slowly using up the funds Li Yuan had given him, cutting corners and making do, trusting that his talent would be enough to pull him through. But now it was make-or-break time. He had to sell some of his ideas – to generate enough money to allow Ch'i Chu to live another year or two.

He shrugged. 'I'm not averse to the idea, but who in their right mind would give me credit?'

Michael smiled. 'Don't worry. I've made discreet enquiries and it seems that the Brothers Hang are willing to do business with you. I've arranged an interview for tomorrow at two.'

Kim laughed, genuinely surprised. 'Okay. But what do I put up for security? I've sunk everything I have into this place. And now that your father has tightened the reins ...'

Michael was still smiling. 'What about the patents? They're worth something, aren't they?'

'Maybe. Once they've been developed.'

'Then use them. You plan to register them tomorrow, right? Good. Then go and see the Brothers straight afterwards. Put the patents up as security. You'll have your funding by six tomorrow evening, I guarantee.'

Kim studied the envelope a moment, then looked back up at Michael. 'Okay. I'll do as you say. And thank you, Michael. Thank you for everything.'

'One last thing. How busy are you?'

Kim laughed. 'I'm always busy. But what do you mean?'

'Tonight, I mean. Could you free some time?'

'I guess so. Everything's prepared for tomorrow. What is it?'

Michael smiled, a broad, warm smile of enjoyment, undiminished by his troubles with his father. 'It's a ball, Kim. A coming-of-age ball for a good friend of mine.' He reached into his pocket and took out a card, handing it across. 'Here. Your invitation. It's fancy dress.'

'Fancy dress?'

Lever laughed, beginning to leave. 'Ask T'ai Cho. And if you've any trouble rustling up a costume, contact my secretary, Mary. She'll sort something out for you.'

Kim studied the gilt lettering of the invitation and nodded, recalling the last time he had been to a ball – the evening the Young Sons had been arrested – and felt a tiny, unexpected thrill of anticipation ripple down his spine.

'Sweetheart?'

Jelka stood there before the giant image of her father's face, smiling broadly. 'Daddy! How are you? When are you coming home?'

The great wall of the Marshal's face restructured itself, the muscles of the mouth and cheeks rearranging themselves, the broad smile becoming a look of dour resignation.

'Something's come up, I'm afraid. A development in the GenSyn case. It's important – something I have to follow up personally – so I might be here another three or four days. Is that all right?'

She smiled determinedly. 'Of course, papa. You do what you have to do. I'll be okay.'

'Good.' He stared at her proudly a moment, his eyes great orbs of steel amidst the craggy cliff-face of his features.

'So how was lunch?'

'Lunch?' He frowned, then, realising what she meant, gave a broad grin. 'Lunch was fine. Young Ward sends his regards. It seems he'll be coming over to Europe quite soon, to be wired.'

'Wired?' She looked up into her father's face uncertainly.

'You know ...' He touched the access slot beneath his right ear uneasily, knowing how she felt about it. 'The standard thing. A direct-processing link. He says it'll help with his work. Make things easier. Anyway ...' he cleared his throat and put on a determinedly cheerful expression, 'you can talk to him directly about it when he's over. I've invited him to dinner.'

She nodded, pretending a polite interest, but beneath it she felt her chest tighten, her pulse begin to quicken. 'That's good. It'll be nice to see him again.'

For a moment the old man's face beamed down at his daughter, drinking in the sight of her, then, with a deep sniff, he sat back slightly, his expression suddenly more businesslike.

'Well, my girl. I must get on. There's much to do here, and I'd like to get it done with as soon as possible.'

'Of course. And take care, all right?'

He nodded, the movement exaggerated by the screen. 'And you, my love.' Then he was gone, the screen blank.

She went across and sat at her father's desk, swivelling the big chair back and forth, staring out across the room thoughtfully. *So the boy was coming here* ...

She frowned, then gave a small, strange laugh. The boy was not a child these days. In fact, if she remembered rightly, Kim was almost a year older than her. It was just that she still thought of him like that. After all, he was so small. So tiny and graceful. So delicately formed ...

She shivered, then stood, disturbed suddenly by the thought of him coming there. But why so? He was just a boy, after all. A friend and colleague of her father's. It wasn't as if ...

She shook her head, then turned, facing the screen once more, staring at the perfect whiteness. It was just that his eyes had burned so brightly that time. As if they saw things differently.

For the briefest instant she saw once more the tiny fox, there in the cave on the island, staring back at her with its dark and feral eyes, the memory so vivid it was as if she stood there, watching it once more. And then it was gone, leaving only the plain white screen, and the memory of some wild, dark thing that did not belong in the world of levels.

Nan Ho was flying east, over the heart of Asia, the sun behind him now, the Altai Mountains beneath. Ahead lay the great desert, beyond it ancient China and, in the shadow of the Ta Pa Shan in Sichuan Province, the estate at Tong-jiang. He had sent ahead that he was coming, but, in the wake of Wei Feng's death – announced on the media an hour into his flight – he was not certain what state things would be in.

Wei Feng had been the oldest, the last of that generation. Even Wu Shih, the eldest of them now, was but a young man by comparison.

The thought troubled Nan Ho as he sat in his padded chair, sorting through his papers. The new T'ang, Wei Chan Yin, was a good man and a sound administrator, who had proved himself already as Regent in his father's stead, but Wei Feng's death had robbed the Council of its last real vestige of experience. Without the old man, they seemed less dignified, robbed somehow of authority. It would not be said, not openly, but it was certain to be thought – to be whispered ear to ear. And, though no outward change would be evident, the Seven would be weaker. For power was something manifested not merely in its exercise, but also in how the people perceived those who ruled them.

For the third time in as many years, the Seven were diminished; first by the murder of Wang Hsien, then by Li Shai Tung's sudden demise, and now this. It was fortuitous, perhaps, that they had made their 'deal' with the Above before the news had broken. Or maybe not. Maybe this news – to be announced this very evening – would be seen as further weakness. As a further erosion of power.

And when power failed altogether?

Nan Ho shuddered, then pushed the papers aside, angry with himself, conscious that Hung Mien-lo's words had got to him. Yet even as he settled back in his chair, a new determination formed in him. Whatever happened from now on he would be prepared for it. For he was forewarned now. It would be no one's fault but his if they faltered in the years ahead. And he, Nan Ho, son of Nan Ho-tse, would do his utmost to ensure that that did not happen. He would make it his sole concern – his life's work.

Even if death were the only payment for his pains.

Li Yuan was waiting for Nan Ho in his study when he arrived, the young T'ang dressed in the traditional clothes of mourning, as if it were his father who had just died. The great desk in front of him was unusually clear, only a small white envelope set to one side. Nan Ho glanced at it as he bowed, then looked again, surprised to find Wei Feng's distinctive seal set firmly in the blood red wax.

'You have done well, Master Nan,' Li Yuan said without preliminaries. 'I have spoken to Wu Shih and Tsu Ma and they are pleased with the terms you have drawn up. I thought we might have had to give much more.'

Nan Ho lowered his head again, but the mystery of the envelope distracted him. What message had the dead T'ang left? And was it to Li Yuan alone, or did all of the Seven have similar envelopes?

'Now that the matter is settled, there is something else I would like you to take on, Master Nan.'

Nan Ho met the young T'ang's eyes, for that brief moment bridging the great gulf in rank that lay between them. '*Chieh Hsia?*'

'I have had news from Tolonen in America. It seems he is on to something out there.'

'Did he say what, *Chieh Hsia?*'

Li Yuan shook his head. 'Don't you find it odd, Master Nan? I mean, it is most unlike the Marshal to keep things to himself. If he has a fault it is usually that he keeps us far too well informed.'

Nan Ho laughed. 'That is so, *Chieh Hsia.* But this is his old friend Klaus Ebert's business. Tolonen saw the man as a brother, and he goes about this business as a brother would.'

'True enough,' Li Yuan said thoughtfully. 'I have noticed that already. He sees this as a debt of honour, neh?'

'That is so, *Chieh Hsia.* He did say one thing to me, however. At Nantes, before he left.'

'And what was that?'

'He mentioned some anomalies in the GenSyn records for their North American operation. When I questioned him about it, he spoke of accounting irregularities, forged shipment details, missing documents and the like. It was a bland, evasive answer. A *safe* answer. Yet when he met my eyes I knew he meant something else. Something is missing, *Chieh Hsia,* and Tolonen has gone to find it.'

Li Yuan sighed. 'I do not like it, Master Nan, but for once I shall have to put up with it. The Marshal is a stubborn old man, but an honest one. We shall find out when he is ready to tell us, I suppose. But in the meantime, I want you to find out what you can. I do not want us caught wholly unprepared.'

Nan Ho bowed low. As ever he was already onto the matter. 'As you wish, *Chieh Hsia.*'

After the Chancellor had gone, Li Yuan leaned across, drawing the envelope towards him. In five hours Wei Chan Yin would be here.

He raised the letter to his nose and sniffed, then, setting it down again, shook his head. What had he expected? The smell of death? Of fear and darkness? Whatever, there was nothing. Nothing but the neutral scents of wax and ink and paper. Even so, he had felt a kind of fear – an almost primal dread – of what lay within that slender pocket of whiteness. It was fate, written in the dark, spidery hand of a dead man. Li Yuan shivered, thinking of it, and pushed it from him.

In five hours ...

Old Man Lever stood on the podium at the centre of the crowd, a full whisky tumbler held in one big, square-knuckled hand, a red, white and blue silk folder in the other. Behind him, a huge stars and stripes banner was draped over the far end of the vestibule, concealing the entrance to the deck. Lever smiled and looked about him, lifting his glass in greeting. They were all gathered here today – all of the original investors – fifty of the most important men in the North American Above, multibillionaires every one of them. But it had been his idea and his drive which had brought this into being. And now, at the inauguration ceremony, it would be he, Charles Lever, who would take the lion's share of the praise.

'Gentlemen ... *Friends* ... Welcome.' Lever combed a lock of steel grey hair back from his eyes and beamed, showing strong, slightly-yellowing teeth. 'You all know why we're here and what we're here for, so let's skip the formalities and go right on in. I'm sure you're all as anxious as I am to see how the money has been spent ...'

There was a roar of approval and, as Lever stepped down from the podium and made his way across, the small crowd followed, talking amongst themselves.

It was not often that they met, and to all it seemed particularly auspicious that it was on such a day, when news of Wei Feng's death and of the triumph at Weimar coincided. The normally placid old men fairly buzzed with the news. It was all linked in, they said; part of the new tide, turning in their favour. From the low ebb of their humiliation on the steps of the Lincoln Memorial they had rebuilt. And now their time was coming. The negotiations at Weimar had been the first step; the elections were the next. And each step would bring them closer to their aim – of a strong and independent America, free of the rule of Seven, taking its rightful place in the world once more. Not an empire, maybe, but a nation. And who knew what might come of that? Maybe they would take up where they had left off and reach out for the stars, the eagle stretching its wings ...

Beneath the huge stars and stripes banner Lever turned, facing them again. 'I realise that you gentlemen have been chomping on the bit, wanting to know what's been going on here, but when you see what has been achieved in the past ten months, I'm sure you'll agree that it was money well spent.'

He lifted a hand. At the signal, the banner drew slowly to one side, revealing a huge entrance tunnel, the walls and ceiling of which had been made to seem like marble. Over the entrance was a massive memorial stone, an inscription cut into the stone in a bold, classical face:

THE RICHARD CUTLER FOUNDATION FOR
GENETIC RESEARCH
Opened this Seventh day of March,
AD Two Thousand Two Hundred and Nine,
by Charles Alexander Lever,
Head of the ImmVac Corporation of North America.

Through the archway could be glimpsed a bright space, landscaped like a great park, and in its midst something huge, like the plinth of a giant statue.

They went through, coming out into a wooded glade from which could be seen the full extent of the Foundation and its grounds.

Lever had had the top three decks 'knocked into one', as he called it, so that the ceiling – a huge screen, programmed to seem like a summer sky – was a good two hundred ch'i overhead. But that was not what first caught the eye. In the centre of the landscaped gardens was an immense building; a structure which was as familiar to the old men standing there as the stars and stripes of the Sixty-Nine States. The Empire State Building.

For a moment there was stunned silence and then uproar as the old men clapped and yelped their approval.

'It's wonderful, Charles,' his friend, the financier, James Fisher said, slapping Lever's shoulder enthusiastically. 'The architect is to be congratulated. He's caught the spirit of the old building to perfection.'

Lever beamed, conscious of congratulations from all sides. 'He has, hasn't he? I gave him the basic idea and he came up with the rest. He had to modify, of course, but the general effect is just what I wanted. The labs and most of the research facilities are beneath this floor, of course – the whole thing stretches down another five decks – but this is the showpiece. The reception area, the main wards and the lecture halls are all within the main building.' He smiled and looked about him once more, 'As you'll see.'

In front of the huge studded entrance doors Lever turned and raised his hands. 'Gentlemen! One last thing before we go in. I am proud to say that only yesterday I received delivery of the latest masterpiece by the greatest painter of our age, Ernst Heydemeier.'

There was a low murmur of surprise. Lever looked about him, savouring the moment, then added, 'Furthermore, let me add that I have donated this specially commissioned painting to the Institute in commemoration of this inauguration ceremony. If you would follow me ...'

As Lever turned, the doors began slowly to ease back, revealing the facing wall-screen and Heydemeier's painting. There was a gasp of surprise and then, as more and more of the giant canvas came into view, a mounting tide of applause.

At the centre of the painting the giant figure of a youth, his muscular chest naked, stood atop a mountain's rugged crest, looking towards the west, the shaft of a huge banner clasped firmly in one hand. His tautly sculpted and beautiful features glowed with a visionary fervour. Behind the youth and the wind-furled flag, a company of youths – young gods, they seemed – climbed towards the summit, their faces gleaming, looking towards the sun that bathed the whole picture in its glorious golden light.

'Gods ...' One of the old men murmured, staring up at the huge canvas, his mouth agape. Nor was he alone. All about Lever the old men had fallen silent as the full scope of the massive painting came into view. There was a moment's hesitation, then, slowly, with a growing sense of awe, they began to approach the screen.

Old Man Lever stood there, looking about him, knowing what they were feeling at that moment. It was what he himself had felt only yesterday when he had first seen the painting. It was astonishing. Once more Heydemeier had taken his idea and transformed it. And now that he had seen it for himself, he knew. This was the Dream. This was what had driven him these past few years. This vision of perfection, glimpsed in the golden light of a new dawn.

He shivered. If it could be done, it would be done here. And this, this masterpiece of visionary painting, was the perfect statement of intent. To be a god and live forever – what was wrong with wanting that?

'It's astonishing,' someone said close by, real awe in his voice.

'You're right, Charles,' another added softly. 'It's a masterpiece. I've never seen its like!'

He looked about him, smiling, accepting the from all sides. Then, raising his voice once mo.. 'Come, gentlemen. Let's not stand here gawping. Let's ᵦ are wonders enough within.'

Two hours later they were standing in the central lecture hall, beneath a massive reproduction of Martin Waldeseemuller's spectacular 'Universalis Cosmographia', the ancient world map, dated 1507, which filled one whole end of the theatre. The original woodcut, the first map to give the new world the name of America, hung in Old Man Lever's study in Philadelphia.

They had seen it all now, and had been impressed. There was no doubt that if a solution to the ageing process could be found, it would be found here, for they had bought the finest state-of-the-art equipment, and hired the very best men in every field. Expert after expert had met them as they'd toured the facility, giving a brief speech of explanation before they moved on, each one impressive in their own right, each building upon the general impression of competence. It looked good. Very good indeed. All that was needed was time and money ... and a little luck. Or so Lever had claimed. Already the research had begun; each of the eight departments looking into their own highly specialised area. Everything had been thought out carefully beforehand, every base covered. Or so it seemed.

The tour completed, Lever went amongst the old men, talking with them, gauging their response, modestly accepting their praise. But all the while something nagged at him. It looked good. Indeed, it was good – the best money could buy. But it wasn't 'the best'. Nor would it be until he had Ward working for him.

He had looked about him as they toured the establishment, trying to see it all as they saw it, with fresh eyes, but all the time he was conscious that it was just a shell – a delightful piece of technological trickery, manned not by geniuses but by lesser men, schooled in old and rigid ways of thought. And he knew – because he had made it his business to know – that it all meant nothing – nothing at all – without that final tiny piece; that spark that would bring this great, magnificent engine of research to life.

It all came back to Ward. He had to have Ward. And if the man could not be bought, maybe he could be hassled into the job. Bullied and threatened and ultimately *forced* into taking on the task. Because, if his advisers were

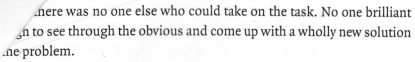

here was no one else who could take on the task. No one brilliant
n to see through the obvious and come up with a wholly new solution
ne problem.

Lever took another glass of whisky and drained it at a shot. No, if Ward
would not come willingly, he would come out of need: because there was
nowhere else to go, no one else to turn to. And that would happen. He
would make sure it would happen. Because the alternative ...

Lever stood there, staring up at the ancient map, conscious suddenly of
the billions of men and women who had lived and died since this chart had
been drawn. Of all those countless souls gone to dust and nothingness.
Then, drawing a long shuddering breath, he turned, smiling, and went
amongst the crowd of old men once again, letting nothing of his unease
show on the surface of his well-lined face.

Michael was silent for some time after Kustow had gone, studying the papers Mary had set before him, then he turned in his chair, looking across at
her.

When he had hired her, three weeks back, he had not been sure how
things would work out. Her record, working in middle management for
MemSys, the biggest of his companies, had been good – first rate, in fact
– but she had had little experience of working as a personal assistant. Nor
would he have hired her had any of the four men he had wanted been available. But they were not. Whether his father had frightened them off or simply
bought them out was irrelevant. He had been left with no choice. It was
Mary Jennings or no one. And maybe he had only got her because his father
had thought it beneath him to buy off a mere woman. But Mary had been
better – far better – than either he or his father had anticipated. She was
sharp, efficient and resourceful. Moreover, she worked well under pressure
– an invaluable trait at present, when the pressure was unrelenting. In many
ways she was the best assistant he had ever worked with.

He sat back, lacing his fingers together. 'Em ... ?'

She looked up, startled. 'I ...' Then she saw the look of surprise on his
face and looked away.

'Why did you call me that?'

'Call you what ... ? Oh. Em, you mean?' He held up a copy of one of her
reports. 'It's how you sign yourself. The letter M. I guess I've seen it so often

now I've come to think of you simply as Em.'

She looked down, her mind still reeling. Of course. M for Mary. Mary Jennings. How strongly she had come to associate herself with that name these past twenty-one months; yet at the slightest reminder it had been dislodged, her real name brought back to her. Em for Emily. *Emily Ascher* ...

She shivered, articulating it clearly in her head. Emily Ascher, late of City Europe and member of the Council of Five of the now defunct *Ping Tiao* – the infamous 'Levellers' – who had brought chaos to the levels and then, foolishly, she thought, had fire-bombed Bremen stack, killing over eleven thousand innocent people. It was twenty-one months now since DeVore had given her false papers and bundled her off onto an inter-City rocket to a new life. Months in which she had maintained a low profile, keeping herself to herself, building up the solid foundations of her life, all the while waiting, biding her time.

For the time would come. And when it did ...

'You know, I think you're right.'

She looked across; saw how he was watching her.

'Pardon?'

He tapped the report. 'About Dunn. I don't think we can trust him. He may have been my father's enemy for a long time now, but that doesn't necessarily make him my friend.' He smiled. 'I know how my father thinks. How he operates. He's a rich man, not averse to buying whatever he needs. And money can make a man – even a Dunn – take stranger bedfellows than his life-long enemy, neh, Em?'

She had it on her tongue to correct him, to ask him not to call her that again, but something in the way he said it touched her. It was like that moment when he had asked her to take over as his assistant. She could have said no. Indeed, the sensible thing would have been to say no. But there had been something in the way he'd asked her – some hint, perhaps, of that vulnerability she had witnessed in him – that had made her agree. And so now.

She smiled. 'It's been my experience that one should trust least those who claim alliance purely on the basis of a shared hatred. There's always a falling out.'

So it was. She had seen the *Ping Tiao* destroyed for that very reason, when Gesell had allied himself with the odious DeVore. But never again. When it came to making alliances, she would set her own terms in future.

Michael was looking at her strangely. 'By the way, what are you doing tonight?'

She laughed, the question catching her totally off guard. 'I'm sorry ...'

He looked away, as if flustered – as if he had overstepped some mark, then sat back, laughing. 'Look, if you've something on, forget it, but I thought, if you hadn't ... well, perhaps you'd like to accompany me to a ball.'

'A *ball*? You mean, like on the trivids?'

He shook his head. 'No. This is real. An old friend of mine. She's celebrating her twenty-fifth, her Coming-of-Age. Her parents died some years back and her estate's been in trust all this time, but now it's all hers and she's throwing a huge party at the family home. I just thought ...'

She sat back, staring at him. 'Why me?' she asked, after a moment. 'I'm sure there must be a dozen beautiful women out there who'd be ...'

'I thought it might be fun,' he said, interrupting her. 'You've worked hard for me and, well, I thought you might enjoy it. I was ...' He laughed. 'Well, I wasn't sure how you'd react. I thought you might mistake my motives. You know, a boss and his assistant ...'

'Especially when the assistant's a woman ...'

He narrowed his eyes, staring at her, then nodded, a faint smile of amusement on his lips. 'Well? Would you like to see how the Supernal let their hair down?'

Did she? Did she really want to mix at this level? For a moment longer she hesitated, and then she smiled; a beautiful, radiant smile. 'I'd like that, Shih Lever. I'd like that very much.'

'Good. But it's Michael ...' he said, returning her smile. 'Tonight you must call me Michael.'

'Is that it?'

Wei Chan Yin looked up from where he sat in Li Yuan's chair and met the young T'ang's eyes. There was nothing in his face to show what he was feeling, nor had he hesitated once in drafting the document. He had sat there, hand-writing it to Li Yuan's dictation, not glancing up, nor aside to where his brother, Tseng-li stood. More like a servant than an equal. Yet Li Yuan knew, better than anyone, the strengths, the qualities of this man. He had often talked with him when they had both been princes and when, in the final period of his father's illness, Chan Yin had acted as his father's Regent on the Council.

'Sign it at the bottom,' Li Yuan said. 'Then have Tseng-li put his name to it as witness. I will sign last.'

Chan Yin smiled and nodded. His hand moved across the thick parchment, signing his name with a flourish of the brush. That done, Tseng-li moved up beside him and, leaning over the desk, inked his brush and signed beside his brother's name.

Chan Yin looked up, and, turning the paper about, offered it to Li Yuan. Tseng-li held out the brush. Li Yuan took the brush and signed, taking a deep breath as he straightened up.

'You understand why this must be?' he said, smiling sadly at Chan Yin.

Chan Yin paused, then shook his head. 'Not yet, Yuan. Not ever, perhaps. But it was my father's dying wish.' His mouth formed a faint smile. 'You understand?'

Li Yuan laughed. 'Maybe. Maybe not. But I am grateful, cousin.'

Chan Yin gave a slight bow. Beside him, Tseng-li was looking down at his elder brother, that same restraint – product of the goodness that was in them all – shaping his features. Seeing the two men thus, Li Yuan felt deeply moved. To have such sons as these. A man might die satisfied, knowing he had bred so straight and true. He sighed, the determination forming in him that he would use this document only if he must.

'Tseng-li,' he said softly. 'There is something else I want from you.'

The youngest looked up, his dark eyes looking out from his beautiful face with a directness and openness that Li Yuan had rarely met. 'What is it, *Chieh Hsia*?'

Li Yuan smiled at the honorific. 'I would like your service, Tseng-li.' He paused, then. 'I want you to replace Chang Shih-sen and be my secretary.'

Chan Yin looked up at him, for the first time a look of surprise on his face. But Tseng-li merely nodded. 'As you wish, *Chieh Hsia*.'

'Good.' Li Yuan smiled, more at ease now that it was all concluded. 'Then we might set the day for your coronation, Wei Chan Yin. It is time you too were T'ang.'

CHAPTER 82

INTO EMPTINESS

Kim stepped down from the hired sedan and looked about him, astonished. A red-painted wall ten ch'i in height enclosed the First Level mansion, a gateway, topped by an ancient bell tower, provided the only way into the grounds. The huge double doors were of burnished bronze, studded with iron, the whole thing flanked by massive dragon pillars, painted a vivid emerald green. It was brutal. Like something from the fifteenth century. A Ming frontier fort, complete with watchtowers. The last thing one expected to find here at the top of the City.

All around him sedans were setting down, their occupants climbing out and making their way across what seemed some kind of horse track to the gateway. The variety and richness of their costumes was fascinating. They had come dressed as gods and goddesses, emperors and concubines, notorious villains and revered sages. All of history had been pillaged for this one night. By comparison his own spider costume was somewhat dour and unimaginative. He had not realised how much time and effort these people would put into something so ... insignificant.

He went across, then stopped, staring up at the great stone lintel that supported the bell tower. At its centre, a single Han pictogram had been carved into the stone: the character Chung, meaning 'The Arbitrator' – the name of the family who owned this great Mansion.

He frowned, conscious that his expectations had once again been turned upside-down. He had thought it would be like that evening at the Lever

Mansion, when the Young Sons had been arrested. To be honest, he had not expected any Han to be present. He turned, looking about him, watching the people filing past. They formed a queue beneath the bell tower, waiting to enter, their invitation cards held out for inspection by two huge, bare-chested Han, who stood before the open doors, barring the way.

Kim joined the queue, catching the air of excitement that was on every side. Reaching the front, he expected the guard to take his card and pass him through, as he had all those before, but the man blocked his way, putting a hand on his chest, restraining him.

'Wait there,' the guard ordered gruffly, then turned his head. 'Chang!' he called, summoning the second guard. 'Get the Captain over. That missing invitation – I think we might have found it!'

Kim looked down, containing his anger. He had met this before. Not often, but enough to recognise it for what it was. To them he was not another human being, he was Clay, the lowest of the low. His large eyes and diminutive stature gave that away at a glance. And some – like the guard – hated the Clay and all those who came from there with a bitter and totally irrational hatred.

He waited, his eyes lowered, listening as the guard and the captain talked between themselves in Mandarin; their assumption that a mere Clayborn couldn't understand the tongue typical of their kind.

'You! Raise your head!'

The Captain's barked command surprised Kim. He jerked his head up, meeting the man's eyes. The Captain studied him a moment, then made a coarse remark in Mandarin. Behind him the guards laughed.

'Well?' he said, thrusting the invitation at him. 'Where did you get this? You're not on the guest list, and one of the invitations was reported missing. It can only be assumed ...'

'What can only be assumed?'

The voice came from behind the guards. They stepped back, revealing the tall figure of Michael Lever, dressed in the bright blue and white costume of an American general of the late eighteenth century.

'Shih Lever ...' the Captain said, bowing low, as if acknowledging both the real and illusory gulf in rank between them. 'Forgive me, but this man was trying to gain admission to the grounds. There was a report this afternoon that one of the invitations had gone missing and ...'

'Be quiet, you imbecile! *Shih* Ward is my honoured guest. He is a great man. A *ch'un tzu*. You will bow low before him and apologise ...'

Embarrassed, Kim spoke up. 'Michael, please, there's really no need. The Captain was mistaken, that's all. Besides, he was right to be cautious. These are troubled times and this is a great house. Its doors should be protected.'

Michael stared at Kim a moment, then shrugged. 'If that's what you want. But I think you're mistaken. I think this shit knew *exactly* what he was doing.'

Almost certainly, Kim thought, *but I'll not be a party to such pettiness. Not while I've a choice.*

They went through, into a huge open space – a garden landscaped in the Han fashion. At the far side, beyond a pair of gently arching, white stone bridges, a large, two-storey Mansion in the southern style rested amidst tree and rock. Already, it seemed, the great house was full to overflowing. Guests crowded the verandah, talking and drinking, while from within came the muted sound of pipes and strings.

Kim turned, looking up at his friend. 'I thought it would be different.'

'You thought it would be like last time, neh? And you're confused, because this is Han. Well, let me explain things, before we meet our hostess.'

He drew Kim aside, moving towards a quiet arbour. There they sat, facing each other across a low table of sculpted stone, Michael's tricorn hat laid to one side.

'Back when the House was still open, Gloria's father was a Senior Representative – an important man, spokesman for his *tong*, the On Leong.'

Kim frowned. The five major *tong* of City America shared an ancestry with the Triads of Europe and Asia, but their recent history was very different. When things had collapsed over here, after President Griffin's assassination, it was the five *tong* who had helped hold things together on the East Coast and in enclaves in California and the Mid-West. And when the City was built across the continent, they had taken a major role in the social reconstruction programme. Their reward was a legitimisation of their organisations. They had become political parties.

'I see,' Kim said, 'but I still don't understand. I'd have thought that the *tong* would be your natural political adversaries.'

Michael sat back, smiling. 'They are. But Gloria is very different from her father. She wants what we want – an independent and outward-looking

America. And she's not alone. There are many Han who think like her. Most of them – the influential ones, that is – are here tonight.'

Kim looked down. 'And there I was, thinking ...'

'That I hated the Han?' Michael shook his head. 'No. Only our masters. Only those who try to keep us from our natural destiny. The rest ... well, there are good and bad, neh? What has race to do with that?'

'Bryn? Can I have a word?'

Bryn Kustow excused himself from the group with which he was standing, then came away, following Michael Lever down the broad corridor and into one of the empty side rooms.

With the door closed behind them, Michael turned, confronting him.

'Well, Michael? What is it?'

Michael reached out and held his arm. 'I've just had news. The bankers have called in the loan.'

'Ahh ...' Kustow considered that a moment, then shrugged. 'Then that's it, I guess. The game's over for the boys.'

'Is that what you want?'

Kustow looked up. 'No. But what's left to us? We've allocated most of my capital, and yours is frozen.'

Michael hesitated, then. 'What if I could get the money somewhere else?'

Kustow laughed. 'Where? Your father has the money market tied up tighter than a fly's arse.'

'That's what he thinks. But I've been checking out a few tips.'

'And?'

'And we've a meeting, tomorrow afternoon at two, with the Clear Heart Credit Agency of Cleveland.'

'And they'll lend us what we need?'

Michael hesitated. 'I don't know. What with this latest development we'll need to reassess things carefully. Work out what we need to pay off the loan and fund new development. The rates are high, but it's that or go under.'

'I see.' Kustow looked away a moment, then turned back, a faint smile on his lips. 'There is one other option. I mean, if we do have to seek alternative employment, there is one sphere we could go into.'

Michael laughed. 'I don't follow you, Bryn. What are you going on about?'

'I've been busy, too, Michael. Making calls. And I've set up a meeting.

Just you and me and an old school friend of ours. Two days from now, out at his place.'

'An old school friend?'

Kustow put a hand on Michael's shoulder. 'Trust me. Meanwhile, let's enjoy ourselves, neh? And smile, dammit. The night's young and you've a pretty woman waiting for you out there!'

A fan fluttered in the pearled light. There was the scent of rich perfumes, the swish of ancient ball gowns, the rustle of silks and satins, the low murmur of conversation, interspersed with bursts of drunken laughter. Emily Ascher stood at the head of the steps, looking down into the Hall of Ultimate Benevolence, amazed by the sight that met her eyes. The great hall was a riot of red, white and blue, decorated with all manner of Americana. Faded flags and ancient banners hung from the surrounding balconies and across the great ceiling, interspersed with huge, carved wooden eagles. At the far end a huge cracked bell rested on a raised platform – the Liberty Bell. Behind it hung a wall-sized map of the American Empire at its height, most of South America shaded blue, each of the Sixty-Nine States marked with a blazing golden star. In the space between, two or three thousand garishly-dressed young men and women milled about, talking and drinking.

Emily turned, wide-eyed, to her companion. Michael was watching her, a smile on his lips.

'Impressed?'

She nodded. 'I didn't expect ...' But what had she expected? 'Are these occasions always like this?'

'Not always. But then, most hostesses don't have Gloria's style. She's done us proud, don't you think?'

'Us?'

'The Sons ...'

'But I thought this was a coming-of-age party.'

'And so it is.' He smiled enigmatically, then offered her his arm. 'Here, let's go down. There are some friends I'd like you to meet.'

Several hours later she found herself amongst a group of young men gathered at the far end of the hall, about the Liberty Bell. There were nine of them in all; Michael Lever, three of his close friends, and five other 'Sons' who had shared the long months of incarceration at Wu Shih's hands. Like

Lever, all were dressed in the style of the early republic – authentic blue and white uniforms that had been purchased at great expense. With their short-cropped blond hair and knee-length boots they brought a strangely sombre note to the occasion, making a striking contrast against the other partygoers.

At first their talk had ranged widely, embracing all manner of things: from the planned reopening of the House and new research into space technologies to developments in the GenSyn inheritance case and the latest round of inter-City trade agreements. But as the evening drew on, their mood had grown darker, their talk focusing-in upon the tyranny of the Seven and the corresponding failings of their fathers.

Lever's close friend, Carl Stevens, was talking, gesturing animatedly as he spoke. 'Our fathers talk of changing things, of a return to Empire. That's something we'd all like to see, but when it comes down to it there's really not much between them and the Seven. Whichever ruled, the Seven or our fathers, we would remain as we are. Dispossessed. As powerless then as we are now.'

Beside him, Bryn Kustow nodded. 'Carl's right. If anything, our position would be much worse than it is now. If the Seven fell and our fathers came to power what would happen? Would they embrace us as their natural partners in the venture? No. Not for a second. We know how they think. We've all had a taste of their treatment these past years. They see us as a threat. As potential usurpers. It's sad to say, but in effect we have become our fathers' enemies.'

There was a murmur of reluctant agreement, heavy with unease.

'But what can be done?' one of the others, Mitchell, asked. 'They have all the power – the *real* power. All we get is the scraps from their tables. And what can we do with scraps?'

The bitterness in Mitchell's voice was mirrored in every face. Kustow looked across at Michael, then looked down. 'Nothing ...' he answered quietly. But there was something about his manner that suggested otherwise.

Standing there at Michael's side, Emily let her eyes move from face to face, conscious of the sudden tension in the circle. Despite what was being said, something about this whole elaborate charade of 'Empire' made her stiffen inwardly against them. They talked of changing the balance of power – of 'liberation' – when all they really meant was grabbing it for themselves.

In that they were no better than their fathers. No. Even after their experience of incarceration, they didn't understand. To them it was still essentially a game. Something to fill the hours and stave off the spectre of boredom.

Even so, it was good to see this – to understand how they thought, how they acted – for in some strange way it made her stronger, more determined.

For a moment she abstracted herself from their talk, looking inwards, focusing on the ideal she had worked for all these years. The ideal of Change – *real* change – free of the old power structures. Something pure and clean and utterly new. That was what she had struggled to achieve all those years in the *Ping Tiao*. A new world, free of hierarchies, where men and women could breathe new air and live new dreams. Yes, and that was what Mach and Gesell had really betrayed when they had chosen to work with DeVore.

She shivered, then looked aside. Michael was watching her, concerned. 'What is it, Em?'

She stared at him a moment, not recognising him, surprised to find herself there in the midst of that gathering, amongst those she would, without a moment's thought, have destroyed. And then, as realisation struck her, she laughed. And he, watching her, smiled, his smile broadening, not understanding, yet liking what he saw in that austere and sculpted face. And as he looked, a strange new determination formed in him, as if from nowhere, making his nerve-ends tingle.

'Well, Michael? Have you enjoyed your evening?'

Michael Lever turned, embracing his hostess, holding her a moment and kissing her cheek before he stepped back. Gloria Chung was a tall, strikingly elegant young woman with the classic features of the Han aristocracy. It was said her ancestors had been related to the great Ming dynasty, and, looking at her, it was not difficult to believe. She had dressed tonight as the famous Empress Wu in sweeping robes of midnight blue embroidered with a thousand tiny golden suns.

They were alone on the broad upper balcony. Below them the last of the guests were making their unsteady way back through the winding pathways to their sedans. She moved past him, standing there at the rail, looking out over the dark, lamp-lit garden.

'I've had a good time,' he said quietly, taking his place beside her at the rail. 'It's been nice to think of something other than the troubles with my father.'

'And the girl?'

'The girl?' He looked blank for a moment, then he laughed. 'Oh, you mean Mary?'

She turned her head, studying him, as if she could see right through him, then she smiled. 'I was watching you, Michael. Watching how you were together. It was ... interesting.'

He turned his head. 'What do you mean?'

'I do believe you're half in love with her.'

'Nonsense,' he said, shocked by the suggestion; yet even as he said it, he saw the truth in it. He stood there a moment, looking at her, then pushed away from the rail, masking his slip with a laugh. 'And what if I were?'

She reached out, holding his upper arm, then leaned close, kissing him. 'Don't get me wrong. I'm not disapproving. If it makes you happy ...' She moved back slightly, her eyes searching his. 'She'd be good for you, Michael. I can see that. She's strong.'

'Yes, but ...' He sighed. No, it was impossible. His father would never approve.

'You've taken the first step. Why not the next?'

'What do you mean?'

'I mean, get out of your father's shadow for good. Show him you're your own man. Marry her.'

He laughed, astonished. 'Marry her?' He looked down, troubled, then turned away. 'No. I couldn't. He'd cut me off ...'

'He'd not dare. But even if he did, how could things be any worse than they are? What else could he do?'

'No ...'

'No? Think about it, Michael. The Old Man's backed you into a corner. He's cut off your finances and tried every which way to prevent you from making a go of it on your own. As things are, you're going to have to make a choice, and soon – either to go back to him and beg forgiveness; to go down on your knees before the Old Man and agree to his terms, or to assert yourself. So why not do it now? Right now, when he least expects it.'

He faced her again. 'No. Not while there are still other options.'

She shivered. 'You mean, like the Clear Heart Credit House?'

He stared at her. 'How did you know that?'

'Because I make it my business to know. And if I know, you can be sure your father knows. In fact, I'm certain of it.'

'How?'

'Because he's the owner of the Clear Heart Credit Agency. As of this morning.'

He closed his eyes.

'So what are you going to do?'

'Do? What *can* I do?'

'You could do what I said. Marry her. Be your own man. As for the money, I'll give you that. It's two million, neh? Good. I'll have a draft ready for you in the morning. My wedding gift.'

He stared at her, astonished, then shook his head. 'But why? I don't understand you, Gloria. Why should you want to do this for me?'

She smiled and leaned close, kissing him again. 'Because I believe in you, Michael Lever. And because I want to see you strong. Strong and independent. For all our sakes.'

Twelve tiny homunculi – hologram figures no more than six *t'sun* in height – were gathered in a half-circle on the desk's surface, blinking and flickering in the faint light from a nearby float-globe. In a tall-backed chair, facing them, Old Man Lever looked down at his Departmental Heads and growled.

'So what's the problem? Why can't we use someone else? Someone cheaper than ProFax? Someone more reliable?'

Several of the figures shimmered, as if about to speak, but it was one of the central holograms – the tiny form of Lever's Head of Internal Distribution Services, Weller, who answered Lever, his image hardening, glowing stronger than before, standing out from the images to either side.

The figure bowed its head. 'Forgive me, Master, but we have had a good record of trading with ProFax. Our association with them goes back over twenty years. In our experience, there is no one more reliable.'

Lever huffed irritably. 'If that were true, we wouldn't be having this discussion, would we?' He sat forward, looming over them. 'So let me ask you once again, what is the problem? I could understand it if ProFax owned the patent to this process, but they don't. And they certainly don't have a monopoly of the market. So why can't we buy the stuff elsewhere? And why can't we cut the rates we pay for it into the bargain? It strikes me that this is the perfect opportunity.'

He sat back, steepling his hands. 'Okay. This is how we do it. We get our legal boys to send ProFax a writ, letting them know that they're in breach of contract, then we withhold all payments for products already shipped, and send out a request for tenders to all of ProFax's major competitors. And we do all this right now, understand me, gentlemen? Right now!'

As he uttered the final words, Lever slammed his right hand down on the 'cancel' button and hauled himself up out of his chair, even as the images faded from the air.

At that very moment, right across the City, his major Departmental Heads would be being woken up and told of the decision. *Yes, and cursing me silently, no doubt,* Lever thought, smiling savagely. But that's how it was in this world: one didn't look back, one got on with things. If something made sense, there was no good reason for delay. Nor was there room for senti-ment. Both were weaknesses. Fatal weaknesses, if one let them be.

He went across to the drinks cabinet on the far side of the study and pulled down a bottle of his favourite malt whisky, pouring himself a large glass, then turned, looking about him.

It was a big, ranch-style study with heavy wooden uprights and low rails dividing the room up into 'stalls'. To his left, beyond one of the rails, stood a mechanical horse, beneath a portrait of himself as a twenty-year-old, bare-chested in buckskins and shiny leather boots.

It was some while – months, if not years – since he had tried himself against the horse, nor had he even thought of it, but now, for some reason, he went across and, ducking beneath the rail, stood next to it, letting his left hand rest on the smooth, cool leather of the saddle while he sniffed in the heavy animal musk of the thing.

Across from him, behind the desk, set back against the far wall, was a big, glass-fronted cabinet, filled with sporting trophies: mementoes of an athletic youth. Beside it, lit softly from above, was a head and shoulders por-trait of his wife, her fine golden hair set like a halo about her soft, angelic face.

Earlier, he had sat in his private viewing chamber, enclosed in the dark-ness there, watching a hologram of his son Michael, wrestling with him beside the pool while his young wife Margaret looked on. It was an old film, taken shortly before Margaret had died. Michael had been eight then, he fifty-four.

He shivered, thinking of the years between. Twenty years this autumn. Long years in which he'd tried hard to forget; to steel himself against all the hurt and injustice he had felt at her death. At the suddenness of it all. He had buried himself in his work, throwing everything into the task of making his Company, ImmVac, the number one economic force in North America. But it had cost him. He had never grieved her properly and inside he was hurting still. Even now, after all these years, he could not look at her without feeling his stomach fall away, a dryness come to his mouth. It had been hard, bringing up the boy without her, but he had done it. And for a time it had worked.

Lever turned his head aside, a sudden bitterness making him grimace. After all he had been through – after all he had done for the boy – how could Michael have turned on him like that? And in public, too! The arrogance of the boy! The ingratitude ...

He shuddered, then slapped the horse's rump, angry with himself. Angry, not because of what he felt, but for the weakness, the sentiment he had allowed to sway him.

Ducking beneath the rail he went across and took the envelope from the table by the door, tearing it open angrily. Inside was the letter he had written earlier; the brief note of reconciliation, forgiving Michael and asking him to come back. For a moment Lever stood there, the letter held in one trembling hand. Then, with a spasm of anger, he ripped the thing in half, then in half again, his face distorted with anger and pain.

'No,' he said softly, looking about him, bewildered, frightened suddenly by the strength, the violence of his feelings. 'Not now, and maybe not ever. Not until you come crawling back, begging my forgiveness.'

And would that be enough? Would that repair what had been broken between them? No. And yet without it there was nothing. Less than nothing, in fact, for this bitterness, this anger ate at him, day by day, hour by hour, giving him no rest. *Like death*, he thought, and shivered again, wondering how it was all connected.

In three days Lehmann had brought the local *tong* boss, Lo Han, to the conference table. Fourteen of his men were dead and six more had joined K'ang A-yin, under Lehmann's lieutenantship. Now Lo Han sat there, three of his henchmen behind him, facing K'ang across the table, making a deal.

'It's too high. Far too high,' Lo Han said, spitting out the end of the cigar he had been chewing on.

'Fifteen per cent or the deal is off,' answered K'ang, turning in his seat to smile at Lehmann, as if to say, 'You can fight, but when it comes to making deals, just watch an expert.'

Lehmann said nothing, knowing that what K'ang was asking for was ridiculously low. The figures Lo Han was showing in his books were rigged. Even at a conservative estimate he must be raking in four or five times as much. And a sixth of twenty per cent wasn't much, seeing that he had been soundly beaten on four occasions now. But it didn't matter. Whatever K'ang agreed to, he, Lehmann, would tear up when the time came, for he wanted a pure one hundred per cent of Lo Han's drug trade.

In his six weeks down here Lehmann had learned much about the Lowers. He had watched carefully and listened to Soucek attentively. He knew now how they thought and what they wanted. He knew what motivated them and how far they would go to get what they wanted. He knew their strengths and their weaknesses – particularly the latter – and had come to see just how he could use both to attain his ends.

And what were those ends?

When he had returned to the City from off the mountainside, he had wanted nothing less than total vengeance against the Seven. He had seen himself as a lone figure, slipping between the levels like a shadow, bringing death to the Families and all who supported them. But that was just a dream. As a single man he could not hope to change things, yet by his very nature he was singular: he could not parcel out his thoughts, his hatreds, and share them. Even so, there was a middle way.

Singular he might be, but not necessarily alone. Already he was forming a solid corps of men about him, Soucek chief amongst them. Men loyal to him alone, however it appeared on the surface. Consulting no one, letting no one into his thoughts, he went about his business, winning allies by the strength of his actions, the single-mindedness inherent in his nature. He did not have to ask; men followed him, recognising in him something they had longed for, maybe dreamed of. Men confided in him, seeking nothing in return. Trusting him. Willing to be used by him. *Wanting* to be used.

Respect and fear. Loyalty and a deep-rooted uncertainty. It was this mixed response to him – there in all who came to know him – that eventually defined for him the means by which he would come to attain that impossible, dream-like end which was the very source, the fountainhead, of his singularity.

He would use their respect and fear, channel their loyalty and uncertainty, knowing that both aspects were necessary and, in their combination, powerful. But at the heart of things would be his own singular desire, deadly and uncompromising, shaping things, moulding those who were attracted and appalled by him into a body – a weapon – through which his will would be done.

He held the thought in mind a moment longer, then frowned. At the table the small men were still haggling and bargaining over nothings – Lo Han's crude arrogance matched by K'ang's petty greed. He looked past them and saw how the eyes of Lo Han's henchmen had strayed to him, troubled by his changed expression. Turning away, he went to the door and tugged it open, ignoring the looks of query from K'ang and Lo Han. Outside he nodded to Soucek and walked on, conscious of his questioning glance.

Soucek caught up with him at the corridor's end. 'What is it, Stefan?' he whispered, concerned.

Lehmann turned, facing the tall, cadaverous man, taking his upper arms in his hands, but for a moment he said nothing.

He knew that they had their rules, their limitations, even here where there seemed to be no rules at all, only brute force. All human life set limits to its actions. There was always a point beyond which they would not go. But he, who valued nothing, had no such rules, no limits. He was beyond good and evil. For him nothing mattered but the accomplishment of his will – the fulfilment of his singular desire.

And if that were so, why then should he wait? Why did he not act at once, not fearing the consequences? Knowing that the consequences were likely to favour him. It was this that he had been thinking as he stood there behind K'ang – this that had made him frown. He squeezed Soucek's arms and stared into his pale green eyes.

'Are you with me, Jiri?'

Soucek nodded, seeming to grasp at once what was happening. 'Right now?' he asked.

'Why not? The two together. They might suspect treachery from each other, but not from us. They'll think we fear an all-out war between the tong.

But with the two of them dead ...'

He let go of Soucek's arms.

The tall man smiled. It was clear that the idea appealed to him strongly; that the thought of killing K'ang scratched a long unsatisfied itch. He drew his gun. 'Okay. I'll take Lo Han's henchmen.'

It was both clever and sensitive of him. In effect he was saying, You, Lehmann, are the leader. To you goes the honour of killing K'ang and Lo Han.

Lehmann nodded slowly and pulled the huge, pearl-white gun from its webbing holster.

'Yes,' he said, his voice cold, brittle like ice. 'Let's do it now.'

Lehmann stood there in the Oven Man's doorway, a tall, unnaturally gaunt figure dressed in white. At his feet lay the corpses of three of the runners who had attacked them. Two more lay dead inside the room. The rest had fled, throwing down their hatchets, as if it were Yang Wen, the God of Hell himself that faced them.

The killing of Lo Han and K'ang A-yin had shocked the local *tong* bosses. But shock had quickly led to the realisation that there was a power vacuum. A vacuum that needed to be filled, and quickly. Within the hour, two of them met and decided to act. A messenger had been sent to Lehmann to set up a meeting to arrange a truce, but the meeting was merely a pretext. The bosses had decided to deal with Lehmann before he became a problem.

Lehmann had known that. In fact, he had counted on it. He had turned up with three men, unarmed, knowing how the *tong* bosses would try to play it. Fifteen runners, armed with silver hatchets. These would administer the 'death of a thousand cuts' – a warning to all other potential usurpers.

But Lehmann had had no intention of dying. He had other lessons in mind.

An hour before the meeting he had set up small groups of men in the approach corridors, making sure they understood that they were not to intercede in any way, merely show themselves when the *tong* runners beat their retreat. Then, when the runners had shown up – hard-faced, arrogant little shits, dangerously over-confident – Lehmann had set his men behind him and faced them alone, taunting them, belittling them, until, one by one, they had come at him.

Soucek stared at him now, remembering.

Lehmann had straight-fisted the first runner before the man had even known the blow was on its way, the force of the punch sending the man staggering back. He was dead before he fell.

The second runner had been more cautious, but Lehmann had taken the hatchets from him as if he were a child, then had lifted him one-handed and snapped his neck. He had stepped over the corpse and made a beckoning gesture with his left hand.

Come on ...

Three more had tried, the last with a kind of fateful resignation, as if mesmerised by the power of the man who stood before him. If man it was. And then, as one, they had broken, running from the figure in white, whose thin, emaciated limbs were paler than ice, and whose eyes were like tiny windows into hell.

He had heard the catcalls of the men in the approach corridors; the jeers and mocking laughter as they goaded the fleeing runners. And then had watched them return, to find Lehmann as he was now, framed in the doorway to the Oven Man's room.

Soucek looked about him, finding his own awe reflected in every face, there in the wide, admiring eyes of every man. He turned, facing Lehmann again, then knelt, abasing himself, laying down his neck before the man, not quite knowing why he did so, only that this was what he ought to do. And, all about him, the others did the same, letting Lehmann move between them, pressing his foot against each exposed neck. Marking them. Making them his men. *His* absolutely. Even unto death. Just as Li Yuan had done on the day of his coronation.

And when Soucek stood again, it was with a sense of rightness, of utter certainty. There was no going back from this. From here on there would be no half measures. It was Lehmann or nothing. And with that sense of rightness came another – a sense of destiny. Of things beginning. It was like being in a dream, or at the beginning of a myth. From this time on they walked a special path. And wherever it took them – to Heaven or down into the very depths of Hell – he would walk it behind the man. For that was how it was from this moment, for all of them gathered there.

It had begun.

It was after four when Emily got back. She kicked off her shoes and went through to the bathroom, humming softly to herself. Reaching up, she placed her hand against the side of the shower unit. Good. It was hot. That meant the servant had remembered to come in earlier. She pulled the dress up over her head and let it fall onto the chair at her side, then slipped out of her chemise.

It had been a memorable evening, and an unexpectedly enjoyable one. She stepped into the shower, casting her mind back over the evening's events as she soaped herself beneath the steady fall of water.

Michael Lever really wasn't so bad, now she had come to know him better. Not that she had always felt that way. When she had first joined Mem-Sys she had viewed the Levers with a distant loathing, not distinguishing much between father and son, seeing only the rapaciousness of the parent Company, ImmVac, and the unheeding damage it did in its eternal quest for profit. But now ... Well, the past few weeks had taught her much. Systems were systems and they ought to be opposed, but it was not so easy with people. You had to take each person as you found them. And in many respects Michael Lever was a good man – honest, reliable, capable of instilling a fierce protectiveness and loyalty in those about him. Was it his fault that he'd been born heir to ImmVac?

Before now she hadn't been sure. She had wondered whether there really was any difference between father and son, but tonight, listening to him talk about what he wanted for the future, she had seen another side of him – one she had never guessed existed. That desire for change – that burning need in him to do something for the ordinary people of America ... was that real or was it merely rhetoric? Despite the warmth of the water, she shivered, just thinking about it. His passion – that fierce, uncompromising fire she had glimpsed when he'd turned to her briefly – had seemed real enough. But how far would he go along that road? As far as she was willing to go, or would his courage fail him in the face of genuine change? Would he shy away from taking that ultimate step?

She cut the flow and stepped out, squeezing her hair, then wrapped it up in a towel. For a moment she stood there, staring sightlessly at the steamed mirror as she dried herself, then turned and went through.

The bedroom was dark. Only the light from the bathroom spilled into the opening. Even so, she saw him before she crossed the doorway.

He was sitting on her bed, a gun in his hand, covering her. A tall, unbearded Han with close-cropped dark hair and a face she had never seen in her life.

She made to step back, but he lifted the gun slightly, clicking off the safety. The signal was unmistakable. She froze, letting her hands rest at her sides, fingers apart, the gesture meant to reassure him. She was naked, the light behind her.

'What do you want?'

She said the words calmly, showing no sign of the fear she felt. He could kill her in a second. Two bullets through the heart. It was what she had been expecting, every day since she had come from Europe. And now, finally, they had caught up with her.

He stood, then crossed the room, the gun covering her all the while, his eyes never leaving her. He lifted something from the dressing table and threw it across to her. It was her robe. With the barest nod of thanks, she pulled it on.

'Who sent you?' she asked, trying another tack.

The smile he gave was strange, almost familiar. And his build. She frowned, trying to place the memory. And then he spoke.

'How are things, Emily?'

She narrowed her eyes, uncertain, then laughed, astonished. 'Jan ... ? Is that you?'

The smile broadened. Slowly the gun came down. It was Mach – Jan Mach – she could see that now, despite the change of face. There was something about the way he stood there – about the way he used the muscles of his face – that could not be disguised.

'What happened?'

He took a breath. 'They were onto me. We were attacked, eleven days back, at third bell. They killed more than twenty agents and took maybe thirty more, six of our cell leaders amongst them – comrades who knew me personally. Who could identify me.'

'Karr?'

He nodded. 'It must have been. I'd heard rumours he was creating a new force, but I didn't think they were ready yet.' He shrugged, his features momentarily formed into a grimace as he recalled what had happened. 'This ...' he touched his face tenderly, 'I had done eight days ago. It still hurts. I should have rested – should have left the bandages on a while longer – but things were too hot in Europe. I had to get out.'

'Do you want to stay here?'

Mach looked at her a moment, then nodded. 'It won't be long. Two days at most.'

'And then?'

He looked down at the gun in his hand, then threw it down onto the bed. 'I've got to go back. There's some unfinished business. An old score to settle. I've set it up, but I've got to be there to make sure it all runs smoothly.' Mach looked back at her, smiling. 'And you? What are you up to over here?'

She was about to answer him when there was a knock on the door. She turned, anxious, then looked back at him. 'In the bathroom. Hide in the shower unit. Take the gun. I'll try and put them off, whoever it is.'

He nodded, then did as she said. Only when he was inside, the door pulled over, did she go down the hallway.

'Who is it?'

'Delivery! For Nu shi Jennings.'

She put her tongue to her top teeth. Delivery? At four seventeen in the morning? She reached out, turning the lock, drawing the door back a fraction and staring out through the thumbnail gap. A small Han was standing there, head bowed, half hidden behind the huge basket of flowers he was carrying.

She gave a small laugh, still suspicious. Then she saw the note and at once recognised Michael Lever's neatly-rounded hand. She pulled the door back. 'Gods ...'

He handed her the basket then stood back, bowing deeply. She turned, reading the note as she pulled the door closed behind her, then went through.

'Well ... ?' Mach began, coming out from the bathroom, then stopped, seeing the flowers. 'A friend?' he asked, curious.

'Yes,' she said hesitantly, closing her hand over the note, for some reason not wanting him to see what was written there. 'A very dear friend.'

They were orchids. Perfect, exotic orchids, worth a thousand yuan apiece, and there had to be – what? – thirty or more of them here. She frowned, disturbed by the gift, then drew the basket to her face, sniffing at them, drawing in their delicate, wonderful scent.

'A lover?' Mach asked, blunt as ever.

'No,' she answered. But even as she said it, she could see him again, smiling, turning to share a joke with her; and afterwards, his dark eyes burning, talking of the great changes to come.

'No,' she said again. 'Just a friend. A very good friend.'

CHAPTER 83

SMOKE RINGS AND SPIDERS' WEBS

You've checked everything?'

Soucek nodded, a feral grin splitting his narrow face. 'Not so much as a cockroach could get out of there unless we willed it.'

'Good.' Lehmann drew a long breath, then nodded. 'All right. Let's go meet them.'

They passed through the cordon, some of the men familiar, others strangers, all of them wary, nervous, but under strict orders to start nothing. If things went wrong today there would be war such as the Lowers hadn't seen in decades. A war that was certain to draw in the Triads.

The deck had been cleared for the meeting, and only the tong were present. The big men – all nine of his rival gangleaders in the Kuei Chuan's territory – were waiting for Lehmann in Main, standing out in the broad open space. They formed two groups, one of five men, one of four. Lehmann paused, taking in every detail, then walked on, Soucek at his side.

He could see in their faces that word had gone before him. His height, his deathly pallor, the whiteness of his clothes, his holstered gun. Some of them feigned indifference, but there was no mistaking what their eyes told him. They were afraid of him. They had only come here today because they were afraid. Like K'ang and Lo Han before them they had tried other means of dealing with him. Now they were forced to come to terms. Or risk a protracted guerilla war that would waste their resources and distract them from the business of making money.

He raised his empty hands as if holding a large bowl, the fingers spread unnaturally wide, like long, fine needles of ice. The gesture seemed to stress his alienness; his long, thin arms held awkwardly, his whole body crouched slightly, like a fighter's. The pose was half challenge, half greeting. It distinguished him from the relaxed, almost slovenly postures of the men facing him.

'Gentlemen?'

He let the archaic word hang in the air between them, its irony unexplained, and saw them frown and look amongst themselves. And though it amused him, he let nothing show in his face, only an intense watchfulness – an almost machine-like attentiveness.

'What do you want?' one of them asked.

It was the first question, the primary question one man asked of another, openly or otherwise. Lehmann turned slightly to face the man, taking in at a glance the fact that they had chosen for their spokesman one who seemed stronger, more aggressive than the rest; a fierce-eyed, bearded man of bull-like stature. Unlike the rest he dressed simply, his fingers free of the heavy rings that seemed a mark of status down here. Lehmann raised his chin slightly, then answered.

'I want what you want. Peace. A truce. Concessions.'

The bearded man smiled, showing strong white teeth. His name was Ni Yueh and Lehmann knew all there was to know about him. All that could be known without entering Ni Yueh's head. It was a surprise to him, however, that they had chosen Ni Yueh. He had expected to have to deal with Yan Yan or Man Hsi, one of the talkers. It made him reassess things and change his tactics. Ni Yueh was a bully-boy. An intimidator. It was obvious that this was the way they thought they could deal with him. Well, he would show them otherwise. Before Ni Yueh could say another word, Lehmann turned away from him and, changing his stance, relaxing the muscles of his face, took a step towards Yan Yan, offering his hand.

'There have been misunderstandings,' he said. 'Bad rumours. We need to clear the air.'

Reluctantly, looking to Ni Yueh then back to Lehmann, Yan Yan took the offered hand.

Lehmann smiled. It was a charming, almost innocent smile. A disarming smile. Slowly, Yan Yan's lips formed a mirror to it, but his eyes still showed uncertainty. Lehmann closed a second hand about Yan Yan's, keeping the handshake warm and unthreatening.

'There's no need for enmity,' he said reassuringly. 'There's enough for all, neh? More than enough.'

Yan Yan looked down at the long, pale hands that held his own, then up into Lehmann's face again, puzzled. But it was Ni Yueh who spoke.

'You say that, but why should we trust you? What's to stop you doing to us what you did to K'ang A-yin and Lo Han?'

Lehmann lowered his head slightly, his expression seeming to say, 'Oh dear, that again ...' He released Yan Yan's hand and half turned, looking across at Ni Yueh.

'I've heard the stories. Heard the tales men whisper to each other, and let me assure you, they are simply not true.' There was an earnestness, a sincerity in his voice as he said it that half convinced them. A plea for belief. The very look of a wronged man. His eyes seemed pained by the misunderstanding. Regretful.

'I didn't want to kill K'ang A-yin. He was a friend. A benefactor. But he made a deal with Lo Han, and my death was part of that deal. Soucek here can vouch for that, can't you, Jiri?'

Soucek nodded and stepped forward, saying the words Lehmann had had him rehearse.

'It was halfway through the meeting. Lehmann and I had gone out to check that everything was secure in the corridors. When we came back, K'ang had moved back against the far wall and Lo Han was sitting there with his big snub-nosed gun in one hand, laughing. It seems that K'ang had given his permission to kill Lehmann. He told me to leave the room. Told me it was simply business. But I stayed.'

'How loyal,' said Ni Yueh in an undertone that suggested he didn't believe a word of it. But Soucek turned on him angrily.

'Maybe. But I saw it like this. A boss looks after his men. He sells one he sells them all, right? So I made a choice.'

There were nods from the other big men. Soucek's outburst had impressed them. If it was as Soucek said, then Lo Han and K'ang had clearly broken the code. It was not done to betray one's own so casually, even for the sake of peace.

'So,' Ni Yueh said, stepping between the two men and confronting

Lehmann face to face, 'there was Lo Han, sat behind the desk with his gun out. How is it he didn't kill you?'

Lehmann held Ni Yueh's eyes. 'Because I was better than him. Quicker. And now he's dead, and I'm alive. It's simple, really.'

'Too fucking simple!' Ni Yueh turned to face the others. 'I don't believe a word of this. I trust this bastard about as much as I'd trust shit to taste good.'

There was laughter, but it was short-lived. Lehmann had split them. The three who had been standing with Ni Yueh were still glaring at him, but the others – Yan Yan and Man Hsi amongst them – were not happy with Ni Yueh's words. Man Hsi spoke up.

'I don't see what proof you have, Ni Yueh. We all know how things get distorted. I say we should forget the past and make things good for the future. That's why we're here, right? Not to bicker and fight. We've done too much of that already and it's got us nowhere. No. We've got to make deals. Patch things up. For all our sakes.'

Ni Yueh was scowling. For a moment he seemed about to answer, then, abruptly, he shook his head and turned away, as if he'd washed his hands of it. Turning to Lehmann, Man Hsi spoke again, his voice growing softer, more conciliatory.

'So what deal have you got for us, Shih Lehmann? What can you offer us to make the peace?'

Lehmann looked past Man Hsi at the others, knowing how things stood. If they had wanted – if they had *really* wanted – they could have wiped him out. It would have cost them dearly, but it had been possible. They *could* have done it. But now? Inside – deep inside – he laughed. Now it was too late. Simply in agreeing to come here and meet him they had made their greatest concession. Had admitted to him their lack of will. Even Ni Yueh, for all his hostility.

Turning to Soucek, he nodded, then waited while his lieutenant brought the documents. As arranged, others brought a long, six-legged table and a stack of chairs and set them down close to where the big men stood. Then, documents in hand, Lehmann put out a hand, inviting them to sit.

There were ten copies of the treaty; one for each of the signatories. He watched as they first frowned, then, with greater interest, began to read the fifteen terms that would bring peace to the Lowers of north-central Europe.

A treaty that divided the *Kuei Chuan*'s territory into ten equal parts. That provided the detailed conditions by which they dealt with one another. Lehmann had modelled it on the commercial treaties he had found amongst his dead father's effects, but the terms were specific to the *tong*.

Man Hsi looked up, met Yan Yan's eyes, and smiled. As Lehmann had expected, they were impressed. They had never seen the like of this before and it pleased them greatly. It gave their activities the seal of legality. It made them feel like businessmen. Like Company executives. Lehmann watched each of them straighten up as they finished reading and seem to puff out, bigger than they'd been only moments before. Kings. If only of the Lowers.

'Well?' he said, looking to Man Hsi.

Man Hsi looked across at Ni Yueh, who nodded grudgingly, not looking at Lehmann. After that it was a formality. Soucek handed out brushes and they signed, Yan Yan with a flourish that strayed over the signatures of three of his fellow bosses. Slowly the documents were passed around the table until each of the copies bore ten signatures at its foot. That done, Lehmann stood, raising his hand for silence.

'By this document – a copy of which will be held by each of us – we have peace in our part of the great City.' He smiled pleasantly, and nodded. 'Yes, peace and prosperity. But ...' his face changed, all friendliness draining from it, '... should *anyone* break this treaty, then all the other parties must and *will* unite to bring the transgressor to account.' He paused dramatically and looked at each of them in turn. When he spoke again his voice was fierce, insistent. 'It is only if each one of us *knows* this and *fears* it that the agreement will work. You understand?'

There was a moment's hesitation, then nods and a murmur of agreement.

'We understand,' Ni Yueh said, his voice heavy with sarcasm. But his eyes showed something different now. The treaty had affected him; had made him question what he had earlier believed. And though the bantering tone remained, deep down he was far less certain. Lehmann had impressed him despite all.

'Good,' said Lehmann, releasing Ni Yueh's eyes. 'Then our business here is done.'

The corridor was packed. People had been gathering for the last thirty minutes outside the offices of the *Chih Chu* corporation, curious to see who had ordered such a grand sedan. Old men and children, young wives and idle youths, Han and *Hung Mao* alike, all stood there, gawping and chattering. Some busied themselves examining the sedan, feeling the thickness and quality of the green ersilk coverings or peeking inside at the big, luxuriantly cushioned chair. There were jokes about how big a man the chair might carry, and then sudden laughter as one of the young boys acted out a mime, pretending to be a fat official, his pomposity matched only by his grossness as he waddled across to take his place in the chair. Others, meanwhile, had formed a crowd about the squatting pole-men, trying to strike up a conversation, but long experience had made the carriers taciturn. The four men waited patiently, saying nothing, their eyes downcast, conscious of the runners who stood nearby.

There was a murmur of surprise as Kim appeared, dressed simply, a slender folder tucked beneath his arm. Many looked beyond him, waiting to see who else was to come, but there was no one, only the employees of *Chih Chu*, who came out and stood there under the arch of the entrance.

Many in the crowd had seen the boy, either in the tea house, or walking the corridors late at night. Few, however, understood who he was, or what his role in the strangely-named *Chih Chu* corporation was. They had thought him just a boy. A messenger, perhaps, or the nephew of a rich man. But now they looked at him anew, redefining him. Or trying to.

Kim stopped, glancing about him uncertainly, then turned back, a smile coming to his face. Bright red good-fortune banners had been draped over the doorway to the offices. Beneath them, all six of his staff had formed up, to say goodbye and wish him luck.

'Here,' T'ai Cho said, coming forward and handing him a small, sealed box. 'You'll need this.'

'What is it?'

'Lunch,' T'ai Cho explained, smiling broadly. 'From what I'm told, it will be a good few hours before they process the patent, and I know you. You would forget to eat.'

Thanks, Kim mouthed, touching his arm briefly, then looked back at the others. The two middle-aged Thais he had hired as researchers were grinning broadly now and waving, excited as children. Beside them, to their right, his assistant, a fresh-faced young Han named Hong Chi, was looking about him, wide-eyed, clearly enjoying it all. Seeing Kim watching him,

Hong smiled then lowered his head, blushing.

Kim's guard, a stocky young *Hung Mao* named Richards met his eyes proudly and shouted a gruff 'Good-luck!', while Nong Yan, his book-keeper, called out, 'Go now! Make us all rich!', which brought a huge shout of laughter from the rest.

'I shall,' Kim said softly, feeling warmed by the smiling faces that surrounded him on every side. 'Be sure I shall.'

With a bow to them all, Kim turned, climbing up into the sedan. As the pole-men lifted the heavy chair, he leaned out, waving goodbye, his voice drowned by the cheering of the crowd and the shouts of the two runners as they cleared the path ahead.

Sitting back, Kim felt a shiver of anticipation ripple through him. So this was it. He looked down at the folder in his lap and gave a little laugh of surprise. Some days he would simply sit there, staring at his hands, astonished that he had survived the darkness of the Clay to come to this. And he would count himself blessed that it was so, in spite of all that had happened in between. Even so, today was special, for today it all came together at last.

'Smoke rings ...' he said quietly, then laughed again, feeling the sedan sway and bob beneath him. 'Smoke rings and spiders' webs.'

Emily turned quickly, the narrow beam of the overhead light picking out the false image in the mirror, then flipped backwards, ignoring the hologram that appeared suddenly to her right, facing the shadowed figure by the door, the knife held out before her. The blade flashed, sank deep into the upper rib cage, then jerked back. She took a step back, breathing deeply, then sheathed the knife, satisfied.

'Cut,' she said quietly. At once the lights came up, the apartment's computer registering her command.

Shuddering, Emily wiped the back of her hand across her forehead. It had been a hard work-out. For the first time in a long while she had forced herself to the very limit.

She looked about the room – at the bloodied figure of the mannequin; at the darted targets she had set up on the walls; at the ceiling-mounted projectors; at the mats and traps and trip-wires – and realised she had missed the excitement of all this. It was time she did something. Time she started organising once again.

Quickly she went about the room, tidying up, stashing the equipment in the storage box at the far end of the room and covering it all over with a pile of sheets and old clothes. Then she went through to the shower, standing there under the flow until the water ran out, considering the way ahead. Mach was out, meeting contacts and making deals: doing what he was good at. She had barely seen him for more than twenty minutes since he'd arrived that night. As for herself, it was two days now since she had been in to the office.

She had called in sick. A brief message on Michael Lever's personal comset. He had called back, less than a minute later, asking if she needed anything; saying that he'd call if she wanted him to. But she had sent back that it was all right. It was just a virus. Nothing serious. Just one of the new forty-eight hour things that had been sweeping the levels recently. She would keep to her bed and come in when she felt better. His second message was brief, almost business-like, except for the way he'd signed it. 'Love, Michael.'

So where did that leave her? She walked about the apartment, towelling herself, recalling how Michael had looked at her the other evening at the ball, and how she'd felt, watching him as he talked, conscious of a growing admiration for him. In the hallway she stopped, standing before the flowers he had sent, and lifted one of the perfect pink and white orchids to her nose. The blooms were still fresh, their scents rich. With the faintest shiver she turned away, returning to the bedroom. There, she stood before the wardrobe, wondering what to wear. She was going down level, so it would have to be something basic. The kind of thing her alias, Rachel DeValerian, might wear.

She looked across. The false ID was on the bed, where she'd left it earlier. A permit card. Employment details. False retinas. Everything she'd need if she were to be stopped and questioned by Security. DeVore had thought it all through. Had made sure to do a fine job for her. But why? Because he knew she would eventually begin again, agitating, causing trouble for the Seven? Was it simply that? Or was it something else? Had he some other purpose that was as yet hidden from her?

Whatever, it was time to take a few risks. Time to make good on the promises she had made herself.

She had changed and dried her hair when a knock came on the door.

Three raps, a pause, a single rap, a pause, and then a further three. Mach. He was back.

She studied herself in the mirror a moment, composing herself, then went through, slipping the bolt from the door, then pressing the key-open. As the door began to slide back, Mach came through, barely looking at her, making straight for the bathroom.

'Hey!' she called after him. 'What's the Hurry?'

She followed him along, then stood there in the doorway watching as he undid his jacket and took out three high-powered Security automatics, each handgun wrapped in sheet ice, and placed them in the now empty water-cabinet above the shower.

That done, he turned, grinning at her, his new face still a shock to her each time she saw it.

'That's good,' he said, noting at once how she was dressed, his careful eyes not missing that her eye-colour had changed, but registering it by the movement of a finger to one of his own eyes. 'Who arranged that for you? DeVore?'

She stared at him, something of her old hostility returning. 'Well it wasn't you, was it, Jan? You wanted me dead.'

Mach laughed strangely. 'Did he tell you that?' He shrugged. 'He told me you'd slipped the net. That he'd tried for you, but that you'd been too good for him.'

She shivered, thinking back. No, it hadn't been like that. DeVore had found her easily enough, and – if he'd wanted to – he could have killed her. But he hadn't. And here she was, two years on, ready to begin again.

'They killed him, you know,' Mach said, moving past her, heading for her bedroom. 'I tried, at Nantes Spaceport, but his man – that red-eyed albino bastard, Lehmann – buggered things up for me. Killed three of my best men. But then the T'ang's man – that big man from the Net, Karr – finally got him. Smashed his head open with a rifle butt, so I've heard.'

Again she followed him through, watching as he took his things from the bottom of the wardrobe and placed them quickly but carefully into a holdall.

'I didn't know,' she said. Then, 'What are you doing?'

He turned, still half crouched, looking back at her. 'I'm moving on, Em. Fresh fields. New ventures. You know ...'

She shook her head. 'You surprise me, Jan. You always did. You're so resourceful. So flexible.'

He stood, then laughed softly. 'Do I detect a note of disapproval in that last comment, Emily Ascher?'

She met his eyes clearly, trying to see him through the mask of new flesh, then nodded. 'We want different things, you and I. We always did, only it took me a long while to see that.'

He studied her a moment then looked away, pressing the lips of the hold-all together and hoisting it up over his shoulder. 'No, Em. It isn't what we want, it's what we're prepared to do to get it. That's what makes you and I different. But now we can go our own paths, neh? Now we've the opportunity to see whose way is best.' He met her eyes again. 'I'll not lie to you, Em. If you'd stood in my way, I'd not have hesitated to have had you killed. But you didn't. And I don't think you ever would. If I did, I'd never have turned up at your door two nights back. So, whether you believe me or not, let me tell you that what DeVore said simply wasn't true. I didn't want you dead. Nor do I now. And if there's anything you need – if there's any way I can help, then just call me. I owe you one, right?'

She stared at him, then shook her head. 'So where are you going? Back to Europe? Or do you plan to move down-level here?'

His smile stretched the new skin about his mouth tight in what seemed almost a parody of a smile. 'Neither, Em, my dear. I'm going to be a house guest. That's where I'm off to right now. I'm staying with Old Man Lever down in Richmond.'

Old Man Lever was standing beside the pool, drying himself, as the two men were led in to see him. He turned, relaxed, watching them approach him around the pool's edge, then threw the towel down, stretching out a hand to greet them.

'Milne ... Ross ... It's good to see you again. You'll have a drink, I hope?'

The two men hesitated, looking to each other, then nodded.

'Good.' Lever turned, snapping his fingers. At once the Steward went across and busied himself, preparing drinks. Lever took a light silk jacket from the back of a chair and threw it across his broad shoulders, then turned, facing them again.

'Well? What have you got for me?'

'Nothing much, I'm afraid,' Ross said, one hand going up to draw a thin wisp of straw-like hair across his balding pate. 'She's a regular Miss Goody-two-shoes from what we can make out. Good at school. A clean College record. And not a mention of her ever appearing, even as witness, before a deck judicial hearing. In short, the public record backs up the company file. Nu shi Jennings is what she says she is. It's all there, except ...'

He hesitated, looking down.

'Except?'

'Except that it doesn't make sense,' Milne finished in his quick, nervy fashion. 'It's all too pat. Too neatly structured. Like someone made it all up. It's ...' He squirmed, his shoulders moving as if he had something up the back of his jacket. 'Well, it's lacking anything distinctive. You know, the kind of things that shape a life. That give it its flavour.'

'Hmmm.' Old Man Lever nodded to himself. 'But it all fits?'

'On the surface,' Ross answered, lifting a hand slightly, signalling the dark-haired Milne to keep quiet. 'But we could dig a little deeper, if you want. We could go back to Atlanta Canton. Speak to a few people who knew her before she moved out east. Find out what she was really like.'

Lever was silent for a time. Then, taking a long swig from his glass, he shook his head. 'What reason could there be for those records being wrong?'

Ross looked at his companion, then shrugged. 'No reason. Just that it feels wrong. We've been doing this job near on twenty years, Mister Lever, and you get to know the smell of wrongness. And this ... well, this just stinks of wrongness.'

Beside him, Milne nodded emphatically.

'Okay,' Lever said, setting his glass down. 'Let's assume the records have been doctored. Let's say that someone's done a number on her official files. Fine. But let me ask you just two questions. Who? And why?'

'I don't know,' Ross said, meeting the old man's piercing gaze. 'I just know that someone has. As Milne says, it's just too neat.'

But Lever was shaking his head. 'No. It makes no sense. It takes a lot of clout to change those records. A lot of clout.' He laughed, then, leaning closer, added softly. 'And who should know better than me, neh?'

He moved between them. 'No, gentlemen. Thanks, but let's leave it at that. I was hoping you might dig up something I could use against the woman – a string of ex-lovers or something – but it looks like I'm just going to have to plain invent something.' He laughed. 'Hell, maybe I should just have done that in the first place!'

'And our file?' Ross asked tensely.

'I'll keep that,' Lever said, meeting his eyes again. 'You'll be paid well, Shih Ross. Very well indeed. But this thing is closed now, understand me? Closed.'

When they were gone, Lever turned, looking up at the balcony overlooking the pool. From behind the cover of a vine a man emerged and leaned against the rail, looking down at him.

Lever called up to him. 'Well, Mach? What do you think?'

Mach smiled. 'It's as you said, Mister Lever. It makes no sense. If this Jennings woman were a sleeper, put in by some rival of yours, she'd have stayed on where she could have done most harm, not gone to Michael.'

Lever nodded. Those were his thoughts exactly. Even so, Ross's conviction had shaken him. He'd used Ross and Milne often these past ten years, and their instinct was generally sound. So what if ... ?

For a moment he entertained the thought, trying to think of a reason – any reason – why her records might have been doctored, then shook his head, dismissing it again. No. It made no sense. No sense at all.

'Well, that's it, then,' Milne said, cradling his ch'a bowl and squinting at his partner across the table of the low-level tea-house. 'Another file closed.'

'Maybe,' Ross said, his eyes following the progress of one of the serving women. 'And maybe not.'

Milne watched his face, waiting, knowing that Ross was chewing something over.

'I've been thinking,' Ross began in a lazy drawl, turning his attention back to Milne. 'Thinking that we could do with a holiday. And with what Mister Lever's paid us, I reckon we could have ourselves a hell of a fun time in Atlanta.'

'Atlanta ... ?' Milne stared back at him blankly a moment, then laughed, understanding dawning on him. 'Atlanta! Hell, sure. Atlanta.'

'Good,' Ross said, sitting back and nodding, a smile of satisfaction splitting his face. 'And maybe we can do a little digging while we're there. I mean ... what harm can it do?'

Li Yuan was at the far end of the gallery, standing beneath one of the five huge portraits that filled the midnight blue walls. As the great doors opened, the young T'ang turned, looking towards them, then smiled, beckoning Tolonen across.

'Knut,' he said, offering the ring finger of his right hand for the old man to kiss. 'You are well, I hope.'

Tolonen came to attention, his head bowed, his close-cropped steel grey hair presented to his T'ang. 'I am fine, *Chieh Hsia*. I ...'

He stopped, conscious of something odd in Li Yuan's manner. Of a strange thoughtfulness in that young, unbearded face, an unnatural stillness to his bearing, that reminded him suddenly of the boy's father, Li Shai Tung. So the old man had been at times, as if something had lodged in his thoughts, like a rock in the middle of a stream.

Tolonen turned, looking up at the portrait Li Yuan had been studying and gave a small smile of recognition. It was Ch'in Shih Huang Ti, the First Emperor. The unifier of ancient China. The tyrant, so-called. In the portrait he was standing on the shoreline of Shandong, staring out towards the east – to P'eng Lai, the Isle of the Immortals. Tall, bearded and arrogant, the peach of immortality clutched in his left hand.

'I have been thinking,' Li Yuan said, moving past Tolonen to stand beneath the portrait once again. 'Trying to see some pattern in the flow of time.'

'A pattern, *Chieh Hsia*?'

'Of what men are, and what they do, and why they never learn.'

Tolonen looked down. 'Do you really think that's so, my Lord?'

Li Yuan nodded. 'I do, Knut. Take our friend here. In many ways he was a great man. A military genius and a visionary administrator, whose actions shaped our land for two thousand years. And yet, as a man, he was ultimately flawed, for he wanted more than life could give him. He wanted to live forever, and that destroyed him. All the good he had done was undone by that. His great empire lasted but a year or so beyond his death.'

The young T'ang moved on, his booted footsteps echoing on the tiled floor, until he stood beneath the second of the portraits. Of the five, this was the most famous, for copies of it hung in every deck, at every level of the great, earth-spanning City.

'Wen Ti ...' Li Yuan turned, looking back at Tolonen, a strange, sad smile on his lips. 'How many times have you heard old men and schoolboys praise him for his virtue? How many times has his name been used like a charm to castigate an errant child or a poor official? In the history books he is portrayed as a rock, a mountain of a man, as just as he was compassionate, as fair as he was stern, and yet, under his rule, the Middle Kingdom almost faltered. Incursions by the northern barbarians, the Hsiung Nu, twice forced him to make accommodations – to cede land and make huge tributary payments. Why, his capital, Ch'ang-An, almost fell to them! And like Ch'in Shih Huang Ti, only a year or so after his death the empire was in chaos, rebellions sweeping the provinces.'

'He did his best, *Chieh Hsia* ...'

'Maybe so, Knut, but it gives one pause for thought, neh? Ch'in Shih Huang Ti was a tyrant, yet beneath him the empire thrived. Wen Ti was a good man, yet beneath him the empire suffered. Which, then, should I model myself upon?'

'Is the choice that simple, *Chieh Hsia?*'

Li Yuan smiled, then moved on to the next painting, looking up at the image of an elegant-looking middle-aged man in golden silks. 'No, Knut. It is never that simple. Take the case of Ming Huang here, sixth of the great T'ang emperors. He was a great man. A wise ruler and a powerful warrior. His reign was a golden age, it is said. The great poets and painters of our history – Li Po, Tu Fu, Wang Wei – such men thrived under his rule. It was a time of great culture, of prosperity and peace, and yet all that was destroyed, the empire torn apart by rebellions, and why? Because of his weakness. Because of his infatuation for a woman.'

Tolonen looked down, uncomfortable with this sudden turn. 'So it was, *Chieh Hsia*. So history tells us, anyway. But what is your point?'

The young T'ang turned. 'My point? Why, that emperors are men, not figureheads or abstract forces, and that what they are shapes the destiny of those they rule. They stretch out a hand and the shadow falls across a continent. So it is. So it has always been. And I, Knut. In what way am I different?'

He turned back, staring up at the handsome features of Ming Huang a moment longer, then, with a small shake of his head, went across to the fourth of the portraits.

'Mao Tse-tung,' he said quietly, his eyes taking in the familiar icon. 'First of the great *Ko Ming* emperors. The Great Helmsman himself. Like Ch'in

Shih Huang Ti – his idol – Mao could be ruthless and tyrannical. Beneath him, the Middle Kingdom was unified again, all invaders cast out. And yet, like Wen Ti – whose values he tried to overthrow – Mao tried hard in his early years to give the people peace and prosperity, to end corruption and reform the bureaucracy. To make the Middle Kingdom strong and healthy after decades of suffering and neglect. In many ways he seems the perfect balance between the two men. And yet he too was flawed. Flawed by a belief in his own infallibility. In his Great Leap Forward, tens of millions died, Knut. And for what? Simply to prove him wrong.'

Tolonen looked down, frowning. 'But you are not any of these men, *Chieh Hsia*. You are yourself. Surely you can learn from their mistakes and be what they were not?'

Li Yuan glanced at the old man questioningly, then turned, making his way across to the last of the five great canvases. For a moment he stood there, staring up at the powerful image of the man his own ancestors had overthrown. Tsao Ch'un. The Tyrant. Founder of the City. Of Chung Kuo itself.

'Coming here, seeing these men, their faces, it makes me wonder. Can I learn from their mistakes? Or am I doomed to take the same path? To go down in history as a weak and foolish man? Or as a tyrant?'

Tolonen went across and stood beside him. 'Does it worry you, Yuan?'

'Worry me?' Li Yuan laughed, then turned, facing his father's General once again. 'Yes, Knut. It worries me. But not as others might think. It worries me that my weakness might prove the death of millions. Or that some excess of desire or pride, arrogance or cold-heartedness might turn my face to tyranny. I look at these faces, these giant figures from our past, and I ask myself. Am I strong enough? Wise enough? You said of Wen Ti just now, 'He did his best'. Well, will *my* best be good enough? Have I, within me, what it takes to mould and shape a world and all its people? Or will ignorance and desire destroy me, as they have destroyed so many in the past? I am determined, yes. But what if determination fails, Knut? What then?'

The old man sniffed deeply, then shrugged, clearly disturbed by the young T'ang's words.

'Never mind ...' Li Yuan looked down, unclenching his fists and staring at them a moment, as if to comprehend them. Then, as if coming to once more, he looked back up at the old man, his dark, hazel eyes less intense than a moment earlier. 'So tell me, Knut. What *did* you find in my cousin's City?'

'Something strange,' Tolonen answered, his voice suddenly clear and resonant. 'Something strange and horrible.'

In what had once been K'ang A-yin's offices, Soucek stood at ease, waiting to be acknowledged. The place had been redecorated since K'ang's death, a simple elegance replacing K'ang's cheap ostentation. A minute passed, then, finally, Lehmann looked up from the screen on his desk, noted the two men his lieutenant had brought back with him, and nodded.

'Good. Did it go well?'

Soucek sniffed. 'I don't think they like us much. But as for our money ... well, that's a different matter, neh? Money is money, Above as Below.'

Lehmann switched off the screen, then came round the table. Ignoring his lieutenant, he studied the two newcomers carefully, reaching out to check the tight, flickering bands about the neck of each. Satisfied, he stepped back.

'Welcome,' he said simply. 'My name is Stefan Lehmann, and you'll be working for me.'

Soucek could see the fear and uncertainty in their faces, just as earlier he had noted their clear disgust at their new surroundings. Lehmann too must have noticed it, for he seemed quick to reassure the men.

'I understand how you're feeling just now. You weren't expecting to come down here, were you?'

They nodded.

'No. Well, I know that what you've seen so far is pretty bad, but I've had special quarters prepared. Something more like what you're used to.'

Soucek narrowed his eyes, fitting another piece into the puzzle. Lehmann hadn't told them yet what he was up to. The first Soucek had known about this was when Lehmann had handed him a special clearance pass and sent him up to Level 180 to meet with a Company Broker. All the documents and payment certifications had been in a sealed package. Soucek had only to ensure that the broker handed over the two men; Lehmann could do all the rest from his newly-installed desk console. But Soucek had glimpsed the figure the broker had tapped into his comset and had whistled to himself. Why, they had paid more than two months' profits for a year's contract on each man!

'There's a lot to do here,' Lehmann was saying, 'but I want you to familiarise yourself with the details of our operation before you get down to things. And I want your input, understand? If you see that a thing can be done better, I want to know how, okay?'

The strangers, still more intimidated than reassured by the look of the tall albino, nodded hastily.

'And understand this ... I've added an extra clause to your contracts.' Lehmann paused, looking from one to the other. 'It's very simple. You do well for me and I look after you. You help me increase my profits and you get a cut. A small one, but significant. And it's non-deductible against your lessee's contract.'

Soucek saw how that changed things. The two men glanced at one another, then looked back at Lehmann, smiling.

'Good,' Lehmann said, turning away, retreating behind his desk. 'Now get some rest. We'll start tomorrow. My lieutenant here will show you your quarters. He'll get you anything you want.'

Lehmann sat, leaning forward to touch the screen, bringing it alive. The audience was over. Soucek ushered the men out.

Walking back to the special area, one of them, a fair-haired man in his early twenties, turned to Soucek and asked him who Lehmann was.

Soucek shrugged. 'He runs things down here.'

'You mean he's a Deck Magistrate?'

'No. Judges he can buy by the dozen.'

He saw how thoughtful they were. How their initial disgust had turned to puzzlement and to a new kind of respect.

Yes, thought Soucek. *After all, he had the clout to bring you two down here. Why, I don't yet know. But I shall soon.*

'And what are you, *ch'un tzu?*'

It was their turn to laugh. 'You mean you don't know?' the blond-haired one said, stopping. 'I thought you understood. We're commodity slaves.' He touched the flickering band at his neck. 'That's what this means. Your boss has bought our services for a year.'

Soucek drew in a breath. He didn't like to be thought ignorant. 'I know that,' he said, brazening it out. 'I meant, what do you do?'

'Whatever he wants us to do. But our specialities are computers and drugs synthesis. I'm the computer man.'

Ah, thought Soucek, *so that's it. But why does he want specialists? What is he planning?*

They walked on, coming to the special area. Guards let them into corridors that had been newly carpeted at great expense. The walls were freshly painted, the two suites furnished with pieces brought down from the Above. It was all in stark contrast to the corridors and rooms through which they had passed. Here it was cool and quiet. No crowds of people crushed against each other. No ragged urchins tugged at you, their dirty faces pleading for a coin, or for something to eat. Now that he had seen it for himself, Soucek saw how like the Above this was. Ordered. Elegant in its simplicity. And Lehmann had known that. Had known what K'ang had only guessed at. As if he had experienced it himself.

Later, alone in his room, stretched out on his bunk, he thought things over. He had known Lehmann only weeks now, but in that brief time he had had the opportunity to study him better than he'd studied anyone before. Even so, Lehmann remained something of an enigma, forever hidden behind those glassy, blood-pink eyes. At times he felt like asking him right out, 'What are you thinking?', but knew how it would be. Lehmann would turn and look at him, then look away, saying nothing. As if to say, 'What business is it of yours?' And yet, for all that, he respected Lehmann more than he respected any man. Maybe even loved him in some strange way. But what *was* Lehmann? Who was he?

He had not seen it at first. Only slowly, gradually, had he begun to notice all the things that were different about him. Not the immediate, obvious things – his height and gauntness, the colour of his skin, his eyes – but other, less readily discernible things. Things seen in contrast only. His scorn for luxuries. His innate austerity. Things that contrasted sharply with the other *tong* bosses. Unlike them he had never even considered moving up the levels. He had laughed contemptuously when Soucek had suggested it. 'They'll pay for their softness,' was all he'd said. But Soucek had thought long and hard about the meaning of those words and had heeded them. Copying Lehmann, he had given up alcohol, drugs and meat, and had begun to spend more time in the practice rooms, honing his fighting skills.

After the meeting with the other nine bosses, Lehmann had sent him up to see Ni Yueh alone, with gifts and letters of friendship. He recalled sitting in Ni Yueh's plush offices and seeing it all with Lehmann's eyes, noting the waste – the 'fat' as Lehmann called it. And he had looked at Ni Yueh anew – perhaps even as Lehmann saw him – seeing not merely his strength and brutality, but also the softness, the small signs of weakness. 'Desire is a chain,' Lehmann had said. 'Only will and discipline can break it.' Well, he had looked at Ni Yueh now and seen a man in whom desire was stronger than will. And had said nothing. That too he had learned from Lehmann. The weak man babbled his thoughts to any that would listen. The strong man kept his silence.

Ni Yueh had liked the gifts, the letters, and he, Soucek, had returned with other gifts and written promises. But Lehmann had scorned the presents and pushed them aside, more concerned with Soucek's view of things. He had listened attentively, then turned away suddenly, nodding to himself. 'We'll bait him,' he had said. 'Hook him and draw him in.' And though Soucek had not understood the exact meaning, he got the drift of it. 'How far can you trust him?' he had asked, and saw how Lehmann turned, studying him closely. 'Trust?' he'd answered. 'I trust no man, Jiri. Not even you. If it were a matter of life and death, a question of choice – of my life or yours – could I trust you? Could I *really* trust you?'

He had wanted to say yes, but with Lehmann's eyes upon him he had not wished to answer glibly, insincerely. He had hesitated, then bowed his head. 'I don't know ... I ...' But Lehmann had only shaken his head and taken his arm, as if to console him. 'Have no illusions, Jiri. Strip what you feel bare. Look hard at yourself. All else means nothing.'

It was the closest he had come to Lehmann, and the moment had seared itself into his memory, but it was the closeness of utter strangers. Even at that moment, he had sensed the utter cold of the vacuum that surrounded Lehmann and kept them separate. Where there were no illusions there could be no warmth. And love, even love, became a thing of ice.

Whiskers Lu's face filled the big overhead screen, his left eye staring down blankly from the pink, crab-mottled rawness of his melted face, his narrow, lipless mouth formed into a fierce grin.

'Wong Yi-sun! Welcome! Come inside! We are all here now.'

Fat Wong hesitated, then, with a nod to his bodyguards, passed beneath the great lintel of the House of the Ninth Ecstasy, entering Lu Ming-shao's territory. Inside, he looked about him, surprised by the understated elegance of the place. When he had first heard that the meeting of the Council was to be held in a sing-song house he had been outraged, wondering whether this were some subtle insult on Whiskers Lu's part, but his advisers had reassured him that this was where Lu Ming-shao did most of his business from these days, and so he had accepted the invitation. Now, seeing it for himself, he understood. Lu's First Level contacts would feel at home in a place like this. It was a good place to do business. Even so, it was of a piece with Lu Ming-shao that he should run the Black Dog Triad from a whorehouse.

There was the faint rustle of a curtain to his left. Fat Wong turned, facing it, one hand on the knife at his belt, then he relaxed. A scantily-dressed young woman stood there, her head bowed.

'Might I take your cloak, Wong Yi-sun?'

Fat Wong studied the girl, noting how delicately she was formed, wondering briefly whether that delicacy were a product of chance or of human manufacture, then he nodded, letting her take the silk from his shoulders. As he turned back, Whiskers Lu appeared on the far side of the room, coming across to embrace him.

'Yi-sun ...' he said, holding Fat Wong at arm's length, as if he had not seen him in a long while. Then, with a flourish of his arm, he turned, inviting Wong to go through.

Again Wong hesitated, the habit of suspicion shaping his response, then let himself be led through. In a room at the centre of the House the other four Bosses were waiting, sat about in huge, comfortable chairs, drinks and trays of sweetmeats on low tables at their sides. As he entered, they called out, greeting him, as if they were old friends and this a chance to drink and eat and talk of women and past times, whereas the truth was that what they were to discuss today was of the utmost importance, heralding a new phase in their relationship with the Above.

Fat Wong smiled, letting himself fall into the role, accepting the tumbler of wine Whiskers Lu held out to him, knowing that his stomach implant would neutralise its effects. He sat, looking about him, conscious yet again of the refinement of the decor. He had had his advisers dig back into the history of this place and had learned what had happened here with the old Madame, Mu Chua, and the Minor Family Prince, Hsiang K'ai Fan. It was Mu Chua who had built this place and established its reputation, running the House for more than thirty years. Her death – her throat slit by Hsiang K'ai Fan even as he was fucking her – might easily have been a disaster for Whiskers Lu, but the intercession of Li Yuan's General, Hans Ebert, had saved Lu's skin. In a secret deal negotiated by Ebert, the Hsiang family had agreed to pay Lu Ming-shao twenty-five million *yuan* in compensation, provided he took no retributive action. With those funds Whiskers Lu had rebuilt the House of the Ninth Ecstasy and installed a new Madame. He had also imported one or two 'oddities', things accepted from the Hsiang family in lieu of cash. Amongst those oddities were one of the GenSyn ox-men and five of GenSyn's famous 'Imperial Courtesan' line – the model with the two additional orifices. Such 'treasures' had won a new clientele to the House and things were almost as they had been.

Whiskers Lu came close, leaning over Wong, his voice lowered to a whisper. 'If there is anything you would like to try while you're here, Yi-sun, you are most welcome.'

Fat Wong smiled, as if pleased by the offer, but it was yet another instance of Lu Ming-shao's poor breeding. Or his naïvety. He studied Whiskers Lu a moment, noting the changes that this last year had brought. Gone was the ragged fur he had once sported about his shoulders; gone too the wild-barbarian look. Lately he had taken to wearing his hair slicked back, his moustache trimmed and waxed. Lu thought it made him look more refined, but the truth was otherwise; it only made his mask-like face look more artificial, more foolish. Wong smiled inwardly then looked past Lu. There, in the corner of the room, was a *wei chi* board, set up as if midway through a game. He had heard that Lu Ming-shao had recently taken up the game and this seemed to confirm it. Rumour had it, however, that Whiskers Lu was very bad at the game and had killed two opponents in fits of temper. If so, it was but another thing against him. The time was coming fast when Lu Ming-shao would prove too great an embarrassment to the *Hung Mun* and when that day came he, Wong Yi-sun, would be the first to act.

It was another hour before they came to business. Between times there was the usual sparring – the sounding-out of positions before the hard bargaining began. This once, however, there was little to debate and they came quickly to agreement. The matter was a simple one. In a year's time the House at Weimar would be reopened. Before then, candidates had to be selected, elections held. It was an ideal opportunity for the *Hung Mun* to buy their way in. Rumour had it that the new House would have real power, real influence. If so, it was to the advantage of them all to gain a foothold. The only question was how big a foothold and how much that would cost.

Li The Lidless was speaking, reading from a special report he had had his advisers draw up.

'... it is also felt that any attempt to spread our net too wide might not only prove a strain upon current resources but might also result in a diminishment of effective influence. It is suggested, therefore, that each of the six brotherhoods concentrate on acquiring the friendship of five Representatives. The resultant pressure group within the House – funded centrally and with the capacity to 'extend' its influence on certain matters within the House; that is, to buy the votes of responsive members – ought to provide a solid foundation for our continued expansion up the levels.'

Li Chin sat back, looking about the circle of his fellow 489s. 'Long years we have waited in the darkness down below. Now our time has come. We must climb. Up, into the light.'

Fat Wong leaned forward, conscious of the receptive mood Li's words had created. 'Then we are agreed? Thirty Representatives, to be controlled directly by this Council. Policy and funding to be as outlined in Li Chin's report.'

He looked about the circle, seeing how enthusiastically they nodded; how willingly they embraced this next step. For once the potential benefits for all outweighed the petty needs of individual Triads. But how long would that last? How long would it be before one or other of them tried to win a greater share of influence than their fellows? Once already he had had to deal with such divisions, enlisting Li Yuan's aid to crush his rival, Iron Mu. But next time would be more difficult. Next time he might have to fight them all. Which was why it was important to pacify them just now, to seem to be working with them closely, hand-in-hand, so that he might build up his strength.

Because ultimately he did not want what Li Chin wanted. No. He wanted it all.

Fat Wong turned, looking across at Whiskers Lu once more, and, smiling, his manner deceptively casual, said what had been on his mind all along.

'I hear there has been trouble amongst your *tong*, Lu Ming-shao. They say there is a new man, cutting in. I wondered ...'

He saw the agitated movement of Lu's good eye, the sense of turmoil beneath the glassy mask of his face, and knew he had touched a nerve. But when Whiskers Lu spoke, it was in the same almost-bantering tone he always used.

'It is so, Wong Yi-sun, but when is there not trouble amongst the lower orders? Besides, the matter is already settled, a new balance found. One must let the little men fight their battles, neh?'

They were good words, and Fat Wong bowed his head, acknowledging them, but all there were aware of the significance of the exchange, for whilst the rest of them had worked their way up the levels of their respective brotherhoods, Whiskers Lu alone had won his post by conquest. He had not entered the brotherhood as a child, nor was he steeped in the ancient rituals of the Hung Mun. No. Like the 'new man' Wong had mentioned, Whiskers Lu was an outsider, a usurper, and had bullied his way into a position of power. The reminder was thus unwelcome.

'Well, brothers,' Whiskers Lu said, standing, his whole manner suggesting that he had already forgotten what had just been said, 'now that we are agreed, let us retire to the next room. I have arranged an entertainment. Something rather special. Something ... *different.*'

His lipless mouth grinned broadly, but as he turned away, Wong noted how Lu's left hand was clenched, the tendons showing at the wrist, as if all of his anger – anger that could not be expressed on the mask-like nullity of his face – had been channelled down into that hard, bunched node of flesh and bone. And, seeing it, Fat Wong smiled.

Yes. Step by step he would undermine them, even as he seemed to be working with them. Step by step, until he was ready. And then there would be War. War such as the Lowers had never seen.

Whiskers Lu let the door close, the last of his guests departed, then turned, his thin smile fading, and glared at the three men who remained in the room.

'How *dare* the fucker discuss my private business in my House!'

Lu Ming-shao kicked out, sending one of the low tables flying, tumblers and bowls of food scattered across the carpet.

'The toad! The fucking insect! What the fuck does he think he's playing at?'

The three men looked to each other but said nothing. When Whiskers Lu was like this, it was best to keep one's head low and wait for the storm to pass.

Lu Ming-shao shuddered, his one good eye burning in his glassy face. 'If it had been any other man, I'd have slit his fucking throat! But I'll have him. See if I don't!'

He turned, anger making his movements jerky, angular. 'Po Lao ... Why was I not told what was going on? What the fuck are you up to, keeping me in the dark?'

Po Lao, Whiskers Lu's 'Red Pole', his second-in-command, bowed his head, accepting the criticism, but inside he was fuming. Lu Ming-shao *had* been told about the new man, and not once but several times, but he had been too busy preparing for the Council meeting – closeted with designers and entertainers – to pay any attention.

'It's not fucking good enough,' Lu went on, standing close to Po Lao, the pink, crab-mottled flesh of his melted face pressed right up against Po's. 'I want you to go down there, *personally*, and see to the matter. To sort things out for good and all, because I don't want any more trouble, understand me? And I particularly don't want any word of what's happening in our territories getting out to that cunt Fat Wong.'

Po Lao felt his face burning beneath its rigid exterior. For a moment he was giddy with suppressed anger. Then, with a curt bow, he turned away. But at the door Whiskers Lu called him back again.

'And Po Lao. No fuck-ups. I want it settled. Right?'

Po Lao turned back, meeting Lu Ming-shao's good eye, letting nothing of what he was feeling show. 'I understand, Master Lu.'

'Good. Now go. I want to hear from you tonight.'

'Shih Ward?'

Kim looked up, beginning to smile, then checked himself, realising that it was not the young official he had been dealing with earlier, but the Supervisor of the section. Beyond the stoop-backed old grey-beard stood two departmental guards, their side-arms held across their chests.

'What is it?' he asked, standing, puzzled by the look of stern anger on the elderly Han's face.

In answer the man thrust a folder at Kim – the same folder he had submitted only four hours back at the counter on the far side of the waiting room.

'It's all done, then?' he asked, staring down at it, wondering momentarily where the completed patent certificate was.

'Are these your documents, *Shih* Ward?' the Supervisor asked, ignoring Kim's comment.

Kim glanced at the folder again. 'Yes. Of course. Why? Is there a problem?'

The man's smile was cold, ironical. 'You might say that. But first let me confirm two things.' He reached across and opened the folder, drawing out the slender, microns-thick official form. 'Is this your signature at the bottom of this patents application form?'

'Yes.'

'And you understand that this form is to be used only for new patents originated by the signatory?'

Kim nodded, concerned now; not understanding why the man should need to ask, nor why he should feel the need to have guards present.

'Then I am afraid to say that this form is invalid, being in breach of Section 761 (D) of the Patents Protection Laws. Moreover, *Shih* Ward, it is my duty to arrest you for making a fraudulent application, infringing a patent already registered at this office.'

Kim laughed, but it was the laughter of disbelief, not amusement. 'It isn't possible. I checked. A week ago. Here at this very office. There was nothing. Nothing even vaguely like it!'

The official smiled, clearly enjoying his role, then produced a copy of a patent protection form. He let Kim study it a moment, watching as the young man's face drained, then took it back from him.

Kim stood there, his hands shaking. 'Someone stole it,' he said quietly. 'They must have.'

The official turned, handing the folder to one of the guards, then turned back, puffing out his chest, as if to display the big, square badge of office there. 'Your comments have been noted, *Shih* Ward and, along with the recording of this interview, will be submitted to the Hearing in two days' time. Until then, I am afraid you will have to be detained.'

'Detained ... ?' Kim shook his head, disbelief tilting over into a kind of stupor. He felt sick and dizzy and hardly heard what the man said next, but then, suddenly, his hands were being pulled behind him. He felt the restraint-lock click into place about his wrists, then he was being pulled backwards out of the room.

'You must send word!' Kim called out, trying to make the official listen. 'You must tell T'ai Cho!' But the Supervisor had already turned away and was talking to the other guard. And then the door slammed shut in front of him and he felt a sharp, sudden blow on the back of his head. And then nothing.

CHAPTER 84

DYNASTIES

The girl was asleep, her long, auburn hair fanned out across her naked back, the thin sheet draped across her buttocks like a shroud. For a moment Old Man Lever studied her, conscious of the contrast between them. Her flesh was so smooth, so *new*, like silk over the taut frame of bone and muscle, no sign of age marring its perfection. He sighed, then pulled himself up heavily, stretching the tiredness from his bones. Suddenly he felt old. Very old. He looked about him, at the simple luxury of the room, a luxury to which he had been born, and shook his head, as if he didn't understand from whence all this had come, then looked down at himself again, at thinning legs and a stomach gone to paunch, a chest to flab – at the changes and distortions time had brought to the landscape of his flesh. All these years he had kept himself trim, had fought Time itself, fleeing from it, like a swimmer in dangerous waters, but Time, patient as a shark, had waited in the depths, staring up at him with cold, impersonal eyes, biding its time, knowing there was no escape.

He padded across to the armchair in the corner of the room and pulled on the dark blue silk dressing gown he had thrown there earlier. The girl had been good – very good indeed – and she had finally brought him off, but it had been a long, uphill struggle, and he had almost sent her away at one point, ashamed of his failure.

It had happened before, of course, and he had blamed it on tiredness or an excess of wine, but it was neither – he knew that now. He was simply getting old.

He drew the sash tight about his waist then went across, standing there at the mirror, looking at himself clearly in the light from the overhead lamp. In four weeks' time he would be seventy-four. One year younger than Tolonen. An old man. Powerful, as old men went, but old all the same.

He turned away, angry with himself. Only an hour ago he had been full of life, buoyant after the news from the Patents Office, standing there, whooping at the screen. Yes, just an hour ago he had felt as though he could run ten li and then take on a pair of serving girls, one after the other, as he'd done in his youth. But now he knew. It was only the adrenalin rush. Only the ragged tide of feeling through an old man's head.

Going across to the room's comset, he tapped out a code irritably. 'Get me Curval on the line,' he said, even before the picture had properly formed. 'And get him *now*, whatever he's doing.'

He looked across at the girl again. She had turned and was lying on her side, one breast exposed above the sheet. Lever shivered. No, it wasn't her fault. She had tried. Had tried her damnedest to be sweet to him. Besides, the girl was mute. So maybe he would keep her. Maybe he would have her assigned here, to his private rooms.

He turned back as Curval's voice came through.

'Curval ... I want you to come here at once. I've a job for you. I want you to go up to Boston for me and see the boy again. I'll brief you when you get here.'

Curval made to answer, but Lever had already cut him off. Turning away, he crossed the room quickly and stood over the girl, shaking her until she came awake.

'Quick now,' he said, pulling her up. 'You must help me dress. I've things to do.'

And as she busied herself about him, he began to feel better; began to shrug off his earlier mood. No, it was no good skulking and sulking. One had to *do* something. First he'd draft a note – an answer to the T'ang of Africa – to be sent by way of Mach, agreeing to his offer. Then he would arrange a meeting of the major shareholders to the Institute and force them to agree to an increase in funding. Last, but not least, he would see Curval, and brief him. For Curval would be his key.

He smiled, letting the girl fuss about him, wondering why he had not thought of it before. At present Curval was Head of the Institute, his reputation as the leading experimental geneticist of his age unchallenged. But Curval, good as he was, wasn't good enough, not when it was a question of squaring-up to death. He had as much as admitted to Lever's face that he considered the problem unsolvable. Even so, he might be the means by which Ward could be wooed back to the fold. Yes, where money and threats had failed, maybe a play at Ward's natural scientific curiosity might succeed. If Curval could show him how wonderful a challenge it was. If he could fire him with a new enthusiasm.

Especially now, when the boy was down and vulnerable.

Lever looked down. The girl had stopped, staring at the fierce erection he now sported. He laughed, then drew her close, forcing her head down onto him.

Yes, he would be young again. He *would* be young.

Two hundred li to the north, in the boardroom of a small company, four men sat about a long oak table, talking.

Michael Lever had been silent for some while, listening, but now he leaned forward, interrupting.

'Forgive me, Bryn, but the point isn't whether it *can* be done, but whether it *ought* to be done. I don't know about you, but I don't want to live forever. It's bad enough thinking of being fifty, let alone being fifty forever.'

Bryn Kustow was hunched forward at the far end of the table, facing Michael, his elbows pressed against the polished surface, his long forearms stretched out along the wood, meeting in a handclasp. His ash-blond hair was cut aggressively short, but the style suited him. He looked like a soldier, sitting there.

'Fifty, no, but what if you could be twenty-five for the rest of time? Wouldn't that tempt you?'

Michael shook his head. 'I know how I feel. Besides, I want sons of my own, and I want those sons to love and respect me. I don't want to be a barrier in their way.'

Kustow nodded and leaned back in the big wheel-back chair. Between him and Michael, to either side of the table, sat their friends and long-time companions, Jack Parker and Carl Stevens. They were dressed simply and sported the same aggressive hairstyle as Kustow. It gave them a kind of uniformity. One look was enough to place them. Sons, they were. Part of the new movement.

'It sounds like you hate him,' Stevens said, leaning towards him. 'Has it really got that bad?'

'No. It's not as simple as that. For all he's done to me these past few weeks, I still don't hate him. But this obsession of his with immortality. It's gone too far. All his energies seem to be channelled into the search for a new serum or for some new way of switching off the ageing process.' He looked across at Kustow, his face filled with hurt. 'I've seen it grow in him these past few years, like a sickness. And I don't want to be that way. Not ever. I don't want to be old in the way he's getting old. Hanging on like a beggar. There's no dignity in that.'

'My father's the same,' said Parker, looking about him at the circle of his friends. 'He's got no time for anything else, these days. The day-to-day stuff he delegates, then goes off to jaw with the old gang.' He paused and shook his head. 'And you know what they're talking about? They're talking about spending a further fifteen billion on the Institute. Fifteen billion! And who loses out?'

'Sure. So what do we do about it?'

They stared at Kustow, as if he'd said something that was difficult to grasp.

'Do?' Stevens asked, shaking his dark, cropped head and laughing. 'What can we do? It's like Mitchell said the other night at Gloria's. They've got all the money, all the real power. All we have is the vague promise of inheritance.'

'Vaguer by the day,' said Parker, nudging him and laughing.

But Kustow and Lever weren't laughing. They were watching each other. Kustow narrowed his eyes in a question, and Michael nodded.

'Okay ... we'll come clean,' said Kustow, standing up and walking round the table until he stood behind Michael. 'The paperwork, earlier ... that was a front. Michael and I called you over today for a special reason. Not to make deals, or anything like that, but to work on this thing that's bugging us all. To see if we can do something.'

'We're listening,' Parker said, leaning back, assuming an air of business-like attentiveness. Across from him, Stevens nodded.

It was Michael who spoke.

'Essentially, you're right, Carl. They have got all the real power. But let's not underestimate ourselves. What have *we* got? Let's look at it. Let's see what we can rustle up between us.'

He separated his hands and sat back, using his right hand to count the fingers of his left. 'One, we've got our personal allowances. Not inconsiderable. There's many a small company who would welcome the same figure in turnover. Don't be offended, but Bryn and I have been checking up. Between the four of us we could count on a figure of some one and three quarter million *yuan*.'

Parker laughed. 'And where would that get us? Your accounts are frozen, Michael, or had you forgotten?'

'Hold on,' said Kustow. 'Michael's not finished yet.'

Michael smiled, his handsome face showing patience and determination. 'Two, there's what we could divert from those funds we control on behalf of our fathers' companies.'

Parker frowned. 'I don't like the sound of that. It sounds vaguely criminal.'

'It is. But let's face that when we have to. From such funds we could probably command upwards of twenty million *yuan*.'

Stevens whistled. Personally he was in charge of three small production companies that serviced his father's near-space development corporation, but they were minnows – sops his father had given him to keep him quiet; more a hobby than a job. He was an engineering graduate and the eldest of them at twenty-eight, but in himself he felt like a boy still, playing when he should have been acting in the world.

'Three, there are Trusts we could borrow against. Even at the most pessimistic rate we could expect to raise something like fifteen million *yuan*.'

Parker interrupted him. 'They'd know.' He laughed briefly, then shook his head. 'Don't you see? If we set about realising all of this they'd know at once that we were up to something.'

Lever smiled. 'Good. Then you're thinking about it seriously?'

The young man sat back, chewing on some imaginary straw, then nodded. But there was a hesitancy in what he said next. 'I think I see what you're getting at. We have the money, so that's not it. That's not our key, right? Because we can't use money against them. They've got it tightly bottled up as far as money's concerned.'

Kustow came forward and leaned over the table, facing him. 'That's right. But the very fact that we *have* the money gives us an edge. The fact that if we wanted to, we could call on some forty to fifty million between us, that gives us power.'

Stevens took his hand from his mouth. 'I don't see it, Bryn. If we can't use it, how does it help us?'

Kustow half turned and looked at Lever. Again, Lever nodded. Slowly, Kustow straightened up, then, without another word, he left the room.

'What's going on?' Parker asked, laughing uncertainly. 'What is this, Michael? Some kind of revolutionary cell we're forming here?'

Lever looked at him calmly and nodded. 'That's just what it is, Jack. But we're joining, not forming it.'

Stevens had tilted back his head and was scratching beneath his neck. For a moment he said nothing, then, slowly, he began to laugh, his laughter getting stronger. 'Well, I'll be ...'

Kustow was standing in the doorway again. 'Gentlemen, I want you to meet an old school friend of mine. A man who, we hope, will some day make America great again.' He stood back, letting a tall, dark-haired man step past him, into the room.

Stevens had stopped laughing. Parker, beside him, gasped and half rose from his seat.

'Hello,' said Joseph Kennedy, smiling and putting out his hand. 'It's good to meet you. Bryn's told me a lot about you two.'

Kennedy leaned back in his chair and stretched out his arms, yawning and laughing at the same time. The table in front of him was cluttered with half-filled glasses and empty wine bottles. Around the table the young men joined in his laughter, pausing to suck on their cigars or drain a glass, the air dense with cigar smoke.

They had all known Kennedy, of course. You could hardly grow up in the North American Above and not know the Kennedys. Even after the fall of the Empire, a Kennedy had overseen the period of transitional government and, through his influence and skill, had prevented the great tragedy from becoming a debilitating catastrophe. This was that man's great-great-grandson, a figure familiar from the élite MedFac channels. When his father had died, eight years back, he had inherited one of the biggest legal firms on the East Coast and had not hesitated to step into his father's shoes at once. Now, however, it seemed he was tired of the legal game. He wanted something bigger to take on.

Which was why he was there, speaking to them.

Joseph Kennedy was a big, good-humoured man, handsome in the way that all the Kennedys were handsome, but with something else behind the good looks; something that made people look at him with respect, perhaps even with a degree of awe. He was powerful and charismatic, like an animal in some ways, but supremely intelligent with it. His mind missed nothing, while his eyes seemed to take in more than the surface of things.

Though he was a good six years older than the men he had come to meet, there was a youthfulness about him that made him seem one of them. He had made them at ease quickly and with a skill that was as much inherited as his vast personal fortune. But he did not play upon his charm. In fact, the opposite was true. When he spelled out what it was he wanted from them, he made certain that they knew the cost of their involvement. It would be bad, he told them. In all likelihood they would be disinherited before the year was out, estranged from their families. At worst there was the possibility that they would be dead. The stakes were high, and only a fool went blindly into such a game.

That said, however, he reminded them of their breeding, and of what there was to gain.

'Freedom,' he said. 'Not just for you, but for all men. Freedom from the old men who chain you, but also freedom from the Seven.

'We will make deals,' he said. 'At first our enemies will think us friends, or, at worst, accomplices. But in time they will come to know us as we really are. And then they'll find us worse than in their darkest dreams.'

And when he said that he paused and looked at them, each in turn, measuring how each one faced him and then, as if satisfied, nodded to himself.

There was more, much more, but in essence they knew what he wanted of them. Loyalty. Obedience when the time came. Support – covert at first, but then, when he asked it of them, out in the open. When the time was right they would mobilise all their resources; four out of hundreds across the great continent who would rise up and change the face of North American politics for all time.

Behind them were discussions about the Edict, about the immortality treatments and the latest terrorist attacks in Europe. Now, at the tail-end of the evening, they were talking of other things. Of women and ball games and mutual friends. Kennedy had been telling them an anecdote about a certain Representative and the daughter of a Minor Family. It was scandalous and close to the knuckle, but their laughter showed no fear. They were as one now; wedded to the cause. And when, finally, Kennedy left, they each shook his hand and bowed their heads, mock solemn, like soldiers, but also like friends.

'Was he always like that?' Stevens asked Kustow when he had gone. 'I mean, was he like that at College, when you knew him?'

Kustow stubbed out his cigar and nodded. 'Always. If we had a problem we went to him, not to one of the teachers or the Head. And he would always sort it out.' He smiled, reminiscing. 'We idolised him. But then, in my second year, he left, and everything changed.'

There was a moment's silence, an exchange of glances.

'Does anyone fancy a meal?' Parker said, breaking the silence. 'I don't know about you guys, but I'm starving.'

'Sure,' Kustow said, looking to Stevens, who nodded. 'And you, Michael?'

Michael hesitated, then shook his head. 'Another time, maybe. Right now I've got to sort something out.'

'Mary?'

He looked back at Kustow, wondering how he knew, then laughed. 'I spoke to her earlier. Said I'd see her sometime this afternoon. I ...'

There was a hammering at the outer door.

'What the hell?' Kustow said, turning to face the sound.

'Do you think ... ?' Stevens began, looking to Michael.

'No,' Michael said quietly as the hammering came again. 'But whoever it is, they sure as hell want to see someone in a hurry.'

He went across quickly and slid the door back, then strode out across the plush expanse of carpet in the reception room. The three men followed him, standing in the doorway, watching as he slid back the bolt and stood back, pulling the double doors open.

Outside, in the dimly-lit corridor, stood a Han. A tall Han in plain green silks with mussed hair and a distraught expression.

'T'ai Cho!' Michael said, surprised. 'What in the gods' names are you doing here?'

'It's Kim!' T'ai Cho said breathlessly, grasping Michael's arm. 'He's been arrested!'

'*Arrested*? For what?'

'At the Patents Office! They say he stole the patent he was trying to register! You have to do something, *Shih* Lever! You must!'

'What is this, Michael?' Parker asked, but Kustow touched his arm and gave him a look, as if to say 'leave it'.

'I'll come,' Michael said, looking across at Kustow. 'Bryn, will you get word to Mary. Tell her that I've been delayed. I ...' He turned back. 'T'ai Cho ... has Kim got legal help?'

'No ... no, he ...'

'Okay.' He patted T'ai Cho's arm, as if to reassure him, then looked back at Kustow. 'Do you know where Kennedy was off to, Bryn?'

'Just home, I think.'

'Good. Then contact him. Tell him I need him. Tell him ... tell him a good friend of mine is in trouble and that I'd appreciate his advice and help.'

Kustow smiled and nodded.

'And Bryn ... tell Mary that I'll see her when I can.'

'So what happened?'

Kim had been standing at the far end of the bare detention room, facing away from where Michael Lever was sitting on a narrow, pull-down bench, but at Michael's words he turned and came across.

'It was my book-keeper, Nong Yan,' he said, looking up into Michael's face. 'It had to be.'

'How do you know?'

Kim shrugged. 'No one else saw it. No one else had even the vaguest idea what I was working on. Even so, I don't know how he did it. He could only have had the briefest glimpse of it. I ...'

Again his eyes drifted off, as they had once or twice already; as if this were a scientific puzzle, to be analysed and solved. Not that it really mattered now.

In less than three hours it had all come apart. The patent was gone – stolen – and with it any chance of securing terms from the Hang Yu Credit Agency. Indeed, news had reached the bankers fast, for a handwritten message had reached Kim an hour back, expressing the regretful apologies of the Brothers Hang. But that was not all. Acting on the news, Kim's present bankers had recalled their development loan and taken immediate action to recover the debt, stripping the facility of all its equipment. At the same time, news had come that a third party had bought up all of the surrounding units – units Kim had made offers for only days before – at four times the normal rental, effectively preventing any physical expansion of Kim's operation. Not that it made any difference now.

'I should have realised ...' he said, after a moment. 'Realised what I was up against.'

'My father, you mean?'

Kim nodded. 'He's toyed with us both, neh? And for what? In my case, so that he might use me to pursue some addle-brained notion of postponing the inevitable. Even though I couldn't do it.'

'He thinks you could. He thinks you could find a way of prolonging life. Of extending it, three, four hundred years. Maybe indefinitely.'

Kim took a long breath, then looked up again, his expression suddenly intense, his eyes burning.

'Technically, perhaps. But that's not what I mean. I couldn't do it because I *couldn't* do it. I wouldn't let myself. The consequences are unthinkable. Once in my life already I've meddled in things that should have been left well alone, but this time I have a choice. So no. The dream of living forever must remain just that. A dream. I mean, just think of it! Unlink the great chain of being, and what would follow? It would be a curse, Michael. Nothing but a curse!'

Michael shuddered, then looked away, disturbed by this sudden glimpse of the young man's potency; by the dark, intense power locked away in his taut, diminutive form.

'So what will you do now?'

Kim smiled. 'It depends on what your friend, Kennedy, can arrange. I was going to go to Europe next week, but what's the point? Whatever I do, your father blocks me. He's obsessed.'

'You should go,' Michael said quietly. 'Really, Kim. You can't let him beat you.' He stood. 'He's been like this all his life. If he wanted something, he'd get it, no matter what. If someone stood in his way, he'd crush them. And no thought for the consequences. Once ... not long ago, really ... I thought that that was how things were. That it was normal to behave that way.'

He stopped, turning to look back at Kim. 'Look, Kim. If I could help you, I would. You know that. Whatever you needed. But he's fucked me, too. Boxed me in. It's how he works. Destroy and control. There's no subtlety to him. No compromise, either. But he doesn't have to win. Not unless we let him.'

Kim smiled. 'Okay. I'll go to Europe. Just as soon as all the legal stuff's sorted out. But I'm finished here. Look...'

He took the four handwritten letters from his pocket and handed them across. Michael studied them a moment, then looked up again, his eyes pained. The stamped timings on the resignation letters showed they had come within an hour of his arrest. Kim took them back from Michael, staring at them a moment, as if they were a mystery he couldn't solve, then pocketed them again.

'I keep trying to tell myself that it's understandable. That I'd do the same. Only it's not true. I ...' He looked away, close, suddenly, to breaking down. 'What's happening, Michael? What in the gods' names is happening?'

'It's this world,' Michael answered softly. 'That's why we have to change it. You in your way, me in mine. We've got to fight the old men who want to keep things as they are. Every step of the way. Because if we don't ...'

There was a knocking on the door. A moment later a lock drew back and the door swung inwards. It was Kennedy. Behind him two men stood to attention, like an honour guard.

'Michael ... Kim ...' Kennedy stepped into the room, tall and imperious, offering his hand for Kim to take. 'Okay. It's all dealt with. I've filed bail for 50,000 yuan, so you're free to go. However, the hearing has been brought forward, to eleven tomorrow morning. Which means we'll have to get our act together, fast.'

'So what do we do?'

Kennedy smiled broadly. 'We produce files. Experimental notes and the like. Things that'll prove beyond all doubt that the patent's your development.'

Kim shook his head. 'They don't exist. It was all up here, in my head.'

'All ...' Kennedy gave a small laugh, then looked to Michael. 'I guess you were right, Michael. He is different.'

'Even so,' Kim said, as Kennedy returned his attention to him. 'I doubt that they've got anything either. In fact, I'd guarantee that they don't even understand yet what they've got, let alone how it works.'

'I see. But how do we use that? The burden of proof is on us, not them. They registered first. We're the ones in default.'

'Unless we counter-claim? Sue them for false registration?'

Kennedy smiled, the smile growing broader by the moment. 'Hey, now that's a good idea. A very, very good idea.'

But Michael was shaking his head. 'It's not on, Joe. I mean, Kim's broke. How can he sue when he's broke?'

'Maybe,' Kennedy answered. 'But I'm not. And I'm sure as hell not letting your father get away with this one, Michael. Unless you've any personal objections?'

Michael looked down, then looked back at the two men, smiling. 'No. None at all, as it happens.'

'Good. Then let's go and get something to eat and talk this through. Somewhere where your father will get to hear of it. The Kitchen, maybe.'

Kim stared at Kennedy a moment, then nodded. 'Yes,' he said quietly, remembering the first time he had visited Archimedes Kitchen, and Old Man Lever's joke about the shark meat they had eaten. Well, now he knew. Finally he understood what the Old Man had meant that evening. They had stripped him bare. Down to the bone. Even so, he had lost nothing. Nothing of substance, anyway. So maybe this was a good thing. To be taught this lesson. To progress from it and build anew. And maybe having the wiring implant put in – maybe that too was serendipitous. Maybe that too was *meant*.

For now he was beaten. Things here were finished for him. But now was not forever. He turned, looking about him at the bareness of the room, remembering all the times he'd been incarcerated, then, smiling, put out a hand, touching Michael's arm.

'Okay. Let's go and be seen.'

Soucek stood in the mouth of the cave, watching while Lehmann moved amongst the deep shadows within, gathering together his belongings. Out here he was afraid – possibly more afraid than he had ever been – but he showed nothing, conscious that Lehmann was watching him. To his back was the slope, that awful uneven surface, shrouded in treacherous whiteness, that in places fell sheer a thousand *ch'i* to the rocks and icy water below. He would not look there, not now, lest his courage fail him. No, the warm darkness of the cave was more to his liking – to the habit of his being. He had never, until two hours back, set foot beyond the City's walls. Had never suspected that such a place as this existed. But now he knew. This was where Lehmann had come from. This place of cold and ice and fearful openness.

Lehmann moved quickly, almost effortlessly about the interior of the cave, taking things from ledges and from small niches hacked into the rock face. Weapons and clothing, tools and food, and, most surprising of all, a complex communications system – unlike anything Soucek had ever seen – in an all-weather case, the logo of SimFic impressed into the hard plastic in the bottom right-hand corner.

'That's it,' Lehmann said, coming out into the brightness once again. 'I'll destroy the rest, then we can get out of here.'

Soucek moved back, taking care with his footing, recalling how unpleasant it had been to fall, then watched as Lehmann set the timer on a small device and gently lobbed it into the cave. He turned at once, as if unconcerned and began trudging back up the mountainside, following the ragged line of deep indentations they had made in the snow coming down. Soucek followed, glancing back once and then a second time. They were thirty ch'i up the slope when it blew, the sound startlingly loud, echoing back and forth between the great peaks, rock fragments scattered far into the valley below. Soucek stopped, looking about him anxiously, his fear getting the better of him. Across from him, half a li distant on the facing slope, a huge spoon-shaped wedge of snow slid, slowly, as if a giant, invisible hand were scooping it up, then settled, throwing up a fine cloud of whiteness, the snow packed high against the tree line.

Soucek turned, looking up the slope at Lehmann. The albino stood there, perfectly at ease, gazing about him, an expression of awe – something Soucek had never expected to see on that narrow, unsmiling face – transforming his features, making him almost handsome. Soucek, seeing that, understood. Here was Lehmann's home. This his element. It was this, this fearful emptiness, that had formed him; that was reflected in the icy mirror of his being. It was from here that he drew his strength, and it was this – this place of stone and ice and sky – that made him singular; made him utterly different from the rest.

Soucek turned back, forcing himself to look around, fighting down the fear that threatened to engulf him, trying – *willing* himself – to see it as Lehmann saw it. And for a moment, for a single, fleeting moment, he saw the beauty, the sheer inhuman beauty of it all.

'Look!' Lehmann said, his voice strangely excited. 'There, Jiri! There, above that peak to the far left of us.'

Soucek turned, looking, shielding his eyes against the brightness of the sky. For a moment he saw nothing, nothing but the empty peaks, the pale blue sky, and then he spotted it – saw the dark speck circling high above the point of rock.

'It's an eagle, Jiri. A T'ang amongst birds! Look how magnificent it is.'

But Soucek had turned, and was watching Lehmann, seeing only him; seeing only how powerful the man seemed, here in his natural element.

Whiskers Lu's 'Red Pole', Po Lao, had left ten minutes back, having shouted at Lehmann for the best part of an hour. Now Lehmann sat there, at his desk, silent, staring at his hands. Soucek, standing in the doorway, could feel the tension in the room. They were all there – all of his lieutenants – and all had witnessed the dressing down Po Lao had given him. He had expected Lehmann to act – to answer Po Lao with a knife or a gun, perhaps – but he had done nothing, merely stared incuriously at the man as he ranted, letting him spend his fury in words.

And there was no doubting that Po Lao had been furious.

He had been waiting for them on their return, sat in Lehmann's chair, his feet up on Lehmann's desk, his runners scattered about the corridors, making sure Lehmann's men made no move against him. And for once the legendary patience of Po Lao had given way to temper, and to an outburst of anger that was a clear sign that Whiskers Lu had been riding him hard.

Lehmann had opposed nothing Po Lao had said, yet there had been a stillness to him – a rock-like imperviousness – that had impressed even Po Lao in the end. Soucek had seen it with his own eyes. Had noted how the Red Pole's eyes went time and again to Lehmann's face, conscious after a while that here was a man he could not intimidate. And with that realisation he had lowered his voice and become more reasonable, more conciliatory, until, at the end, it had seemed almost as though he and Lehmann had come to some strange, unspoken agreement between them.

For a moment longer Lehmann sat there, deep in thought, then, with a strange, almost lazy motion, he drew a sheet of hardprint towards him and, taking the ink brush from the pot, drew the schematic outline of a running dog on the back of the paper, the figure starkly black against the white. He looked up, his eyes moving from face to face, as if measuring each of them, then, taking his knife from his belt, he nicked the top of his right index finger, so that a bead of blood appeared. Slowly, applying the gentlest pressure to the cut, he placed the tip of his finger against the paper, drawing a bright red circle about the figure of the dog.

Soucek, watching, looked about him, seeing the understanding, the sudden excitement in every face and felt his heart begin to hammer in his chest.

Old Man Lever turned from the screen, speechless with fury, then hurled his goblet into the old stone fireplace.

As a servant scrambled to clear up the shattered glass, the old man paced the room like a wounded cat, cursing, his eyes blazing, oblivious, it seemed, of the men who stood in the shadows to either side, watching.

'How could he?' Lever said, stopping before the screen once more. 'How *dare* he!' He clenched a fist and raised it, looking about him, as if searching for something to hit out at. 'And Kennedy ... what's Kennedy's involvement in this?'

There were blank expressions on all sides, shrugs and apologetic bows. But no one knew. This had come as a surprise to them all.

Lever raised his voice. 'Does no one know *anything?*'

'There are rumours that Kennedy plans to move into politics,' Curval answered, stepping out from beside one of the pillars.

Lever fixed him with one eye. 'Politics?'

'They say he wants to form his own party. To challenge the old guard when the House reopens.'

Lever studied the geneticist a moment, then began to laugh; a scornful, dismissive laughter that was like the braying of a wild beast. In an instant the big room was filled with laughter as Lever's men joined in, sharing his joke. But beneath the laughter was relief that the old man's rage had been defused, his anger deflected. For the time being.

'Politics!' the old man exclaimed, wheezing with amusement. 'Who would have believed it? And my son?' He turned back, facing Curval again, his eyes suddenly much colder. 'Is my son involved in this?'

Curval shrugged. 'I wouldn't have said it was Michael's thing. But if Kennedy stood bail for Ward, maybe there's something in it. I mean, why else should he get involved?'

Lever stared at him a moment longer, then went across and sat behind his desk. For a while he was deep in thought, then, looking up, he set to work.

'Okay. Harrison ... I want you to find out all you can about young Kennedy and his plans. James ... I want a team posted to cover my son's activities. I want to know where he is and what he's doing every hour of the day from now on, understand? Robins ... I want you to compile a list of all Kennedy's contacts – business and personal – along with their financial strengths and weaknesses. Spence ... I want you to take over the winding-up of Ward's business affairs. I don't want any last minute hitches, okay? Good. And you, Cook, I want you to find out a bit more about this trip to Europe our young friend is apparently making. I want to know if he has any plans to set up over there. If he has, I want to know who he meets and what's agreed.'

Curval stepped forward, catching Lever's eye. 'And my meeting with the boy? Is that still on?'

Lever shook his head. 'Not now. Later perhaps. When things are better known. Right now it might prove ... counter-productive, let's say. Ward has ridden this one. He's survived. Right now he has friends, supporting him, buoying him up. But that won't last. Besides, there's nowhere for him to go now. No one to turn to after this. We have only to isolate him once more. To harry him, like dogs at his heels, until he tires and falls. And then ...' Lever smiled, broadly, savagely, like some wild thing scenting victory. 'And then we'll have him.'

Soucek stood there over the cot, rocking it gently, cooing to the now-sleeping child. Across from him, Lehmann was tidying the room. The woman lay face down on the bed, as if asleep, the single stiletto-wound to the back of the neck hidden beneath her long black hair.

Lehmann had explained nothing, simply told him to come. As on the last occasion, when they had gone outside, Lehmann had taken him into the service shafts, this time climbing the pipes fifty, maybe a hundred levels, until Soucek had begun to wonder whether they were going up onto the roof itself. But then Lehmann had turned off, following the map in his head, finding his footing easily, confidently. They had come out thirty *ch'i* from here, in a maintenance corridor. There Lehmann had handed him a uniform from his pack, then put one on himself. The orange of deck maintenance. ID in hand, he had come directly to this door, as if he'd done it several times before, and knocked. There had been the sound of a baby crying, a woman's spoken query, and then they were inside, Lehmann talking to the woman, reassuring her. A moment later she was dead.

Soucek had watched as Lehmann turned the woman over. He had taken a thin sheet of printout from his pocket – a sheet with her picture on it – and checked it against her. Then, satisfied, he had lifted her and placed her face-down on the bed. When the baby began to cry half-heartedly, Lehmann had turned, looking directly at Soucek, and made a rocking gesture.

What are we doing here? Soucek wondered, looking about him. It was a normal Mid-Level apartment, modestly furnished. And the woman. She was simply a wife, a mother. So what the fuck was Lehmann up to? What did he want here?

His answer came a moment later. There were footsteps outside in the corridor, then a brisk knocking and a cheerful call.

'Sweetheart! It's me! I'm home!'

Lehmann signalled for Soucek to go out into the kitchen, then went across. Moving to one side of the door, he pressed the lock. As it hissed back and the man came into the room, Lehmann moved between him and the door, his knife drawn.

He was a tall, almost cadaverously thin man, with dark, short-cut hair and of roughly the same height and build as Lehmann.

'Becky?' he asked, confused, seeing the woman on the bed, apparently asleep. Then, understanding that someone else must have operated the doorlock, he jerked round.

Soucek, watching from the kitchen, saw, in the mirror on the far side of the room, the look of horror in the man's face; saw Lehmann glance at a second paper. Then, letting the paper fall from his hand, he leaned in towards the man, as if embracing him. A moment later, the man fell back, the smallest sound of surprise escaping his lips.

As Lehmann knelt over the body, Soucek stepped out into the room again. 'Who is he?'

'There,' Lehmann said, concentrating on what he was doing. 'The paper on the floor.'

Soucek went across and picked it up. It was a printout giving brief personal details of the man. Thomas Henty. *Hung Mao*. Married. One child. Age thirty. A technician. Soucek turned back, looking across, then grimaced. Lehmann was using a narrow scalpel now, and was carefully cutting the man's eyes from his head. As Soucek watched, he severed the optical nerve and gently dropped the eyeball into a special tube-like carrier he had taken from his pack. There was the faintest hiss as the soft eye slid into the cold compartment, then the lid clicked over. Moments later the other eye joined its companion in the narrow box.

Eyes. He was stealing the man's eyes.

'What about the child?'

Lehmann leaned back, looking across at Soucek. 'Forget the child. He's dead. They're all dead now.' And, as if in explanation, Lehmann took a small device from his pack – an incendiary – and, setting the timer for sixty seconds, placed it between the two corpses on the bed.

'Quick now,' he said, going across to the door. 'We've another call to make and only forty minutes to get there.'

But Soucek paused at the door, looking back into the room. The sight of the dead couple on the bed and the soft snuffling of the sleeping child tore unexpectedly at his feelings. For the briefest moment he stood there, as if paralysed, wondering what special torments the demons of hell would have in store for him when his life above the Yellow Springs was done. Then, with a tiny shudder, he turned away, following Lehmann out into the corridor.

That night the dream came once again.

Again, as once before, Jelka stood alone upon that tilted, shattered land, trapped beneath a low, impenetrable sky of steel. It was dark, an oppressive, elemental darkness lit now and then by sudden flashes of light. All about her the storm raged violently, growling and shrieking at her with a voice of primal evil. Before, she had felt only fear; a gut-wrenching fear that had rooted her to the spot. This time, however, it was not fear she felt but excitement.

Excitement, and a sense of expectation.

Beneath her the tower slowly climbed the slope, its wooden, spiderish limbs folding and stretching inexorably, its dark mouth grunting and wheezing as it came on. With each searing flash of light she saw it gain on her, its shattered, glass-like eyes glittering malevolently, its jagged, toothless maw crammed with splintered bone.

Closer it came, and closer yet, and as its foul breath rolled up the hill towards her, she cried out, her voice high and clear above the noise of the storm. There was a moment's silence, a moment's utter stillness, and then, as once before, the earth between her and the tower cracked and split.

She shivered, watching, knowing what would come. Knowing and yet fearful in case, this time, it would be different.

Slowly, like a shadow forming from the dark mouth of the earth, he emerged; a stooped little creature with short, strong limbs and eyes that burned like coals. Turning, he looked at her, his wet, dark skin glowing with an inner light.

She smiled, greeting him, recognising him for the first time. It was Kim.

For a moment he was still, watching her, his dark yet fiery eyes seeming to pierce her to the bone. And then, slowly, his lips parted in a smile, like a pocket opening in the blackness of his face, light – a brilliant, burning light – spilling out, falling like molten gold from the mouth of a furnace.

He smiled, and then, with an agility that surprised her, he span about, facing the tower, his arms held up before him, as if to ward it off.

'Avodya!' he said clearly. 'Avodya!'

Slowly the tower heaved itself up, creaking beneath its own bloated weight, a furious whispering and muttering coming from within its hideous maw. Then, with a rush, it came up the slope at him, its cracked eyes glinting, its thin legs straining, a low moan rising to a screech as it ran.

'Avodya!'

On it came and on, rushing at him through the half-dark. On, like some vast, unstoppable machine, until, with a fearsome cry, it threw itself at him.

And as it fell, the darkness seemed to explode. Where the small, dark creature stood was now a web of brilliant, coruscating light that pulsed between the fingers of his outstretched arms.

Slowly, ever so slowly, the tower fell, tumbling, shrieking, into the fierce, pure fire of the web. And where it touched it sparked and vanished, flickering into nothingness.

For a moment longer, its shrieks echoed across the shattered land, flapping like bats against the ceiling of the sky. Then, as they faded, a pure, high ringing tone grew, until it filled the sudden stillness.

She blinked and looked, but he was gone. Slowly, fearfully, she went across. The earth from whence he'd come no longer gaped, but was smooth and seamless. And beyond it, there where he'd stood – there, where the tower had tumbled shrieking into the fiery web – was nothing. Nothing but a huge circle of ash.

Jelka shuddered and then woke, remembering. Kalevala and the storm. And the morning after – the circle of darkness in the woods and the seven charred tree stumps. And Kim. All of it linked somehow. All of it tied in to the future. But how or why she did not know. Not yet.

CHAPTER 85

PLUCKED EYES AND SEVERED HEADS

olonen was stripped to the waist, exercising, when Kim came into the room. He turned, nodding to Kim, then continued with his routine, bending to touch his toes, then throwing his arms up above his head, twisting his torso once, twice to either side, before ducking down again. It was a vigorous, impressive routine that even a much younger man would have found strenuous, but at seventy-five the old man made it look easy. He was in fine physical condition and, but for the bright, golden sheen of his artificial arm, seemed in perfect health.

Kim waited, watching respectfully, in silence. Only when the old man had finished and was standing there, towelling himself down, did he cross the room and stand by the broad oak desk that dominated the study.

'Hello there,' Tolonen said, coming across. 'How are you, boy?'

He reached out with his good hand and held Kim's hand a moment, meeting his eyes squarely, challengingly, as he always did.

'I'm fine,' Kim answered, taking the seat the Marshal offered him. 'I wasn't sure you'd have time to see me.'

Tolonen smiled, making his way round to the other side of the desk. 'Nonsense. You're always welcome here.'

Kim bowed. 'Thank you. But I wouldn't dream of keeping you from your business.'

The old man laughed. 'There's no chance of that, my boy. I've got to be off in twenty minutes. Li Yuan himself has summoned me. I'll have to shower and change before then, but we've time for a chat, neh?'

Tolonen turned, taking a tunic from the back of the big, leather-backed chair, then pulled it on in one swift motion. To Kim, watching wide-eyed from his chair, he seemed like a god, there was so much power and authority in every movement.

He turned back, facing Kim again, and sat, leaning towards Kim across the broad expanse of the desk's surface. 'So how's business? Did you finally get round to registering those patents?'

Kim hesitated, not wishing to burden the old man with his problems. 'There were difficulties,' he said, after a moment. 'Complications with the patent...'

'Complications?' Tolonen sat back slightly. 'You mean the thing didn't work, after all? But you were so confident.'

'No ...' Again Kim held back, loath to discuss the matter. But Tolonen was staring at him now, curious. 'The device works. That's not the problem. The problem is that someone beat me to it. They registered a day before me.'

'I didn't think anyone was working on the same lines. I thought you said ...' Tolonen stopped, his face changing, suddenly realising what Kim was actually saying. 'But that's outrageous! Does Li Yuan know of this?'

'Not yet.'

'Then maybe he ought. We should *do* something ...'

Kim looked down, shaking his head. 'Forgive me, Marshal, but I would rather the T'ang knew nothing of this. He has much on his mind as it is. Besides, the problem is mine, not his, and I shall find ways and means to solve it.'

Tolonen stared back at the young man a moment, taking in his words, then gave an emphatic nod. 'All right. But if this should happen again ...'

'I'll let you know.' Kim smiled. 'But enough of my troubles. How did your investigations go?'

Tolonen gave a small sigh and put his hands together, metal and flesh interlaced. 'They say that those who look shall find, neh? I can say very little just now, I'm afraid. I ...' He stopped, studying Kim's face a moment, then reached into the drawer to his left and took out a slender computer-file, placing it on the desk between them.

'Can I trust you to be discreet, Kim?'

Kim narrowed his eyes. 'This has to do with what you found?'

'It has. At present only three people know what is in that file. With your-self and the T'ang, it'll make five. And so it must remain, for the time being. You understand me?'

'I understand.'

'Good. Then take the file and read it. And let me know what you think. In return I shall have a special team investigate this matter of the patent.' He lifted a hand to still Kim's objections. 'I heard what you said, my boy, and I respect you for it, but sometimes it does not hurt to have a little outside help, neh? All I ask is that you keep the information in that folder to yourself and return it once you have had time to consider its significance.'

Kim leaned towards the old man, about to ask him about the file, when the door to his right swung open and Jelka came hurrying into the room. She was talking, already three or four steps into the room, when she stopped and fell silent, realising that her father was not alone.

She bowed her head. 'Forgive me, father. I didn't realise you had com-pany.'

Jelka turned, looking across at Kim. He was sitting there, like a large-eyed child in the big, tall-backed chair, the very smallness of him making her frown involuntarily then look back at her father.

He smiled, amused, not hurt by her reaction. Across from him, Tolonen stood, turning to his daughter with a kindly, indulgent smile.

'This is Kim,' he said. 'Kim Ward. A valued servant of Li Yuan. And this, Kim, is my daughter, Jelka.'

Kim stood, offering his hand, seeing how she had to bend slightly to take it. Her hand was warm, its pressure firm against his own, enclosing his, her eyes friendly, welcoming.

'I know who Kim is, daddy,' she said, releasing Kim's hand. 'He was on the Project.'

Kim's eyes widened, surprised that she remembered. But Tolonen mere-ly laughed.

'Of course! I'm forgetting, aren't I?' He came round, putting an arm about his daughter's shoulders. 'Why, you might almost say that she found you, Kim, after the attack. We had given up any hope of finding survivors, but Jelka insisted that you'd escaped. She made us search the vent for signs that you'd got out that way. And you know what? She was right!'

Kim stared, his mouth open. He hadn't known.

He looked down, suddenly abashed. That first time he had seen her – when she had come with her father to visit the Wiring Project – he had stared at her in awe, thinking her some kind of goddess. Never, even in his wildest imaginings, had he thought she would remember him. But she had. More than that, she had made them look for him.

Kim looked down at his hand. He could still feel the gentle warmth, the firm but pleasant pressure of her hand enclosing his, and shivered, surprised once more by the strength of what he was feeling. And when he looked up, it was to find her watching him still, a strange intensity in her vividly blue eyes.

The file lay on the desk beside him. For a brief moment both men had forgotten it, but now Tolonen reminded Kim, pointing to it.

'Take it with you, Kim. And look at it closely. You don't have to answer at once. The end of the week will be soon enough.'

Kim stared at the file a moment, then, impulsively, answered the old man. 'I don't need that long. I'll give you my answer tomorrow.' He smiled. 'Whatever Li Yuan wants, I'll do. If I *can* ...'

At that Tolonen laughed, and, as if letting his daughter in on a joke, began to explain. 'Kim here is a physicist. Our experts say he's the best, despite his years. Maybe the best we've ever had.'

He could see how she glanced at him, then back at her father, as if she couldn't quite take it in. Indeed, to Kim, sitting there watching her, nothing seemed more implausible than the fact that men like Tolonen and Li Yuan should need him, seeing in him something that they could not match, and using words like 'the best'. To the part of him that was Clayborn – that had come up from the darkness beneath the City – it seemed absurd. And when this girl, so tall and beautiful that she seemed somehow unreal, narrowed her eyes and asked him if it were true, if he *was* the best, he could only laugh at her and nod, watching her face change slowly until it mirrored his own delight at the absurdity of things.

'If I can ...' Tolonen murmured, echoing Kim's words, then laughed. But Kim didn't hear. He was still staring at the girl, seeing how she looked away from him, then back, something strange happening in her face even as he watched.

He looked down at the unopened file and nodded to himself. But the gesture had nothing to do with what was in the folder. Had nothing to do with physics, or projects or Li Yuan's needs. It was the girl. In an instant he had decided something, irrevocably and without further doubt. He would not rest. Not until he had married her.

In the Imperial Shower Room of Tongjiang, the maids of the inner household, Fragrant Lotus and Bright Moon, were preparing to wash the young T'ang's hair. Taking soft woollen towels from the big cupboards above the sinks, they laid them out beside the glazed bowls of unguents and shampoos, the silver combs and brushes, the trays of brightly-coloured beads and silken thread, then, returning to the sinks, they opened the great dragon mouths of the taps and sprinkled a fine, nut-brown, aromatic powder into the steaming crystal fall.

As they worked, Li Yuan watched them from his chair, at the centre of the great tiled floor, enjoying the sight of the two young women, the sound of the ancient songs they hummed as they busied themselves about him, the sweet scent of their softly-veiled bodies as they brushed past.

He sighed, for once not merely content but happy. For a long time he had denied himself such things as this, attempting to harden himself against the world, but now he understood. This too was part of it. Without these moments of soft luxury – of surrender to the senses – there was no balance to life, no joy. And without joy there could be no real understanding of the flow of things. No wisdom.

For a long time he had struggled to be what he was not. To be some purer, finer creature. But it was all in vain. From the day of his betrothal to Fei Yen, the balance of his life had been lost. Casting off his maids, he had cast off that part of him that needed warmth and comfort, a mother's touch. He had tried to shape himself, as a tailor cuts cloth to make a gown, but the gown he'd made had been too tight. It had stifled and disfigured him.

He looked down, remembering those times. To have one single, perfect love; that had been the dream. To have a woman who was all to him, just as he was all to her – like Yin and Yang, or night and day – that had been the dream. But the world was not a dream. The world was harsh and true to itself alone. In it there was falseness and betrayal, sickness and hatred, cruelty and loss. Loss beyond the strength of hearts to bear.

And yet there was this. This simple light of joy to set against the darkness of the times. The joy of a woman's touch, a child's embrace, the laughter of a loving friend. These simple things, weightless as they seemed in the great scale of things, were the equal of a hundred deaths, a thousand cruel blows. Feathers and iron. Joy and grief. Balanced.

Li Yuan laughed softly, then looked up, conscious suddenly that the maids had finished and were standing there before him, watching him.

'*Chieh Hsia* ...' they said as one and bowed low, their smiles betraying how much they too enjoyed these moments alone with him.

'Here,' he said, standing and putting out his arms to them. 'Hsiang He. Ywe Hui. Come here, my little blossoms. Come here and tend to me.'

Tolonen was waiting for him in his study, standing by the door to the eastern garden, his golden hand glinting in the sunlight as he turned to face his master.

'*Chieh Hsia*,' the old man said, bowing low. 'Forgive me if I came too early.'

Li Yuan shook his head and laughed. 'Not at all, old friend. The fault is mine. I spent too long in the shower this morning and now everything is running late.'

'Then I will be brief, *Chieh Hsia*, and come directly to the point. You asked me to have my discovery checked out and analysed. Well, I now have the preliminary findings and they are most disturbing. Most disturbing indeed.'

Li Yuan looked across and saw the folder on the edge of his desk. 'Is this it here, Knut?'

'That is it, *Chieh Hsia*.'

Li Yuan stared at the Marshal a moment, then went round his desk and sat. Drawing the thickly-padded folder towards him, he flipped it open. On top of the pile was a picture of the thing he had seen last time Tolonen had visited him. The thing he'd brought back with him from North America. In the picture it looked like a giant walnut, the size of a young child's hand. Just looking at it, Li Yuan could recall the scent of the original, the dry spicy mustiness of it.

A brain it was. An artificial brain. Smaller and less complex than a human brain, but a marvel all the same. In many ways it looked like the brains Gen-Syn produced for many of their top-range models, but this was different. GenSyn brains were limited things, grown from existent genetic material – painstakingly nurtured in baths of nutrients over a period of years. But this brain had been made. Designed and built, like a machine. A living machine.

When he had seen it first, a week ago, he had been unimpressed. The thing was long dead – the only one of five to have survived in its storage case. But the experimental notes – a small library of computer records – had been saved intact. Using them, Tolonen had spent the last week piecing together what had happened. Now, reading through his summary, Li Yuan felt himself go cold.

'Kuan Yin!' he said, looking up at Tolonen. 'What put you onto this?'

The old man bowed stiffly. 'Gaps in the record, *Chieh Hsia*. Things that didn't make sense. There was too much wastage of basic materials, for instance. The percentages were far higher than in previous years, so I did some digging, found out where the 'waste' was being shipped and followed the trail. As I suspected, it was being sold off cheaply, the funds being used to finance a small R & D establishment in the far south. That's where I found it all. Untouched. The room sealed up.'

'A mistake, do you think?'

Tolonen shook his head. 'I think we were just lucky. My guess is that whatever this was, it was almost ready to go. And the only reason it didn't is because we hit them first.'

Li Yuan frowned. 'What do you mean?'

'Look at the dates on the final research entries. They're all late Autumn 2207. That's significant. That means this thing was coming to fruition at the same time that we dealt with Hans Ebert and DeVore. If I'm right, we settled with them before they could get this under way. Before they could *use* one of these things.'

'I see. So you think this was Hans Ebert's doing?'

Tolonen sniffed deeply. 'I'm certain of it. Not only are his initials on a number of the documents, but the whole thing has the twisted feel of one of his schemes. That said, I think he was making these things for DeVore. Maybe even to DeVore's specifications. From the shipping documents we've found, they were going to be shipped to Mars.'

'Mars?' Li Yuan stood, then walked slowly across to the window. 'Why Mars?'

Tolonen turned, watching the young T'ang. 'I'm not sure, *Chieh Hsia*, but I feel sure it has something to do with those copies that came in from Mars that time.'

'But my father's investigations drew a blank.'

'Maybe so. But perhaps we should look again. More thoroughly this time. Send Karr perhaps.'

Li Yuan glanced at him, then looked back out at the sunlit garden. 'Perhaps.'

Tolonen hesitated a moment, then spoke again. 'There is one other thing, *Chieh Hsia*. Something which isn't in the summary, Something we're still working on.'

'And what's that?'

'The brain. It wasn't like anything else GenSyn ever produced. For a start, it wasn't connected to any kind of spinal cord. Nor did it have to be sited in a skull. Moreover, it's a lot more compact than a normal human brain, as if it was designed for something else. It makes me think that this was only a single component and that the rest was being made elsewhere, maybe at sites all over Chung Kuo.'

'To be sent to Mars for assembly, you think?'

'Maybe.' The old man frowned and shook his head. 'Maybe I'm just being paranoid about this, *Chieh Hsia*. Maybe it's all dead and gone, like the brain itself. Maybe we killed it when we killed DeVore. But I'm not so sure. The fact that this could be built in the first place worries me immensely. If you were to put a number of these inside *Hei* bodies, for instance, you could do a lot of damage. No one would be safe. Not if those performance statistics are correct.'

'So what do you suggest?'

'That you meet with Wu Shih and Tsu Ma and let them know of this at once.'

'And the rest of the Council?'

Tolonen shook his head. 'For once I think you need to keep things tight. Master Nan will need to know about this, certainly. But if Wang Sau-leyan were to find out, who knows what he would do? If this thing was built once, it could be built again. And in your cousin's hands, who knows what evil might result?'

'That is so,' Li Yuan said quietly. 'Yet why not simply destroy all record of it? That would be simplest, surely?'

'Maybe it would, *Chieh Hsia*. But can we take the risk? Can we be certain that these are the only records of the experiments, or are there copies elsewhere? On Mars, perhaps? Or somewhere else, hidden away?'

Li Yuan looked down. 'So we must live with this?'

'It seems so, *Chieh Hsia*. At least, until we can be sure.'

'Sure?' Li Yuan laughed bleakly, recalling with surprise his earlier mood of joy. When could they ever be sure?

Old Man Lever turned, the dark, curly-haired head held firmly between his broad, square-fingered hands, and smiled.

'Well, what do you think?'

Lever held out the severed head, as if offering it to the three men stood before him, but they merely grimaced, their fans fluttering agitatedly before their faces.

'Really, Charles,' one of them, a tall, morose-looking man named Marley, answered. 'It's grotesque. What is it? GenSyn?'

Lever shook his head, but the smile remained in his eyes. He was enjoying their discomfort. 'Not at all. It's real. Or was. As far as I know there are only three such heads in existence, but this is the best. Look at it. Look how well preserved it is.'

As he thrust the head out towards them, there was a sharp movement back; a look of revulsion in their faces so profound it was almost comical.

Lever shrugged, then turned the head in his hands, staring down into the dark, broad features. Lifting it slightly, he sniffed the black, leathery skin.

'It's beautiful, neh? Slaves they were. Negroes, they called them. They were brought over to America from Africa four, five centuries ago. Our forefathers used them like machines, to toil in their fields and serve in their mansions. They say there were once thousands of them. Sub-human, of course. You can see that at a glance. But men, all the same. Bred, not made.'

Marley shuddered and turned away, looking about him. The room was cluttered with packing cases from a dozen different auction rooms, most of them unopened. But those that were displayed treasures beyond imagining. Clothing and furniture, machines and books, statues and paintings and silverware. Things from the old times none of them had dreamed still existed.

He turned back. Old Man Lever's eyes were on him again, as if studying him, gauging his reaction to all this.

'I thought we might have a special exhibition suite at the Institute, George. What do you think? Something to boost morale. To give us a renewed sense of our heritage. As Americans.'

Marley shot worried glances at his fellows, then looked back at Lever, a faint quiver in his voice. 'An *exhibition*? Of this?'

Lever nodded.

'But wouldn't that be ... dangerous? I mean ...'

Marley's fan fluttered nervously. 'Word would get out. The Seven would hear of it. They would see it as a kind of challenge, surely?'

Lever laughed dismissively. 'No more than the Waldeseemuller map that already hangs there. No, and certainly no more of a challenge than the Kitchen. Besides, what would our friend Wu Shih do if he knew? What *could* he do?'

Marley averted his eyes before the fierce, challenging gaze of the other, but his discomfort was evident. And maybe that was why Lever had invited them this morning – not to show off his most recent acquisitions but to sound out their reaction to his scheme. The ancient map of the world that hung in the great hall of the Institute, that was one thing, and Archimedes Kitchen and its anti-Han excesses, that was another. But this – this scheme for an exhibition, a *museum* of ancient Americana – was something else entirely. Was an act of defiance so gross that to ignore it would be tantamount to condoning it.

And Wu Shih could not afford to condone it.

So why? Why did Lever want to bring things to a head? Why did he want a confrontation with Wu Shih? Was he still burning at the humiliation he had suffered on the steps of the ancient Lincoln Memorial, or was this something else? In setting up this exhibition was he, perhaps, attempting to create some kind of bargaining counter. Something he might trade off for some other, more worth-while concession?

Or was that too subtle a reading of this? Mightn't the old fool simply be ignorant of the likely result of his proposed action? Marley stared at the severed Negro head in Old Man Lever's hands and shuddered inwardly. It would not do to offend Lever, but the alternative for once seemed just as bad.

He met Lever's eyes firmly, steeling himself to ask the question. 'What do you want, Charles? What do you *really* want?'

Lever looked down at the head then back at Marley. 'I want us to be proud again, that's all, George. Proud. We've bowed before these bastards all our lives. Been *their* creatures. Done what *they* said. But times are changing. We're entering a new phase of things. And afterwards ...' he lowered his voice, smiling now, 'well, maybe they'll find occasion to bow their heads to us, neh?'

Yes, Marley thought, *or have ours cut from our necks …*

He was about to speak, about to ask something more of the Old Man, when there was a banging on the door at the far end of the room. Lever set the head down carefully, then, with a tight smile that revealed he was loath to be interrupted, moved past them.

While Lever stood there at the door speaking to his First Steward, Marley looked to his two companions – like himself, major contributors to the Institute's funds – and saw his own deep reluctance mirrored there. But how articulate that? How convey their feelings without alienating Lever?

He turned, looking back at Lever, and caught his breath, surprised by the look of unbridled anger in the old man's face.

'Send him up!' Lever barked, dismissing the servant with a curt gesture. Then, composing himself as well as he could, he turned back, facing them again.

'Forgive me, *ch'un tzu*, but my son is here. I forbade him to come without my express permission, but he is here nonetheless.'

'Ah …' Marley looked down, understanding. The rift between Old Man Lever and his son was common knowledge, but until now he had not known the depth of their division. Things were bad indeed if Lever had barred his son from the family home.

'Should we leave, Charles? This matter of the exhibition … we might speak of it another time. Over dinner, perhaps?'

He had hoped it would be enough to extricate them from a potentially embarrassing situation and buy some time to discuss the matter privately amongst themselves, but Lever was shaking his head.

'No, George. If the boy has the impertinence to disturb me while I am in conference with my friends, he is hardly to be rewarded for it with a private audience, neh?'

Marley bowed his head slightly, the bitterness and determination in Lever's voice warning him against pursuing the matter. A moment later the son himself was there in the doorway; a tall, athletic-looking young man so like his father that they might easily have been taken for brothers.

'Father,' the young man said, bowing his head dutifully, waiting to be asked into the room. But Old Man Lever gave no word, made no gesture of admittance. He merely stood there, stone-faced and implacable.

'I asked you not to come. So why are you here, Michael? What do you want?'

Michael Lever looked to the three men, then back to his father, as if expecting something of him. Then, understanding how things were, he lowered his head again.

'I had to see you, father. To speak to you. This thing between us ...' He hesitated, finding it hard to say the words, then looked up, meeting his father's eyes. 'I wish to be reconciled with you, father.'

Old Man Lever stood there a moment, unmoving, silent, as if carved in granite, then, turning away abruptly, he gave a tight little laugh. A derisory, dismissive laugh.

'Then you will marry Louisa Johnstone, after all?'

'Marry her ... ?' The younger man faltered, at a loss. He glanced uncertainly at the others then took a step towards his father. 'But that's behind us, surely, father? I'm talking of the future. Of being your son again, your hands ...'

'My *hands!*' Old Man Lever whirled round, his face ugly now, one angry look from him enough to make his son step back beyond the room's threshold again. 'And if my hands will not do as I ask them?' He shook his head contemptuously and waved the young man away. 'Pah ... Go and play with your dreamer friends, boy. Go sleep with your low-level whores. I'll have nothing to do with you, boy. Nothing at all!'

For a moment the young man said nothing. Then, with one final, precise bow – a bow that showed immense self-control – he withdrew. 'So be it, then,' then,' he said softly, turning away. 'So be it.'

But Marley, standing there, had seen that initial look of angry bewilderment on the young man's face and knew he had been witness to a final breach. Whatever the rights and wrongs of this – and Lever was certainly right to insist that his son obey him – there was no doubting that the old man had set out deliberately to humiliate his son, speaking thus to him before those who were not of his kin. He turned, looking at Lever, expecting to see that stern and unrelenting expression maintained on his features, and found, to his surprise, not anger but regret and – underlying all – a hurt so profound, so all-embracing, that it threatened momentarily to engulf the old man.

For the briefest unguarded moment it was so, and then, as if a steel door had slammed down over it, it was gone.

'Well, *ch'un tzu*,' Lever said, clearing his throat, 'as I was saying ...'

While Milne stood at the counter, asking questions of the clerk, Ross looked about him at the walls and furnishings of the Records Office, as if they might give some kind of clue.

It was a dirty, shabby place, empty drink-bulbs and crumpled paper forms littering the spittle-stained floor, while on the walls of the public space were torn and faded posters, over-painted with slogans and graffiti, one symbol – a simple black palm print – dominating all others.

'Who's this?' Ross asked, leaning over an old Han seated on the bench. 'Are they popular here in Atlanta?' But the ancient stared straight through him, as if he wasn't there.

'Terrorists, I guess,' Ross murmured, straightening up and looking about him once more. Not that there was much to know about places like this. They were all much of a muchness these days.

He went back across, standing beside Milne at the counter. A young Han clerk was talking animatedly to Milne in Mandarin, running his finger along the open page of one of the big official Records books.

'So what have we got?' Ross whispered. 'Anything good?'

The clerk glanced at Ross, then, removing his finger, slammed the book shut. 'That's it,' he said, in halting English. 'That's all there is.'

'Shit,' said Milne quietly. 'Just our luck.'

'What's the problem?'

Milne looked away nervously. 'There was a deck fire, three years back. All of the local records were destroyed. Back-ups, too, in a separate fire. The deck itself was cleared. Re-seeded with new settlers. They've been rebuilding the files ever since, but there's not much. Only what we've seen already.'

Ross looked down. 'Hmm. Bit of a coincidence, neh? I mean, when was the last time you heard of something like that? Two fires?'

'It's not impossible. Fires happen.'

'Maybe. But it's all too neat, don't you think? I mean, if you wanted to put in a sleeper, what better way?'

'And you think that's what happened? You think Mary Jennings is a sleeper for one of Lever's enemies?'

'And you don't?'

Milne hesitated, then gave a reluctant nod.

'Right. So what we do is this. We find out where the survivors of the fire were moved to, and then we go and speak to some of them. Find out what they remember about our friend Mary Jennings. That is, if they remember anything.' Ross turned back, facing the counter again, a fifty *yuan* bill held out between his thumb and forefinger.

'And then?'

Ross looked back at his partner and smiled. 'And then we do something we should have done right at the start. We make a facial check on our friend. Not just here in North America, but right across the seven Cities.' He laughed. 'It's time we found out just who Mary Jennings really is.'

Emily sat before the mirror in her room, brushing out the long dark tresses of the wig. It was a tight fit, but that was good. Unlike the other she had bought, this one looked natural. As well it might, for it reminded her of how she had once looked, twelve years ago, when she was seventeen.

Seventeen. It was not long as the world measured things, and yet it seemed another lifetime. Back then things had seemed so simple. So black and white. She had known then where she stood in the world and what she wanted. Meeting Bent Gesell, she had become his woman, faithful to him alone, sharing his ideals; that vision of a better, purer world. A world without levels, free of hatred and corruption. For eight years that vision had sustained her. Had driven her on. But then Gesell had been seduced: won over by the dream of power DeVore had seeded in his head.

The vision had died. And yet DeVore had saved her. After the débâcle at Bremen, it had been DeVore who had come to her, offering her a new identity and a passport to a new life – that same life she had led these past twenty-one months.

Yes, but what had she done in that time? What achieved?

Nothing, came the answer. For almost two years now she had sat on her hands, serving her natural enemies, doing nothing for the cause she'd once believed in.

So maybe it was time to begin anew. To go down the levels and organise again:

She stood, looking about her at the tiny room. Her bag was packed, her jacket laid neatly across it. Beside it on the bed rested the second of the two IDs DeVore had given her. Stooping, she picked it up and studied the tiny image within. *Rachel DeValerian*, it read. *Maintenance Engineer.*

She smiled. Even Mach knew nothing of this. Only DeVore. And he, if Mach could be believed, was dead now, his skull smashed into tiny pieces by the T'ang's man, Karr.

Only she didn't believe that. From what she knew of the man, she couldn't believe he would have let himself be caught so easily. No. He was out there somewhere. Waiting. Biding his time.

And Michael?

She sighed. The note had gone by messenger more than three hours back. He would surely have read it by now. In fact, she had been expecting him to call these last few hours. But nothing. It was as she'd thought – as she'd said in the letter – he was too preoccupied with other things to see what he had done to her. Too bound up in his father's business. For a while she had thought him cured of all that, changed, free to pursue his own straight path through life, but she had been mistaken. Kennedy's visit had opened her eyes to that.

Yes, and the news that he had gone to see his father – to beg forgiveness and become his 'son' again – had hit her hard. Had woken her to the reality of her life.

She had delayed too long. Had let herself be blinded by her love for him. Well, now she knew. It was no good waiting for Michael Lever. No use relying on any man. Surely she had learned that lesson once already in her life, with Gesell?

Even so, some instinct kept her here, waiting for him to call, to knock on the door and tell her it was all a mistake. That what he'd said to her was true. That he *had* changed.

That he loved her.

'Ten minutes,' she said softly to herself, glancing at the timer on her wrist. Ten more minutes, and then she would go.

She tucked the ID into the inner pocket of the jacket, then went across and stood before the mirror once again, carefully removing the wig and replacing it in the carrier.

She had booked her flight already, under the name of Mary Jennings, taking the rocket to the West Coast and then a fast-track south. There, in the teeming Lowers of old Mexico, she would switch identities. To begin again. As Rachel DeValerian.

She looked about her nervously, going through all she had done these past few hours. All bills were paid three months ahead, all commitments met. Only Michael would miss her. And then maybe not.

She closed her eyes, wishing, hoping against all reason, that he would call, at this late hour, and put things right between them. That he would simply walk through the door and take her in his arms and ...

There was a banging on the outer door, so sudden that it made her jump. *Michael* ...

She went across and stood there, trying to calm herself, but her pulse was racing, her heart pounding in her chest. As the hammering came again, she called out, her voice tiny, barely in control.

'Who is it?'

'It's me! It's Bryn!'

Bryn? And then she understood. It was Bryn Kustow, Michael's partner. Thumbing the lock, she stood back, letting him in.

'You've got to help me,' he said breathlessly. 'Michael's gone. He went to see his old man and they had a big bust-up. I got a call. I don't know who it was. One of the old man's cronies, I suspect. Marley, maybe. But it seems that Michael was very upset. The Old Man really gave it to him. Making demands. Insisting that he marry the Johnstone girl. Humiliating him in front of strangers. I tried Michael's apartment but he wasn't there. No one's seen him for hours!'

Taking his arm, she made him sit on the edge of the bed, then stood over him, her mind in a whirl, trying to take in what had happened. 'Okay. Slow down. Let's think this through. You say you went to his apartment. Had he been there?'

'I think so. I mean yes. Yes, he had. The manservant said he'd called in. Very unlike himself. Very distressed.'

'And did he take the note?'

'The note?'

'I sent him a note. It's important. It might explain things.'

Kustow shrugged. 'I don't know. I ... Yes. Hang on. The man said something about ... about a special messenger coming.'

'Shit.' She shuddered, knowing now that she had got it wrong. Whatever

Michael had been doing, going back to see his father, it had had nothing to do with her. And that was Kennedy's fault. Kennedy who had misled her.

'Look,' she said, 'he won't have gone far. I know what he's like. He won't want to face anyone he knows. Not now. I reckon he's gone down. Down to the Lowers. If I were you, I'd check the bars in all the local stacks. Somewhere dark and anonymous, where he's not likely to be known. That's where you'll find him.'

'Michael? Down there?' Kustow laughed, but then he saw how she was looking at him and his laughter died. 'You think so?'

She nodded. 'Yes. And when you find him, tell him this. That the note was a mistake. I didn't understand. I thought ...' She shrugged. 'Look, just tell him that I'll wait for him. If he wants me, he knows where I am. And Bryn ...'

'Yes?'

'Tell him that I love him. And that I need him, even if his father doesn't. Tell him that, neh?'

Kim was standing with his back to her when she came into the room, his dark head tilted forward as he looked down at something in his hands. She set down the tray, she was carrying, then, quietly, knowing he had not heard her, went across and stood there, behind and slightly to the side of him, looking down at the object he was holding.

It was a globe of yellowed ivory, carved with intricate towers and orna-mental bridges, crowded with tiny figures, yet small enough for him to cup in one of his tiny, childlike hands. She watched him set it back carefully, then half turn, realising suddenly that she was there.

'I'm sorry, I ...'

She smiled and shook her head. 'No, don't apologise. Handle them if you want.'

He looked at her strangely, his lips parted, the pupils of his eyes form-ing large dark circles that surprised her with their intensity. There was a wild, untamed quality about him that both frightened and attracted her. His eyes seemed to fix and hold her with a power she didn't quite understand, yet when she found her voice again all that she said was, 'You've nice eyes. They're so dark ...'

'They're green,' he said, laughing, looking up at her.

'No ... not their colour ...'

She hesitated. She had been about to say that they were like the surface of the northern sea; that their greenness seemed to mask an unfathomed depth of darkness, but he knew nothing of seas and so she kept silent, watching him, knowing only that she had met no one like him before. His dark hair was cut neat against his large but not unattractive head, and his skin had the pale smoothness of a child's. He was dressed simply, so simply that in that single respect alone he was distinct from anyone she knew. Even her father's young soldiers wore jewellery and made up their faces. Yes, even the austere and distant Axel Haavikko. But Kim wore nothing special, added nothing to his natural self.

He looked past her at the tray. 'Is that *ch'a*?'

'Yes.' She laughed, feeling a sudden warmth come to her cheeks. She had forgotten. For that brief moment she had forgotten everything. 'There are some sweetmeats, too. But you'll stay for dinner, I hope. My father should be back ...'

He nodded, then moved around her, bending down to take one of the sweetmeats from the tray.

She turned, watching him. In some indefinable way he was beautiful. Quite beautiful. Nor was it the kind of beauty she was accustomed to. He was not tall, nor broad, nor handsome in the classical Above sense of that word. Even so, something shone out from him. Some quality that was more sensed than seen. Some powerful, uncompromising thing that simply wasn't there in other people. She felt that he was somehow ... *in touch*. Was that it? In touch. But in touch with what? She shook her head, watching him bend to take another of the sweetmeats, his smallest movement different, somehow *connected*. She watched, frowning with the intensity of her watchfulness, but she could say no more than that.

He turned, looking back at her, smiling. 'Won't you join me?'

She laughed, embarrassed, realising how awkward, how gawky she must have appeared at that moment, but he seemed not to notice. He merely stood there, smiling, one hand raised to her in invitation, waiting for her.

She crossed the room and took his hand, the movement so easy, so natural, that it seemed to her that she had somehow always done it. But the feel of his palm against her own stirred her so deeply that she shivered and glanced down to where their fingers met and interlaced. When she looked up again he was watching her.

She frowned, suddenly conscious of how frail, how small he was beside her, how her hand enveloped his, her strong, slender fingers thicker, longer than his. Like a mother with her child.

His face was serious, unsmiling now, his eyes still questioning her. Then, unexpectedly, he lifted her hand to his lips and kissed it, brushing it with his lips gently before releasing it. Again she shivered, then turned away quickly, a sweet but painful sensation filling her, physical in its intensity. And as she turned, the memory of her dream came back to her, so that she saw it vividly – saw again that small, dark creature, whose eyes burned like coals and whose wet, dark skin shone with an inner light. She saw it climb from the darkness of the cracked and scarred earth and lift the mirror at the tower. Saw it and gave a small cry, as if in pain. But it was recognition.

She turned back. He was watching her, concerned, not understanding why she had made the sound.

'Are you all right?'

She made to speak, but at that moment there were noises in the hallway outside. Kim was still watching her, confused, unable to comprehend the pain, the sudden intentness of her glances at him. 'I ...' she began, but it was all she could say. It was *him*. Now, the dream returned to her, she saw it. Saw how his eyes saw through her to the bone and the darkness underneath. Saw it and knew – even as her maid came into the room – that this was her fate. This childlike man. This fierce and gentle creature.

'Jelka?' He was looking at her strangely now. 'Are you all right?'

She took a breath and nodded. 'I ... I'm fine.' But she felt faint, felt both ice cold and fiery hot, as if a sudden fever had taken her. Forcing herself to be calm, she looked across at her maid and smiled, as if to reassure the girl.

'You'll stay for dinner, Shih Ward?'

'If you want me to.'

She nodded. 'I ... I must go now,' she said, looking down. 'But please, make yourself at home. My maid ... my maid will see to you.' Then, with one final glance at him, she turned and left the room.

And after, as she lay on her bed, thinking back on what had happened, she saw him differently: saw not the man nor the creature of her dreams, but the two transposed, inextricably mixed. And knew, with a sudden certainty that surprised her, that she wanted him.

Three hours had passed. Kim sat there in the Marshal's study, listening to her talk.

Jelka was standing on the far side of the room, beside the huge window wall, staring out into the artificial depths of the past and recreated country of Kalevala, a wistfulness in her face that seemed to mirror the light in that other land. And as she talked, he leaned in towards her, entranced, hanging on her every word.

'You can't help yourself, that's the worst of it. It's like a constant betrayal of yourself. You feel nothing, and yet you go on smiling, talking, laughing, all to fill the vacuum, to mask the nothingness you're feeling.' She glanced at him. 'At least, that's how it was.' She laughed, showing her perfect teeth, her chin slightly raised.

Kim, watching her, caught his breath, pained by the beauty of that one small movement. She was like something from a dream; so tall and straight and lovely.

'As for the rest of them, they don't even seem to notice how things are. It's as if they're dead to it all. I mean, perhaps they really can't tell the difference between this and real life. I don't know ...' She shrugged, her eyes suddenly pained, 'But it seems to me that there's a falseness, an intrinsic flaw in them. It's as if the City's swallowed them. Eaten them up, souls and all. And yet they seem happy with that. It's as if they really don't need anything more.'

She turned, facing him, a fierce determination in her eyes. 'That's how it is here, Kim. Like a living death. Yet when I saw you I knew at once that you were different.' She shivered, the intensity of her words forcing her face into a grimace of pain. 'Do you understand what I'm saying? It's not your size. It's not even what you do – that talent that my father values so highly. It's *you*. You're different from the rest. And I want that. I want it so much it hurts.'

She looked away, her eyes releasing him. But her words had seared him. He looked down at his trembling hands, then answered her.

'You have it,' he said, meeting her eyes. 'All of it.' He laughed strangely. 'I think I wanted you from the first moment I saw you. Your eyes ...'

She turned, surprised. 'Then it wasn't just me? You felt that, too?'

'Yes ...' He was silent a moment, then, quietly. 'I love you, Jelka Tolonen. I have done from the first.'

'You *love* me?' She laughed, surprised. 'You know, I thought all that was done with. That nothing would ever touch me again. I thought ...'

Again she shivered, but this time she came across and knelt beside him, taking his hands.

'You see, I wasn't expecting anything. I didn't think that anything more could happen to me. There was the engagement to Hans Ebert, of course, but, well, it was as if I was living inside a kind of shell, in a magic theatre where things only seemed to happen, and nothing real ever took place. I thought that that was all there was ever going to be. And then I saw you ...'

He turned, meeting her eyes. It was like looking into the sky. He could sense the depths of blackness beyond the blue and remembered suddenly his vision – of that great web of brightness spinning out through the surface of her eyes into the darkness beyond.

'And your father?'

Her eyes moved away, then came back again. 'Papa ... ?' She shook her head, real anguish behind the tiny movement. 'He's a darling really. I just can't tell you ...'

He nodded. He had seen for himself how Tolonen doted on his daughter. 'And yet?'

'Well, it's just that he can't see that there's a difference. To him it's all politics. Deals. Who's in and who's out. And death underpinning everything. I love him, but ...'

He saw just how much that 'but' had cost her and touched a finger to her lips to prevent her from saying more. She smiled, grateful to him, and gently, tenderly kissed his fingers. It was the prelude to a proper kiss. Their first. He broke from it, surprised, his eyes wide, seeing his own astonishment mirrored in the perfect blue-black of her pupils.

'You're beautiful,' she said, her fingers touching his cheek. 'So dark and perfect.'

He laughed softly. 'And you're mad. Utterly mad.'

She nodded, but her eyes were filled with that same fierce determination he had witnessed earlier. 'Maybe. But I'd fight the whole Above to have you.'

The two men stood before the unmarked door, waiting to be admitted. Soucek turned, reading the plaque on the wall nearby. 'Level One Hundred And Eighty-Six' it read; 'North 2 Stack, Canton of Düsseldorf'. He looked about him, trying to get some clue as to what they were doing, why they were here, but there was nothing. This far up the levels the Seven were still firmly in control. Things were neat and tidy. As if the chaos of the Lowers were a dream and nothing else but this existed.

For a moment Soucek stared past his feet, trying to picture the levels stacked up beneath him, layer above layer; to imagine all those people – young and old, Han and *Hung Mao* – eking out their lives in the packed and degenerating strata of the City. Narrow, blighted, desperate lives. He had not really thought of it before, not until he had begun to travel between the levels on Lehmann's business, but now he could not shake it from his mind. He had seen the City from outside; had gone up the levels and seen what existed up Above, and knew – with a certainty he had never had before – that it was wrong. There had to be a better way.

He looked back at Lehmann, seeing how patiently he waited; how he held the flask loosely in one hand, as if it contained nothing of value. And yet three men had died, not counting the woman and her child, to get what it held.

Soucek shuddered, remembering. But just then the door hissed back, and a tiny, boyish-looking Han in a black, ersilk *pau* stepped through. He smiled, offering both hands in greeting to Lehmann. Tiny, golden hands that were like the hands of a mechanical toy. His head was shaven, a faint purse-like scar just behind and beneath his right ear revealing that he had been wired. He wore a sweet, aromatic perfume, but beneath it one could discern the strong scent of chemicals.

'Feng Lu-ma,' Lehmann said, acknowledging the man, but he ignored the offered hands.

The Han shrugged, then moved past them, looking up and down the corridor before he ushered them inside.

'You're early,' Feng said, toying nervously with the tiny lenses that hung like a necklace of delicate glass pendants about his neck and shoulders. 'I didn't expect you until four.'

He led them down a narrow, unlit passageway and out into a bright, crowded workshop. The walls were covered with row upon row of tiny translucent box files, while the nearby worktops were cluttered with dissecting instruments and culture dishes, stacks of slender ice-covered folders and strange, spiderish-looking machines. Four young Han – thin-faced, malnourished-looking youths – glanced up from behind their high desks on the far side of the room as they entered, then quickly returned to their work; delicate, silvered instruments flashing between their fingers. There was the sharp, almost tart odour of chemicals; the original of the scent that lay beneath Feng's perfume. Moreover, it was cold; surprisingly so after the warmth of the corridors outside, but that was to be expected. Soucek looked about him, taking it all in, surprised to find this here. Before now he had only been guessing, but now he knew. It was a lens shop.

He turned, looking at Lehmann, seeking something more – some final piece to the puzzle. On the surface of things it made no sense coming all the way up here to a lens shop. No, if Lehmann had wanted a lens shop there were plenty beneath the Net who would do as good a job and ask only a tenth of what they charged at this level, so why come here? But even as he asked himself he began to understand. It was of a piece with the murders. Lehmann had gone to inordinate lengths in selecting his victims. He had read the files Lehmann had handed him. Besides the physical match, Lehmann had gone out of his way to ensure that all of them, even the married technician, had been without complicating family connections. That meant, of course, that there was no one to mourn their deaths. No one to ask awkward questions. After which, it had been simplicity itself to bribe an official and falsify the public record – to make it seem as though the men were still alive.

Which, of course, was necessary if Lehmann were to use their eyes. For no matter how good a copy might be made of their retinas, no one – no, not even a Plantation Guard – would pass a dead man through a checkpoint.

Anonymity, that was what Lehmann sought. That was why he had chosen his victims so carefully; why he had come here rather than trust to the dubious 'confidence' of one of the Net shops. Yes, he had heard tales of how certain tong bosses had bought information about their rivals, then had them tracked and trapped.

But Lehmann was too clever to have that happen. That was why the official at the public record office had subsequently had his throat cut; why his colleagues had been pacified by an anonymous 'sweetener'.

He watched as Lehmann haggled with the man, then handed over four large denomination credit chips and the flask. The Han took the flask round to the other side of the nearest worktop and sat, unscrewing the lid and tipping the frozen eyes out into a sterilised cold dish. He poked at them delicately with his tiny, golden fingers, lifting each in turn and studying it beneath the light. Then, satisfied, he looked back at Lehmann.

'These are fine. There's two, three per cent damage at most. Certainly nothing I can't repair. You haven't, by any chance, the original retinal mappings?'

Lehmann took the copy files from the inner pocket of his tunic and handed them across. All references to names and whereabouts had been removed. Again, Lehmann had taken great care not to let the lensman know any more than he had to.

Soucek saw how the man's eyes narrowed, scanning the files, noting the erasures, then returned to Lehmann. 'I should charge you more.'

Lehmann stared at him impassively. 'I can take them elsewhere if you wish, Feng Lu-ma. To Yellow Tan, perhaps. Or your friend, Mai Li-wen. Maybe I should ...'

The Han studied Lehmann a moment longer, then looked down. 'When do you need them by?'

'Tomorrow.'

There was a moment's pause, then. 'All right. You'll come yourself?'

'No. My man here will come.'

'But you ought ...'

Lehmann leaned across the worktop threateningly. 'I know what I ought to do, *Shih* Feng, but I'm a busy man. Besides, I've worn lenses before. I don't need your help to fit them. You just do your job and everything will be fine, neh?'

The Han stared at him thoughtfully, then nodded. 'Tomorrow, then. After ten.'

But Soucek, watching him, could feel the weight of curiosity at the back of the man's words and knew – without needing to be told – that he would have to kill the man.

Bryn Kustow stood there in the doorway of the crowded club, looking about him anxiously as customers elbowed past. It was dangerous this far down the levels and normally he wouldn't have come here alone, but just now things weren't normal. Michael was down here somewhere.

Kustow squinted, trying to make out faces in that long, ill-lit room, but it was hard. The Blinded Eye was packed tonight, the noise from the big speakers in the corners deafening. *Ta*, it was – 'beat'; a stripped-down form of Han folk music, amplified heavily; the music of these parts. Kustow stood there, grimacing against the sound, searching the crowded tables for a face he knew, but they were mainly Han here. Ugly little bastards, too. *Tong* runners and minor criminals, for sure. As he craned his neck, a big, pug-nosed Han planted himself directly in front of him.

'What you want, fuck face?'

'A friend,' he shouted back, keeping his tone measured. 'I'm looking for a friend. A big guy. Short blond hair.'

The man glared at him a moment then turned, pointing across the room. On the far side of the bar a light flickered fitfully. Beneath it, at a packed gaming table, a tall Hung Mao was slumped across the table, face down. To either side of him, eager Han faces watched the dice fall and tumble across the baize, ignoring him.

Kustow felt his stomach tighten. Was it Michael? And if it was, was he all right? He reached in his pocket and took out a ten *yuan* chip, pressing it into the big man's hand, not certain it was the right thing to do down here. But it seemed it was. With a glance at the ten-piece, the man stood back, letting him pass.

'Over there,' he said again, as if Kustow hadn't taken it in first time. 'Take the fucker home, neh? Before he gets his throat cut.'

Kustow made a tiny bow, then, pushing through the crowd, made his way across. As he came out in front of the table, another Han, smaller yet more vicious-looking than the last, barred his way.

'What you want?' he shouted against the wall of sound.

Behind the thin-featured Han the gaming had stopped. A dozen Han faces were watching Kustow coldly.

'My friend,' Kustow shouted back, indicating the slumped figure of Michael Lever. 'I've come to take him home.'

The Han shook his head. 'Your friend owe money. Five hundred *yuan*. You pay or he stay.'

Kustow looked about him, trying to read the situation. Was it true? Had Michael lost that much to them? Or was the Han trying it on?

'You have his paper?' he yelled back, meeting the Han's eyes once again.

The Han sneered. 'What fucking paper? He owe me money. You pay or you fuck off!'

Kustow took a long breath. Five hundred. He had it on him. Twice that, in fact. But it wouldn't do to let them know that. He felt in his pocket, separating out three of the big fifties and three tens.

'I can give you one-eighty. It's all I have. But I can give you my note for the rest, if that's okay?'

The Han hesitated, eyeing him suspiciously, then nodded. 'Okay. But get him out of here right now. And don't come back. Not if you know what's good for you!'

Forty minutes later and a hundred levels up, Kustow held Michael Lever steady as he leaned over the sink, heaving. Michael's hair was wet where Kustow had held his head beneath the flow, but the two tablets he'd forced down his throat were beginning to take effect.

Michael turned his head slightly, looking back at his friend. 'I'm sorry, Bryn. I ...'

Kustow shook his head. 'It doesn't matter. Really it doesn't. But what the fuck were you doing down there? You could have been killed.'

Michael turned back, staring down into the bowl again. 'Maybe that would have been for the best.'

'Don't say that. It's not true.'

'No?' There was a strange movement in Michael's mouth and then his whole face creased in pain. 'It's finished, Bryn! It's all gone fucking wrong!'

'No, Michael. No. There's the Movement, remember? And there's Mary ...'

Michael shook his head. 'She's gone. I got her note.'

'No, Michael. You're wrong. She wants you. She told me so. The note ... it was a mistake. She didn't understand what had happened.'

Michael snorted. 'She understands all right! I'm washed up! A failure! And my father hates me!' He shuddered violently. 'There's *nothing*, Bryn! Nothing!'

Kustow gripped his shoulders firmly. 'You're wrong. You don't know how wrong. She needs you, even if the old man doesn't. And I need you, too, you silly bastard. Don't you understand that?'

Michael turned, looking up at him uncertainly. 'She *needs* me? Are you sure about that? What did she say?'

'She loves you, Michael. Don't you understand that? She loves you. So stop all this belly-aching and go to her. And for fuck's sake do it, before you end up dead in some clapped-out, five-piece drinking den!'

Michael stared at him. 'Do what?'

Kustow stared back at him a moment, then laughed, surprised at his naïvety. 'Why, marry her, of course. Marry her. Now, before it's too late.'

'*Marry* her?' Michael laughed sourly and shook his head. He shivered, then, straightening up, pushed away from the sink. Kustow tried to stop him, but, breaking free of his friend's grip, Michael stumbled towards the door. For a moment he stood there, his forehead pressed against the door's surface, then he turned back, swaying unsteadily, meeting Kustow's eyes.

'Look, I know you mean well, but just leave me alone, Bryn, understand? Just fucking leave me alone!'

CHAPTER 86

MONSTERS OF THE DEEP

The sweeper paused, leaning on his broom, staring across at the scene outside Hsiang Tian's Golden Emporium. Black dog banners were everywhere one looked, the triangular silks fluttering gently in the false wind generated by the big fans sited above the storefront. There was a low buzz of expectation and then the crowd began to move back, Triad runners pushing them back from the front of the store. There was a moment's angry jostling and then the crowd settled again, watching as Whiskers Lu strode out, his stylishly-cut black silks glistening in the bright overhead lights.

Lu Ming-shao was a big, exceedingly ugly man, with a melted, misshapen face and an air of uncouth brutality. He spat, then turned, summoning Hsiang Tian from within. Hsiang came, his head lowered, ingratiating himself, yet uncomfortable all the same.

'Bring them out,' Lu Ming-shao ordered, his rough voice booming. 'The four I liked best. I want to see them out here, in the light.'

Hsiang turned, snapping his fingers. At once there was hurried movement within. A moment later the first of the sedans emerged, a long, sleek model with delicate satin coverings, carved, dragon-head lamps and a high-backed 'wooden' chair, designed to seat two; a *tien feng*, or 'Heaven's Wind'. It was carried by six of the Emporium's runners, their dark mauve one-pieces emblazoned front and back with the bright red pictogram, a box within a box, 'Hsiang', and their status number. Setting the sedan down close to

Whiskers Lu, they knelt, heads bowed, waiting patiently while he mounted the chair and settled his huge bulk across both seats. Then, at Hsiang's signal, they lifted slowly, taking the sedan in a slow, smooth circle.

Whipped up by the Triad runners, the crowd yelled and cheered, genuinely enjoying the sight, but when Whiskers Lu stepped down, it was with a curt shake of his head.

'Next!' he barked, turning his back on Hsiang.

There was a further commotion inside, and then the second sedan appeared. This was a bigger, seemingly more substantial model; an eight-man *yu ko*, or 'Jade Barge'. Broader and squatter than the previous model, Lu Ming-shao looked less out of place in its huge, throne-like chair. What's more, the extended canopy, with its blood-red ersilk covering, gave the whole thing a slightly regal appearance, reminiscent of the state carriages of the Minor Families. Even so, when Whiskers Lu stepped down again, it was with an expression of distaste.

Seeing that look, Hsiang turned quickly, summoning the next sedan. As it came out under the bright exterior lights, the sweeper made his way across and, pushing his way through the fringes of the crowd, stood near the front of the press, close to the line of runners, watching as Lu Ming-shao mounted the sedan.

He had heard many tales of Whiskers Lu, of his legendary fearlessness, of his heartlessness and casual brutality, but his eyes saw something else. Whatever Whiskers Lu might once have been, he was no longer the man of legend. Sharpness had given way to self-indulgence, brutishness to a kind of uncultured hedonism. Oh, there was no doubting that Lu Ming-shao was a big, fearsome-looking, monster of a man, and not one casually to make an enemy of, yet those special qualities that had made him a 489 – that had allowed him to wrest power from the hands of his deadliest rivals – were phantoms now. He saw how Whiskers Lu looked about him, aware not of the possible danger from the crowd – the ever-present danger of assassination – but of the impression he was making on them. He noted the big, expensive rings the man wore, the elegant First Level fashions, and understood. Three years of unopposed leadership had changed Lu Ming-shao. Had made him soft. Worse, they had made him vain.

As he watched, Whiskers Lu climbed up into the wide, deeply-cushioned seat and settled back amongst the padded silk. Yes, only a fool paraded himself this way before the *hsiao jen*, the 'little men'. Only a fool closed his eyes, relaxing, when an assassin's bullet lay only a fraction of a second from his heart.

Lehmann turned, then made his way back through the throng, satisfied. He had seen enough. It would be easy to take Whiskers Lu. Easier than he'd anticipated. But it was best not to be too cock-sure. Best to plan it properly and make sure the odds were wholly in his favour.

Returning to his cart, Lehmann folded down the handle of his broom and fixed it to the two clips on the side. Then, for all the world like a common sweeper going off shift, he swung his cart in a sharp half-circle and began to push slowly towards the side corridor, making for the down transit.

The nurse handed Jelka back her pass and came round the desk. Behind her, in the glass-fronted booth that over-looked the spacious reception area, the clinic's security guard relaxed, returning to his game of chess.

'Is he expecting you?'

Jelka smiled. 'No. But I think he'll be pleased to see me.'

'Well, follow me. He's awake, but he may be working.'

'Working?'

The nurse laughed. 'He never stops. The morning after the operation he was sitting up, looking at files. But we've kept him from using the input as yet. It takes a while for the implant to take, even with the latest drugs.'

Jelka gave a vague nod, frowning. It sounded horrible. Behind her, her bodyguard, Zdenek, looked about him, ill at ease without his gun. Only Jelka's strongest pleas had made him agree to come in here.

'Were there any problems?'

'No. It's a standard enough operation, these days. More than three million last year. But he has to rest. Otherwise he'll be back in here with an embolism. And that would be *very* serious.'

'Ah ...' But Jelka was far from reassured.

'He's a friend of yours?'

It was none of her business, but Jelka answered her anyway, aware that Zdenek was listening, and that whatever the bodyguard heard would be reported back to her father. 'He works for my father. And for Li Yuan.'

The nurse glanced at her, her eyes widening, then nodded. 'Ah, so that's why he's here.' She laughed. 'I thought it was strange.'

They came to the end of the corridor and turned left. At the second door the nurse stopped and tapped out a code on the panel beside the door. A screen lit up at once, showing an overhead image of a patient in a bed. It was Kim. Leaning forward slightly, the nurse spoke into the grill.

'Shih Ward, you have a visitor. Jelka Tolonen. Will you see her?'

Kim smiled broadly, looking up at the camera. 'Of course. Please ... show her in.'

As the door slid back, the nurse stood aside, letting Jelka go inside. Zdenek made to follow, but Jelka turned, facing him. 'Please, Zdenek, stay here. I'll be ten minutes, that's all.'

He hesitated, then shook his head. 'I'm sorry, Nu shi Tolonen, but your father would have me court-martialled if I did. My orders are never to leave you alone.' He paused, clearly embarrassed at having to be so heavy-handed. 'You understand why ...'

She was quiet a moment, then turned to the nurse again. 'Have you an audio unit? Just the earphones.'

The nurse hesitated, then nodded. 'You want me to get a pair?'

Jelka nodded, then turned back, smiling at Kim. 'I'm sorry. This won't take a moment.'

He smiled, drinking in the sight of her. 'That's all right. It's really nice to see you. How did you know I was here?'

She glanced at Zdenek, then smiled broadly. 'I'll tell you ... in a moment.'

The nurse returned, handing Jelka the headphones and a small tape machine; an under-ear sling. Jelka handed it to Zdenek. 'Will you wear this for me?'

The big man looked at the earphones and laughed, relenting. 'Okay. But when your father asks me I want to be able to tell him something. All right?'

She smiled and leaned forward, pecking his cheek. 'I'll make something up. Okay?'

Zdenek nodded, then went to sit in the far corner, the earphones balanced awkwardly on his large, close-shaven head. Satisfied, Jelka went across. She pulled out a chair, sitting beside the bed, her back to the guard.

Kim was sitting up in bed. The comset he'd been working on was pushed aside on top of the bedclothes. He leaned forward, intending to kiss her, but she made the smallest movement of her head.

'What's the matter?' he asked quietly, then looked past her at the guard.

'Is this your father's idea?'

'He thinks it's necessary when I travel.'

'And you?'

She nodded. 'They've made three attempts on my life already. It's unlikely they'll stop now. They can get at him through me. That's why it's best to take no chances.'

'I see.' But it was clear that he hadn't realised before how tightly circumscribed her life was.

She smiled, her mood brightening. 'Anyway. How are you?'

He looked past her, then met her eyes again, smiling. 'I'm fine. It's still sore, and the headaches are bad, especially at night, but they say it's healing well.'

She leaned closer, looking at the silvered stud that jutted from the flesh beneath his ear. The skin surrounding it was red and chafed, but the single, thread-thin scar above it looked good. Even so, the thought of the implant made her feel queasy. She had never been happy about her father's, and though he had had it long before she was born, it still seemed unnatural. More so than his artificial arm.

'Well?' he asked softly.

She drew back her head and looked at him. The uncertainty in his voice was clear. He hadn't been sure how she would take it. After all, he hadn't even told her he was going to have it done.

'You *need* this?'

He looked at her intently a moment, then nodded. 'It'll make my work much easier.'

She looked at the silvered stud again. 'It's a neat job.'

'The best. Li Yuan's own surgeon.'

'Then I'm glad. Really I am.' She hesitated, then looked down. 'Your work ... it means a lot to you, doesn't it?'

He was quiet, watching her.

'No ... I mean, I know it does. My father said. But more than that, I can see it in you. It's what you are. You can't separate yourself off from it.'

'And you don't mind?'

She met his eyes. 'No. Why should I? It's what you are. It's what makes you what you are. I can see that.'

'Can you?' He watched her a moment, then nodded. 'Yes. I can see you can.'

They were silent a moment, then she reached out and took his hand. 'I understand. I ...' She lifted her shoulders slightly, looking away from him, then met his eyes again. 'It's like my father, I suppose. He loves me, fiercely, almost possessively, but there's more to him than that. He *has* to do what he does. When he was exiled – when he couldn't be General any more – it was like he was dead. Or like a shell, paper-thin, the mere pretence of a man. Seeing him like that made me understand. Like you, he is what he does. The two things are inseparable. Without it ... well, maybe he would be less of a man than he is. And maybe I'd love him less than I do.'

'Maybe,' he answered, his eyes watching her carefully, a strange tenderness in their depths. 'And you?'

She laughed and sat back, cradling his hand now in both of hers. 'Me?'

'Yes, *you*. Isn't there something *you* want to do? Some part of you that needs something more?'

She shook her head slowly, squeezing his hand between her own, her face suddenly more serious. 'No. There's nothing I want to do.'

'Nothing?'

She smiled. 'No. I've already found what I want.'

From his seat in the corner Zdenek watched everything. Jelka had her back to him so he could see nothing of what passed on her face, but he could see the Clayborn, Ward, clearly. He saw how the child-man smiled, and looked down, disturbed, knowing he would have to tell what he had seen.

And then?

He felt sorry for Jelka. This would hurt her. Badly, perhaps. But it was necessary. Her father would end this thing, for there was no way she could marry Ward, and a mistake here might spoil her chance of marrying well elsewhere. Besides, Ward was Clayborn, and Clay was Clay, it could not be raised.

And Jelka? He watched the back of her head, seeing how the overhead light caught in the golden strands of her hair. For a moment he was distracted by it, then, smiling, he looked down at his big, ugly hands. Jelka Tolonen was something special. Something high and fine and ... well, above Ward, anyway. Far, far above him.

'Well? What should we do?'

Tsu Ma turned, facing his cousins, his broad, manly figure framed in the moon door. Beyond him, through the broad circle of the entrance, the sun lit up the western garden. 'To be frank with you, Yuan, I think we should dig much deeper. Find out where the brain came from, and who designed it. What Tolonen says makes sense. We should send Karr out to Mars again. Have him turn the Colony inside out until he finds what's going on out there. This ...' he shook his head, 'this frightens me, Yuan. The fakes that came in to kill your brother, they were bad enough, but these!'

'I agree,' said Wu Shih. 'Tolonen's findings are the most significant thing to have come to our notice these past twelve months. To think that they were that close to developing and using these things. It only goes to prove how right our forefathers were in clamping down on research into these areas. Indeed, it makes me have second thoughts about our plans. We must be careful how we change the Edict. Careful what we permit within our Cities.'

Li Yuan looked from one to the other, then nodded. 'Then we are agreed. We will keep this to ourselves. As for Karr, I will think the matter through. Just now he is doing important work for me, keeping an eye on what is happening down below. But that may have to wait. As you say, Cousin Ma, we must find out where these things came from, and it may well be that Karr alone can do that for us.'

They walked on slowly, following the path towards the lake.

'And this evening?' Wu Shih asked quietly. 'Shall we still go ahead, as planned?'

Tsu Ma looked up, meeting his eyes. 'Our path is set. The announcement must be made. Even this cannot alter that.'

'Maybe so,' said Li Yuan sombrely, 'but I have slept badly since learning of these things. It is as if we are being warned.' He sighed, then stopped, turning to face his fellow T'ang, the great expanse of the lake behind him. 'Our ancestors argued that there could be no compromise with Change. So we were taught to believe, from the cradle on. Yet now we seek to make a deal with Change. To let it run, like a fish on a line. But what if the line breaks? What if we lose control?'

'There is no option,' Tsu Ma answered bluntly. 'You know that, Yuan. If we falter now we are lost. A deal must be made. Something given, something taken back. No one said it would be easy. But that is why we are T'ang.

To make such decisions and carry them through. And to face the problems as they arise. It is our great task, and I, for one, will not shirk from it.'

Wu Shih reached out, touching his arm. 'We did not say you would, cousin. I am merely thinking that perhaps we ought to delay a while – to give us time to find out more about this other matter – before we announce the reopening of the House.'

'And if we did?' Tsu Ma shook his head. 'No, cousin. Too many people know of this already. Ministers and their assistants. Representatives and leading businessmen. To delay would have them question our determination. It would cause more problems than it would solve. No. Our path is set. We must grasp the reins and hold on for dear life!'

'So it is,' Li Yuan said, acknowledging the truth of what Tsu Ma had said. Yet in the last day his reluctance had taken on a clear and solid form. It was as he'd said. Tolonen's discovery was like a warning. A sign of things to come. The steps they were about to take – the changes to the Edict and the reopening of the House – were irrevocable. And whilst they might think they knew what would transpire, there was nothing in past experience to say for certain what would happen. From here on the future was unknowable, like a page from an unread book.

Once before the world had fallen into chaos.

He shuddered and turned away, staring out across the ancient lake towards the orchard. And as he looked, the image of a sprig of white blossom snagged in the darkness of his memory, then blew away, turning, turning in the wind.

'And that's all you heard?'

When Zdenek nodded, Tolonen sat back, his left hand placed flat against the desk, his right rubbing at his neck, metal against flesh. There was no doubt that Zdenek's report had disturbed him, but the old man's response was not quite what the bodyguard had anticipated. For a while he simply sat there, his granite-like face clouded, uncertain. Then, sniffing deeply, he shook his head.

'I don't know. I simply don't know.'

There was a kind of precedent, of course. Once before Tolonen had interfered directly in his daughter's life. Then he had tried to marry her – against her will – to Klaus Ebert's son, the traitor, Hans. The old man had been wrong, and he knew it, but was that what was affecting him now? Or did he hesitate for another reason? After all, it seemed he rather liked the young man, Clayborn or no. Admired him – forasmuch as he could admire some-one who wasn't a soldier. But was that important when the question was one of marriage to his daughter?

'You will keep this to yourself.'

It was command, not question. Zdenek bowed his head curtly, coming to attention again.

'Shall I continue to watch them, sir?'

Again Tolonen seemed in two minds. A bodyguard was necessary in these troubled times, but he had not foreseen the need for a chaperone. Zdenek had his own thoughts on the matter, but kept them to himself. It would have been impertinent of him to say more than he had already.

Tolonen was frowning, his top teeth pulling at his lower lip. Then, as if the indecision were too much for him, he stood and came round the desk, stopping an arm's length from where Zdenek stood, looking at him steadily.

'You will do as you have done in the past and no more. Understand?'

Zdenek parted his lips, as if to speak, then gave a curt nod. Tolonen was silent a moment, then spoke again, his voice softer than before.

'I'll admit that what you say makes me ... uneasy. If her aunt were living still ...'

Tolonen's voice trailed off. He turned away abruptly, going back round his desk. Seated again, he looked up at Zdenek.

'All right. That's all. And Zdenek ... thank you.'

Alone again, Tolonen went and stood by the viewing wall, thinking things through. For a while he stared sightlessly away through the artificial land-scape of trees and mountains, then turned and went back to his desk, his decision made. This time he would be subtler. Yes, he would let time be the cure of this.

Leaning forward, he spoke into the intercom, summoning his private secretary. The young equerry came into the room a moment later, coming to attention in the doorway, his head bowed.

'General?'

'Come in, lad. Close the door and come over. I want to ask you some-thing.'

The young soldier hesitated, then did as he was told, surprised by the unusually personal tone in the General's voice. 'Sir?'

Tolonen smiled, indicating that he should take a chair. 'At ease, lad. I need to pick your brains.'

The equerry drew up a chair and sat. It was the first time in eight months' service with Tolonen that he had done so, and he sat up straight, as if at attention, his head held rigid.

'You come from a good family, Hauser,' Tolonen began, smiling warmly at the young soldier. 'Your uncle was a Major, was he not?'

The equerry nodded, then found his voice. 'In the colonies, sir. And the mining satellites.'

'And your eldest brother ... he's there now, isn't he?'

'Yes, sir. On a five year tour of duty.'

'And does he like it out there?'

The young soldier smiled for the first time, relaxing. 'He loves it, sir. Says it's beautiful out there.'

Tolonen sat back, studying his equerry with some care. The young man sat up even stiffer than before, conscious of the Marshal's eyes on him.

'Have you ever thought of a colonies posting?'

The equerry looked down, his tongue touching his top teeth momentarily; a gesture Tolonen had noticed before.

'Well, lad?' he coaxed, more gently than before.

The young soldier met his eyes. 'I do what is asked of me, sir. But ... well, yes, I would welcome such a posting if the opportunity arose.'

'And if it arose now?'

The young man allowed himself a smile. 'Now, sir?'

Tolonen laughed. 'Let me explain ...'

It was cold in the Dissecting Room, colder than Maryland in January, yet Old Man Lever stood there, bare-headed and without a jacket, staring down at the row of corpses laid out on the long slab. Nearby, Curval, the Chief Geneticist, stood watching him. The two men were alone in the room, the investigation team dismissed for the moment while the Old Man saw things for himself.

'What went wrong?' he asked, turning to meet Curval's eyes.

'We're not sure,' Curval answered, looking past Lever at the eleven shaven-headed bodies. 'It seems like some kind of virus, but we're not certain.'

Lever licked drily at his lips. 'Why not?'

Curval shifted awkwardly. 'Because it might not be that. All of the corpses show traces of the thing, but the virus itself doesn't seem harmful. My personal belief is that it's a long-term side-effect of the drug treatment. But we'll know that for sure as soon as we've tested a few of the living immortals.'

Immortals ... Old Man Lever shuddered and turned back, staring down into the blank face of one of the dead. There had been deaths before, of course, mainly from accidents, but nothing on the scale of this. No. Once this got out ...

'Does anybody know? I mean, apart from the staff here?'

Curval nodded. 'I'm afraid so. The clause in the original contracts allowed us to bring all the bodies back here – for tests – but there's been trouble with some of the relatives. I got a team onto it at once, but it looks like a group of them are going to go public, tonight at ten.'

Curval waited, tensed inside, for the Old Man to explode with anger, but there was nothing. Lever simply stood there, as if in shock, staring down at the nearest corpse.

'There's no choice, then,' he said, after a moment. 'We have to go public before they do.'

'Is that wise? I mean, what will we say?'

'That the treatment is a failure. And that we're working on something new. Something better. Something that we've just invested a further ten billion yuan into.'

Curval blinked. 'We've got new sponsors?'

Lever shook his head. 'No. The money will come direct from ImmVac. At the same time we'll be making substantial payments to all those on the present programme to ensure that they receive the best medical treatment possible in the coming days.'

Curval bowed his head. 'I see.'

So the rumour was true: some of the major sponsors had pulled out. If news of that broke at the same time as this then the Project was as good as dead. And even if it survived, it would be the object of wide-scale public derision. Faced with that possibility, Old Man Lever was willing to double the stakes and risk all on a further throw of the dice. To make a brave face of it and ride out the present storm, hoping to limit the damage.

And who knew? – it might even work.

Curval looked up again, meeting the Old Man's eyes. 'So what do you want me to do?'

'I want some kind of research outline. Something that'll sound impressive. And I want some visuals of our best men at work in the labs. You know the kind of thing.'

Curval nodded. 'And the boy? Ward?'

Lever stared back at him, eyes narrowed. 'Offer him what he wants. *Whatever* he wants. But get him.'

When Curval had gone, Lever walked slowly up the line, then back, stopping beside the last of the corpses, that of a fifty-seven-year-old woman.

For a long time he stared down at her, at the cold, pale shape of her, unable to take in what had happened. Her name was Leena Spence and she had been one of the first of his 'immortals'. He had slept with her once or twice, before she'd had the treatment, but lately, tied up in the business of the Institute, he had seen little of her.

And now it was too late.

He shivered, the cold beginning to get to him at last. So this was death. *This.* He swallowed, then leaned closer, studying the fine blue tracery of lines that covered the pale, smooth flesh of her skull like the hand-drawn pictograms in an old Han notebook.

He reached out, running his fingers over the faint blue lines, as if to gauge the mystery of it, but it was like a map he could not read of a country he did not know. Queequeg's back, Curval had called it once, for some reason, and that came back to Lever now, making him frown then shake his head, as if to deny what had happened here. But they were dead. His immortals were dead. Eight yesterday, a further five today, like machines being switched off one by one.

A virus, Curval had said. But what kind of virus? Something harmless. Harmless and yet deadly. If that *was* what had done this.

Old Man Lever drew his hand back, shuddering, then turned and walked swiftly away, rehearsing words and phrases in his head, beginning at once upon the task that lay ahead.

Ross lay on the narrow bed, reading, files scattered all about him. Nearby, at the table, Milne was hunched over his comset, working through the transcripts of the interviews they had done that morning.

The stay-over was a small, spartanly furnished room that had cost them ten *yuan* for the week. Not that they planned to stay a week. No. For with what they'd got that morning, they could probably wrap things up by that evening.

They had tracked down more than thirty of the former inhabitants of Mary Jennings' 'birth-deck', including a midwife who had worked there more than forty years. Not one of them had any knowledge of the girl. That, in itself, might not have been conclusive. There were between five and ten thousand people in an average deck, and it was possible – just possible – that their sample was insufficient. But the results of the facial identification check had confirmed what they had suspected all along. Mary Jennings was a fake. In reality she was Emily Ascher. A European.

'Listen to this,' Ross said, sitting up, then turning to face his partner. 'It seems that her father was involved in some kind of scandal. He was an official in the *Hu Pu*, the Finance Ministry. It looks like he made some kind of cock-up on the interest rates. There was a Hearing and he was kicked out. The family fell. One hundred and twenty levels. Six months on, the father was dead. The mother had to cope with the child on her own.'

Milne looked down. 'How old was she?'

'Nine, I think.'

'Then maybe that's why.'

Ross frowned. 'Why what? I don't follow you.'

'Why she became a terrorist.'

Ross laughed. 'Are you serious, Mike? I mean, what evidence have we got?'

'Instinct,' Milne said, glancing at him nervily. 'I've been thinking about it. She's not your usual kind of sleeper. I mean, she's a woman for a start. And most industrial espionage is short-term. The sleeper gets in, does his job and gets out – as quick as possible. They're in a year at most. I've not known one to be in there as long as her. And then there's the background. Maintenance and economics. The combination fits the profile. Remember that report we read about the make-up of the *Ping Tiao*. I reckon that's what she was. *Ping Tiao*. The timing fits, too. She vanished only weeks after

Bremen. And then here she is, over here, in the Levers' employ. There has to be a reason for that.'

'Coincidence,' Ross said, putting his feet down onto the floor. 'For a start the Ping Tiao had no foothold over here. Besides, it would take real clout to destroy a deck and all its records.'

Milne shook his head. 'I think the fire was genuine. An accident. But someone took advantage of it. Someone with Security training, perhaps. And a lot of influence.'

Ross's eyes slowly widened. 'You mean DeVore, don't you?'

'They say he was working with them at the end. So why not this? It's the kind of thing he was good at.'

'But why? What's his motive?'

'I don't know. Just that it all fits. Her background. The timing. The nature of the deception. And it makes sense, too, of the spare ID of Rachel DeValerian. I think she was put in as a terrorist sleeper. Biding her time. Waiting to set up over here, when the time was right.'

Ross was quiet a moment, considering things, then he nodded. 'It would certainly make sense of why she left Old Man Lever to join up with the son. That was bothering me. But if DeVore put her in over here ...' He laughed. 'Hey. Maybe you're onto something.'

'Then maybe we should get it all written up and get back to Richmond straight away.'

Ross looked down. 'You think we should take this to Lever, then?'

'Why, who were you thinking of?'

'Wu Shih, perhaps?'

Milne laughed uneasily, but before he could answer there was a faint rapping at the door.

Ross looked at Milne tensely, then stood. Drawing his gun he crossed to the door.

'Who is it?'

'Room service!'

Ross glanced at his partner. *Did you order room service?* he mouthed.

Milne shook his head, then stood, drawing his own gun.

Ready? Ross mouthed. Milne nodded. Moving to the side, Ross reached out and thumbed the door-lock. As the door irised back, a tall Han stepped into the room, carrying a fully-laden tray, covered in a cloth.

'Compliments of the management,' he said, setting the tray down on the bedside table, then turned, a look of surprise and shock coming into his eyes as he saw the drawn guns. '*Ch'un tzu?*'

Ross looked to Milne then back at the Han. Only then did he lower his gun and, with a faint, embarrassed laugh, went across and lifted the cloth from the tray. There were six bowls of steaming food.

'I'm sorry,' he said, turning back and meeting the Han's eyes. 'You can't be too careful. I thought ...'

The movement of the Han's arm was deceptively fast. Ross felt himself being lifted and turned, something hard and acid-hot slicing deep into his back. There was the sound of a gun's detonation, followed instantly, it seemed, by the searing pain of a bullet smashing into his collarbone. Then he was falling towards Milne, the darkness enfolding him like a tide.

Mach looked about him at the room, then, setting the detonator on the incendiary, stepped back. He had what he'd come for. The rest could burn.

For a moment he paused, smiling, pleased with himself. His instinct was still good, despite what had happened in Europe. If he had not followed these two, the game would have been up for Emily. And for him too, perhaps. As it was, he knew now what had happened that time with DeVore.

Yes. Milne had been right. A clever man, Milne, but no good with a gun. As for Emily, what he'd found out today might one day prove invaluable.

'Rachel DeValerian,' he said softly, noting how closely the surname mimicked the form of DeVore's own. He laughed and tapped the file against his side, then, turning away, he thumbed the doorlock and stepped out into the corridor. Richmond was two hours away.

The place stank. But this was not the normal stink of the Lowers, this was a powerful, strongly animal stench that seemed to fill and thicken the close, warm air, pressing like a foul cloth against the mouth and nostrils. Soucek had gagged at first and turned to look questioningly at Lehmann, but the albino had shown no reaction.

'Gods, what is this place?'

Lehmann glanced at him. 'It used to be a pen.' He indicated cages, the silvered snouts of the feeding tubes, retracted now into the walls. 'Some friends of mine have emptied it for a while.'

Soucek nodded, understanding. He had never seen one of the great meat animals – the *jou tung wu*, as they were called – but he had seen pictures. He looked about him, imagining the huge, brainless creatures, one on each side of the central walkway, the vast pink bulk of each crammed tight into the rectangular mesh, the dozens of tiny, eyeless heads guzzling at the trough. He made a noise of disgust. No wonder the place stank.

He was about to say something more when he saw the figures at the far end of the pen; three of them, each of them holding a hand up to their mouth. He almost laughed, but checked himself, letting nothing show on the blank of his face. It was a sign of how much he had changed since knowing Lehmann. *Show nothing,* he thought, recalling what Lehmann had said. *The man who shows what he's thinking is weak. He allows his opponent an advantage.* And never more than when the stakes were as high as they were today.

There was a moment's hesitation as the three men looked amongst themselves, then they came forward. They were big men, their bare arms heavily-muscled. Together they seemed to form a type, but no one knew better than Soucek how different from each other these three were.

The three stopped a body's length from where Lehmann and he stood. Everything about them was wary. They had committed themselves heavily simply by coming. If Whiskers Lu found out, they were dead. But that didn't mean they were won over. Far from it.

'You've chosen a sweet place for our meeting, *Shih* Lehmann.'

The speaker was Huang Jen. As lieutenant to Po Lao, Red Pole of the *Kuei Chuan*, he was the most senior of the three. It was not surprising that they had chosen him as their spokesman. But the bovine look of him was misleading, for he was a clever, subtle man – though not entirely. He had a reputation for sadism. To his left stood Meng Te, a big Han with a large, shaven head who had joined the *Kuei Chuan* from one of the northern *tong* a year back. Making up the three was a sullen-faced *Hung Mao* named Visak.

'Sweet enough,' Lehmann answered, stepping forward, taking each of them in turn by the hands. 'Like what we do here, neh?'

Lehmann was holding the hands of Visak as he said this, and Soucek, watching, saw how the man's eyes widened marginally, trying to fathom the albino. Visak was the most interesting of the three. It was rare – almost unique – for a *Hung Mao* to rise in the ranks of the Triads and said much for his ruthlessness and ability. Though beneath Huang Jen and Meng Te in the

Triad hierarchy, he was, without doubt, the most dangerous of the three. Before Lehmann had asked him to sound the man out, Soucek would have considered him the most loyal of Whiskers Lu's henchmen. Fiercely loyal. But here he was.

Security-trained, Visak's prowess in hand-to-hand fighting was legendary throughout the Lowers. In stature he was one of the few men Soucek had met who were as tall as Lehmann, and seeing the two of them together, he noted how big Visak really was, for the sheer breadth of his chest and shoulders made the albino seem frail. But Lehmann appeared undaunted. He met the other's gaze unflinchingly.

'You understand the need for secrecy?'

Huang Jen lifted his chin disdainfully. 'Your man promises much, if I take his vague inferences to mean anything. Will you spell it out for us? Make it clear?'

Soucek glanced at Lehmann uneasily. What if this were a trap? What if Whiskers Lu knew about their meeting? It would mean War, surely, for all Lehmann said of Lu's softness, his lack of will. But Lehmann seemed contemptuous of such fears.

'I am the coming force,' he said, looking from one to the other. 'The very fact that you are here means that you understand this. That you know where the future lies.'

He stood there imperiously, relaxed but commanding, as if every word he said were incontestable fact. And though Soucek had seen this side of him before, he felt his nerve-ends tingle with a strange excitement as he listened. At these moments it was like hearing the voice of some dark, unnatural power. It both terrified and awed him.

'In time it will all be mine. From the north to the south. From west to east. Every last corridor. You know this. You hear what is whispered amongst your men. Even now they see it clearly. Lehmann, they say. Lehmann's the one. And they're right.'

Visak glanced at the others, then laughed. But Soucek could see that even he was awed.

'I want proof,' he said. 'Something more than words.'

The words seemed strange, rehearsed, and Soucek, watching, narrowed his eyes suspiciously. Was Whiskers Lu behind this? Was he listening even now? But Lehmann was shaking his head slowly.

'No, Visak. No sideshows. No games. What we do we do in the utmost seriousness. You are here because you have already chosen. Children want proof. Children and old men. But men such as you and I ... we work in certainties, neh?'

Visak raised his chin challengingly, then relented, giving a grudging nod. Huang Jen, who had been watching him, looked back at Lehmann.

'You are right, Shih Lehmann. There are whispers. But you have still not answered me. What do we get out of this? And what do you want from us?'

Lehmann was silent a moment, his pink eyes seeming to hold and judge each one of them in turn. Then, satisfied, he answered.

'I want you to swear loyalty to me. Here. Right now. I want each one of you to be my man. To serve me. And, in the time that is to come, to do what I ask of you.'

'And in return?'

'You live. You rule with me.'

Huang Jen smiled. 'And that's all?' But the smile quickly faded.

'The choice is simple,' Lehmann said coldly. 'All or nothing. Which is it to be?'

For a moment there was silence, stillness. Then, hesitantly, Meng Te went down onto his knees and bowed his head. Slowly, and with one final questioning look at the albino, Huang Jen also knelt.

For a time it seemed that Visak would choose against, but then, with a suddenness that was strange, he too knelt and lowered his head. Only then did Lehmann go down the line, offering his foot for them to kiss, speaking the words he would have them offer him in token of their loyalty.

He moved back, calling on them to stand.

'I want you to prepare yourselves. To gather about you those loyal to you and put aside those who might waver. When things are ready, I'll send and tell you what to do.'

Soucek shivered, understanding how they were feeling at that moment. He too had knelt and sworn his loyalty. *Yes*, he thought, watching them bow and turn away, *I understand this better now.*

It was not simple force or cunning they responded to, but something stronger, deeper than those; something so different from what they were used to that to encounter it was to be changed, as he, Jiri Soucek, had been changed. To be in Lehmann's presence was to cast off all masks, all illusions.

It was to grasp the raw essence of things. It was like ... like pressing through the flesh and touching bone!

All ... or nothing. It was so potent an offer that to refuse it was almost impossible for men such as they. Even so, he wondered whether it were enough. Whether they were bound to Lehmann as he himself was bound?

He turned, looking at Lehmann. The albino was staring at the tunnel's mouth, concentrating, his features fixed, like a mask. Then he turned, looking at Soucek. 'That will make Whiskers Lu think, neh? He'll try to kill me, I warrant.'

It was so unexpected that Soucek laughed. 'Then Visak was acting?'

Lehmann shook his head. 'Not all the time.' He sniffed loudly, then cleared his throat. 'Still, times are sad when such *hsiao jen* are legend. You'll watch him, neh?'

Soucek nodded, but he was thinking through what had happened, trying to see it all anew.

Lehmann turned, starting towards the tunnel's mouth. 'Come, Jiri. Let's go. It stinks here.'

Soucek looked up, his eyes widening, surprised that Lehmann had even noticed.

To the sound of martial music, the golden curtains swept back, revealing the dragon throne, mounted on a platform of seven broad steps. To each side, vast pillars rose up into depths of darkness, while in the great chair itself Wu Shih, T'ang of North America and spokesman for the Seven, sat cloaked in silks of imperial yellow. As the camera panned in, his face grew until it filled the screen, its stern authority staring out at the watching billions.

'People of Chung Kuo,' he began, his dark eyes clear and certain. 'Today I have great news to tell you. An announcement of the utmost importance to everyone in the seven Cities. For the first time since the dark cloud of War fell over our great civilisation, there is peace in the levels. Both high and low can look forward to a future of safety and prosperity, of growth and stability. But to ensure that stability, certain measures must be taken.'

Wu Shih paused, his lined and bearded face emanating a strength, a calm assurance that was impressive. Rock-like and yet fair he seemed at that moment. A father to his people.

'First of all, the State of Emergency which has been in place these past nine years is immediately revoked. From this day on, the law will be as it was before the troubles began. Furthermore, all political prisoners will have their cases reviewed by civil tribunals, these matters to be concluded, at the latest, six months from now.'

There was a faint softening to the features, the merest hint of a smile. 'Secondly, the House of Representatives at Weimar will be reopened one year from now, elections to be held in three stages in the six months prior to that. Further announcements regarding the dates of such elections and of franchise rights will be posted throughout the Cities in the days to come.'

He paused once more, letting that sink in, then continued, his eyes staring out unblinking at the gathered masses, commanding their attention.

'Thirdly, and perhaps most significantly, we have decided upon a package of revisions to the present Edict of Technological Control. In five important areas we shall be allowing new developments. Developments which, it is hoped, will be of benefit to everyone living within our great society. Changes.'

Throughout Chung Kuo there was a murmur of surprise. *Changes.* Never had they thought to hear the word from the lips of a T'ang. But Wu Shih was not finished.

'Finally, there is one last great matter we must face as a people. One challenge which we must let unite us in the years to come. For many years now we have chosen not to speak of it. To ignore it, as if by itself it would go away. But it will not go away. And so, finally, we must tackle the great question of our time. Are we to be a single people, free and safe and prosperous? Or are we to see ourselves riven by division, our great Cities destroyed, our institutions falling into anarchy and chaos?'

There was a slight upward movement of the great T'ang's head. His eyes burned now with a fierce challenge.

'We cannot let that be. We cannot let our children suffer. Therefore we must confront the fact that has stared us in the face too long. Our numbers are too great. Chung Kuo groans beneath the burden of that weight. That is why, in the years to come, we must work together, People and Seven, to find a solution to this last great problem that confronts us. This is a new beginning. A new chance for us to set things right. People and Seven. Our chance to be strong again. To ensure stability and a good life for all.'

As the final words echoed out across the great world of levels, the camera panned back, revealing once more the dragon throne, the pillars and the steps. Slowly the golden curtains closed.

Wu Shih rose from his seat and, coming slowly down the steps, made his way through the kneeling technicians and out into the hospitality suite at the back of the studio. Guards opened the doors before him, their heads bowed low. He went through. Inside, his fellow T'ang, Tsu Ma and Li Yuan, were sitting on the far side of the room, facing a giant screen. They turned as he entered, standing up to greet him.

'That was good,' Tsu Ma said, coming across and holding Wu Shih's arm briefly.

'Yes,' added Li Yuan, smiling. 'The people will sleep soundly tonight, knowing what is to come.'

'Maybe so,' Wu Shih answered, taking a seat between them, 'and yet for once the words felt hollow even as I uttered them. All that talk of a new age. Of peace and stability and of working together, People and Seven. I would that it were so, that we could call on them and they'd respond, yet I fear we must face dark days before things get better.'

Tsu Ma looked down thoughtfully. 'Maybe. And yet to say as much would only bring it that much quicker. No, you spoke well tonight, cousin. For once we must pray that what we say will come about, even as we prepare ourselves for the worst.'

'Prayers, cousin Ma?' Li Yuan laughed gently. 'Has it come to that?'

Tsu Ma met his eyes sombrely. 'Maybe that's the answer, Yuan. Prayers and chanting, bells, icons and incense ... as in the old days.'

Wu Shih, watching him, frowned. 'Are you serious, Tsu Ma?'

Tsu Ma turned, smiling bleakly. 'No, my dear friend. I would sooner allow our cousin Wang to cut my throat than have us return to those dreadful times. Yet from recent reports it seems that such thinking is rife, even as high up as the Mids. There is a need amongst them. Something that the City does not satisfy.'

Li Yuan nodded. 'I, too, have heard such things. Of new cults, new movements in the Lowers. My forces try the best they can to uproot such growths, yet the garden is long untended, the weeds many. I fear the day will come when we must relinquish such regions to the darkness.'

Wu Shih sighed. 'I confess that is how I also feel. I tell myself that we must prevail, yet in my heart of hearts I am uncertain.'

Tsu Ma nodded. 'We must face the truth, cousins. It is as Wang said, that day at Astrakhan when we first saw how things were to be amongst us. We live in new times. There are new ways of thinking and behaving. It is said that in my great-grandfather's day everything under Heaven, yes, even the *wan wu*, the ten thousand things themselves, would bow before the sound of his voice, the solemn glare of his eye. But now?' He laughed sourly. 'Well, our eyes have lost their fierce glow, our voices their terrifying power. Or so it would seem, neh? And our Cities ... our Cities are filled with the shadows of fear and ignorance and hatred. And how can one fight such shadows?'

'And yet we must.'

'Yes, cousin Yuan. And we must also guard against these other, inner shadows – the shades of fear and despair. For we who rule are not as other men. If we fall, who will stand in our place? If we fall, all is lost.'

A heavy, brooding silence fell, and then, unexpectedly, the screen behind them lit up once more.

'Cousins ...'

It was Wang Sau-leyan. His moon-shaped face filled the great screen, smiling, as if he saw them.

'Wu Shih ... you spoke well tonight. Indeed, you spoke for us all when you said that this was a new beginning, a new chance to make things right. So it is, cousin. So it is. But time alone will show just how important this moment is. It is a joyous moment, a truly great moment for the Seven and for the people of Chung Kuo. Let us go forward from this moment and build upon that vision of a new age. I, for one, will not hesitate to strive towards that goal. You can be assured of my continued support in Council for all measures designed to bring that aim about.'

The smile broadened momentarily, like a fracture in that pallid expanse of flesh, and then, unexpectedly, Wang bowed his head.

'And so I bid you good night, cousin Wu. Likewise to my cousins, Tsu Ma and Li Yuan. May the gods protect you and your loved ones.'

The screen blanked. Below it the three T'ang sat in stunned silence, staring at each other. At last Tsu Ma broke the spell.

'Now what in the gods' names was that about? What is that calculating bastard up to now?'

'Whatever it is,' Wu Shih said irritably, 'you can be certain of one thing –

that our effusive cousin means not a single word of what he said.'

'Maybe not,' said Li Yuan thoughtfully, 'but now, at least, we are fore-warned.'

'True,' said Tsu Ma, leaning back in his chair, a sudden twinkle in his eye. 'And there's one, at least, who casts a shadow large enough to fight.'

There was a sudden, violent banging at the door. Emily woke, groping for the gun she always kept at her bedside, her heart hammering. For a moment she thought herself back in her tiny apartment in Munich Hsien, then she realised where she was – America – and sat up, suddenly alert.

There was no gun, only the bedside timer. It was after four and the apartment was in total darkness. For a moment she sat there, breathing shallowly, listening, wondering if she had imagined it, and then it came again.

Mach. It had to be. Security wouldn't have bothered knocking.

She hissed out her anger, then got up quickly and threw on a robe. He had better have a good excuse for waking her at this hour. A fucking beauty of an excuse.

She stabbed the view button angrily, studying herself briefly in the wall-length mirror beside the door, then looked back at the screen.

'Michael ...'

Michael was leaning against the wall beside the door, his closely cropped head lowered, his body slumped forward, as if he were ill. As she watched he swayed back slightly and looked up at the camera, bleary eyed.

No, not ill. Drunk.

She studied herself in the wall-length mirror, wondering what he wanted of her, then, with a tiny shudder, slammed her hand over the door-release pad.

He stood there unsteadily, simply looking at her. She made to chastise him, then stopped, catching her breath.

'Michael ...' she said, pained by the sight of him. 'What is it?'

He looked away, then looked back at her, tears welling in his eyes.

She had never seen him like this. Never seen him anything but strong, resourceful, positive, even when things had seemed hopeless. But that look in his eyes had been dreadful. She had never seen such misery, such a vast, despairing sense of loss.

'Come on,' she said gently, putting her shoulder under his arm to support him. She drew him inside and closed the door behind them. 'Let's have some ch'a. You can tell me all about it.'

'It's finished,' he said, shuddering, his face screwed up in sudden torment. 'There's no going back. It's ended between us.'

She stared at the side of his face, wondering what he meant.

'Who ... ?' she began, then understood.

'He pissed on me, Em. The old fucker pissed on me.'

The words were angry, accusing. But the anger of the words was underlaid with a raw hurt that genuinely surprised her.

She sat him down in the kitchen in one of the big chairs, then began to prepare the ch'a, her mind racing.

'It was Kennedy,' he said, telling her what she already knew. 'It was his idea. He thought it would help things. Take the pressure off. Give us some breathing space in which to raise some funds and develop our campaign. It seemed like a good thing to do at the time. But I didn't ...'

Again his voice broke, betraying him. He closed his eyes, squeezing the lids tightly shut, but still the tears came, defying his every effort to hold them back.

'I didn't know,' she said softly, sympathetically. 'I thought you hated him.'

'Hated him?' He laughed and opened his eyes again, staring at her almost soberly. 'I could never hate him, Em. Never. He's my father. He's ...'

Again he could not go on.

'So what happened?' she asked, coaxing him gently. 'What did he say?'

He took a deep, shuddering breath, then shook his head. 'It wasn't what he said, it was how he did it. He had his cronies there. You know, that crowd he's roped in to fund his immortality project. I wanted to speak to him alone, but he wouldn't have it. He wouldn't even let me into the room. And then ...' He licked his lips, then carried on. 'Well, it was hopeless. He doesn't want to know.' He looked up at her forlornly. 'He wants me to be a slave to him – to do everything he says. And I can't do that, Em, I can't! He asks too much. He always has.'

'I see ...' But she didn't. Not yet. This was something specific. Something he was holding back from her.

She turned away, busying herself a moment, pouring the ch'a. When she turned back it was to find him leaning forward in the chair, watching her strangely.

'What is it?' she said, setting the bowl down on the table beside him. 'What aren't you telling me?'

He laughed, but it was a strangely forlorn sound. 'You're a good woman, Em. And not just good at your job. There's something about you. Some quality ...' He shrugged and sat back slightly, his movements awkward, slightly exaggerated, as if he were trying hard to control himself. 'I saw it from the first. Even before you started working for me. I noticed you. Did you know that? I used to look out for you in my father's offices. I ...'

He looked down at his hands, as if it were suddenly hard to say what he was about to say, then looked back at her again, his whole manner suddenly changed.

'Gloria Chung ... remember her, Em? The hostess at that party we went to. She told me something that night. Something I should have known for myself but hadn't really seen until then. Well, tonight, facing my father, what she said came back to me. You see, I had to make a choice. Oh, I don't think the Old Man was even aware of it. Anything else he'd have asked of me I would have done. Anything. But that ...'

Emily shook her head, exasperated. 'What, for the gods' sakes? What the hell are you talking about?'

'It was you,' he said, his gaze suddenly piercing her. 'That's what it was all about. He wanted me to marry the Johnstone girl and I refused. As before, only I didn't know it back then. But tonight I was certain of it. Anything else, and I'd have agreed. Anything. But to lose you, Em ... No. I couldn't do that. Not that.'

He stood unsteadily, taking her hands. 'Don't you understand it yet? I want to marry you, Em. To spend my life with you.'

The words surprised her; caught her totally off guard. She was silent a moment, then recollecting herself, she shook her head. 'But what about your father? You love him, Michael. You need him. If you marry me, he'll cut you off for good.'

He shuddered, the full weight of his hurt there briefly in his eyes. 'Maybe. But it's done already, Em. It's finished between us. Really. There's no going back. So now it's just you and I. That's if you'll have me. That's if you feel even the tiniest bit the way I feel towards you.'

She laughed, but beneath her laughter was a kind of numbed surprise –

almost awe – that he had done this for her; that he had cast it all off simply to have her.

'I'll have you, Michael Lever,' she said quietly, surprised by the strength of what she felt for him at that moment. 'Just you and I. For life. And no going back.'

CHAPTER 87

LOST

I t had been a long time since they had entertained and Jelka felt awkward, unpractised in her role as hostess. Their guests, the Hausers, were friends of her father's from years back, the husband ex-Security and a one-time Colonial Governor, the wife a soldier's wife, silent and dutiful in all things. Their son, Gustav, had come to work for the Marshal as his equerry and was shortly to be re-posted. Jelka often saw him about the house, though he kept much to himself. He seemed a pleasant enough young man, though, like all of them, bred with a certain stiffness to him.

At table she busied herself, turning to have a word with the servants, making sure things went smoothly, then turning back to ensure that the conversation kept flowing. Not that there was any real problem with that, for the two men monopolised the talk. First it was pure reminiscence, then, after their wine glasses had been topped up and the dessert was out of the way, they moved on to that perennial topic amongst the old: how things had changed.

'It was far simpler back then,' Hauser began, nodding and looking to his wife. 'Values were stronger. Positions were much clearer cut than now.' He sipped and leaned forward, giving Jelka the benefit of his gaze. 'There was no question of divided loyalties. A man was what he said he was.'

She wanted to question that. It struck her that men had always been as they were now – a mixed bunch, and some more mixed than others – but she kept her silence, smiling, as if she agreed.

Hauser smiled back at her, pleased by her acquiescence. 'Our job was simple, back then. We rounded up a few malcontents. Made sure things ran smoothly in the levels. None of this 'Who's my friend? Who's my enemy?' business.'

Tolonen sighed and wiped at his lips with his napkin. 'That's true, Sven. Why, if I could but tell you ...' He shook his head sadly and reached for his glass. 'Honour is not a thing you can buy. It must be bred. Must be there from birth in the immediate environment of a man. And if it's not ...' He drank deeply, then set his glass down again, pursing his lips.

Jelka, watching him, thought of Kim. Was it true, what her father said? Was honour simply a thing to be bred into a man? Couldn't a man be naturally honourable?

'Unfortunately,' continued her father, 'we live in an age where such standards are vanishing fast. Young men like your son are rare, Sven.'

She looked down once more, keeping the smile from her face. The old governor had pushed out his chin at her father's remark and nodded sternly, the gesture so like a character in a trivid historical that she had it on her lips to remark about it. But there were rules here, and she would obey them, dislike them as she might. She said nothing, merely looked past the governor's wife to the waiter, indicating that he should fill the woman's glass again.

'You must be excited.'

Jelka looked back at the ex-governor and realised he had been talking to her. 'I beg your pardon, Major Hauser?'

'About the trip. It must be wonderful. Seeing all that so young. I was in my late forties before I first went out.'

She still wasn't following him. Confused, she looked to her father for explanation, but the Marshal was staring fixedly down at the table, as if deep in thought.

'Yes,' went on the governor, 'I can remember it clearly, even now. Seeing the moons of Jupiter for the first time.'

She laughed. 'I'm sorry. I'm afraid you must be mistaken.'

It was the old man's turn to look confused and turn to her father. 'What's this, Knut? I thought you'd settled things?'

There was a slight colour to Tolonen's cheeks. He met his old friend's eyes firmly, but his voice was quieter than usual. 'I haven't told her, Sven. Please ...'

'Ah ...' There was a moment's clear embarrassment, then the old man turned and looked back at Jelka. 'Well, as it's out, I guess you might as well know. I suppose your father wanted to surprise you, neh?'

Jelka had gone cold. She was looking at her father steadily. What had he done now? 'A trip?' she asked, ignoring their guests momentarily.

'I would have told you,' Tolonen said, still not looking at her. 'Tonight. When our friends here had gone.'

There was a slight emphasis on the word friends that was meant to remind her of her duty as hostess, but she ignored it.

'You're doing it again, aren't you?'

She could sense how both their guests had stiffened in their seats. Her father, however, had turned to face her.

'Doing what?'

'Interfering ...' She said it softly, but the impact of the word couldn't be softened. She was thinking of Hans Ebert and her father's pressure on her to marry him. He had been wrong then, and he was wrong now. She *loved* Kim. And she would not be separated from him. Not for some soldier!

She shivered, realising the point to which her thoughts had brought her. Did she really hate all this talk of duty and breeding? Hate all this soldiering?

'Jelka ...' her father said softly. 'You must listen to me. In this I know best.'

She folded up her napkin and threw it down on the table, then stood. Turning to the governor and his wife, she gave a small bow and a faint smile of apology. 'I'm sorry. I really don't feel well. If you'll excuse me ...'

She made to turn away, but her father called her back.

'Where do you think you're going, girl?'

She took a deep breath, then turned to face him. He was angry with her. Furiously angry. She had never seen him quite like this. But the sight merely steeled her to what she was doing. She faced him out, for the first time in her life openly defying him.

'What is it?'

He waved a hand at her, indicating that she should sit. But she remained as she was, standing away from the table, the chair pushed out behind her. He saw this and narrowed his eyes.

'You'll sit down, and you'll apologise to our guests for your behaviour.'

She opened her mouth, astonished by him. Slowly, she shook her head.

'No. I'll *not* go.'

'Sit down!'

There was real menace in his voice this time. She sat, slightly away from the table, making no effort to draw her chair up. 'I'll not go,' she said again, as if he had not heard her the first time.

Hauser was silent, looking from her to her father. But his face was the mirror of her father's.

'You'll go because I tell you to. Understand?'

She went very still. Then, looking up at him again, she shook her head.

This time he stood and yelled at her. 'You'll go, dammit! Even if my men have to bind you and carry you on board. *Understand?* You're still my daughter, and until you're of age, you do what I say!'

She shuddered, looking away from him. He was so ugly like this. So ...

Not meaning to, she laughed.

It went very quiet. She could feel the chill of the atmosphere about her. She looked up at him again. He was looking at her strangely, almost as if he didn't recognise her.

'What are you afraid of?'

'What?' He didn't seem to understand. 'Afraid?'

'Kim,' she said. 'Why are you so afraid of him? Why would it be so wrong if I married him?'

She had said nothing before now, but this was the nub of it. The reason for all this heavy-handedness.

Her father laughed oddly. 'You'll not marry him. Not *him*.'

She met his eyes and saw that he was determined in this. But he had reckoned without her opposition. Like before, he had thought she would bow meekly to his wishes.

'I have your blood,' she said softly. 'If needs be, I'll fight you on this.'

'You'll go,' he said, with an air of finality.

For a moment longer she hesitated, then nodded. 'I'll go,' she said, 'because you make me go. But it will change nothing. I'll marry him, see if I don't.'

His eyes widened and his mouth opened as if he were going to argue more with her, but then he nodded, and sat down. He had her agreement. That, for now, was enough for him. The rest would take its course. Why fight tomorrow's battles before they came?

'Now may I go?' she asked, still sitting there.

He looked back at her again, then across at his guests. The ex-governor gave a tight little nod and a half-smile. Beside him, his wife sat stiffly, looking down at her hands, as if in shock.

'Go on, then,' Tolonen said softly, and stood for her, as if nothing had happened. But, watching her go, he knew that something had broken between them. Some last link of childish trust. He shivered, then turned back to his guests.

'I'm sorry, Sven,' he said. 'I should have warned you ...'

The boardroom was tense, silent, as Old Man Lever, at the head of the table, read through the figures on the loan document. To his left along the great oak table sat the financiers, eight in all, to the right his team of advisers. All eyes were focused on the old man as he turned the page and, looking up, tapped the document in front of him.

'The top-up's too high. I thought we'd agreed on two point six.'

'Two point eight, Mister Lever,' Bonner, the Chief Negotiator answered quietly. 'I have it minuted.'

Lever stared at him a moment, as if Bonner had taken leave of his senses, then, taking his ink brush from the stand beside him, he put a line through the figure and wrote the new figure beside it, initialling the change.

There was the briefest exchange of glances to his left, a small shrug of acceptance from Bonner. The matter was decided. As ever, Lever had got his way.

'And what about this matter of extended term insurance?' Lever added casually. 'I think we should share the expense, fifty-fifty. What do you think?'

Bonner looked down. 'It's unusual, Mister Lever. The borrower usually bears the cost of any loan insurances, but if that's what you want.' He looked back up at Lever and smiled. 'Besides, I'm sure the project will come in on time.'

Lever smiled, then reached out to pat Bonner's arm. 'Good. Then we'll get this signed and witnessed, neh?'

Bonner let out a breath, the tension draining from him. The two points on the top-up would cost them over fifty thousand, and the insurance might add up to one hundred and fifty thousand more, but in terms of the total deal that was nothing.

Eight billion *yuan!* Bonner's mind reeled at the thought of it. It was the biggest loan his Finance House had ever set up. And even at the fine rates Lever had insisted on, it would bring handsome profits. Personally, as Chief Negotiator, his own share was a quarter point, but a quarter point on eight billion was nothing to sneer at.

And every last *fen* secured by prime ImmVac stock, the best on the market. Bonner stood, bowing to the old man. Behind him, in a line, his team did the same, keeping their heads lowered as Bonner walked round the table to append his signature to the bottom of the agreement, then flicked back, initialling the two changes. A second copy of the document would be retinally-imprinted and registered later in the day, but for now their business was concluded, the deal done.

Old Man Lever turned and, looking across at his Chief Steward, clicked his fingers. At once, the Steward turned and pulled open the doors. Waiting there in the corridor beyond were six servants, bearing trays of wine and delicacies. Quickly they went about the table.

'Come,' said Old Man Lever, looking about him with a broad smile, 'let's celebrate! For today the Cutler Institute for Genetic Research is mine. Lock, stock, and barrel, as my grandfather used to say.'

He laughed, then nodded to himself. Standing, he took a wine cup from the nearest servant and raised it. 'This is a great moment, and *nothing* ... nothing, can spoil it!'

All about the table, cups were lifted, voices raised in the traditional toast. '*Kan pei!*'

'Mister Lever ...'

The Steward stood at Lever's shoulder, leaning close, his voice a whisper, low but insistent.

Lever turned a fraction. 'Yes?'

'News has come, Master. Moments back. It's Michael, Mister Lever. He's married. Married the Jennings woman.'

Mach and Curval were standing in the ante room when Lever came storming out, his eyes bulging with anger. They had heard the tray go crashing down, and Lever's angry shout, but the sight of him, his face set into a fierce grimace, his fists bunched tight, surprised them both.

'What is it?' Mach said, catching up with the old man. 'What in hell's name has happened?'

Lever stopped abruptly and turned, facing Mach. 'It's Michael. He's betrayed me.'

'Betrayed you?'

Lever shuddered. 'He's married her. The bastard's gone and married her!'

Mach stared at him, shocked. Emily, he meant. Michael had married Emily Ascher.

'Not possible,' he said, after a moment. 'She wouldn't. I mean ...' He shook his head, unable to explain it. 'Are you certain?'

'Not certain, no, but fairly sure. I'd put a trace on him, you see. I ...' Again Lever shuddered. 'He's betrayed me, Jan. Pissed on me! First with the Ward boy, and now this!'

'Maybe they've got it wrong.'

'No. This time he's really done it. Done it to spite me. To piss on me. My son ...'

'Charles ...'

'No. This is my fault. I should have expected this. Should have known he'd do this.' He shivered, lowering his voice. 'I should have had her killed.'

Mach glanced at Curval, then shook his head. 'No, Charles. It would have solved nothing. You have to live with this. To show him it means nothing to you.'

'Nothing?' Lever closed his eyes, the sudden pain in his face something awful to see. 'That boy meant everything to me. *Everything.* And now ...'

'You must show him he means nothing,' Mach said, insistent now. 'It's the only answer, Charles. The only answer.'

Whiskers Lu, Big Boss of the *Kuei Chuan*, stood, letting out a great roar. Fat Wong's handwritten note lay on the desk before him, its curt, six word summons the reason for his anger.

'How *dare* that jumped-up little cock-sucker tell me what to do! How dare he summon me like one of his runners!'

Lu's men kept their heads lowered, their eyes averted. They had been poring over a plan of the Lowers, discussing the recent incursions by the 14K in the eastern stacks and the movements up-level of the Red Gang to their north, trying to work out counter-moves, but this had pushed all that from Lu Ming-shao's mind. For ten minutes now he had raged, taxing the limits of his invention with the names he had called the United Bamboo's 489. And yet everyone there knew that Whiskers Lu would go. He had to. For Fat Wong was currently strong, his alliances in Council secure, whereas the last year had seen the decline of the *Kuei Chuan's* fortunes, the erosion of their once firm links with their neighbouring Triads.

Yes, and that too had been Fat Wong's doing, no doubt. Lu Ming-shao had no proof of it, but how else could it have happened? Why else would the 14K have dared encroach on *Kuei Chuan* territory unless Fat Wong had given his tacit agreement? And now this.

'Why not kill him?' Visak said suddenly, speaking into the stillness between Lu's rages.

Whiskers Lu laughed humourlessly and fixed Visak with his one good eye. 'Kill him? Kill Fat Wong?' He laughed again, this time in disbelief. 'How?'

'An assassin,' Visak said, meeting Lu's ferocious stare. 'I know a man. He's special.'

'Special?' Whiskers Lu leaned forward, holding the edge of the table, and laughed. 'He'd have to be a ghost and walk through walls to get Fat Wong.'

Visak lowered his head. 'With great respect, Master Lu, this man is special. He could get Wong Yi-sun. Wong and all his top men.'

Whiskers Lu was breathing shallowly now, his hands gripping the table's edge. His mottled, mask-like face twitched violently. Then, relaxing, he pushed back again, composing himself, drawing his silks tightly about him. He turned, making a show of studying the glass cases on the wall behind his desk – the cases that contained the heads of his three great rivals – then nodded.

Lu Ming-shao took one of the heads down, studying it a moment, a brief smile flitting across his glass-like features as he recalled the moment he had killed this one – that look of dumb incomprehension in the man's eyes as he had choked the breath out of him, and the great surge of satisfaction he had felt afterwards. Unconsciously he smoothed the tip of his thumb across the surface of the blinded eye, then reached up again, setting the head back in its place.

'All right. But it has to be tonight. Understand? I'll be fucked if I'll let that bastard live to see another day. Not after the way he's insulted me. Contact your man at once. Offer him whatever he needs. Then bring him here, understand? I want to see this ghost. An hour from now if possible, but tonight, at any rate. Before the meeting.'

He turned, meeting his lieutenant's eyes. 'Oh, and Visak. You will make sure of your friend, won't you? Very sure.'

Visak nodded, then, bowing low, turned away. Whiskers Lu watched him go, then sat, thoughtful now, his rage spent. For a moment he was silent, staring at the handwritten note, then, reaching out, he crumpled the note into a tiny ball, popped it into his mouth and swallowed.

For a moment there was nothing. Then, as if all the tension in the room had been suddenly dispelled, Whiskers Lu began to laugh, his laughter echoed back at him.

Lu Ming-shao pushed the young girl aside unceremomously, then eased his huge bulk up off the bed. He pulled on the robe his man was holding and tied the sash tightly about his waist, eyeing his lieutenant.

'So he's here, then?'

Visak lowered his head. 'In the audience room, Master.'

'Unarmed, I hope.'

'Yes, Master. And under guard.'

'And the task I want of him. He understands what it entails?'

'He does, Master.'

'How did he react?'

Visak hesitated, his eyes straying briefly to the young Han girl on the bed, who lay there, naked, watching the exchange, her eyes curious. He looked back at Lu Ming-shao, meeting his one good eye.

'Our friend is rather a cold fish. He is not one to ... *react*.'

Whiskers Lu stared at him a moment, then laughed delightedly. 'Good! I warm to him already.'

They went through, Visak leading the way, Whiskers Lu's runners kneeling, bowing low before him as he approached. The door to the audience room was barred by two of his best men, Meng Te and Huang Jen.

'Okay,' Lu said, looking about him and smiling. 'Let's meet our special friend.'

Inside, the unexpected. A tall man dressed totally in white, his back to them, his head tilted slightly, looking down, as if he was cradling something. As he turned, they saw what it was. A baby.

Whiskers Lu glared at Visak, angry that he'd not been prepared 'What is this?'

The tall man looked down at the baby, then, looking back at Whiskers Lu, threw it at him.

Lu Ming-shao, taken totally by surprise, raised his arms in reflex, catching the child. As he did, the man drew his gun and fired twice. Whiskers Lu heard the choked cries and felt the floor shake as the bodies fell either side of him, but he himself still stood there, untouched.

The stranger put the gun away. 'The unexpected is a powerful tool, don't you think, Lu Ming-shao?'

Lu Ming-shao swallowed, his anger something cold and hard. 'What the fuck do you think you're doing, *friend*?'

'Those two were traitors,' the tall man answered calmly. 'They made deals behind your back. They sold you to another.'

Lu Ming-shao turned, looking down at the fallen bodies of Meng Te and Huang Jen. Was it possible? Yet even as he asked the question he knew that it was perfectly possible. After all, *he* was the outsider here. There were no blood ties as existed between the other 489s and their men. They were his men through force alone, not loyalty.

He looked down at the child that rested, strangely silent in his arms. A *Hung Mao*, it was. An ugly little brat, weeks old at most. He lifted it slightly, as if to test its weight, then threw it back at the stranger.

The tall man stepped back, letting the child fall, screeching, to the floor. He had a knife in his hand now. A huge, wicked-looking thing with a white pearl handle.

Whiskers Lu drew his own knife and, bellowing loudly, lunged at the other man, knowing now that he had been set up. But he had taken only two steps before he sank down onto his knees, his breath hissing painfully from him, Visak's knife buried to the hilt in his upper back, Visak's weight bearing him down.

The baby was silent now. It lay beneath Lu Ming-shao, crushed by the weight of the two men.

Visak got up and moved away, leaving the knife embedded in his former Master's back, his eyes going to the tall man.

The stranger moved closer, standing above Whiskers Lu, listening to the pained wheezing of his final breaths, the soft gurgle of the blood in his pierced and damaged lung. Then, with the sole of his left boot, he forced Lu's head down brutally into the floor, turning his foot, the heel gouging into the melted, mask-like face of the dying man, cracking open the brittle mottled plastic of his flesh, as if he were crushing an insect.

Lehmann looked up past the dying man, meeting Visak's eyes. 'Summon the Red Pole, Po Lao. Bring him here at once. And if he asks, tell him he has a new Master.'

Main had been emptied. Beneath the clock tower, the decapitated bodies of those who had opposed Lehmann were laid out in rows, more than three hundred in all, their severed heads stacked in a huge pile close by.

Lehmann stood there, gaunt yet imperious, looking about him at the heartland of his new territory, his face betraying nothing at that moment of triumph. Twenty *ch'i* away, in the shadow of the tower, stood Soucek, Visak at his side. The two men had fought hard these last few hours, quelling the last pockets of resistance; making sure no news of this got out before its time. Now it was done, Lehmann's rule made certain. At a signal from the albino, Visak bowed and went across, calling the men in from the main corridor.

The runners crossed the great floor slowly in a great tide, approaching the tower timidly, their eyes wide, staring at the rows of headless corpses, the gruesome stack of bloodied skulls nearby. Then, at Visak's shouted command, they went down onto their knees, lowering their foreheads to the floor. More than four thousand men in all. *Kuei Chuan*, every one.

Lehmann stood there a moment, looking out across their lowered backs, then went amongst them, lifting this man's chin and staring into his face, and then another's, moving between them all the while, fearless and magisterial, like a T'ang, his every movement emphasising his command.

For long minutes there was silence; a silence in which, it seemed, they dare not even breathe, then, coming out from their midst, Lehmann went over to the stack of heads and, taking one in each hand, turned to face the watching mass.

'These were my enemies,' he said, his voice calm and cold and measured. 'And this will be the fate of all my enemies, from this day on. But you ... you have the chance to be my friends. My men.'

He set the heads down and took a step towards them.

'There is a price for disloyalty. So it is. So it has always been amongst our kind. But loyalty ... how do you earn that? What is its price?' Lehmann turned his head slowly, his pale pink eyes encompassing them all. 'I understand your shock, your confusion over what has happened. But I know that many amongst you were unhappy with how things were under Lu Ming-shao. That many of you welcome change. As for me ... well, you do not know me yet. Only, perhaps, by reputation. That, too, I understand. You might fear me right now, but there is no reason for you – any of you – to owe me any loyalty. Not yet. But in the months to come I shall ask much of you. Things Whiskers Lu never dreamed to ask. And in return?'

Lehmann paused and nodded slowly, thoughtfully, as if in reverie; yet when he spoke again, his voice was suddenly powerful, echoing across the great open space. 'In return I will give you everything. Everything you ever dreamed of.'

Kim removed the jack from the face of the terminal, letting the wire coil back into the stud beneath his ear, then sat back, breathing shallowly. 'It's good. Very good. And easy to use. I thought it would take a while to get used to.'

The surgeon smiled. 'Everyone thinks that. And there's a degree of truth to it. What you've just experienced – that's just the beginning. You see, whilst it uses the same skills you've always had – you can't, after all, slow down the speed that messages travel at in the nervous system – you're used to limiting your thought processes to the speed at which you can read or speak language. Once those limitations are removed, the brain can process raw data at phenomenal speeds. Anything up to a thousand times as fast as it could unaided. But it takes a while to adapt.'

Kim nodded, his eyes looking inwards. He was remembering how it had felt: the *power* of that feeling. Information had flashed into his head at an almost frightening speed. He had had a feeling of exultation, of tightness – of utter clarity. He had felt himself grow by the moment, achieving a degree of sharpness he had never experienced before. Sparks of pure insight had flickered between points in his head, like electrical discharges, and he had struggled to hold on to them as others filled his head.

He looked at the surgeon again. 'You should do this yourself. It would help you, surely?'

The surgeon laughed. 'They all say that. We call it conversion syndrome. Those who haven't got it, fear it; those who have have a proselytising urge to make others have the operation. But I don't have it because I can't.'

'Why?' Kim's fingers traced the shape of the stud unconsciously. It was a gesture that betrayed the newness of the implant. The surgeon saw it and smiled.

'For you there are no drawbacks. You're a theoretician, not a practitioner. But experiment has found that there's a slight decay of motor control. A loss of sharpness in that area. As if the increased use of the memory draws upon other sections of the brain and weakens their functions. A sort of compensatory effect, if you like. As a surgeon I can't risk that. My work is with my hands as much as with my knowledge of the mind's workings. I can't afford to impair my motor responses. Besides, they'd not allow me to.'

Kim nodded, considering. 'There would be other difficulties, too, wouldn't there?'

The surgeon smiled. 'Interfacing,' he explained quickly. 'That's the term we have for it. From old computer jargon. Interfacing is the difficulty you experienced moving from one state to another. Why you couldn't say anything for the first few seconds. The mind has grown accustomed to responding at what is, for it, a more natural speed. Dropping down from that it stumbles and finds great difficulty in adjusting. The effect lasts only five to ten seconds, but it would be utterly debilitating for a surgeon.

'You only get that effect when you cut out, and there seems no way of preventing it. When you plug in, the mind speeds up gradually. It's almost two seconds before it reaches its full operating speed. Cutting out, there's no gradual assimilation. The change of state is immediate and, to an extent, shocking.'

'Harmful?'

The surgeon shook his head. 'The mind's a resilient machine. It defends itself against damage. That's what the interfacing effect is – a defence mechanism. Without it there would be damage.'

There was a knock on the door. A moment later an orderly entered and, after bowing to the surgeon, handed Kim a 'sealed' notecard, the tiny slip of plastic winking blankly in the overhead light.

'Excuse me a moment,' Kim said, getting up from the chair and moving away from the terminal.

'Of course,' the surgeon answered. 'I'll make my other calls then come back later, if you like.'

Alone again, Kim placed his thumb to the seal and activated the release. At once a message appeared on the blank plastic card. He read it slowly, moving his lips to form each word, realising, even as the message sank in, how painfully slow this normal way of doing things was. Then that was forgotten. He read it through again, astonished, his mind struggling to understand.

'He can't ...' he said, turning sharply to face the door, his whole stance suddenly changed; his body tensed now, crouched like a fighter's. 'No ...'

The message was brief and to the point, signed with Tolonen's personal code.

'Shih Ward,

You are not to see my daughter, nor should you try to see her. There is no future for the two of you, and certainly no possibility of a match. You will keep away from my living quarters and deal with me only through my office in future. Finally, let me warn you. If you persist in this matter, I shall do all in my power to break you.

    Knut Tolonen.'

The hairs on his neck bristled as he read the note again. He threw it down and went to the terminal. Sitting there, he tapped in the 'Reach' code she had given him. Her private code, known only to her and him. He waited, anger and fear and something else – something he knew but could not put a name to – churning in his stomach. For a long time there was nothing. The screen remained blank, the delay pulse the only sign that the machine was attempting to connect them. Then, almost imperceptibly, the screen changed, showing not her face, as he'd hoped, but a message. Briefer than Tolonen's and less personal, but something: a sign for him that she had no part in this.

'Nanking. South Port 3. Meridian.'

Nanking was the great spaceport that served the colonies. South Port 3 must be the departure point, the Meridian the ship. But why had she given him these details?

He went cold. Quickly he signed off, then summoned up details of departures from Nanking, South Port 3 and found the *Meridian* listed on the second page. He shivered. Seven hours. Less than seven hours. That was all the time he had to get to her and ...

And what? He sat back, his heart hammering, his hands trembling. He could do nothing. Tolonen would make certain of that. Even now, perhaps, he was being watched. But he would have to try. He would never forgive himself unless he tried.

He stood up slowly, feeling weak. Turning, looking down at the tiny slip of card where it lay on the floor across the room from him, he recognised at last what the feeling was he had failed to put a name to. It was dark and vast and empty like a pit; a feeling so dreadful and debilitating that it seemed to drain him even as he stood there; making him feel hollow and close to death. It was loss. He had lost her.

But even as it swept over him, another feeling grew – of anger, and determination. He would go after her, Tolonen's threats notwithstanding. He would try. Because nothing else mattered to him as much as Jelka. Nothing in the whole vast universe.

Soucek was walking beside the sedan, Po Lao and Visak several paces in front of him at the front of the procession as they approached the end of the corridor and the rendezvous point beyond. Lehmann had hand-picked the tiny force that marched along beneath the black dog banners, yet there were only two dozen of them, including the pole men, and Soucek felt uneasy, hideously exposed, here in Red Gang territory.

The meeting had been rearranged at short notice. The note sent to Fat Wong had stated bluntly that the Big Boss of the *Kuei Chuan* would meet him on Red Gang territory or not at all. It had specified a time and a place, and had informed Wong Yi-sun that copies of the note were being delivered simultaneously to each of the other four Bosses. That last was an elementary precaution, yet if Fat Wong *was* contemplating a move against the *Kuei Chuan*, this seemed as good a place as any to make it. If what Visak had said were true, the last six months had seen Fat Wong's United Bamboo Triad grow very close to Dead Man Yun's Red Gang. Why, they had even gone so far as to support Red Gang encroachments on *Kuei Chuan* territory. To

Soucek, then, this seemed a strange thing to do – tantamount to putting one's head in the tiger's mouth. But Lehmann had ordered it.

They slowed, Soucek not alone in counting the guards on the barrier up ahead and noting the great array of banners beyond. They were all here – 14K and Yellow Banners, United Bamboo, Red Gang and Wo Shih Wo – and here in some force, too. The *Kuei Chuan*, a meagre two dozen fighting men, were clearly the last to arrive.

He felt his pulse quicken, his chest tighten at the thought of the encounter ahead. For once he felt a slight uncertainty about what Lehmann was doing. This was a different league. A different league entirely. It was one thing to kill a Big Boss, another to establish oneself in his place. And yet Po Lao, like Visak, had bowed to Lehmann, accepting the inevitable. So maybe ...

A figure appeared at the barrier. A small, dapper-looking Han in cream and lilac silks. Behind him four other middle-aged Han waited, watching the sedan come on.

'That's Fat Wong at the front,' Visak said quietly, talking from the corner of his mouth. 'The bald one to his left is Dead Man Yun, our host. The pop-eyed one next to him is Li Chin, Boss of the Wo Shih Wo – Li The Lidless, as he's known. The starchy old man is General Feng, Boss of the 14K. Beside him – the tall one with the crippled hand – is Three-Finger Ho, Boss of the Yellow Banners.'

Soucek narrowed his eyes, taking it all in. He had never thought to see these men, not separately, let alone together like this, but here they were, gathered at his Master's summons. His fear now was a solid thing at the pit of his stomach and part of him wondered if he would ever see another morning, but the thought of letting Lehmann down made him keep his fear in check; made him look about him with cold, clear eyes.

They were powerful men, there was no doubting it. He could see it in their stance, in the calm aura of superiority that hung about them as they waited, and in the cold, passionless depths of their eyes. Men died at their slightest whim, at their smallest gesture. And yet they were men, for all that. They could be killed. As Whiskers Lu had been killed.

And Lehmann? He too could be killed, for he was simply a man when it came down to it. And yet the thought of someone bettering Lehmann seemed wrong somehow – almost an impossibility – and that sense of wrongness gave Soucek new confidence, for at bottom he believed in Lehmann.

They stopped ten paces from the waiting group. Slowly the sedan set down. Soucek tensed, seeing how Fat Wong's hands were clenched, how his eyes were hard and cold. Lehmann's counter-summons – that terse, unsigned message – must have angered Wong Yi-sun greatly. Coming here was, in itself, a kind of loss of face. And yet he had come.

There was the rustle of heavy silks as the plain black curtain was lifted by the two attending pole men, and then Lehmann stepped out from the darkness within, straightening up slowly, his tall, emaciated figure ghost-like in the glare of the overhead lights. As ever he was dressed from head to toe in white.

White, the colour of death.

A great gasp went up from the men manning the barriers. A gasp of fear as much as surprise. In front of them Fat Wong, his mouth fallen open, shook his head slowly in disbelief. For a moment he was at a loss, then he turned, looking to the Red Pole of the *Kuei Chuan* for an explanation.

'What in the gods' names is going on, Po Lao? Where is your Master? And who the fuck is this?'

But Po Lao held his tongue. He merely turned, his head bowed low, facing his new Master, his whole manner subservient.

'Our good friend, Whiskers Lu, is dead,' Lehmann said, stepping forward, Wong's slur seemingly ignored. 'So let me introduce myself. My name is Stefan Lehmann and, as of two hours ago, I became the new Big Boss of the *Kuei Chuan* brotherhood.' He turned slightly, meeting Fat Wong's eyes from no more than an arm's length away, his voice soft, his face unsmiling. 'Fat Wong ... it's good to meet you at last.' His eyes held Wong's a moment longer, then he looked past him at the others gathered there. 'And you, *ch'un tzu*. It's good to meet you all. I've heard so much about you ...'

Moving past Wong Yi-sun, Lehmann joined the circle of the 489s, looking about him coldly, imperiously, defying them to contradict his claim to power. And Soucek, looking on, saw how they stared back at him, impressed despite themselves, maybe even awed – even the great Wong Yi-sun. In a few moments he had won through sheer audacity what no force of arms could ever have achieved: their respect.

Soucek shivered. It was done. Lehmann, the *Hung Mao* – the usurper – was one of the Six now. A Boss. A 489. One of the great lords of the underworld.

And in time he would be more. Yes, Soucek burned now with the certainty of it. In time he would be more.

The barriers were down, the ship sealed. Kim stood there, staring up at the departures board, the figures on the clock, his stomach falling away as he realised that he was too late. Then, forcing himself to go on, to carry things through to the very end, he crossed the big lounge quickly, making for the Security desk in the corner.

The young guard looked up at him as he approached and frowned. 'What do you want?'

Kim held out his all-levels pass. 'I've got to get a message through!' he said breathlessly. 'It's vitally important.'

'What ship is it?' the guard asked, studying the pass a moment, then looking back at Kim, eyeing him curiously, clearly recognising him for a Clayborn.

'The *Meridian*. South Port 3.'

The guard smiled and sadly shook his head. 'I'm sorry, *Shih* Ward, but it's too late. The *Meridian* is already sealed.'

'I know,' Kim said, impatient now. 'But I have to get a message through. It's terribly important.'

'I'm sorry,' the guard began again, all politeness, 'but that's simply not possible. Not until the ship is in orbit.'

Kim looked away, wondering what he could do, what say, to persuade the guard to help him, then turned back, leaning across the barrier, deciding to confide in the young officer.

'The truth is that the girl I love is on board the *Meridian*. Her father wants to prevent us from getting married, so he's sending her off to the Colonies. I only heard about it a few hours back, so I must speak to her before she goes. I simply must.'

The young guard sat back slightly. His chest patch showed that he was a lieutenant, but from his manner Kim could tell he was not long out of cadet school.

'I'd like to help you, *Shih* Ward, really I would, but I can't. The communications of the *Meridian* are locked into the launch sequence now. Even the great T'ang himself couldn't communicate with the *Meridian* right now – not unless he wished the countdown cancelled.'

'I see.' Kim turned away.

He had lost her.

'Shih Ward ...'

Kim turned back. 'Yes?'

The young man came from behind the barrier, his eyes softer than before. 'I'm off duty here in five minutes. If you want, I can take you up into the viewing tower. You can watch the ship go up from there. As for your message, well, maybe I can pass something on for you. Amongst the technical stuff. Fifty words maximum, mind you, and I can't guarantee it'll get through, but it's the best I can do.'

Kim bowed his head, a feeling of immense gratitude flooding through him. 'Thank you. With all my heart, thank you.'

Twenty minutes later, watching the tiny point of flame disappear into the upper atmosphere, Kim looked away, touching his top teeth with his tongue. Seven years he'd have to wait until she could be his. Yet even as he thought it, he knew how he would fill those long years of waiting. They would be hard, but he would get through them. And then she would be his, meddling old men or no. His.

CHARACTER LISTING

MAJOR CHARACTERS

Asher, Emily — Trained as an economist, she was once a member of the *Ping Tiao* revolutionary party. After their demise, she fled to North America where, under the alias of Mary Jennings, she got a job with the giant ImmVac corporation, working for Old Man Lever and his son, Michael. Ultimately, however, what she wants is change, and the downfall of the corrupt social institutions that rule Chung Kuo.

Lehmann, Stefan — Albino son of the former Dispersionist leader, Pietr Lehmann, he was briefly a lieutenant to DeVore. A cold, unnaturally dispassionate man, he seems the very archetype of nihilism, his only aim to bring down the Seven and their great earth-encompassing City. His move 'down level' into the 'underground' world of *tong* and Triad marks a new stage of his campaign.

Lever, Charles — Head of the massive ImmVac pharmaceuticals corporation, 'Old Man Lever' is a passionate 'American' and one of the instigators of the Cutler Institute's Immortality project. A bull-necked, stubborn old man, he will let nothing get between him and what he wants. And what he wants is to live forever.

Lever, Michael — Son of Charles Lever, he was incarcerated by Wu Shih for his involvement with the 'Sons of Benjamin

Franklin', a semi-revolutionary group formed by the sons of wealthy North American businessmen. Cast from childhood in his father's mould, he has yet to break from his upbringing and find his own direction.

Li Yuan

T'ang of Europe and one of the Seven, as second son of Li Shai Tung, he inherited after the deaths of his brother and father. Considered old before his time, he nonetheless has a passionate side to his nature, as demonstrated in his brief marriage to his brother's wife, the beautiful Fei Yen. Having remarried, he is determined to find balance, both in his private life and in his role as T'ang.

Shepherd, Ben

Son of Hal Shepherd, and great-great-grandson of City Earth's architect, Ben was brought up in the Domain, an idyllic valley in the south west of England where, deciding not to follow in his father's footsteps and become adviser to Li Yuan, he pursues instead his calling as an artist, developing a new artform, the Shell, which will one day transform Chung Kuo's society.

Tolonen, Jelka

Daughter of Marshal Tolonen, Jelka has been brought up in a very masculine environment, lacking a mother's love and influence. Despite a genuine interest in martial arts and weaponry, she feels a strong need to discover and express the more feminine side of her nature; a need matched by a determination not to succumb to the gender demands of her world.

Tolonen, Knut

Former Marshal of the Council of Generals and one-time General to Li Yuan's father, Tolonen is a rock-like supporter of the Seven and their values, even in an age of increasing uncertainty. In his role as father, however, this inflexibility in his nature brings him into repeated conflict with his daughter, Jelka.

Tsu Ma

T'ang of West Asia and one of the Seven, the ruling Council of Chung Kuo, Tsu Ma has thrown off a dissolute past to become Li Yuan's staunchest supporter in Council. A strong, handsome man

Wang Sau-leyan

in his late thirties, he has yet to marry, though his secret affair with Li Yuan's former wife, Fei Yen, revealed a side of him that has not been fully harnessed.

T'ang of Africa. Since inheriting – after the suspicious deaths of his father and elder brothers – Wang Sau-leyan has dedicated every moment to bringing down Li Yuan and his allies in Council. A sharp and cunning adversary with an abrasive, calculating manner, he is the harbinger of Change within the Council of Seven.

Ward, Kim

Born in the Clay, that dark wasteland beneath the great City's foundations, Kim has a quick and unusual bent of mind that has marked him as potentially the greatest scientist on Chung Kuo. His vision of a giant starspanning web, formulated down in the darkness, drove him up into the light of the Above. But, despite the patronage of Li Yuan and the friendship of powerful men, life has proven to be far from easy for Ward, either in business or in love.

Wong Yi-sun

Big Boss of the United Bamboo Triad, 'Fat Wong' – a tiny, birdlike man – has won the favour of Li Yuan. Yet his ambitions reach beyond mere patronage. He wants to unite the lower levels of City Europe under his rule.

Wu Shih

Middle-aged T'ang of North America, he is one of the few remaining members of the old generation. A staunch traditionalist, nevertheless he has found himself allied in Council with Li Yuan and Tsu Ma against the odious Wang Sau-leyan. Yet with the resurgence of American nationalism he finds himself confronted by a problem none of his fellow T'ang have to face; a problem he must find an urgent and lasting solution to.

THE SEVEN AND THE FAMILIES

Chi Hsing — T'ang of the Australias.

Fu Ti Chang — third wife of Li Yuan.

Hou Tung-po	T'ang of South America.
Lai Shi	second wife of Li Yuan.
Li Kuei Jen	son of Li Yuan and heir to City Europe.
Li Yuan	T'ang of Europe.
Mien Shan	first wife of Li Yuan.
Tsu Ma	T'ang of West Asia.
Wang Sau-leyan	T'ang of Africa.
Wei Chan Yin	first son of Wei Feng and heir to City East Asia.
Wei Feng	T'ang of East Asia.
Wei Hsi Wang	second son of Wei Feng and Colonel in Security.
Wei Tseng-li	third son of Wei Feng.
Wu Shih	T'ang of North America.
Yin Fei Yen	'Flying Swallow'; Minor Family princess and divorced wife of Li Yuan.
Yin Han Ch'in	son of Yin Fei Yen.
Yin Tsu	head of the Yin Family (one of the 'Twenty Nine' Minor Families) and father of Fei Yen.
Yin Wu Tsai	Minor Family princess and cousin of Fei Yen.

FRIENDS AND RETAINERS OF THE SEVEN

Bachman, Lothar	lieutenant in Security.
Bright Moon	maid to Li Yuan.
Brock	security guard in the Domain.
Chan Teng	Master of the Inner Chambers at Tongjiang.
Chang Shih-sen	personal secretary to Li Yuan.
Ch'in Tao Fan	Chancellor of East Asia.
Chu Shi-ch'e	*Pi-shu chien*, or Inspector of the Imperial Library at Tongjiang.
Coates	security guard in the Domain.
Cook	duty guard in the Domain.
Fen Cho-hsien	Chancellor of North America.
Fragrant Lotus	maid to Li Yuan.
Franke, Otto	*Wei*, or Captain of Security for Zwickau *Hsien*.
Gerhardt, Paul	Major; Head of Tracking, Northern Hemisphere.
Gustavsson, Per	Captain of Chi Hsing's personal guard.
Gustavsson, Ute	wife of Captain Gustavvson.
Hauser, Eva	wife of Major Sven Hauser.
Hauser, Gustav	private secretary/equerry to Marshal Tolonen; son of Major Sven Hauser.

Hauser, Sven	Major; ex-Colonial Governor; father of Gustav Hauser.
Henssa, Eero	Captain of the Guard aboard the floating palace Yangjing.
Ho Chang	valet to Wu Shih.
Hung, Yan	'Wiring' surgeon to Li Yuan.
Hung Mien-lo	Chancellor of Africa.
Karr, Gregor	Major in Security.
K'ung Feng	Third Official in the *Ta Ssu Nung*, the Superintendency of Agriculture, for City Europe.
Lofgren, Bertil	lieutenant and aide to Marshal Tolonen.
Mo Yu	Security lieutenant in the Domain.
Nan Ho	Chancellor of Europe.
Read, Helmut	Governor of the Saturn system.
Rheinhardt, Helmut	General of Security for Li Yuan.
Shepherd, Ben	son of the late Hal Shepherd; 'Shell' artist.
Shepherd, Beth	widow of Hal Shepherd; mother of Ben and Meg Shepherd.
Shepherd, Meg	sister of Ben Shepherd.
Tolonen, Jelka	daughter of Marshal Tolonen.
Tolonen, Knut	ex-Marshal of Security; Head of the GenSyn Hearings committee.
Tu Mai	security guard in the Domain.
Virtanen, Per	Major in Li Yuan's Security forces.
Zdenek	bodyguard to Jelka Tolonen.

THE TRIADS

Chao	runner for K'ang A-yin.
Feng Shang-pao	'General Feng'; Big Boss of the 14K.
Feng Wo	lieutenant to K'ang A-yin.
Ho Chin	'Three-Finger Ho'; Big Boss of the Yellow Banners.
Hua Shang	lieutenant to Wong Yi-sun.
Huang Jen	lieutenant to Po Lao.
Hui Tsin	Red Pole (426, or Executioner) to the United Bamboo.
K'ang A-yin	gang boss of the Tu Sun *tong*.
K'ang Yeh-su	nephew of K'ang A-yin.
Kant	runner for K'ang A-yin.
Li Chin	'Li The Lidless'; Big Boss of the Wo Shih Wo.

Li Pai Shung	nephew of Li Chin; heir to the Wo Shih Wo.
Ling Wo	Chief Adviser to K'ang A-yin.
Liu Tong	lieutenant to Li Chin.
Lo Han	tong boss.
Lu Ming-shao	'Whiskers Lu'; Big Boss of the Kuei Chuan.
Man Hsi	tong boss.
Meng Te	lieutenant to Lu Ming-shao.
Ni Yueh	tong boss.
Peck	lieutenant to K'ang A-yin (a ying tzu, or 'shadow').
Po Lao	Red Pole (426, or Executioner) to the Kuei Chuan.
Soucek, Jiri	lieutenant to K'ang A-yin.
Visak	lieutenant to Lu Ming-shao.
Wong Yi-sun	'Fat Wong'; Big Boss of the United Bamboo.
Yan Yan	tong boss.
Yao Lu	lieutenant to Stefan Lehmann.
Yue Chun	Red Pole (426, or Executioner) to the Wo Shih Wo.
Yun Yueh-hui	'Dead Man Yun'; Big Boss of the Red Gang.

YU

Anne	Yu assassin.
Donna	Yu assassin.
Joan	Yu assassin.
Kriz	senior Yu operative.
Mach, Jan	maintenance official for the Ministry of Waste Recycling, former Ping Tiao member and founder of the Yu.
Vesa	Yu assassin.

OTHER CHARACTERS

Ainsworth, James	lawyer for Charles Lever.
Barratt, Edel	SimFic employee at Sohm Abyss.
Becker, Hans	side-kick of Stefan Lehmann.
Bonner, Alex	Chief Negotiator for the P'u Lan Finance Corporation.
Bonnot, Alex	Scientific Supervisor for SimFic at Sohm Abyss.
Campbell, William	Regional Controller of SimFic's North Atlantic Cities.
Carver, Rex	Reformer candidate for Miami Hsien and friend of Charles Lever.

Chan Long	security guard, working for Lever and Kustow.
Chang	guard on the Chung estate.
Chang Li	First Surgeon in the Boston Medical Centre.
Chiang Su-li	Master of the House of the Ninth Dragon tea-house.
Chung, Gloria	heiress; daughter of the late Representative Chung Yen.
Curval, Andrew	leading geneticist; employee of the ImmVac Corporation.
Dann, Abraham	steward to Charles Lever.
Deio	Clayborn friend of Kim Ward from 'Rehabilitation'.
DeValerian, Rache	alias of Emily Ascher.
DeVore, Howard	Major in Security, and Dispersionist.
Dunn, Richard	business rival of Old Man Lever.
Feng Lu-ma	lensman.
Feng Wo-shen	protein designer and scientific assistant for SimFic at Sohm Abyss.
Fisher, Carl	American; friend of Michael Lever.
Fisher, James	financier and friend of Charles Lever.
Gratton, Edward	friend of Charles Lever and Reformer candidate for Boston *Hsien*.
Haller, Wolf	side-kick of Stefan Lehmann.
Harrison, James	employee of Charles Lever.
Hart, Alex	Representative at Weimar.
Hartmann, William	friend of Charles Lever and Reformer candidate.
Hay, Joel	leader of the Evolutionist Party of North America.
Henty, Thomas	technician.
Heydemeier, Ernst	artist; leading exponent of *Futur-Kunst*, 'Science Art'.
Hilbert, Eduard	head of cryobiology for SimFic at Sohm Abyss.
Ho Chao-tuan	Representative for Shenyang *Hsien*
Ho Yang	reporter for the *Wen Ming* media channel.
Hong Chi	assistant to Kim Ward.
Horton, Feng	American; a 'Son'; also known as 'Meltdown'.
Hsiang Tian	merchant; store-owner.
Jennings, Mary	alias of Emily Ascher.
Johnstone, Edward	friend of Charles Lever; father of Louisa Johnstone.
Johnstone, Louisa	long-standing fiancée of Michael Lever.
K'ang Hung-chang	professor at the Kunming Institute of Comparative Genetics.
Kennedy, Jean	wife of Joseph Kennedy.
Kennedy, Joseph	American lawyer, and founder of the New

	Republican Party.
Kennedy, Robert	eldest son of Joseph Kennedy.
Kennedy, William	youngest son of Joseph Kennedy.
Koslevic, Anna	schoolgirl friend of Jelka Tolonen.
Kustow, Bryn	American; friend of Michael Lever.
Lanouette, Henri	banker.
Lehmann, Stefan	albino son of Under-Secretary Lehmann.
Lever, Charles	'Old Man Lever', head of the ImmVac pharmaceuticals company of North America; father of Michael Lever.
Lever, Michael	son of Charles Lever; Head of the MemSys Corporation, a subsidiary of ImmVac.
Li Min	'Brave Carp', an alias of Stefan Lehmann.
Luke	Clayborn friend of Kim Ward from 'Rehabilitation'.
Mai Li-wen	lensman.
Marley, George	business associate of Charles Lever.
May Feng	*Hung Mao* Head of EduCol.
Milne, Michael	private investigator.
Mitchell, Bud	American; a 'Son'; associate of Michael Lever.
Munroe, Wendell	Representative at Weimar.
Nong Yan	book-keeper to Kim Ward.
Pai Mei	stallholder.
Parker, Jack	American; friend of Michael Lever.
Ping Hsiang	Representative for the Above in discussions for the reopening of Weimar.
Reiss, Horst	Chief Executive of the SimFic Corporation.
Richards	guard at Kim Ward's *Chih Chu* company.
Robins	employee of Charles Lever.
Ross, James	private investigator.
Schram, Dieter	Administrator for SimFic at Sohm Abyss.
Snow	alias of Stefan Lehmann.
Spence, Graham	employee of Charles Lever.
Spence, Leena	'Immortal' and one-time lover of Charles Lever.
Stevens, Carl	American; friend of Michael Lever.
Stewart, Greg	American; NREP candidate for Denver *Hsien*.
Symons	SimFic employee at Sohm Abyss.
T'ai Cho	friend and former guardian of Kim Ward.
Tewl	'Darkness'; chief of the raft-people.
Thorsson, Wulf	settler from Iapetus Colony in the Saturn system.
Tong Ye	young Han sailor (a 'morph') used by Ben Shep-

	herd.
Tuan Wen-ch'ang	SimFic employee at Sohm Abyss.
Underwood, Harry	Representative at Weimar.
Ward, Rebecca	Commercial Adviser to SimFic at Sohm Abyss; Clayborn friend of Kim Ward from 'Rehabilitation'.
Weller, John	Head of Internal Distribution for ImmVac.
Will	Clayborn friend of Kim Ward from 'Rehabilitation'.
Yellow Tan	lensman.
Yi Pang-chou	schoolgirl friend of Jelka Tolonen.
Yueh Pa	official in the United Bamboo heartland.

THE DEAD

Barrow, Chao	Secretary of the House at Weimar.
Bercott, Andrei	Representative at Weimar.
Berdichev, Soren	Head of SimFic and, later, leader of the Dispersionist faction.
Ch'in Shih Huang Ti	the first emperor of China (ruled 221–210 BC).
Chung Hsin	'Loyalty'; bondservant to Li Shai Tung.
Cutler, Richard	leader of the 'American' movement.
Ebert, Klaus	head of the GenSyn Corporation.
Feng Chung	Big Boss of the Kuei Chan (Black Dog) Triad.
Fest, Edgar	Captain in Security.
Gesell, Bent	leader of the Ping Tiao terrorist organisation.
Griffin, James B.	last president of the American Empire.
Han Huan Ti	Han emperor, (ruled AD 168–189), also known as Liu Hung.
Hou Ti	T'ang of South America; father of Hou Tung Po.
Hsiang K'ai Fan	Minor Family Prince.
Hwa	master 'blood', or hand-to-hand fighter, below the Net.
Kao Jyan	assassin; friend of Kao Chen.
K'ung Fu Tzu	Confucius (551–479 BC).
Lehmann, Pietr	Under Secretary of the House of Representatives and first leader of the Dispersionist faction; father of Stefan Lehmann.
Lever, Margaret	wife of Charles Lever and mother of Michael Lever.
Li Ch'ing	T'ang of Europe; grandfather of Li Yuan.
Li Han Ch'in	first son of Li Shai T'ung and once-heir to City Europe; brother of Li Yuan.

Li Hang Ch'i	T'ang of Europe; great-great-grandfather of Li Yuan.
Li Kou-lung	T'ang of Europe; great-grandfather of Li Yuan.
Li Shai Tung	T'ang of Europe; father of Li Yuan.
Lin Yua	first wife of Li Shai Tung.
Mao Tse Tung	first Ko Ming emperor (ruled AD 1948–1976).
Ming Huang	sixth T'ang emperor (ruled AD 713–755).
Mu Chua	Madame of the House of the Ninth Ecstasy.
Mu Li	'Iron Mu', Boss of the Big Circle triad.
Shang	'Old Shang'; Master to Kao Chen when he was a child.
Shepherd, Amos	Great-great-great-great-grandfather (and genetic 'father') of Ben Shepherd.
Shepherd, Augustus	'Brother' of Ben Shepherd, b. AD 2106, d. 2122.
Shepherd, Hal	Father (and genetic 'brother') of Ben Shepherd.
Shepherd, Robert	Great-grandfather (and genetic 'brother') of Ben Shepherd, and father of Augustus Shepherd.
Tsao Ch'un	tyrannical founder of Chung Kuo (ruled AD 2051–2087).
Wang Hsien	T'ang of Africa; father of Wang Sau-leyan.
Wang Ta-hung	third son of Wang Hsien; elder brother of Wang Sau-leyan.
Wen Ti	'First Ancestor' of City Earth/Chung Kuo (ruled 180–157 BC), also known as Liu Heng.
Wyatt, Edmund	company head; father of Kim Ward.
Ywe Hao	Yu terrorist.
Ywe Kai-chang	father of Ywe Hao.

GLOSSARY OF MANDARIN TERMS

Most of the Mandarin terms used in the text are explained in context. However, as a few are used more naturally, I've considered it best to provide a brief explanation.

ai ya!	common exclamation of surprise or dismay.
ch'a	tea. It might be noted that *ch'a shu*, the Chinese art of tea, is an ancient forebear of the Japanese tea ceremony *chanoyu*.
chang shan	literally 'long dress', which fastens to the right. Worn by both sexes. The women's version is a fitted, calf-length dress, similar to the *chi pao*. A South China fashion, also known as a *cheung sam*.
chan shih	a fighter.
Ch'eng Ou Chou	City Europe.
ch'i	a Chinese foot; approximately 14.4 inches.
chih chu	spider.
chieh hsia	term meaning 'Your Majesty', derived from the expression 'Below the Steps'. It was the formal way of addressing the Emperor, through his Ministers, who stood 'below the steps'.
chi pao	literally 'banner gown'; a one-piece gown of Manchu origin, usually sleeveless, worn by women.
Chou	'state'; here the name for a card game based on the politics of the state of Chung Kuo.
chung	a lidded serving bowl for *ch'a*.
ch'un tzu	an ancient Chinese term from the Warring States period, describing a certain class of nobleman, controlled by a code of chivalry and morality known as the *li*, or rites.

Here the term is roughly, and sometimes ironically, translated as 'gentlemen'. The *ch'un tzu* is as much an ideal state of behaviour – as specified by Confucius in the *Analects* – as an actual class in Chung Kuo, though a degree of financial independence and a high standard of education are assumed a prerequisite.

erhu   two-stringed bow with snakeskin-covered sound box.

fen   unit of money (a cent); one hundred *fen* make up a *yuan*.

han   term used by the Chinese to describe their own race, the 'black-haired people', dating back to the Han Dynasty (210 BC – AD 220). It is estimated that some ninety-four per cent of modern China's population is racially Han.

hei   literally 'black'; the Chinese pictogram for this represents a man wearing warpaint and tattoos. Here it refers to the genetically manufactured (GenSyn) half-men used as riot police to quell uprisings in the lower levels.

hsiao jen   'little man/men'. In the *Analects*, Book XIV, Confucius writes: 'The gentleman gets through to what is up above; the small man gets through to what is down below.' This distinction between 'gentlemen' (*ch'un tzu*) and 'little men' (*hsiao jen*), false even in Confucius's time, is no less a matter of social perspective in Chung Kuo.

hsien   historically an administrative district of variable size. Here the term is used to denote a very specific administrative area; one of ten stacks – each stack composed of thirty decks. Each deck is a hexagonal living unit of ten levels, two *li*, or approximately one kilometre in diameter. A stack can be imagined as one honeycomb in the great hive of the City.

Hsien L'ing   'Chief Magistrate'. In Chung Kuo, these officials are the T'ang's representatives and law enforcers for the individual *hsien*, or administrative districts. In times of peace, each *hsien* also elects a representative to the House at Weimar.

Hung Mao   literally 'redheads', the name the Chinese gave to the Dutch (and later English) seafarers who attempted to trade with China in the seventeenth century. Because of the piratical nature of their endeavours (which

	often meant plundering Chinese shipping and ports) the name has connotations of piracy.
Hung Mun	the Secret Societies or, more specifically, the Triads.
hun tun	'the Chou believed that Heaven and Earth were once inextricably mixed together in a state of undifferentiated chaos, like a chicken's egg. Hun Tun they called that state' (from 'Chen Yen', Chapter 6 of The White Mountain). It is also the name of a meal of tiny sac-like dumplings.
jou tung wu	literally 'meat animal'.
kan pei!	'good health' or 'cheers'; a drinking toast.
Ko Ming	'revolutionary'. The T'ien Ming is the Mandate of Heaven, supposedly handed down from Shang Ti, the Supreme Ancestor, to his earthly counterpart, the Emperor (Huang Ti). This Mandate could be enjoyed only so long as the Emperor was worthy of it, and rebellion against a tyrant – who broke the Mandate through his lack of justice, benevolence and sincerity – was deemed not criminal but a rightful expression of Heaven's anger.
k'ou t'ou	the fifth stage of respect, according to the 'Book of Ceremonies', involves kneeling and striking the head against the floor. This ritual has become more commonly known in the West as kowtow.
Kuan hua	Mandarin, the language spoken in mainland China. Also known as Kuo-yu and Pai hua.
Kuan Yin	the goddess of mercy. Originally the Buddhist male bodhisattva, Avalokitsevara (translated into Han as 'He who listens to the sounds of the world', or 'Kuan Yin'), the Han mistook the well-developed breasts of the saint's for a woman's and, since the ninth century, have worshipped Kuan Yin as such. Effigies of Kuan Yin will show her usually as the Eastern Madonna, cradling a child in her arms. She is also sometimes seen as the wife of Kuan Kung, the Chinese God of War.
li	a Chinese 'mile', approximating to half a kilometre or one-third of a mile. Until 1949, when metric measures were adopted in China, the li could vary from place to place.
min	literally 'the people'; used (as here, by the Minor Families) in a pejorative sense (that is, as an equivalent to 'plebeian').

Ming	the Dynasty that ruled China from 1368 to 1644. Literally, the name means 'Bright' or 'Clear', or 'Brilliant'. It carries connotations of cleansing.
niao	literally 'bird'; but here, as often, it is used euphemistically, as a term for the penis, often as an expletive.
nu er	daughter.
nu shi	an unmarried woman; a term equating to 'Miss'.
pai nan jen	literally 'white man'.
pau	a simple long garment worn by men.
Ping Tiao	levelling. To bring down or make flat.
p'i p'a	a four-stringed lute used in traditional Chinese music.
san kuei chiu k'ou	the eighth and final stage of respect, according to the 'Book of Ceremonies', involves kneeling three times, each time striking the forehead three times against the floor. This most elaborate form of ritual was reserved for Heaven and its son, the Emperor.
shan shui	the literal meaning is 'mountains and water', but the term is normally associated with a style of landscape painting which depicts rugged mountain scenery with river valleys in the foreground. It is a highly popular form, first established in the T'ang Dynasty, back in the seventh to ninth centuries AD.
shao lin	specially-trained assassins; named after the monks of the shao lin monastery.
Shih	'Master'. Here used as a term of respect somewhat equivalent to our use of 'Mister'. The term was originally used for the lowest level of civil servants, to distinguish them socially from the run-of-the-mill 'Misters' (hsian sheng) below them and the gentlemen (ch'un tzu) above.
Siang Chi	Chinese chess.
tai	'pockets'; here used to denote Representatives bought by (and thus 'in the pocket of') various power groupings (originally the Seven).
t'ai chi	the Original, or One, from which the duality of all things (yin and yang) developed, according to Chinese cosmology. We generally associate the t'ai chi with the Taoist symbol, that swirling circle of dark and light, supposedly representing an egg (perhaps the Hun Tun), the yolk and the white differentiated.
T'ai Shan	the great sacred mountain of China, where emperors

have traditionally made sacrifices to Heaven. T'ai Shan, in Shantung province, is the highest peak in China. 'As safe as T'ai Shan' is a popular saying, denoting the ultimate in solidity and certainty.

Ta Ts'in the Chinese name for the Roman Empire. They also knew Rome as *Li Chien* and as 'the Land West of the Sea'. The Romans themselves they termed the 'Big Ts'in' – the Ts'in being the name the Chinese gave themselves during the Ts'in Dynasty (AD 265–316).

T'ing Wei the Superintendency of Trials. See Book 3 (*The White Mountain*), Part 2, for an instance of how this department of government functions.

ti tsu a bamboo flute, used both as a solo instrument and as part of an ensemble.

tong a gang. In China and Europe, these are usually smaller and thus subsidiary to the Triads, but in North America the term has generally taken the place of 'Triad'.

ts'un a Chinese 'inch' of approximately 1.44 Western inches; 10 ts'un form one *ch'i*.

wan wu literally 'the ten thousand things'; used generally to include everything in creation, or, as the Chinese say, 'all things in Heaven and Earth'.

wei chi 'the surrounding game', known more commonly in the West by its Japanese name of 'Go'. It is said that the game was invented by the legendary Chinese Emperor Yao in the year 2350 BC to train the mind of his son, Tan Chu, and teach him to think like an Emperor.

wen ming a term used to denote civilisation, or written culture.

wuwei non-action; an old Taoist concept. It means keeping harmony with the flow of things – doing nothing to break the flow. As Lao Tzu said, 'The Tao does nothing, and yet nothing is left undone'.

yamen the official building in a Chinese community.

yang the 'male principle' of Chinese cosmology, which, with its complementary opposite, the female *yin*, forms the *t'ai chi*, derived from the Primeval One. From the union of *yin* and *yang* arise the 'five elements' (water, fire, earth, metal, wood) from which the 'ten thousand things' (the *wan wu*) are generated. *Yang* signifies Heaven and the South, the Sun and Warmth, Light, Vigour, Maleness, Penetration, odd numbers and the Dragon. Mountains are *yang*.

yin	the 'female principle' of Chinese cosmology (see *yang*). Yin signifies Earth and the North, the Moon and Cold, Darkness, Quiescence, Femaleness, Absorption, even numbers and the Tiger. The *yin* lies in the shadow of the mountain.
yu	literally 'fish' but because of its phonetic equivalence to the word for 'abundance', the fish symbolises wealth. Yet there is also a saying that when the fish swim upriver it is a portent of social unrest and rebellion.
yuan	the basic currency of Chung Kuo (and modern-day China). Colloquially (though not here) it can also be termed *kwai* – 'piece' or 'lump'. One hundred *fen* (or cents) make up one *yuan*.
yueh ch'in	a Chinese dulcimer; one of the principal instruments of the Chinese orchestra.
Ywe Lung	literally, the 'Moon Dragon', the wheel of seven dragons that is the symbol of the ruling Seven throughout *Chung Kuo*: 'At its centre the snouts of the regal beasts met, forming a roselike hub, huge rubies burning fiercely in each eye. Their lithe, powerful bodies curved outwards like the spokes of a giant wheel while at the edge their tails were intertwined to form the rim' (from 'The Moon Dragon', Chapter 4 of *The Middle Kingdom*).

AUTHOR'S NOTE

The transcription of standard Mandarin into European alphabetical form was first achieved in the seventeenth century by the Italian Matteo Ricci, who founded and ran the first Jesuit Mission in China from 1583 until his death in 1610. Since then several dozen attempts have been made to reduce the original Chinese sounds, represented by some tens of thousands of separate pictograms, into readily understandable phonetics for Western use. For a long time, however, three systems dominated – those used by the three major Western powers vying for influence in the corrupt and crumbling Chinese Empire of the nineteenth century: Great Britain, France, and Germany. These systems were the Wade-Giles (Great Britain and America – sometimes known as the Wade system), the Ecole Française de L'Extrême Orient (France), and the Lessing (Germany).

Since 1958, however, the Chinese themselves have sought to create one single phonetic form, based on the German system, which they termed the *hanyu pinyin fang'an* (Scheme for a Chinese Phonetic Alphabet), known more commonly as *pinyin*, and in all foreign language books published in China since January 1st, 1979 *pinyin* has been used, as well as being taught now in schools along with the standard Chinese characters. For this work, however, I have chosen to use the older and to my mind far more elegant transcription system, the Wade-Giles (in modified form). For those now used to the harder forms of *pinyin*, the following (courtesy of Edgar Snow's *The Other Side Of The River*, Gollancz, 1961) may serve as a rough guide to pronunciation:

Chi is pronounced as 'Gee', but *Ch'i* sounds like 'Chee'. *Ch'in* is exactly our 'chin'.

Chu is roughly like 'Jew', as in *Chu Teh* (Jew Duhr), but *Ch'u* equals 'chew'.

Tsung is 'dzung'; *ts'ung* with the 'ts' as in 'Patsy'.

Tai is our word sound 'die'; *T'ai* – 'tie'.

Pai is 'buy' and *P'ai* is 'pie'.

Kung is like 'Gung' (a Din); *K'ung* with the 'k' as in 'kind'.

J is the equivalent of r but slur it, as rrrun.

H before an s, as in *hsi*, is the equivalent of an aspirate but is often dropped, as in Sian for Hsian.

Vowels in Chinese are generally short or medium, not long and flat. Thus *Tang* sounds like 'dong', never like our 'tang'. *T'ang* is 'tong'.

a as in father
e – run
eh – hen
I – *see*
ih – her
o – look
ou – go
u – soon

The effect of using the Wade-Giles system is, I hope, to render the softer, more poetic side of the original Mandarin, ill-served, I feel, by modern *pinyin*.

This usage, incidentally, accords with many of the major reference sources available in the West: the (planned) sixteen volumes of Denis Twichett and Michael Loewe's *The Cambridge History of China*; Joseph Needham's mammoth multi-volumed *Science and Civilisation in China*; John Fairbank and Edwin Reischauer's *China, Tradition and Transformation*; Charles Hucker's *China's Imperial Past*; Jacques Gernet's *A History of Chinese Civilisation*; C. P. Fitzgerald's *China: A Short Cultural History*; Laurence Sickman and Alexander Soper's *The Art and Architecture of China*; William Hinton's classic social studies, *Fanshen* and *Shenfan*; and Derk Bodde's *Essays on Chinese Civilisation*.

The Luoshu diagram, mentioned in the Prologue, is a three-by-three number square

4	9	2
3	5	7
8	1	6

and was supposedly seen on the shell of a turtle emerging from the Luo River some two thousand years before Christ. As can be seen, all the numbers in any one row or column or diagonal add up to fifteen. During the T'ang dynasty its 'magical' properties were exported to the Muslim world where they were used – as here – as a charm for easing childbirth.

Wu Shih's mention (in Chapter 1) of 'the three brothers of the Peach Garden' is a reference to Lo Kuan Chung's classic Chinese novel, San Kuo Yan Yi, or The Romance of the Three Kingdoms, in which the three great heroes, Liu Pei, Chang Fei and Kuan Yu swear brotherhood.

The translation of Ch'u Yuan's T'ien Wen, or 'Heavenly Questions', is by David Hawkes from The Songs Of The South: An Anthology Of Ancient Chinese Poems, published by Penguin Books, London, 1985.

The quotation from Jukka Tolonen is from a song on the album, Lambertland, by the Finnish band, Tasavallan Presidentti, and the lyrics from the song 'Last Quarters' are reprinted with the kind permission of Sonet Records.

The passage quoted from Book One [V] of Lao Tzu's Tao Te Ching is from the D. C. Lau translation, published by Penguin Books, London, 1963, and used with their kind permission.

The quotations from Rainer Maria Rilke's Duino Elegies are from the Hogarth Press fourth edition of 1968, translated by J. B. Leishman and Stephen Spender. Thanks to the estate of Rilke, St John's College, Oxford, for permission.

The translation of Tu Fu's 'After Rain' is by Sam Hamill from his wonderful anthology of Tu Fu's verse, Facing The Snow, Visions Of Tu Fu, published by White Pine Press, Fredonia, New York, and is reprinted here with their kind permission.

Once again, I find I have quoted extensively from Samuel B. Griffith's translation of Sun Tzu's The Art Of War, published by Oxford University

Press, 1963. I reprint the four passages used herein with their kind permission and only hope I have directed a few readers to this most excellent work.

Finally, for those of you unfamiliar with the pidgin Cornish used in Part Two of the book, here are translations of the relevant passages. First, the utterances of the Clay-men:

Avodya! Get back!
A-wartha! Up above!
An chy. Kerdhes! Tenna dhe an chy! The house. Go! Take the house!
Ena ... Ena ha ena! There ... There and there!

And Ben's whisperings:
Of ancow. I am death.
Gwelaf why gans ow onen lagas. I see you with my one eye.
Ow golow lagas dewana why! My bright eye pierces you!
Ow enawy a-vyn podretha agas eskern ... My light will rot your bones.
Furthermore, when the hologram of the Ox-faced angel says 'Dyesk-ynna!' ('Come!') there is a faint echo of the Revelation to John (6:1).